THE
GIRL
AND THE
MOUNTAIN

THE
GIRL
AND THE
MOUNTAIN

The Second Book of the Ice

MARK LAWRENCE

ACE
NEW YORK

ACE
Published by Berkley
An imprint of Penguin Random House LLC
penguinrandomhouse.com

Copyright © 2021 by Bobalinga Ltd.
Penguin Random House supports copyright. Copyright fuels creativity, encourages diverse
voices, promotes free speech, and creates a vibrant culture. Thank you for buying an authorized
edition of this book and for complying with copyright laws by not reproducing, scanning,
or distributing any part of it in any form without permission. You are supporting writers
and allowing Penguin Random House to continue to publish books for every reader.

ACE is a registered trademark and the A colophon is a trademark of Penguin Random House LLC.

Library of Congress Cataloging-in-Publication Data

Names: Lawrence, Mark, 1966– author.
Title: The girl and the mountain / Mark Lawrence.
Description: New York: Ace, [2021] | Series: The book of the ice; book 2
Identifiers: LCCN 2020042962 (print) | LCCN 2020042963 (ebook) | ISBN 9781984806024
(hardcover) | ISBN 9781984806031 (ebook)
Classification: LCC PS3612.A9484 G566 2021 (print) | LCC PS3612.A9484 (ebook) |
DDC 813/.6—dc23
LC record available at https://lccn.loc.gov/2020042962
LC ebook record available at https://lccn.loc.gov/2020042963

Printed in the United States of America

1st Printing

Book design by Alison Cnockaert
Title page image by BLAGORODEZ/Shutterstock

Dedicated to the memory of George Lebon,
with whom I misspent some of the best parts of my youth

THE STORY SO FAR

✦ ✦
✦

FOR THOSE OF you who have had to wait a while for this book I
provide brief catch-up notes to Book One, so your memories may
be refreshed and I can avoid the awkwardness of having to have
characters tell each other things they already know for your benefit.

Here I carry forward only what is of importance to the tale that follows.

Yaz and her brother Zeen found themselves in the Pit of the Missing as a
result of developing powers that, while useful, made them too weak to
survive the extreme cold of Abeth's icy surface. There are four old bloods
that show in a small minority of children:

GERANT, which means you grow very big

HUNSKA, which makes you very fast

MARJAL, which can give you some of a variety of lesser magics,
like command over shadows, water, air, rock, fire, etc.—sometimes
more than one of these

QUANTAL, which can give you major magics, including accessing
the vast power of the Path, and the ability to weave the threads of

existence to achieve more subtle manipulations of people and things

Under the ice Yaz met the Broken—a tribe formed from those who survived the fall down the pit. She also met the Tainted—members of the Broken who had been taken over by devils/spirits that dwell in the black ice.

In the rock under the ice are the remains of Vesta, a city built by the Missing—a race that left Abeth before the four tribes of man (gerant, hunska, marjal, and quantal) arrived. The Missing purified themselves before they vanished—they carved out their impurities, their undesirable traits: anger, selfishness, jealousy, and other evils. These evils have since escaped the vaults and polluted both the ice and now the Tainted. The leader and most powerful of these spirits is called Theus.

The Missing's city is also the source of stars and iron, both of which the Broken mine and scavenge. The stars are glowing spheres that seem to be a power source used by the Missing. Yaz has an ability to manipulate the stars, an ability seemingly shared only by a small number of the priests. The priest who threw Yaz's brother down the pit wanted Yaz to join the priesthood and has worked to recover her from the Broken.

Before Yaz escaped from the pit she drove the spirits out of the Tainted, returning the possessed people to the Broken. Theus was defeated.

Important figures from Book One:

YAZ: ~16 years old, part of the Ictha clan, quantal with the special ability to control the stars.

ZEEN: ~12 years old, part of the Ictha clan, hunska, Yaz's brother.

THURIN: ~18 years old, born under the ice, marjal with powers over water and fire. Thurin was possessed by Theus. Theus later agreed to leave him after striking a bargain with Yaz.

ERRIS: ~5,000 years old. As a young man he was lost in the undercity, millennia ago before the sun weakened further and ice covered the planet. The city adopted him. It's unclear whether Erris is really alive or just a memory kept by the city. He now inhabits an artificial body that he built with the city's help.

QUINA: ~15 years old; hunska; a quick-witted, sharp-tongued girl.

MAYA: ~13 years old, marjal, a shadow-worker, a member of the ice's most warlike clan and no stranger to killing.

KAO: gerant, well over six feet tall and powerfully built though only 12 years old.

QUELL: ~17 years old, part of the Ictha clan. Quell was going to ask Yaz to marry him just before she jumped into the pit. He followed her in later.

THEUS: age unknown, a spirit made from most of the undesirable traits of one of the Missing.

TAPROOT: age unknown, an ancient simulation of a man named Elias Taproot—brought to Abeth by one of the four tribes of men that settled the planet together after the departure of the Missing.

THE REGULATOR: age unknown, an oldish priest, responsible for selecting children to be thrown down the pit.

EULAR: age unknown; an old, eyeless man who appears to be part of the priesthood that lives in the Black Rock but he also spends time living among the Broken, who believe him to be one of them.

The priests of the Black Rock—the only mountain known to rise above the ice—exercise authority over the ice tribes. They are the only ones with access to iron and trade it with the ice tribes for furs and food.

During her time in the pit Yaz discovered that the priests give the

Broken vital salt and in exchange the Broken recover iron and stars for the priests.

In addition to the small-scale conflict between Yaz, the Broken, the Missing, and the priests of the Black Rock, there is a much-larger, older underlying conflict. Parts of many of the Missing's cities survive under the ice, and each has its own controlling mind, though these have fallen into madness in the millennia since the Missing left. The most powerful of these city minds is called Seus. Seus is engaged in a conflict with Taproot. Taproot has told Yaz that there remains a thin green corridor around Abeth's equator that the ice has yet to swallow. Seus wants the ice to cover it—Taproot wants to stop that happening. They're fighting each other through the ancient networks though Seus is much more powerful. Yaz has a needle that contains a fragment of Taproot's personality and will guide her to a more complete copy of the man.

Book One ended with an escape from the pit via a long shaft that Thurin helped melt through the ice. Yaz and others were lifted in an iron cage via a long cable. The priests of the Black Rock were hauling the cage up.

In the cage were: Yaz, Zeen, Erris, Maya, Kao, and Quell. Quell has a knife in his side. Thurin was unable to get into the cage and has been left behind. Quina is missing, presumed captured by one of the priests' mechanical star-driven hunters.

Maya climbed up the cable as the cage was rising. Yaz went up after her. When Yaz got to the top, ahead of the cage, she found the regulator and Eular there and no sign of Maya. Eular used magic to send Yaz to sleep and the regulator told the acolytes raising the cage to let it drop the two miles back into the caverns below.

1

✦ ✦
✦

THURIN

THERE HAD BEEN a great fire and there had been a great flood. Both are forces of nature that sweep clean, that wipe the slate and promise a new beginning. Thurin had been the cause of the fire and of the flood. And yet both had failed to wash away his desire to be with Yaz of the Ictha: the girl for whom the stars shone brighter.

Thurin stared up at the miles-long hole stretching vertically through the ice to a world that he had never seen. It seemed impossible that he had driven the fire that melted it. The release of his fire-talent, of energies that had built inside him for years and years, had hollowed him. The subsequent battle with the Tainted had left him bruised, bitten, and torn. And almost immediately after that he had used the full extent of his ice-work in a desperate attempt to ensure Yaz's brother joined her escape.

Even as he wondered what it was that still kept him upright, Thurin found himself collapsing to the floor. The last image to remain with him was of Yaz's impossibly white eyes locked on his as the cage rose ever further and vanished into darkness.

"WAKE UP!"

Thurin rolled to his side, groaning. A pleasant heat wrapped him and for a beautiful moment he thought himself at home in his mother's house within the settlement. He tried to cling to the illusion but it slid through his grasp, leaving only pieces of the darker dreams that had haunted his sleep, ones in which Theus stood above him pulling puppet strings to make him dance to a tune that was not his own.

"Still with us? Good."

Thurin cracked open an eye. A fierce glow, distorted by his blurry vision, stole detail from the scene but he saw enough to tell that he was lying in one of the forge sheds. Lengths of chain and a variety of tools hung from the support beams. "Kaylal? That you?"

"It is." The young smith clapped a hand to Thurin's shoulder. "Takes more than a hundred screaming Tainted to put me down."

Thurin struggled to sit. All of him hurt. Bites and scratches that he hadn't noticed before now cried for his attention. "You're alright?"

"Well, I lost both legs . . ."

Thurin smiled at the old joke. Kaylal looked as bad as Thurin felt, both eyes blackened and puffy, his ear torn and bleeding, bruising round his neck. Still, the greatest of his hurts was the loss of Exxar. The rest of his wounds would heal. "It's good to see you. How did I get here?"

"Arka had the wounded carried to shelter. The worst of them are at the settlement." Kaylal hauled himself up a chain to gain his work stool. "Your friend Yaz left in spectacular fashion, I'm told."

"She's your friend too." Thurin scowled, angry at his own evasion.

Kaylal shook his head. "I lost Exxar and there's no getting him back. Yaz has only been gone half a day. She's up there." He pointed. "It's a journey that took even me almost no time at all."

"I'm told it's harder on the way up." Thurin stood, groaning at the stiffness in his limbs.

"Seriously, though, you need to do something, Thurin. I saw how you looked at her. What will it be like spending the years to come always wondering where she is, what she's doing?"

Thurin stretched, imagining he could hear his leg bones creaking. He knew Kaylal was right and it scared him. He moved closer to the forge pot, still radiating residual heat despite being empty. "The Broken need me."

"That's just an excuse. We have Arka. We have our people back from the taint. And if this whale is really there . . ."

"It is. Getting it out of the black ice will be a problem, but I saw it. I never believed the stories when they said how big those things are!"

Kaylal grinned. "I want to see it too!"

Thurin echoed his friend's smile. It seemed madness for the two of them, neither having any memories of the ice, to be discussing his going to the surface. But if ever there had been a time for madness it was here in the days since Yaz's arrival.

"I don't know how to follow her." Thurin said it in a small voice. It seemed a sorrier excuse than being needed here. But the truth was that two miles of ice was a daunting barrier. It wasn't as if anyone had ever overcome it before Yaz made her escape.

Kaylal laughed. "They say you're the one who made that hole in the first place. If that's true then surely you can get yourself up it. I doubt they've been able to close it off yet."

Thurin frowned. "Maybe . . ." He bit his lip. "It would be dangerous though. Very."

"Oh, well. Better stay then." Kaylal took down one of his hammers and began to inspect the open chain links scattering the table before him.

"Heh." Thurin shook his head. "Everything has been dangerous since she came. I guess I've got a taste for it now."

Kaylal reached out behind him and took hold of something dark and heavy that he tossed to Thurin.

"Exxar's cape?" Thurin stroked a hand down over the garment: double-layered rat skin. It had taken an age for Exxar to barter for the furs.

Kaylal managed a smile. "He was never warm enough."

"I can't—"

"Take it. I heard it's chilly up there."

Thurin swirled the cape around his shoulders and started towards the door. He paused to set a hand on Kaylal's shoulder. "You'll look after them all for me, won't you?"

"I will, brother." Kaylal put down his hammer and laid a calloused hand on top of Thurin's. "And we'll be here if you need a place to come back to. Now go and get her."

THURIN RETURNED TO the city cavern, passing through cave after cave where the Broken wandered in numbers greater than he'd ever seen them. Those reclaimed from the taint outnumbered the Broken who had remained free, but they were intermixed now, families reunited. There were greetings from people who remembered Thurin as a baby, and others he recalled from his childhood. Some, taken more recently, rushed to hug him, trying to drag him off to this or that celebration. The joy that Yaz had left in her wake was just starting to sink in. The Broken were only now beginning to truly believe that this was no dream, that it was something real that couldn't be taken from them.

Each invitation, each reunion, weakened his resolve; each was a hook sunk into his flesh and needing to be torn free if he was to continue to his goal. It would be so easy to stay, so easy to resume the familiarity of his life, to enjoy the improved future within the company of his extended family. But Thurin knew that if he turned from his course, if he surrendered to what was easy, then Yaz would haunt him all his life, however long it might be. The great "what if" hanging over his head year after year.

And so he came to the city cavern and crossed the puddled expanse of stone, the iced-over remnants of the flood cracking beneath his feet. He walked among the abandoned wealth of iron, the wreckage of broken hunters, discarded armour, weapons cast aside. He gave a wide berth to the pit into which Theus and the other tainted gerants had fallen when Yaz collapsed the floor beneath them into a chamber of the undercity. He assumed that the pit remained full of the bodies of those who had fallen amid a tumult of shattered rock, but he had no wish to see the truth of the matter for himself. The families of the dead would come for them soon enough.

Thurin spotted a lone figure poking among the debris of Pome's hunter, Old Hanno, who after Eular had to be the oldest of the Broken at well over fifty. He raised his hand in greeting. Apart from the two of them the ruins stood deserted.

Thurin came to a halt beneath the wide throat of the hole that stretched up through the roof of the city cavern to the surface of the ice, allegedly miles above. The stardust marbling the ice illuminated the first twenty or thirty yards of the shaft in a dim multi-hued glow. Beyond that, only darkness, no hint of the sky that the stories told of. Most of Thurin's friends had memories of the surface, but none of their words really painted a picture in his mind, or even made sense. What held this "sky" up? How high above the ground was it? Where were the walls? Thurin sighed and guessed that if his plans succeeded, then he would soon see for himself and being an adult he would understand what the Broken had failed to explain from their childhood recollections.

A deep breath calmed him a little. Another deeper breath, exhaling the tension. Thurin's power to work the ice came from his marjal blood. Next to shadow-work the elemental skills were the most common to manifest in marjals. He had been strong with water and ice since his early years. By the age of ten he had been able to weaken the cave walls, allowing the gerants to dig through much more swiftly in their hunt for stars. The talent had slowly strengthened as he grew and used it daily with the mining crew, but it still hadn't been anywhere near as strong as Tarko's.

That had changed when Thurin returned from the Tainted. Something had shifted within him; some barrier had broken. He found himself capable of new feats. And in the week since Yaz's arrival it had seemed that some hitherto unsuspected internal wall had surrendered to each day's mounting pressure. In the fight with Hetta he had held her off by seizing the water that suffuses all humans. Yaz's arrival had heralded a sequence of life-or-death situations, and in each new extremity Thurin had clawed his way to some fresh height, unlocking more strength, his ice-work at last becoming equal to that of their former leader. Perhaps even surpassing it.

Another deep breath and Thurin reached for his power. The idea had come to him when he thought about how he had saved Zeen. The boy had lost his grip as the cage accelerated upwards towards the shaft. Thurin had reached out with his ice-work, his mind taking hold of Zeen's blood. Thurin had lifted the boy and sent him in pursuit of the cage, letting him grab the bars once more.

Now Thurin turned his ice-work inwards, taking hold of the water in the blood that ran through his own veins, the water that suffused his flesh. You only had to see how solid a corpse would freeze to know how much of us is water. With a small grunt of concentration Thurin lifted his feet clear of the rock. It was easier than he had feared, yet still hard enough to make him worry that sustaining the effort for as long as was necessary might be beyond him.

He rose slowly into the air with the sense that he was balancing on the narrow top of an invisible, ever-growing tower. The pressure needed to raise his bodyweight pushed back on some elastic part of his mind, some focus of his talent that would stretch and stretch again, providing whatever effort was demanded of it . . . right up to that moment when suddenly too much had been asked and without warning it might snap.

Empty yards piled up beneath his feet. The ground grew more distant, the roof closer. With the ice ceiling looming above him on every side, Thurin found himself seized by a swift and unexpected terror. The distance yawning beneath his feet seemed to exert a pull all of its own. The invisible tower on which he balanced became an unstable stack of loosely connected parts, piled way too high. The rocky expanse bearing the city's scars demanded that he rejoin it with crushing speed.

A panicked burst of power sent Thurin rushing into the shaft, and in its rapidly narrowing, rapidly dimming confines the distance beneath him was quickly tamed. Within a short time, all that could be seen below him was a shrinking circle of light that yielded no impression of the fall it concealed.

Within a hundred yards the darkness wrapped Thurin completely and from then on he was simply a dot of warmth rising blind through the night, grazing the ice walls from time to time, and wondering if the seemingly endless shaft would spit him out into the world above before gravity's pull overcame his willpower and dragged him screaming back to a quick but ugly death.

Up, always up. Thurin lost track of time. The pain built behind his eyes until he also lost all sense of where he was going and why. Up and up. And the hurt kept getting worse.

2

✦ ✦
✦

QUELL

QUELL LAY IN the rising cage surrounded by stacked boards from the settlement and carelessly heaped fungi. The knife in his side pinned him to each moment, the pain both sharp and at the same time a dull, pervading ache. It hadn't hurt going in. The sight of the hilt, tight against his flesh, had astonished him.

The weakest among the Tainted had been more dangerous than Yaz thought, but she had been right to try to stop him swinging his axe at them. Even now he would rather be lying here, waiting to die, than sitting unharmed and carrying the memories of children he had hacked apart. There are prices worth paying to stay alive, and others not worth paying.

The regulator's price for saving Yaz's life had been one Quell had been prepared to pay. He had thought her dead already. The weight of sadness that he'd had to carry from the Pit of the Missing on the day she fell had been more than he thought he could bear. He still told himself that she fell. For her to have thrown herself down seemed to speak of a willing destruction of the bond that he thought had grown between them. He had been going to ask her to walk with him for the rest of their days. To share a tent and raise children of their own. If she had jumped rather than fallen . . . what did that mean? He should have been the rock she clung to, her com-

fort in the face of Zeen's death. Instead it seemed that her own life had
been the price that she was ready to pay to escape him.

Yaz's mother had climbed from the crater as though she were a dead
woman walking only out of habit. Yaz's father, a man given to silence, had
cracked open in a way he had not before, even when the dagger-fish took
his youngest son. Yaz's uncle and her mother's cousins had had to wrestle
her father from the crater while all the time he fought and raged against
the Gods both in the Sea and in the Sky.

Lies and deceptions had seemed a small price when Regulator Kazik
had taken Quell aside and spoken those two golden words. "She lives."

Quell's task had been a simple one. To locate Yaz and then use the tiny
star the regulator had given him to summon an early collection of iron in
the city chamber. He was also to introduce himself to the blind man, Eular,
and pass on the regulator's regards and cryptic messages, saying nothing of
that to anyone else.

For the price of that small deception Quell would get to return a
daughter of the Ictha to stand beneath the sky once more. A daughter re-
stored to grieving parents. And then, only then, when they stood free upon
the ice again, would he be able to ask the questions that had burned inside
his chest ever since she fell. Only then would he have been able to ask her
to share his life.

Of course now he lay dying. Even if the priests returned him to the
Ictha he would just be a source of sorrow for them as they enacted the ritual
of farewell and left him alone on the ice with salt and a cube of harpfish for
his hunger.

Worse still, he lay dying while forced to look up at the stranger who so
fascinated Yaz, dark of eye and skin where the Ictha were copper-skinned
and so pale of eye that the white and the iris became almost the same thing.
The man seemed both impossibly strong and impossibly fast, matching
Zeen's superhuman swiftness and exceeding the strength of the Ictha
manyfold. And the cruellest blow might be that he had the calm confidence Quell had sought all his life. Quell's own reserve had cracked at Yaz's
fall and had started to desert him in earnest the moment his rope had
snapped and he began his own fall into the midst of the Broken.

Even now, Erris was examining Quell's wound, probing around the knife with his fingers as if they could somehow see deep into the surrounding flesh.

"I was wrong," Erris said. "Given what's been cut it would be better to leave the blade in place until we are somewhere warm with more resources."

"Just take it out," Quell grunted.

Erris shook his head. "You would bleed to death. Quite likely before we even get you out of this cage."

"Go and help Yaz then!" Quell's anger rose. Erris had stayed only to help him. And that had meant leaving Yaz to climb the cable on her own in pursuit of Maya.

"I can't see her at all now." Zeen sounded worried, staring up the cable after his sister, towards the distant circle of sky above them. During the long, slow ascent the boy had oscillated between joyous excitement at his return to the surface and abject terror that the regulator would simply deliver him to the depths again. In the excited moments Quell saw glimpses of the child who had marched south to the Black Rock with him. He hoped that child would return in full back on the ice and manage to leave the horrors of the Tainted in the hole in which they belonged. Though how Zeen might survive in the teeth of the wind, broken as he was, Quell didn't know. Perhaps Yaz could persuade the priesthood to find a place for him within their mountain halls. She would have to deal with the priests of course. Quell had never thought her plans of a trek into the vast expanse of the southern ice anything but fantasy. The regulator would be waiting for them at the head of the shaft. And the magics of the priests were known to be unstoppable. Even this Erris would be put on his knees before it. The enchantments of the priests had held two dozen clans in check for generations.

"How far above us do you think she is?" Zeen asked again.

"Too far," rumbled Kao. He held up a hand against the far-off circle of light and tried to squint past it. He too sounded scared. Despite the boy's great size Yaz had assured Quell that he was hardly older than her brother.

The cage continued its smooth upward journey. The walls of the shaft were close on every side now and the cage scraped along one wall, spitting pulverized ice over all four of them. The white circle of sky grew ever larger, breaking the darkness into twilight. Quell began to see detail in it, some kind of structure over which the cable must run. He knew a moment's fear for Yaz then—had she been dragged over the crossbar? But no, if she had come to grief in such a manner she would have fallen back.

The sound of the wind moaning across the open mouth of the shaft began to reach them. Already it seemed colder. Quell gave thanks that this was not the north. His skins were still damp from the flood that had poured out when Thurin had melted the passage. In any true cold it would be a death sentence.

With less than a hundred yards of shaft remaining, the cage came to a sudden halt.

"What's happening?" Zeen got to his feet.

"Nothing good," Kao muttered.

Quell struggled to sit but Erris laid a hand to his chest. "Remain still."

Quell would have told him to find a sea and jump in it, but the pain from the knife became so sharp that he had to lie back in any event. He remembered the crash as the empty cage had hammered down on the city after the flood. He remembered the emptiness in the regulator's eyes as he pushed children into the Pit of the Missing. "They're going to drop us."

Quell's words seemed to crystallize a truth that they all already knew. Erris was first to act. Almost too fast to follow he snatched up one of the stakes with which Yaz had planned to anchor their shelter. Next he took the heavy iron mallet that had fallen between two stacks of boards. With a single blow and a strength that even the largest gerant surely could not match, the man drove the stake a good two-thirds of its eighteen-inch length into the wall of the shaft, leaving the remaining six inches jutting out through the gridded bars of the cage wall.

"Zeen, you help." Erris stuck another into place on the other side with two swift blows.

Zeen, moving as fast as Erris, began to supply the man with stakes, allowing him to focus on placing them and driving them home.

"That will hold us!" Quell tried to raise his voice between the hammer blows as Erris set a fifth stake. The cage was heavier than its contents, but even its substantial weight should be secure with five deep anchors.

"You're forgetting the cable!" Erris said, accepting a sixth stake from Zeen.

Even as he spoke the cage jolted and settled heavily on the stakes. The cable above them began to fall, dragged down by its own weight, bowing against the shaft walls and then coiling down on top of the cage in a shower of broken ice. The metal cable began to mount up on the cage housing with frightening speed. The weight of it must be incredible and there were the best part of two miles' worth of it still to come. Within moments the light had died to a fraction of what it had been.

Erris drove the last of their stakes home. Already the ice around them groaned as the increasing weight strained against the hastily sunk anchors.

"I have to get up there before too much cable comes down." Erris snatched up both awls they'd brought with them in case new holes had to be made in the boards during repairs.

Quell watched Erris climb. He wondered if the man would be able to find a way out of the rapidly growing mass of cable overhead. If not the weight would increase until the six stakes tore loose and they all made the long fall to their deaths.

Erris moved fast and exerted his enormous strength to push a way through the coils of iron cable. More quickly than Quell had imagined possible, he was gone, leaving them in darkness with the continuing thunder of descending metal overhead.

"Can he do it?" Zeen asked.

"Climb out, you mean?" Kao asked.

Quell tried to imagine it. A hundred-yard wall of smooth ice with cable rushing down just a yard from it. Erris would be relying on the two thin awls, hauling himself up by strength of arm alone, his whole weight, which according to Kao was far more than it should be for a man that size, depending on first one of the spikes and then the other. "Yes, he can do it." It seemed a reasonable lie to tell, bringing comfort to the two boys, and if he was wrong, then it would all be over soon enough.

They waited, blind and helpless. The sound of piling cable grew muffled as the thickness built above them. The stakes groaned alarmingly, the ice around them beginning its inevitable surrender to the mounting pressure. Quell could feel that he was bleeding again. Something had moved the knife. Perhaps the jolt earlier as they tried to drop the cage, or maybe Zeen had knocked it while scrambling for the stakes. Either way, his lifeblood was running from the freshly opened wound once more.

"What does it mean?" Zeen asked the darkness. "Yaz wouldn't have let them drop us."

"They must have taken her," Kao answered in a hopeless voice.

"Or lost her and done this out of spite or to lure her back." Quell spoke in gasps around the pain of his injury. He had never thought to die stabbed by a knife worth more among the Ictha than all of the possessions he had gathered in his life. But now it seemed instead that his end would come beneath a weight of metal greater than that owned by all the clans of the three tribes combined. He doubted anyone from the ice had ever died a grander death. And still he wanted to live, to fish the hot seas, to wait out the long night, to father children of his own.

The cage lurched downwards, just a fraction, but enough to bring cries of alarm from all three of them. One of the stakes must have gone. The other five were holding. For now.

"It's stopped . . ." Zeen croaked.

Quell wondered what he was talking about. Of course it had stopped, or they would all be falling.

"The sound," Kao said.

Save for the groaning of ice there was no noise from above.

"It might—" Quell bit off the words. It might be just that too much now lay atop them to hear through. But why not let the other two think Erris had made it out? Maybe he truly had.

They waited in the dark with the creak and complaint of the ice all around them, sometimes a deep far-off sound that reverberated in his chest, sometimes high-pitched and close, like the sudden fracturing of something brittle. Already, even after just a few days, Quell had grown as used to the sounds as he had been to the ceaseless moan of the wind.

With a groan of his own he raised himself a little, resting his shoulders against the board stacks. He could feel Kao and Zeen's silent fear, and as the only adult among children he felt he should offer what comfort he could, even if it was only distraction from their fate. "More adventure than you ever wanted, eh, Zeen?" The boy had lived for tales of danger and discovery.

"Hells yes . . ." Zeen managed a broken laugh. "I could use some boring right now. Just set me to repairing tent hides or waxing runners. I don't mind." He sighed. "I want Yaz back."

"Don't you worry about her," Quell said. "She's strong. Stronger than all of us."

"She let the dagger-fish take Azad . . ." Zeen's voice trailed off.

Quell growled: "I didn't see your brother get taken. I heard the cry and he was gone when I turned. I saw Yaz leaning over the side with her arms in the waves. Then I saw the boat turn over. And then I saw it go down. Now, I'm not saying it wasn't a dagger-fish, just that no dagger-fish I've ever seen or heard about could take an Ictha canoe under. It had to have been the biggest damn dagger-fish to swim the sea. More likely a whale-eater looped a coil round your brother and pulled him under. What amazes me isn't that something like that would snatch Azad but that anyone, even an Ictha, had the strength to hold on to him so tight that the whole boat would be dragged under. The aprons were in place. No water was getting in past Yaz and not even that much where Azad had been. You've no idea how much force it takes to pull a canoe down when it's full of air. I'd be astonished if a dagger-fish could manage it, but think of this: it had hold of Azad, not the boat, so the only thing dragging that boat down was Yaz, by not letting go. I know I couldn't have held on."

"What happened next?" Kao asked in an awed breath. "How did she get out?"

"I thought she was gone too." Quell winced at the memory. "The sea was calm, just a few bubbles rising. I couldn't even see the boat. I knew she was gone. I was shouting for the others. I . . ." His voice caught in his throat. He hadn't the words to say how it had felt just watching the water where she vanished. It had been as if he were drowning too.

"Jex and Jax had arrived in their boat and were shaking their heads. She'd been gone forever. She had to have drowned by then even if she wasn't eaten. Jex was just saying how sorry he was and suddenly something broke the water nearby, like a breaching whale, launching nearly clean out of the waves. We paddled towards it through the mist. And there she was, unconscious, flopped over in the canoe. The air trapped inside had shot it back up once she let go. That's Yaz for you. That's how strong she is. And she tells it like a dagger-fish just took a bite, dragged Azad off and she left him to his fate." He shook his head in the darkness. "I think something broke in her that day. I think that was the day she started to change. Started to become . . . what she is now."

They sat in silence for a long moment after that. Just the blind dark all around them and the groan of the ice. Quell gathered himself. "What about you . . . Kao, isn't it? What clan are you?"

"Golin!" A halfhearted Golin chest-thump sounded in the dark. "Best there is . . ."

Quell knew the boy was wondering if they might ever take him back. Privately, Quell thought there was more chance of finding the green on Yaz's crazy quest. The Golin were famous sticklers for rules and regulations. The code had kept them alive in the wastes and they in turn kept the code alive.

Quell changed the subject to keep the lad from brooding. "What do the Golin fish in those southern seas of theirs?"

"Southern?" Kao bridled, as Quell had known he would. "The Golin are the best fishers on the ice. We follow the Wandering Sea and our boats are longer than a full-grown red shark."

Kao carried on, talking about species both known and unknown to Quell, boasting as boys will, showing his enthusiasm for the hunt, telling of the time a sheerfish had bitten off his paddle without even enough of a jerk for him to know that the blade had gone.

Time passed, and Zeen was telling Kao about the pranks young Ictha played with the dry ice at the end of the long night, when Quell realized that for the first time in an age he could make out a dim outline of the boy.

Their own long night had come to an end. Looking up he saw a weak light fingering through gaps in the coiled mass of cabling. Even as he stared the illumination grew stronger, more yards of cable lifting.

"Quick, Kao. Find that hammer and be ready to pull those stakes when the cage tries to rise. A solid upstroke on each should work them free."

The cable above them continued to snake away, until at last the final coil unwound and the whole thing became taut. The cage jolted upwards.

"Get them free!" Quell coughed.

"What if it's a trick? To get us loose then drop us again?" Kao hesitated.

"Just do it!" If Quell had to lie in the cage with a knife in him for the rest of his life then he would rather that be a short time than a long one.

Kao hammered and tugged and a dozen blows set them free. Immediately they began to rise.

The daylight intensified rapidly. Quell found himself shocked by its brightness and was soon squinting at the world through the gaps between his fingers. The noise of clanking metal grew louder and louder as they rose. Suddenly they were in the open, the wind knifing through the bars to steal their body heat. Kao and Zeen began to shiver immediately, but Quell, even in his damp skins, welcomed the freshness of it. The air in the caverns had felt dead to him; the air in the city smelled of decay. The wind, though, that was a living thing. Not a friend but an adversary that reminded him he too was alive, even with the blade bedded in his side.

A dark hand reached out and slipped a hook through the cage bars. The clanking that had ceased now resumed and the cage was dragged to the side, beginning to lean at an angle away from the iron frame that stood over the shaft mouth and about which the cable slid on a wheel.

"Don't let anything fall out!" Quell barked. "Quick!"

Zeen took him at his word and moved with lightning speed to prevent the fungi and smaller tools rolling across the now-sloping boards and out through the cage bars.

Erris climbed the outside of the cage and fixed another hook, higher up this time. He returned to a huge piece of winding gear, toothed iron wheels stacked in brain-aching complexity. Erris set both hands to an iron bar standing out horizontally from the central mechanism and placed his feet in small pits in the ice for traction. He began to circle the device, pushing the capstan bar; there was more clanking. His progress turned the wheels within wheels, and somehow released some of the main cable while drawing the newly attached cable in close. The net result was to stand the cage on its base beside the shaft.

Quell struggled to sit, cursing all the gods he knew by name. The expanse of the ice greeted him, endless, white, haunted by the wind. The only landmark was the Black Rock, thrusting through the glacial sheet, a vast fist of stone not more than a few miles distant. The shaft mouth with its winding gear and gantry was deserted, though Quell noticed a smear of crimson not far from the mechanism, and a scatter of droplets around it. Someone had bled here.

"Why is it so cold?" Zeen hugged himself. It looked wrong, one of the Ictha bothered by a southern breeze, but Quell had seen great changes in both Yaz and her brother over their week or so beneath the ice. He could see no reason, though, why such changes should crowd into the space of a few days when for the year before their drop neither sibling had shown anything but the slight signs of their difference creeping upon them. Perhaps it had been the stars.

"Kao and Zeen, if you could climb out first, I can help Quell." Erris's voice broke the landscape's spell and both began to climb, Zeen practically running up the bars. Kao, moving more slowly, found his hands sticking to the freezing iron.

Erris climbed in and Quell, knowing the feeling unworthy of him, began to hate the man even as he descended into the cage. Erris would carry him out of there as though he were less than a child, lifting a full-grown man of the Ictha with one arm, while Quell hung useless, trying not to scream as he jolted against the bars.

"This isn't good." Erris knelt to inspect where the knife stuck into Quell's side. "I'll have to try something." With a grimace he held his hand between them, squeezing thumb and forefinger together. Within a few heartbeats both digits began to smoke. With his other hand Erris pinched the side of the wound closed then ran the tip of his smoking finger along the joined edges. Where his finger passed, a dark brown strip the same colour as Erris's skin now covered the redness of Quell's skin and sealed the gash around the knife.

"That should hold you." Erris reached around Quell and, with a father's care, lifted him; then began to climb.

The nightmarish pain was thankfully brief and Quell lay gasping on the ice with Kao and Zeen watching anxiously over him while Erris returned for something from the cage.

"What happened here?" Quell asked when Erris came out again carrying boards and wire.

"When I emerged there was no sign of Yaz or Maya." Erris set to work wiring three boards together. "Only six robed priests standing by the capstan. They ordered my surrender and then took up iron bars against me when I would not." Erris shrugged. "When they found that they couldn't overwhelm me they retreated, dragging their wounded. They went that way." He pointed towards the Black Rock.

"I think . . . I can see them." Kao shaded his eyes and squinted out over the fractured landscape of pressure ridges separated by ice flats. "Far off, still heading away."

Erris worked to fashion a sled on which Quell could be dragged. "We'll have to follow them."

Zeen nodded, his mouth a flat, worried line.

"Go to the Black Rock?" Kao seemed aghast at the idea.

"Yaz must have been taken there." Erris cast a dubious eye over the ice. "Besides, where else is there to go?"

"I . . ." Kao twisted his mouth. "I could strike out to the west and meet the Golin on the shores of the Lesser Sea."

Erris looked incredulous but extended his arm out towards the west. "I wish you the best of luck with that. But I bet it's warmer inside the Black Rock. In any event, I have to take Quell there. His only chance is to have the knife removed and then to rest somewhere warm with access to food and water."

Kao bowed his head, still shivering. "I guess if Yaz needs us . . ."

And before long Quell found himself being dragged across the ice on boards made by the Missing from gods knew what, towards a forbidden mountain full of mystery.

3

✦ ✦
✦

YAZ

YAZ WOKE WITH a groan. For a blessedly long moment she had no idea where she was. She wondered if she had somehow fallen back into the city, for wherever she had ended up there were no familiar sounds, no wind worrying at the tent hides, no cavern walls creaking as the ice edged forward, no drip drip drip of meltwater. No sounds at all.

She sat up, still wrapped in ignorance, and found herself in a chamber not unlike those in the city of the Missing but hewn from the rock rather than walled with poured stone. She lay on a platform rather like a table with very short legs, the bedding a luxury of furs such as all of the Ictha together would be hard-pressed to muster from their tents. A small iron pot of stardust provided very muted illumination.

The chamber had one exit, sealed by a heavy iron door with a small window in it. The sudden memory of Eular drove Yaz to her feet. The old man had been in league with Regulator Kazik all along. More than that, he seemed to be in charge!

Yaz reached the door in three strides. She stopped herself, fist raised to pound iron, a demand for release on her lips. Instead she pushed on it to confirm that it wouldn't open. Nobody seals you in a room just to let you out when you tell them to. She returned to sit on the bed and gather her thoughts.

Eular couldn't have spent his whole life with the Broken and yet be a high-placed priest, possibly the highest of all and commanding the Black Rock. She had met him beneath the ice in that cave on the very margins of the air gap melted by the stars. He had lived alone, summoning his visitors and seldom mixing with the Broken . . . What had Thurin said about him? Eular could go for months without being seen. That had to mean he had a way between the surface and the caves. Maybe something like the iron-collection route but secret. Though how such an exit could be kept hidden from the Broken Yaz had no idea.

As Yaz sat, fractured memories began to emerge from the darkness that Eular had forced upon her, reassembling themselves into the story of her recent past. With sudden shock, Yaz remembered the cage. Her brother, Erris, Quell, and Kao hadn't been far behind her, coming to the surface. The phrase "have them drop the cage" returned to her, the last words that she'd heard before she passed out. In an instant she was there at the door, hammering on the metal, shouting for Zeen. If she could have touched the Path she would have blown the door off its hinges. But she'd drawn on her power too much recently and the Path lay beyond reach.

Yaz could see a rock-hewn tunnel and several more doors like hers, but nobody came to their dimly lit windows. She shouted until her voice grew hoarse, her cries echoing away down the passage. Scared and angry, she turned from the door, rubbing the side of her hand. Her eyes came to rest on the only thing of interest in the room. The small bowl of glowing stardust.

Yaz walked slowly towards the bowl, attuning her mind to the faint buzz of innumerable heartbeats. The tiny stars sang in harmonies, their song spiralling past the upper edge of Yaz's hearing, even though she wasn't listening to them with her ears. She held her hand out flat about a foot above the bowl and made the twinkling dust rise in streamers to gather beneath her palm. When the bowl lay empty, its contents hanging in a shifting mass below her fingers, Yaz slowly turned her hand and let the dust flow across her skin, a glowing glove of muted colours.

The door grated open and the dust fell from her hand, grey and lifeless. A man stood in the doorway, silhouetted by the lanterns of the two armoured figures behind him.

"I heard you were awake." Eular stepped into the room, seemingly confident in his blindness.

For a vivid moment Yaz saw herself wearing the iron pot on her fist and punching the old man full in the face. The vision faded, but not the anger. "Where are my friends? Where's Zeen?"

"Back in the undercaves with the Broken." Eular's words were mild where Yaz's had been hot.

"I heard you say to drop them!"

"A figure of speech." Eular waved the idea away. "The descent is fast but the cage slows towards the end and comes to a gentle rest."

The tension in Yaz's jaw eased a fraction, backing away from the level where it felt her teeth might shatter at any moment. She hoped what he'd said was true. "Why?"

"Why?" Eular echoed. He advanced into the cell and one of the armoured men followed him in.

"Why . . . everything?" Yaz realized she wasn't cold. The air held a warmth at odds with all the stone heaped around her.

"Straight to the big questions." Eular's smile was fatherly, gentle beneath the eyeless horror of his face. Yaz found herself torn between pity and trust, but rejected both. She had been lied to by this man from the first moment they met.

"So tell me the big answers to my big questions," she said.

"You were wearing a new glove when I came in." Eular patted his way towards the bed and sat on it.

"You can see?" Yaz hadn't imagined that he'd lied about that too, not with his hollow sockets to back his claim.

"I can see stars."

Yaz frowned. "Just stars?"

Eular shrugged. "Sometimes they illuminate a fraction of their surroundings for me. I knew about your experiment with the dust from the shape the stars formed."

Yaz shook her head. "You're not answering me!"

"About the big questions?" Again that smile, which was so easy to believe in. "I'm stepping towards them by example. You were desperate and afraid. It drove you to experiment. I have little doubt that given enough time you would have found your way through that door and forged a new skill in the effort."

"So?" Yaz had treated elders with respect her whole life. It was the Ictha way, to honour those who survived so long when the wind was a whetted knife always seeking to skewer those in its path. But Eular was like no elder she had ever met. And thinking of the wind as a knife brought with it the chilling reminder that Quell had been stabbed. She became aware that Eular had given up talking in favour of watching her with his empty stare. "So I would have found a new skill. So what?"

"Have you not changed, Yaz? Changed beyond recognition in your short stay with the Broken, full of hardship and extreme peril as it was?"

"I . . ." She nodded.

"And your friends? Have they not changed? Who was it that fired the coal seam? There were none capable of such work when I left."

"Th—" Yaz bit off Thurin's name, not wanting to offer Eular any answers. "They have changed, yes."

"Well, that's the purpose of the caverns. That is the why." He spread his hands. "To change you. The truth is that it is not training which brings the old bloods to their full potential. The barriers that lie between us and what we could be are ones that can only be broken in the most extreme circumstances. True fear, true agony, true striving at the very edge of existence to save yourself, your friends, your family. There must be hope too. Always a sprinkling of hope.

"We don't mine stars or iron in the Pit of the Missing. We mine you. We make heroes. We make warriors."

"The hunters . . ." breathed Yaz.

"The hunters are there to chase you, to scare you. And when you're ready, they are there to collect you."

"Quina's alive? She's here?"

"Quina? The hunska girl from the Kac-Kantor clan? She came to the caves fast and left faster. Hunskas can be very quick to make the break-through. Always in a hurry." He smiled at his own joke.

A weight lifted off Yaz's heart. She hadn't spent long with Quina but somehow she felt like a truer friend than the few Ictha girls her age ever had. "Can I see her?"

Eular nodded slowly. "Later."

"And Quell! Quell's hurt. He has a knife in him. How could you send him back down there?" Yaz took an angry step towards the bed and the guardsman matched it with a step of his own. A large man, though not a gerant. He had pale eyes and a face that, like those of the Broken, had not been carved by the wind. "You sent Quell to die!"

Eular shook his head. "The Broken have healers, marjals with a talent for it. Gella is the best. You met her, yes? Quell is better off with the Broken than with any of the clans, the Ictha least of all. The Ictha would take the knife for the iron and leave the man bleeding on the ice with empty words about his heroic sacrifice."

Yaz held her tongue at that. It was true that the Ictha could offer noth-ing to those too injured to pull a sled and pitch a tent. The harshness of their existence left no room for such compassion. "You still haven't explained—"

Rapid footsteps approached down the passage and a woman arrived, hurrying past the guard outside. She came to a halt, her priest's robes flap-ping, trying not to pant. "Strangers. Approaching the east gate."

Eular stood smoothly, as though he were not an ancient whose knees should creak with every move. "Strangers?" He smiled. "Remarkable."

And with that he turned to go. "I must ask you to stay here, Yaz."

Yaz made to follow. "I don't want—" But the guard pushed her back and the heavy door slammed shut.

"Strangers . . ." Eular turned at the window. "I may have spoken more truly than I knew when I called you an agent of change."

4

✦   ✦
✦

THURIN

A WHITE DOT broke into Thurin's unending pain. A white dot
that grew slowly as Thurin drove himself towards it. To begin
with he thought it a hole in his mind, the first indication that
the effort of lifting himself was starting to tear him apart. Later he remembered how the city cavern had shrunk to a circle of light that had diminished into a point and then winked out, swallowed by the darkness.

"The sky." The sound of his own strained voice surprised him. The roof
of the world cavern lay above him, lit by its own stars. Though he vaguely
recalled that those only came out at night. Whatever that was.

Thurin drove himself upwards, the agony of the effort bone-deep now.
It felt as though he were still tethered to the rock so very far beneath him,
and that each yard stretched the tether a little more, building the tension
that sought to reclaim him. The stones of the city continued to reach for
him with a blind, insatiable greed.

The ceiling of the world grew larger, closer, brighter, a blue-white disk
threaded with faint lines of crimson. A moaning sound grew too, like the
bitter complaint of some great beast. And almost from one moment to the
next Thurin was out among it all. The disc of the sky sprang away in all
directions to become a dome so vast it defied both belief and understand-

ing. The beast, whose whistling voice had heralded Thurin's approach, remained invisible but somehow the air itself came alive and took him in a freezing fist, wrestling him from his course, pushing him from the hole until ice lay beneath his feet.

The light beat at him. Eyes that had known only starlight squinted and wept against the red sun's glare. Blind and disoriented, he flailed for something to hold on to.

Thurin had been pushing upwards for so long that he hardly knew how to stop. The ice retreated below him and it seemed that he might be exchanging one fatal fall for another. But at last he managed to unclench the muscle in his mind that pain had locked solid, and began to fall, though less swiftly than if the world had had its way with him.

The ice met him with a hard jolt and he collapsed onto it. This ice was not like the ice he had known all his life; it was rough and dry where the caves were smooth and wet. It was colder too, colder than the farthest-flung caves. And the wind! Thurin stood quickly, wrapping Exxar's rat-skin cloak tight about him. Already he was shivering. The shock of the frigid air in his lungs made his chest hurt. He squinted against the brightness, now coming at him from the ice as well as the sky. Tears leaked from his eyes, freezing on both cheeks.

Thurin made a slow turn. The spike of pain driven into his brain by recent efforts discouraged him from any sudden move. He turned with his body, not twisting his neck. Apart from the iron gantry, the cage, and the winding gear, there was nothing. Not one thing to rest the eye on until his turn brought a distant mountain into view. It took an age for his mind to make sense of what his eyes presented it with. Even then he wasn't sure of the distances. How far to the point where sky met ground? How far to the mountain? It depended how large the pile of rock was, and Thurin had no real idea.

He turned instead to the familiar. To the empty cage that had carried Yaz and the rest. Their food and shelter had been left inside. He reached through the bars for one of the yellow-cap mushrooms and found it frozen solid, welded to the others in a fixed mass. When he withdrew his arm his wrist brushed the iron and even that brief contact seared him, taking skin with it.

Thurin pulled his hands into his sleeves and hugged them beneath his armpits. Already his face was a mask of numb flesh that no longer seemed to belong to him.

"The mountain." There wasn't anywhere else to go.

Thurin bent his head and began to walk. The ice near the winding gear had a large smear of blood across it; more splatters led away. He wondered if the blood was Quell's. Perhaps they took the knife out of him there.

He trudged forward with his gaze on the ice, lifting his eyes only to check that he hadn't strayed from his course. The great emptiness on every side haunted him, filling his mind with obscure existential fears. The expanses of space, the freedom to walk arbitrarily far in any direction, didn't threaten him so much as wholly undermine the foundations of a life lived in confinement.

From time to time he risked a glance at the sun, a crimson orb low in the west. It seemed to him that it might be a vast star not unlike the ones that drove the hunters. Though, like the mountain, it defeated his mind's attempt to balance the equation of size and distance. It offered no warmth but somehow it felt closer to friend than to foe and he was glad to have seen it at last.

The wind shocked him with its cold persistence. There seemed no end to it and no doubt that it was a deadly enemy. Already his feet were unresponsive blocks in their inadequate casings of skins and furs. How Yaz could ever have imagined they might trek south for weeks and months Thurin had no idea. He was far from sure that he would make it to the mountain. Already he was thinking about a retreat to the peace and relative warmth of the Broken's caves. The forge's heat seemed a distant dream.

As he walked, that part of Thurin's mind responsible for his ice-work began slowly to hurt less, and started instead to tingle at the sense of the ice all around him. He started to see into the opaque whiteness before him, understanding the frozen flows and fractured depths of it.

The Black Rock grew larger and larger, increasing its share of his vision until he had to crane his neck to look up at the distant peak. It seemed to Thurin that the only explanation for the shaft head being deserted was that the priests must have taken Yaz and the others to the mountain. The fact that their food and shelter had been abandoned was a clear indication that they had not gone willingly.

If the priests had been able to overpower Yaz and Erris that was bad news. Yaz had worked wonders with the stars, and Erris . . . Erris was something else again. Thurin hadn't said anything but during Yaz's escape his ice-work had told him that Erris was not a man, not a person, or any live thing. There was no water in him. Whatever he was his outer appearance was a lie. He was no more human than a hunter was.

The mountain grew nearer and Thurin began to struggle with the idea of how big it was. It seemed impossible that there could be space in the world for anything so large. And in between his wonder and his fear and his suffering he began to question what sort of reception might be waiting for him not far ahead.

The stories had it that the priests lived inside the Black Rock. Thurin understood the concept of caves far better than he did the idea of the "outside" and he was looking forward to finding himself in close confines once more. But in his experience of cave systems there were many ways to get from one place to another, and many entrances.

Thurin started to veer left. Whichever way the others had been taken would still be watched. Perhaps he could find an alternative route into the mountain. He knew, though, that he had better find it quickly or this monster they called the wind would kill him and his body would lie forever in the ice's grip.

THE TALES TOLD that the Black Rock resisted the ice's advances, and that its stones were hot to the touch. The former claim was only partly true, the latter an outright lie. At the foot of the Black Rock the ice surged around the roots of the mountain, cladding the rock yards deep in some places, chasing any gorge or fissure up the steepness of the slope. But it did seem that something kept the rock a fraction above freezing, even where the wind wrought its cold anger on the heights. And thus, as the elevation grew, the ice became confined to fissures where the slow process of melting and refreezing allowed gravity to haul it back to the plains.

Thurin soon realized the scale of the task ahead of him. He would have to search the steep flanks of the mountain where the wind blew still harder, though that seemed barely possible. Before him lay a vast expanse of sullen rock that deceived the eye into thinking every hollow a cave mouth.

Thurin had to climb only a few ridges to know that if his feet hadn't lost all feeling he would be in agony from the cruel angles of the rock biting through the soft hides wound about them.

Twice within the first hundred yards he had to reach for his ice-work to save himself from falling. The cold had robbed his hands of all cleverness, reducing them to claws barely capable of holding, and his numb feet tripped over every outcrop.

Thurin soon resigned himself to the fact that his self-appointed task was an impossible one and that it would be better to trek around the mountain's base in search of the entrance that Yaz must have been taken to. For a brief while he had imagined himself a hero come to save his friends. That had been foolish pride. He should throw himself on the mercy of the priests. At least he would be with Yaz. If he set off immediately he might make it before the cold killed him.

Thurin hugged himself and took a last look up the mountain. Far above, his gaze caught on what might well be a cave mouth, huddled at the base of a daunting cliff. It was too far, too high, and it hardly seemed credible that—if it truly did connect to the priests' caverns—it would be unguarded.

With a grunt of despair, Thurin turned and stumbled back down the slope, frozen and defeated. He would have to seek the main entrance and hope that the priests wouldn't turn him away. Though to judge by the tales of the Broken there was precious little mercy on offer up in the world of sun and sky.

On the lower slopes the ice lay thicker, climbing up over rock as if eager to reach Thurin. Wary of falling, he stretched out his ice-work to find a sure path. His perception fingered through the ice with practiced ease, discovering faults and voids. Thurin was reaching out to roughen the surface along his chosen route when he became aware of a void that dwarfed all the others. Behind a few yards of ice there seemed to be the mouth of an ice-choked tunnel leading into the rock.

Thurin came to stand where the ice levelled off, facing the hidden tunnel. He wasn't sure he had enough strength left in him to reach the entrance to which Yaz and the others had been taken. He was fairly sure he didn't have enough strength to break through the ice and investigate the void he'd sensed. He was *very* sure he hadn't the strength to do both.

In the end it was the wind that decided for him. It changed direction and blew harder than ever before. Thurin's skins and Exxar's fur cape seemed helpless against the gale's assault. Wanting only to escape the wind's teeth, Thurin sank his power into the ice. Here at least he was on familiar ground. Most days of his adult life had been spent reducing ice to fragments for the gerants to clear, and then searching them minutely for stars. Ultimately even the dust would be recovered.

Thurin worked quickly, finding the natural flaws and applying the pressure that would make them spread. The fractures that reached out forked, and forked again, turning the ice milky, dividing it into fragments all interlocked in a complex puzzle. Rather than rely on the absent muscle of a half-dozen gerants to overcome the puzzle with pick and shovel Thurin applied his own ice-work, breaking the mass apart in a crackling white explosion of pieces. The wind hauled all but the largest fragments to one side in a spreading white cloud.

The effort, on top of the exertion that brought him to the surface, left Thurin's brain ringing like a cracked bell. He staggered beneath the burden of his weariness and picked his way over the larger chunks, advancing into the cavern of broken ice he had created. He moved with the caution of an old man wary of his own fragility. It felt to him as if any sudden move might shatter his skull. Even tilting his head was enough to slosh the pain from one side to the other, making him cry out in a high-pitched keening.

In this manner he advanced several yards. Almost immediately the wind died down, howling its complaints around the mouth of the tunnel. Thurin forced himself to keep moving rather than to sag into the relief and let it take him to the floor. Even without the full blast of the gale it was still bone-achingly cold and with the red sun settling towards the horizon behind him he could only imagine that it was going to get even worse.

The ice gave way to stone. The slanting rays of the sun threw Thurin's shadow ahead to join with the gloom further back along what proved to be a hand-hewn tunnel. With a gasp of relief he hurried forward until the darkness left him blind. He took from one pocket a collection of small stars, none bigger than a baby's tooth but together enough to make a dim glow about him, and, lighting his own way, he made a slower advance.

Almost immediately he began to feel better, though his head still ached fiercely as if to warn against any further exercise of his talents. The tunnel sloped upwards at a modest gradient and seemed to grow warmer every ten yards. The moan of the wind faded from hearing and before long he could almost imagine himself on a scavenging trip in the undercity.

The life gradually returned to his extremities. His feet especially hurt like all the hells, burning and tingling, but after the stories he'd heard of the cold biting off toes he was very glad to feel his own complaining.

Thurin pressed on. Like the undercity, the passages and occasional chambers he passed had a feeling of having been deserted long ago. He wondered that the priests would take the enormous effort to carve such space from the mountain and then not use it.

The rock was in the main the same hard dark stone he had seen on the mountain's flanks, but another kind of stone littered the ground in places, more fragile and darker still, a true black from which his handful of starlight could coax no variation.

"Coal," Thurin whispered, lifting a fist-sized chunk of the stuff, which was less heavy than any other kind of rock he knew.

In one spot he found a thin coal seam running through the harder stone. He wondered then if the priests mined coal from stone in the same sort of way the Broken mined stars from ice. It could be that these chambers and tunnels were part of an exhausted mine.

In a low-roofed side chamber later on he found a rusting iron truck, a container large enough to hold several men and set on four wheels. Thurin had never seen wheels before except on toys that Madeen sometimes made for the children from pieces the scavengers brought back. The scatter of broken coal at the bottom of the empty truck hinted at its purpose.

He moved on, cautious and quiet, aware of his hunger and thirst now that his body had recovered from the wind's assault. The passage he was following had widened and begun to head downwards. The air continued to warm. A small noise from the darkness ahead brought Thurin to a halt. He stilled his breathing, closed his fist about his stars, and pressed his shoulders to the wall. The noise came again. A wet, tearing sound.

Thurin inched forward. He had come to learn this place. To find Yaz. Not to hide. The same task had faced Quell when he entered the unfamiliar world of the Broken, and he had not shied from it. Thurin determined to do just as well if not better, admitting to himself that he considered the man a rival.

Thurin kept to the wall, placing his feet carefully. A chamber lay ahead, lit very faintly by three small stars seemingly abandoned on the floor. The space was little more than a widening of the passage, a passing point perhaps for loads of coal and empty trucks. To one side of the chamber a figure squatted with its back to Thurin. A figure so shapeless in its mound of ragged furs that he could only guess that it was human. A very large human.

The tearing sound came again. Whoever it was . . . whatever it was . . . they seemed to be chewing something.

Thurin knew he was in danger. He didn't understand how he knew but he did. Without releasing his next breath he took a slow step backwards. Others might think it fear that pushed him away, and it *was* fear that filled him, making his hands shake and his brow sweat, but his retreat was driven by common sense rather than terror.

Even as Thurin stepped away the stranger raised a shaggy head and sniffed at the air, then again, more sharply as if catching a scent. The person turned as they rose, and continued to rise, huger and wider than Thurin had feared. One vast hand clutched the sorry carcass of what might once have been a rat. The other fur-laden arm sported a metal bar wrapped around it in a spiral. The sniffing face revealed by parting locks of filthy, thickly coiled hair split in a grin that put on show an array of teeth filed to points.

Now Thurin's fear truly overmastered him. How could she be here? How could he escape? He had imagined all manner of horrors that might await him within the Black Rock but this horror had not been among them.

"Hetta . . ."

5

✦　✦　✦

QUELL

QUELL HAD NEVER felt cold in a southern wind before but with damp skins, just thin boards keeping him from the ice, and a length of cold iron jammed into his side, there was a first time for everything.

Kao and Zeen shivered too as they flanked Erris, bowed against the wind. Erris, however, despite the flimsy nature of his garments, which were now stiff with ice, seemed unaffected. He pulled Quell along on his makeshift sled without complaint, his pace set by their slowest member, who was Zeen, generally the fastest of them all.

The Black Rock grew inexorably nearer and Quell, who had seen it several times though never closer than from the Pit of the Missing, marvelled at how much bigger it was than he had ever imagined. Vastly, impossibly huge.

The sun hung low in the sky, staring at them from above the western flanks of the mountain, which it had only recently crested. Their shadows trailed behind them as if reluctant to follow. On the east flanks thin trails of smoke escaped the rocks, streaming away at a sharp angle before being dispersed by the wind, these few signs of hidden industry being the only clue to the fact that the Black Rock was inhabited.

Quell shivered again and tried to imagine what welcome awaited them beneath the mountain. The priests were the guardians of the three tribes. The glue that kept the many clans together in their loose but enduring peace. True, the cage had been dropped. But perhaps that had merely been a very rapid descent. Kao and Zeen's weakness was self-evident. Their exile to the undercaves was a merciful second chance, dictated by the harsh realities of life on the ice. Accepting those cruel truths was an essential part of becoming an adult, but that acceptance didn't make you cruel. He loved Zeen, the younger brother he'd not had. But what life was there for him with his people now?

When it seemed they had perhaps a quarter of a mile to go before they met the rock rising through the ice, Erris came to a halt. "Where do you think the entrance is?"

"Should we just be walking up to it anyway?" Kao asked.

"We want to rescue Yaz, like she rescued us," Zeen said. "We should try to find an entrance they're not watching and—"

"If we don't get inside soon and find Quell some help he is going to die." Erris turned to look down at Quell. "Do you know the way in?"

Quell shook his head. "When we came out of the shaft we were already closer than I've ever been. If we're heading in the same direction as the priests you chased off, then they're going to find us. They're going to be coming back, you know. These are the priests of the Black Rock. They run things. They don't run away."

"He's right." Kao had a hand raised to shield his eyes and was peering beneath it at the base of the mountain. "There's someone coming."

SOMEONE TURNED OUT to be around twenty someones. Ten of them were armoured, iron plates secured over their furs, not unlike the armour worn by the Broken. They had spears in their gloved hands and swords at their hips. There were half a dozen in the black robes that Erris had described, younger men and women bearing iron staves. The last four wore the ribbon-edged capes that Quell associated with the travelling priests who visited the clans to dispense lore, conduct ceremonies, and trade iron for the best of what they had. Two were hard-faced women, one silver-haired and shrivelled by the years, the other a brutal-faced young woman with mismatched eyes. The other two were men, the younger one with skin as pale as the ice and blue veins mapping his face, and lastly Regulator Kazik, hands bundled inside his cape, wearing his usual sour expression.

Erris stepped aside as the priests approached, allowing them a clear view of Quell on the ground. "We have an injured man who needs treatment."

The pale man leaned to mutter into Regulator Kazik's ear. Kazik glanced at Quell and then returned his gaze to Erris. "I don't recall giving you the push."

Erris shrugged. "I fell a long time ago and I am much changed by the years." He gestured to Quell with a bare hand. "You recall Quell, though. He's been stabbed. The knife is still in him."

Quell raised his voice, tired of being talked about, tired of watching from the ground with legs rising around him on every side. "What have you done with Yaz?"

The regulator ignored both Quell and his question. "You attacked my acolytes."

"They attacked me," Erris said. "I defended myself. Also, by that point they had tried to drop us back down the hole."

"Perhaps you should have let them." The regulator gave a small smile. Erris did not echo it. "Strangers are only brought to the Black Rock in chains. They remain in custody until they have been tested and identified."

"You know me, Kazik," Quell called. "I'm no stranger. You know Zeen and Kao too. You pushed them down the pit with Yaz."

The regulator curled his lip. "Quell we will take. The rest of you have broken the covenant and may enter the Black Rock in chains or not at all."

Erris cast a calculating look across the array of priests and their servants. Kazik raised a hand. "I hear you're quite the brawler, man-I-don't-remember, but you have friends both here and inside the mountain who may suffer for your actions, so think again."

Erris pressed his lips into a flat line, still considering. "Here." He raised his wrists.

Quell watched as two men came forward and set heavy chains about Erris, securing them with an iron device that closed around the links with a loud click. Two more pairs of guards took chains from around their waists and used them to secure first Kao then Zeen. Both boys flinched at the searing cold of the metal where it touched skin.

"Quell?" Zeen looked to him as the men bound him.

"It will be alright." Quell didn't know what else to say. He could have told Zeen to run, but where was there to go? The ice would kill him long before he found the Ictha, and the Ictha wouldn't have him back in any case. The chains were not an unreasonable precaution for escapees from the pit. Their breed was as dangerous as wounded whales. Who knew what magic would burst from them from one moment to the next? Even so, he hoped they had not chained Yaz.

WITH THE GUARDS and priests on every side Quell and the others were taken to the mouth of a cave so large that it seemed impossible they had not seen it from a mile away. The dark rock and black interior probably explained their blindness.

Quell endured the pain and ignominy of being dragged across progressively rougher ice and then, with more effort, rather smoother rock. The cordon of bodies around them had already muzzled the wind but Quell still felt the difference as they moved into the maw of the cave. Within a few dozen yards the air was almost still, the wind reduced to yowling its frustration out on the ice. Given time, it promised, it would tear down the mountain.

Regulator Kazik set a hand to the pale man's shoulder. "Bring the Ictha boy to me when you're done with him, Valak."

"Yes, regulator." The man inclined his head. The dark veins spreading across his face seemed almost to lie above the skin and Quell was sure his own veins didn't spread in such a manner, like encompassing fingers.

Some of the guards fell away as Kazik and the older of the two female priests took their leave. Quell was dragged into a side chamber, which was far smaller and lower-roofed than the entrance. Erris and the boys followed, prompted by their captors. On the ceiling a board not unlike the ones Quell lay on had been secured to the rock. A layer of stardust had somehow been applied to the board and provided a familiar glow. The air was warmer here and the boys unclenched their bodies.

Two priests accompanied them now: the pale man, Valak, and the woman with gerant features but normal height. She studied them with one brown eye and one blue, both of them cold. The cave had been furnished with table, chairs, and several chests, all made from material that must have been scavenged by the Broken from the city of the Missing.

Valak reached a white hand into one of the chests and brought out a box made of bone, which he set on the table. The others all backed off a pace or two as he lifted the lid and was immediately lit from below by a mix of bright colours, the upcast shadows making something sinister of him. "My name is Father Valak. This"—he gestured to the woman—"is Mother Krey. We expect your obedience in all things. Your gods remain outside this mountain. Within, there is only the Hidden God. And we are his voice."

He passed his hand over the box and the glow dimmed to almost nothing. He took out the first star and held it between finger and thumb, the tentative hold of a man worried it might burn him. The star had that quiescent, sky-behind-clouds look to it that Quell had seen Yaz induce before, a silvery luminescence.

"You first, I think." Valak brought the star close to Erris. Mother Krey moved behind Erris as if to catch him when he tried to flee, but he stood his ground, unflinching.

The priest frowned as if he had been expecting something, then moved on to Zeen, who pulled away. Even as Zeen tried to back into the guards the star in Valak's grip began to shine brighter, the silver light becoming something sharp that needled Quell's skin. Two guards held Zeen's arms while trying to keep their own distance from the star. Krey, though, grasped his neck from behind in a cruel grip, unconcerned by the star's aura.

"It's hurting me!" Zeen gasped.

Krey tightened her grasp, sneering.

"Just a little longer . . ." And Valak set the stone to Zeen's narrow chest, where it burned with the fiercest light yet. "Impressive." Valak stepped away just as it looked as though Zeen would scream. "A fully woken hunska prime at least. Quite possibly a full-blood."

The priest quieted the star again. He brought it towards Kao and then Quell, neither of whom sparked the slightest reaction in it. Krey moved behind both of them but kept her hands to herself. Valak replaced the star and selected another, this one a muted green. Zeen had no effect on it but as the priest drew it closer to Kao the gentle green became a deep and penetrating emerald. Four guards were needed to help Krey hold the boy in place until the star touched his skin.

"You have some growing to do yet, young man." Valak replaced the star, not bothering with Erris or Quell. "Gerant prime."

"W-what does that mean?"

"Just as he said. You'll grow bigger. More than a half-blood, less than a full-blood." Mother Krey walked around from behind, managing somehow to make a smile ugly. "You'll be a valuable asset in the mines."

"Mines?"

But Valak ignored Kao's question and took a violet star from the box, the third of four. This one Quell guessed would measure the marjal talent. It remained unresponsive for all of them save for Erris, where it pulsed erratically, its glowing surface patterned in black with shifting geometries.

Valak seemed puzzled. "Some kind of unrealized marjal trait? Not a strong one in any case."

"Worthless." Krey dismissed the indication with a wave of her hand. "Another one for the mines."

The final star was a touch larger than the other three and gave off a faint golden light, the stone looking as though it were a ball of liquid gold in slow but constant motion, with darker areas forming on the surface before being dragged inside by the circulation of hidden currents. A guard took this one from the box using long iron tongs, and whenever she allowed it to come near either of the priests it began to burn brighter. When pressed to the flesh of the prisoners, however, it produced nothing but a sense of profound discomfort. It made Quell feel as if his skin were not his own but was instead something parasitic that had engulfed him while he slept. The urge to scratch it off became nearly overwhelming before the star was withdrawn.

Valak shook his head and held out the box for the return of the final star. "Much as expected." He pointed a long pale finger at Erris. "This one and the gerant to the mines."

Erris made a slow shake of his head, a smile on his lips. "What are we to dig?"

"You'll dig what you're told to dig," Krey said.

"Coal." Valak waved the guards forward. "Take them."

As Kao and Erris were led away, Kao protesting that he needed to go back to the Golin, Valak turned to Zeen. "Take this one to the holding cells. Level three. We don't want him too near the sister."

Krey returned her hand to Zeen's neck and steered him roughly towards the exit before striding ahead of him. Zeen set off without a fight, rattling in his chains, making no objection. Quell was proud of the boy. The Ictha didn't complain or waste their energy. They endured and acted decisively at the moment when their effort would yield greatest results.

"And finally . . ." Valak peered down at Quell, still lying on the boards he'd been dragged in on. "The regulator says you have performed the service required of you. So we will treat your wound."

"And then send me back to the Ictha with Yaz and Zeen." Quell wanted to face the man standing, or at least to sit, but he doubted he could do either and decided not to waste his energy in the name of pride.

"Whether you can be returned to your people will depend on the high priest's judgment of your discretion. The girl and her brother will remain here."

There are some truths that you know already but hearing them spoken is a punch to the gut. Quell had known there was no place for Zeen or Yaz on the ice but somehow having that fiction shredded still tore at him. "My discretion?"

Valak nodded. "What we do here is for the future of all the peoples of the ice. There is a greater good being served beneath this mountain. A long-awaited change is almost upon us but word of it must not spread until the time is right."

Quell knew that if the priest gave him an answer to his next question it might anchor him to the Black Rock. They might never let him return to the Ictha. But Yaz was here and they weren't letting her go either. "A change?"

The priest waved the guards forward and turned away. Quell felt a certain guilty relief in receiving no answer. He held his side and braced himself against the pain of being moved.

"War," came Valak's reply. "We're going to war."

6

✦ ✦
✦

YAZ

ABANDONED IN HER cell once more, Yaz stood staring through the small window of the iron door. Strangers had come. Something so rare that it had taken Eular from his inspection of his prisoner. She imagined that clan members would occasionally visit the Black Rock for trade or to obtain rulings on matters that couldn't be settled without higher authority. But these would not be strangers: they would be recognized by any one of a score of signs—their numbers, the design of their sleds, even the pattern of their walking. Some clans actually carried banners cut in distinctive ways, though the Ictha considered this wasteful vanity. So who could the strangers be?

To meet a stranger on the ice was a once-in-a-generation occurrence. When Yaz's mother had been a young girl a man from no known clan had been spotted in the west, near the Hot Sea. He came from a tribe that the clan father of the time had never heard of. The stranger's people had a version of the Ictha's rite of passage, just as the known tribes did. Like Zin, the first of men, and Mokka, the first of women, each adult would, at a time chosen by the wind, go out and walk the ice alone. The aim of such journeying was to find the kyzat, the perfect place, a spot that on all the ice had been ordained by the Gods in the Sky and in the Sea for that individual alone as the place where all the elements of their life find meaning, giving a vision of such clarity that the air itself becomes ice and the wisdom of Sky and Sea finds a place in the seeker's heart, allowing them to endure the hardships of the years ahead.

Quell had admitted to Yaz in a private moment that his own journey to find his kyzat, a walk that had lasted four days, had brought him to an ice spike at the juncture of three pressure ridges. Here he was visited by the epiphany that, having run out of his allotted ration of angel-fish, if he did not turn back he would lose first his toes then his fingers to the wind. Yaz had wondered if that wasn't the wisdom that the ritual was designed to impart. That there is nothing but ice and more ice, and that if you are too stubborn to admit it and turn back, you will die and your malcontent will no longer burden your clan.

The stranger from the curiously named Lamarkan clan had clearly not been open to this message and had travelled so far beyond his strength and common sense that he no longer knew the way back to his people. The man limped to the Ictha's camp at the clifftops where the wind swirls the great fog from the Hot Sea and beards every line with trailing ice.

"This sea is my sea. Its fish are my fish. This is the wisdom I have found." The man had no fear, for the wind had taken it from him along with the end of his nose, the edges of his ears, and the flesh of his lips.

The Ictha had offered the stranger the warmth of a tent, though properly any who come to the Hot Sea of the North should be turned away, for it had been given to the Ictha on the day that Zin died, and belonged to no other. The man lasted four more days before the cold that had entered his bones stopped his heart. And in that time he shared with the elders some of the wisdom and lore of his people. So it is with strangers. They can bring gifts and they can bring danger. And ever after the Ictha had set a watch on the east when they took to the Hot Sea against the day that more Lamarkians might come, for part of the lore that the dying man shared was that the seas his people visited were all shrinking and that their gods had told them they must one day go in search of others.

IN TIME, YAZ went back to her bed and returned her attention to the stardust that now scattered an area of the floor close to the table. Eular had sent it to sleep in the same way that he had silenced the star she had brought with her from the city cavern. Yaz felt a sudden pang of loss for that star. She had no possessions other than what she wore. She patted herself to check that her iron knife had not been missed, but no, it too had been taken.

A gleam caught her eye and she saw that they had missed one thing, or considered it beneath them to take. A silver needle remained stuck through the skins above her collarbone. She set a finger to it. The only physical evidence she had that Elias Taproot existed—a man she had met under the strangest of circumstances in the city of the Missing. He had said the needle would lead her back to him. It wouldn't be leading her anywhere with the door locked, though.

As enigmatic as Elias was, it comforted Yaz to know she had a friend in the world beyond, the world that Erris had dwelt in before he had committed himself to the body he had spent so many years making for himself. But if Elias had not been a fever dream, then the monstrous Seus was real too. The mind of an entire city, albeit a distant one, bent on her destruction and the destruction of all those like her. That was not a comfort. Though Seus too acted in the world beyond and offered no threat that Yaz could see within the confines of the Black Rock or out in the teeth of the wind where no extra threat was needed in order to bring a swift end.

Yaz ran her fingertip once more along the needle's length and then turned her mind to matters more concrete and pressing. The stardust was a puzzle. Had Eular left it to test her? Yaz knew how to quiet a star but this was something new. Closer to death than to sleep. Only by straining her senses to the utmost could she tell that some tiny spark remained active in the dust. She collected some in her palm and returned to the bed to study it.

Eular had done something akin to when water turns to ice. Just as a falling tear will come liquid from the eye, full of flow and possibility, but become solid before it hits the ground, something had been stolen from the star grains in her hand. Yaz needed to warm them up, to remind them of the life they once had, to teach them each their song again. She had no idea how to do it.

What she did have, she discovered, was time. A commodity that had been in scant supply down in the ice caves of the Broken where danger intruded into every quiet moment. She sat, trying to concentrate on the dust, attempting to poke it back into life with her mind. She even considered singing to it, but felt too self-conscious to try to croon a broken version of star song to a handful of dust.

Instead of focusing on the dust, Yaz's thoughts slipped continuously away to dwell on the fates of Zeen, Quell, and Erris. Had Eular lied again about the cage being slowed as it reached the city chamber, or were they all safe, reunited with Thurin in the warmth and new security of the caves? And what of Maya, who had gone up the cable before her? Was the girl trekking across the ice in search of the Axit clan to report her findings as the first of their spies to escape the Pit of the Missing?

Yaz was still turning over possibilities when the sound of approaching footsteps drew her gaze to the door again. She shook away the image of Thurin being crushed by the falling cage and stood to receive her captors.

The door rattled and the sound came of something being fitted into the small hole she had spotted near the edge. The door's opening was preceded by a loud click and the sound of the object being taken back out. Two armoured guards walked in, Eular following behind.

"Still here?" He smiled.

Yaz said nothing, though her eyes strayed to the exit.

An old woman entered behind Eular, her face deeply lined, her hair, long but thinning, the colour of iron. She wore a priest's robe, with the hide strips trailing from both arms, and a lustrous silver-grey fur around her shoulders despite the heat. She fixed Yaz with black eyes that were hard as stones, then showed her teeth in a kind of smile. "I'm Mother Jeccis, my dear. Father Eular has told me so much about you."

Eular swung the door shut behind them. "I remarked on you still being here, Yaz, to make a point. It's a sad fact that when we're warm and fed and safe we humans shy away from the barriers that stand between us and our full potential." He rapped his knuckles on the metal. "If, instead of going about the business that called me away, I had spent the last hour in the corridor, torturing a loved one of yours on the other side of this door. Your brother, say. Do you think you would still be in this cell now?"

Yaz shrugged, feeling strangely guilty. "You said you put us in the pit to make us into warriors. It didn't work for Jaysin. He died. A lot of them died."

Mother Jeccis tutted, and Eular winced in a way that might not be sincere. "There's a saying that you can't make an omelette without breaking eggs. But you don't know what an omelette is, do you, Yaz? And you're thinking of fish eggs."

"I . . ." Yaz held her tongue but the image entered her mind of an ungainly bird strutting on the ground, and of an egg bigger than an eye, and not round as eggs are but an off-centred oval, with a skin that was hard and brittle . . . a shell. She shook her head to clear it of these images from Erris's world. "No. What is an omelette?"

Eular regarded her curiously from empty sockets. "We are a poor people."

"We?" Yaz rejected the familiarity. Eular was not Ictha.

"We. The ice tribes." The old man waved his arms expansively as if he were at the gathering and all the clans stood within a spear throw of him.

Yaz shrugged. It wasn't a concept she had considered before. The ice tribes were *all* the people that were, and they were not poor. Some had many furs. Others hoarded iron. Even in the hard north the Ictha managed to wring riches from the sea. Mother Mazai lit her tent with a whale-oil lamp all through the long night.

"We are poor," Eular repeated. "Starvation is common, we die young, the seas are smaller and less frequent from generation to generation."

"Poor." Mother Jeccis nodded, smiling in her fine robe.

"We can't care for our sick," Eular continued. "We can't keep those born with the old bloods alive, let alone nurture and train them. The pit is the only place where we can even approach what is needed."

"You said you mined warriors there." He had said "heroes" but Yaz wouldn't use that word. She had blood on her hands. She had made hard choices that stained her soul. "Why do you need warriors?"

"We need them, Yaz. *We.*"

"The Ictha don't fight." Yaz scowled. "The Axit talk of it. But those days are gone."

"What would the Ictha do if the Golin came north to fish the Hot Sea?" Eular asked.

"They would not."

"The Golin follow the Wandering Sea. When they lose its trail they go hungry. If they grew hungry enough they might turn their eyes north. What would the Ictha do then?"

"We would turn them back," Yaz said. "The Gods in the Sea gave—"

"The gods gave the Ictha their sea." Eular nodded. "Did you know that I was not born like this?" He touched his fingers to the edges of his eye sockets.

"You said . . ." Yaz slumped. Eular had told her that he had been cast into the pit as a baby. "You lied. Perhaps you are lying now too."

Mother Jeccis's smile vanished. "How dare—"

Eular silenced her with a raised hand.

"Perhaps." His smile held a certain sadness. He left Jeccis's side to stand next to Yaz by the bed. "In my youth I was restless. My clan roamed far to the south, beyond even the Kac-Kantor. A stranger's story took me from my family and saw me journey ever further south. I found the green lands. I saw their riches and knew that all my life I had known only poverty and hardship. I saw grass and I saw trees. And for that crime the men of that green world took my eyes. They said that their god had given them the grass and the trees and the rivers and the beasts of the land. They said if I brought my people there, then they would die two steps from the ice and the grass would drink their blood." Eular reached out, patting for Yaz, and found her hand. She flinched away but he closed his fingers about her forearm, his skin gnarled around the knuckles and withered between. "So yes, there is a green world and I saw it when I still had sight, and my hands remember the touch and the warmth of it, Yaz. But it is a place of blood and death and if we want any part of it we must carve it out for ourselves with the blade of a knife. Like slaughtering a whale. And that is why we need heroes, Yaz. The people of the ice need an army because all men make their own gods and those gods tell them only what they want to hear. But the truth is that the cold continues to grow deeper and soon even the Ictha will need to run before it. The truth is that only in the green belt of Abeth beneath the light of the sun and moon can our people hope to live and live to hope."

And Mother Jeccis, whose smile had slowly returned, nodded and showed her yellow teeth. "A war's coming. A war that will paint the green lands red."

7

✦ ✦ ✦

THURIN

THURIN SHRANK BACK against the tunnel wall as Hetta sniffed the air again. How she might scent him above the ruined rat carcass in her hand Thurin had no idea, but life in the caves did educate a nose and she had lived under the ice longer than most. Without drawing breath Thurin began to inch away. Hetta rose to her feet. Her face and both hands were stained black, all her exposed flesh bore the marks, as if she were no longer the home of just two or three demons but had been overfilled with a multitude.

Eidolon. The word surfaced through the lake of Thurin's fears. The worst of the Tainted, creatures that even Theus had been unable to control. When a mind truly broke then the demons flooded in and made a battleground of the body.

How Hetta had reached the mountain Thurin had no idea. She hadn't been in the city cavern when the Broken had fought each other and then battled the Tainted. No one had reported seeing her since her attack on Maya when Yaz had laid her low with magics that none of the Broken had ever seen before.

Thurin backed as quickly and as silently as he could but his foot scraped on loose rock and suddenly Hetta's gaze nailed him to the spot. And slid over him. Amazed, Thurin managed to swallow. He stared as

Hetta made a slow, almost fearful turn, one hand held out to the darkness as if to ward off any attacker.

Had the monster gone blind? The Tainted could see in the dark whenever their demons were in their eyes, and every part of an eidolon was filled to bursting. But somehow the shadows were hiding him from her.

"Who's there? I can hear you!" Hetta's voice held none of the malicious humour evident when they'd last met and she'd taunted Yaz. She sounded like she looked. Scared and unable to see past the limits of her scant illumination, though still with a hard core of defiant anger.

Once upon a time, when Thurin had been too young to remember, Hetta had been Jerrig's wife. The two of them were the only gerant full-bloods among the Broken. The crueller tongues had said the pair had no other choice for they would crush any other partner while coupling, but Thurin's mother had said that it was a true love and that when Hetta was taken by the taint Jerrig fell into the enduring silence that was all Thurin had ever known of the shy giant.

Thurin backed another few paces, but a fragile scrap of coal crunched beneath his heel and suddenly Hetta was charging at him, vast and unstoppable, eyes wild above a gaping maw of pointed teeth.

Knowing his ice-work was nowhere near recovered enough to hold off over nine feet of roaring gerant, Thurin turned and ran, his escape relying on the hope that he could remember the tunnel he'd just come down better than she could.

For a few terrifying moments Hetta almost had him, then the sound of her collision with the wall cut off her howling, and the noises of pursuit fell behind. When he thought it was safe, Thurin opened his hand a little and let enough starlight leak out to aid his navigation. Hundreds of yards and many turns later, Thurin came to a stumbling halt with the breath labouring in his lungs. He'd come to a suspiciously familiar junction where several tunnels met. He leaned over, hands on knees, panting to recover his wind.

Hetta came from nowhere, a huge shape rising at his side, and with a single sweep of her arm she threw him into a blackness that no star, however bright, could lead him out of.

✦ ✦ ✦

THE FIRST OF Thurin's senses to return to him was smell. The stench that assaulted his nose reminded him of the rank caverns of the Tainted, the acrid, eye-watering stink that humanity can reach only by years spent wholly neglecting all forms of hygiene. Next he became aware that along with his ongoing sources of pain he had two new complaints. The side of his head ached, his left ear feeling five times its normal thickness, and something heavy lay across his back, pinning him to the ground, the body of a large man perhaps.

A groan escaped Thurin's lips before he found the presence of mind to play dead and gather his strength.

"You're going to show me the way out of here." A rumble deeper than most men could manage, but enough to let him know who his captor was.

"Hetta?" He tried to keep the fear from his voice.

"You know me, boy?" She didn't sound like the Hetta from the ice caves—she sounded changed, like the Hetta who'd chased him blind and yet had somehow caught him.

"That's why you haven't eaten me yet?" Thurin asked. "You're lost?"

"Eaten you?" Hetta sounded disgusted at the idea. "I don't eat—" She broke off, suddenly unsure. "How did you know my name?"

"All the Broken know your name." Thurin tried to lever himself off the stone floor but got nowhere. What he had taken for a large man lying across him was one of Hetta's legs. In the dimness of his scattered star grains he could make out an enormous foot, heel to the ground, long as his arm from fingers to elbow and wrapped in stinking hides. "How did you get here?" Even at the monster's mercy curiosity ate at him and he didn't want to take it to his death with him.

"I . . . got lost." She sounded uncertain. "I didn't know we'd tunnelled into the rock like the Missing." A massive hand fastened around the back of his neck, and the leg lifted from him. "You can lead me back." She got to her knees and stood him on his feet as a child might stand a toy man.

"You think you're still under the ice?" Thurin stared up at the face, so close to his. What he had taken for demon stain was a mix of damp, caked-on coal dust, mottling her face, neck, and hands.

"Where else is there?" Hetta's eyes, small, deep-set, and dark, scanned the blackness around them. The topology of her skull raised thick bone to form brutal features: broad cheekbones, a jutting jaw, a forehead that looked capable of crushing rocks. The sharpened teeth still terrified Thurin but he now saw something unexpected, something he had never thought to see on the cannibal's face. In place of the Tainted's rage was an angry defiance, and, beneath that, not the customary hunger but uncertainty. Perhaps even fear. "Show me how to get back." She shook him, hard enough to make his teeth rattle.

"We're inside the Black Rock," Thurin managed. "Stop! If you kill me I won't—"

"Kill you?" Hetta sounded shocked. She shifted her grip to his arm and let him stand.

"You . . . You're not tainted anymore?"

"Tainted?" Hetta spoke the word with soft horror. Thurin heard the sound of her tongue sliding behind her lips over the serrations of her teeth.

"How did you get here? What do you remember?"

"I . . . I had an evil dream." Hetta's deep voice cracked. "I need to go home. Where's my Jerrig?"

Thurin felt an unexpected stab of sympathy deep in his chest, the breath in his lungs hitching. He too had been ridden by the evils of the Missing, though the spirits that had invaded him had been less wild and had stayed for a much shorter period. "I'm Thurin. You know me from when I was a child. I'm looking for my friends. If you come with me we can leave together."

"Thurin?" Hetta rubbed the back of her hand across lips still smeared with rat gore. She still looked confused but nodded. "Gatha's boy?"

"Yes."

"I remember . . . you were tiny. I could sit you in my hand."

Thurin thought she probably still could. "I grew."

Hetta made a slow nod. "Show me the way."

THURIN LED, WITH Hetta's hand heavy on his shoulder. Not once had she released her hold on him. In her place Thurin wouldn't either. He wondered how long she had been wandering the tunnels. Long enough to learn about the loop that brought him back to her when he had first run away. From time to time she would rumble a "no" when he made to take a turn.

"That goes nowhere."

The Black Rock had a lot of tunnels that Hetta said went nowhere. It seemed to support Thurin's idea that they were wandering deserted mine-shafts. Some of the tunnels led steeply up; others plunged. Twice they had to climb long shafts using iron rungs set into the rock. And then, after an age in darkness, a circle of light.

Thurin had to go right up to the source of the illumination to make sense of it. It was a lone disc of board no wider than a hand span, coated with stardust. It barely illuminated the stone roof to either side of it but it could be seen for many yards and once they reached it another was visible, far off.

"To guide us," Thurin said.

"To trap us?" Hetta asked.

Thurin shrugged his weary shoulders. In the black depth of the sea it was said that there were fish that carried their own light to lure prey. "We'll get nothing done wandering deserted tunnels." He set off in the direction of the second light, looking for a third.

Soon the discs of light were spaced so closely that Thurin could see the walls and the floor. The trail of light forked in several places, winding away down other tunnels. Hetta had no opinion regarding the route now, and Thurin opted to head upwards at each opportunity. Here and there signs of active mining could be seen, stacked picks in one place, a spill of coal in another. But these became rarer as Thurin led the way ever upwards.

Several times, at tunnel junctions, they passed stars hanging within wire-mesh cages, large enough to light the whole space clearly. Hetta shied away from the stars as if they were fierce sources of heat, but Thurin saw no sign of demons in her and guessed it was a habit built up over the long years of her nightmare. He hoped that other of her habits would not return. Especially eating people.

Thurin had imagined he would be hugging the walls, keeping to the shadows, spying on the priests to find out what they had done with Yaz.

Instead he'd arrived with almost ten feet of hulking gerant in tow and she was providing most of the shadows as she loomed behind him, head bowed to keep from scraping it on a ceiling that he would have to stretch for on tiptoes. What he would do when they encountered a priest Thurin had no idea. Just ask to see Yaz, most likely. But at least with Hetta at his shoulder anyone they met would feel inclined to agree with his requests. That or run screaming.

The tunnels became smaller and warmer, the walls straighter, the floors and ceiling flatter, pressing on Hetta's bowed shoulders. There were caged stars everywhere now. A great wealth of them. In a few hundred yards Thurin passed the best part of what he might find in ten years mining the ice.

"Someone's coming," Hetta said.

Thurin turned to see that the gerant had stopped at the junction he had just passed and was now several yards behind him. The light of four stars threw her shadow in four different directions with her feet the stake that joined them all. The left turn held her attention, her stare fixed on something distant. Then, swift as fractures spreading beneath a blow, terror claimed her face, and she came thundering towards Thurin, filling the corridor.

Thurin ran too. It was that or be flattened, and Hetta's obvious fear made an eloquent argument for running in any case. And so, for the second time in a scant few hours, Thurin found himself pursued by Hetta through the tunnels of the Black Rock.

This time the pursuit didn't end with Thurin stumbling into a blow but by being yanked off his feet from behind. He found himself hauled into a side chamber as if he were a small child. Hetta pressed him to the wall while he clenched his teeth against crying out at the pain from a bitten tongue.

Time passed. Enough for Thurin to regain his breath and become restless, trapped between Hetta and the wall. He opened his mouth to complain but the light in the corridor began to change character, becoming bloody, and Hetta shrank back. Footsteps approached at an even pace. A man passed by, trailing a dark cloak. Thurin got only a glimpse of his face from the side and it took him a few moments to understand what he had seen.

The stranger stopped some yards past the entrance to the chamber. Thurin could only see his right shoulder and he stared at it, the breath trapped in his lungs, his heart hammering against the cage of his ribs. A long moment passed. The light shifted this way and that, then faded as the creature walked away.

"What *was* that?" Thurin hissed. It had been a man but not a man. Where his eyes should have been, two stars had burned, set into the sockets, suffusing his flesh with a crimson glow. "Hetta?"

The gerant made no answer and Thurin turned slowly towards the dimly lit gloom of the chamber behind him.

They stood in silent rows, stretching away down the long gallery. Scores of them. Some huge, some small, some dark, some fair, but all of them staring ahead at an unseen infinity, all of them secured by two iron bands that wrapped them tightly, anchored at the back by a cable stretching to the ceiling, not allowing them to fall. All of them wore an iron circlet from which black wires ran beneath their skin. And where the bands crossed over each heart, and where the circlets sat upon their foreheads, was set a star as large as a thumbnail, and all of them burned a dull crimson.

8

✦ ✦
✦

QUELL

THEY CALLED THE lesser priests acolytes. The pale priest, Valak, directed four acolytes to take up the boards that Quell lay on and carry him.

"Quickly. Let's get out of this gods-damned cold." Valak watched impatiently as the acolytes readied themselves around Quell.

The priest led them off through a tunnel at the back of the chamber in which he had used the four stars to test Quell and the others. The air, which Quell had already considered warm, grew warmer still with each turn.

Quell had been both pleased and curiously disappointed to learn that no trace of any of the old bloods manifested in him. The Ictha prided themselves on possessing that peculiar alloy of strengths which bound together so uniquely to shape them to survive the polar north. Any deviation meant admitting a weakness that would see them die during the long night. On the other hand, Quell had seen the wonders that the Broken could work. Some were like the Children of Sea and Sky, godlings capable of magics that could defeat a whole clan. Yaz herself owned a power that astounded him. She could kill him with a thought, reduce rock to fragments, turn ice to steam. How did she see him now? Now that the curse of her gifts while making her too weak to live on the ice also reduced him to a child beside her strengths? If they truly were to marry could she respect him in such an unequal partnership? It saddened Quell on many levels, not least that he couldn't find within himself the faith to believe that Yaz wouldn't change.

A jolt brought Quell out of his thoughts. He realized he had been sliding away into some kind of delirium, too weakened by the knife wound to retain his grip on the world. He bit down on the pain and wiped the sweat from his brow. With a cold shock he knew that if he let himself slip away into dreams he might well never emerge from them again.

The acolytes had come to the top of a flight of stairs. The corridor they bore him along was well carved, not a rough tunnel. Caged stars shone in muted hues of green, red, blue, and many other colours not seen on the ice. Some were wholly new to his eye, not even to be found on the scales of any fish that Quell had ever hauled from the Hot Sea. The black rock of the walls swallowed the light away but the competing shades found their voice as they slid across the whiteness of Valak's skin.

Quell didn't know how far they had come into the mountain but the air had become much warmer. Hotter even than in the ice caves of the Broken. He found himself sweating even as his body trembled.

They laid him on the floor in a chamber that seemed undecided whether it was a place to sleep or to store curios. A raised bed stood at the back, but on stands cluttering the floor and in niches around the walls rested all manner of objects scavenged from the city of the Missing. Toothed wheels, complex pieces of the shining silver metal that the forge pot couldn't melt, abstract shapes made from the stinking gooey mess that the boards Quell lay on would turn into if heated. Elsewhere hung patterns that trapped the eye woven from strands of the orangey metal that Eular had once called copper, and beneath them the unmelting ice that the Broken called glass, fashioned here by unknown artistry into flowing forms of heart-aching beauty, some perhaps vessels in which oil might be carried, others more reminiscent of the ice flowers the Ictha elders made at the end of the long night. And beside Quell's head, two great black springs that even a gerant couldn't compress by the smallest fraction. Whatever their function, the collection was clearly precious beyond the wealth of all the tribes combined.

A single golden star hung on a thin wire from the ceiling, chasing the shadows into the room's corners. Closer at hand the starlight danced through glassware and gleamed on curving metal, even coaxing sparkles from the sculptures made from melted boards.

"See to your duties." Valak dismissed the acolytes.

Quell guessed that there was to be no more carrying. He would walk out of the chamber on his own legs, or be dragged out by them as a corpse.

"Touch nothing," Valak instructed before turning from Quell and following on the heels of the last acolyte. "These are my personal treasures, gathered over many years."

Quell lay back with a groan. He had no inclination to touch any of the Missing's works even if he could manage to sit and reach out to one. He doubted very much, however, that Valak had had anything to do with the gathering of the objects other than by inspecting the contents of the cages hauled from the ice. Even so, the priest had had the air of a mother watching over precious children. His eyes had slid across the objects with an affection wholly absent while watching the acolytes.

Quell let his head roll back on the board. His thoughts, looking to escape being pinned by the knife and the likely consequences of his wound, drifted to Yaz again. He remembered standing at the fissure that led down into the undercity. Yaz hadn't returned among the others that he saw her go down with. It had been his chance to find her alone and bring her back.

It had taken more of Quell's courage than he liked to admit to descend into the undercity to hunt for her. It was perhaps true—though he had yet to fully admit it to himself—that if recovering Yaz had not been his only way to return to the surface he might never have lowered himself into that ancient darkness.

A rattling noise pulled Quell from his memories and drew his eyes to the far corner of the room. He could see nothing there to account for the sound. A large cube of dull metal served as a table on which to display more of the delicate glassware recovered from the city. Quell tried to imagine how the glass had been packed to survive being hauled up through the ice amid the mass of metal pieces that the Broken heaped into each cage.

The rattle came again, definitely from the vases on the table. Something like a sharp inhalation followed, a sniff fierce enough to set an elegant spray of glass fronds rolling about on the rim of its heavy base.

"Hello?" Quell called. "Who's th—" His voice suddenly fell into a hiss. "Maya?" Had the girl escaped detection and followed Yaz into the Black Rock?

The table tilted, shrugging off the object with its collection of glass fronds. It hit the ground and shattered into innumerable pieces. A vase followed immediately, graceful curves catching the light before it too pulverized itself on the stone floor, scattering fragments a remarkable distance. Preserved for untold thousands of years, then lost in an instant.

"No!" Quell tried to reach out a warning hand, wincing, both in pain and at the unfolding disaster.

The table, which resembled a round-cornered cube about which overlapping iron plates had been riveted, began to unfold. The last two pieces of glassware fell off as what looked like blunt-fingered limbs opened out on heavy hinges. A rounded rectangular head lifted from the cage of its limbs, revealing dark and gleaming eyes, one set to either side. The thing began to walk towards Quell, somewhat unsteady on its feet as if relearning a long-forgotten talent.

In the process of crossing the room the metal monster managed to topple three more stands, spilling precious artefacts to the floor. The only land animals Quell had ever seen were the dogs of the southern clans. He'd seen whalebone carvings of the six-legged hoola that preyed on unfortunates around the margins of certain seas, but had been lucky enough never to meet a real one. The creature approaching him had elements of both the dog and the hoola about it, even some aspects that seemed human: blunt fingers and toes, for example, instead of the padded paw of a dog or the three long claws of a hoola. The main difference being of course that it was made entirely of metal. Even so, Quell felt it had more in common with an animal than with the hunters that had attacked him and Yaz in the city. No starlight burned through its joints or shone from its eyes. And something about its uncertainty suggested a living creature more than an automaton.

The . . . thing . . . reached Quell's side, setting one more plinth rocking on its base as it drew near. It nuzzled at him with its blunt head, its touch surprisingly warm. It swung its thick, articulated neck and Quell cried out as it came within a finger-width of knocking against the hilt of the knife in his side. Instead, with a delicacy at odds with its clumsy crossing of the room, it moved its featureless muzzle back and forth across the wound where Erris had bound Quell's sliced skin together with a dark strip of his own. For an instant two black slots opened in the metal muzzle and the sharp inhalation came again, as if they were the slits of a nose. The black eye on Quell's side of the head regarded him with solemn intensity.

The creature tilted its head on one side and made a vibrant, mournful sound from somewhere deep within its body, like the noise the wind can make when left alone outside an empty ice cave.

"W-what are you?" For some reason Quell wanted to reach out and lay his hand on that heavy head, but common sense kept him motionless. Although the creature was smaller than him it was considerably bigger than a dog and must have outweighed a gerant.

The metal monster repeated its moan, perhaps with a slight questioning tone this time, then began to shuffle away.

"Wait!" Quell tried to reach for it, an effort that turned him over and sent him sprawling off the boards onto his front. He collapsed in agony, cheek to the stone, watching the creature lumber back to the corner it had come from. Shards of broken glass crunched under its iron feet. Quell felt his grip on the world beginning to slip as he grew ever more faint with pain and blood loss. As his sight began to darken he noted absently that the metal dog thing had a stumpy segmented tail at its rear and that, as it walked, the tail wagged.

"DEAR GODS!"

Quell found himself being shaken awake. Valak loomed over him, both white hands twisted in furs over Quell's chest, trying and failing to drag him up. He looked horrified. "What have you done?"

Quell glanced around at the glittering wreckage. The iron-plated cube stood in its original spot, backed into the far corner with the broken remnants of the glassware it had supported now scattered around its base. "It wasn't m—"

Quell broke off as he sighted a second person over Valak's shoulder. A woman wearing ragged hides, her hair hanging in dirty straggles. Three things caught his attention, the third of them seizing it so hard that it stole the protestations of innocence from his tongue.

The first thing to draw Quell's eye was the star burning bloodily at the junction of the two iron bands that crossed at the centre of the woman's chest. The second thing was that she was Ictha. And the third thing was that he knew her. This was the girl who had gone south to the gathering with his parents when he was almost too small to stand. The girl who had not returned and of whom they had never spoken again.

He said her name for the first time in more than ten years and his voice broke around it. "Qwella?"

9

✦ ✦
✦

YAZ

I'VE GIVEN YOU a lot to think about." Eular got up from the bed. "I'll
give you some privacy to consider what you've been told."

"Time to consider that you throw our children into a hole in the
ice so they can suffer and die?" Yaz asked. "Or suffer and survive, at which
point you collect the strongest for an army to attack the green lands? Have
I got it right so far?" She couldn't keep the anger from her voice.

Mother Jeccis stood looking from Eular to Yaz, grinning as if a great
joke were being told. Eular smiled apologetically. He held his hands before
him and moved his fingers as if he were delicately plucking floating hairs
from the air before him. "We make the best of the bad choices before us,
Yaz." He turned towards the doorway with Jeccis following, and the two
guards moved to flank them. "Give it some thought. That's all I ask. And
when I return we can talk some more."

Yaz found herself nodding. The rage that had been boiling in her stomach was gone. Her hands that had been clenched into fists now hung loose
at her sides. She blinked in surprise. "Wait . . ."

"Yes?" Eular turned to her over the shoulders of the two guards.

The questions and accusations queuing on her tongue had gone. For a
moment she stood openmouthed before finding something else to ask.

"You've been doing this for decades, slowly collecting these soldiers for your army—"

"Our army, Yaz."

"So . . . won't those chosen a generation ago all be too old to fight?"

"Ah." Eular shook his head, a faint smile on his lips yet again. "There you have us, Yaz. You've discovered my secret sorrow. While I've grown old steering this endeavour to its conclusion, those who will have the honour to fight for the cause, those who will take the green lands and revel in a new life, they all wait in timeless slumber, untouched by the years." He looked down at his gnarled hands. "Me though, I have work to do. I might rest for a few years here and there. Sometimes a decade. But I need to let time have its way with me every now and then. I'm like a stone skipping across the water, but with each splash I'm getting older."

With that he turned and left. The door swung shut behind him with a heavy clang. It was only after the guards had locked the door and retreated beyond earshot that Yaz even thought to ask how she was to relieve herself.

The light departed with Eular and his men, leaving Yaz blind once more. A fumbling search by hand, however, discovered more than she had seen when she'd had the light of the stardust to aid her. She discovered a covered bucket under the bed and a jug of water. But these arrangements just revived her anger. She was of the Ictha, a free people, and these priests expected thanks for sealing her in a small chamber without flame or food. They expected her to sit amid her own stink until they returned to wrinkle their noses at her.

Yaz quenched her thirst then lay back on the bed to do what Eular suggested. To think. The months-long nights of the north had taught her the value of patience in the darkness.

She considered Eular first, pondering both the many lies and the many truths he had told her. He had said that he was cast down into the Pit of the Missing as an eyeless infant, and yet he must have first arrived there as a man. Had he not thought she would share that story with the Broken or did they too believe he had arrived among them as a child? Either he was careless with his lies, which seemed unlikely, or the Broken believed his story. And how was that possible?

She considered the absences that the old man must take from the Broken. If he were so highly placed among the priests of the Black Rock then he must spend considerable time here, surely. How were these departures not questioned among the Broken? Their caves were numerous and the Tainted made exploring the margins dangerous, but even so, it was inconceivable that his ability to simply vanish wouldn't be questioned.

Yaz thought again of the children thrown into the pit to become strong enough for Eular's army or die trying. She had been so angry about it when Eular stood to go and yet now when she reached for that outrage she found only disquiet and mild confusion. Had the old man talked away her objections so easily?

Yaz sat and tried to shake the fog from her head. Rather than dwell on the mysterious priest she reached out in search of the handful of stardust she had set down when Eular returned from meeting the strangers at his doorstep. She found the dust with her mind more than with her fingertips, beginning to understand how Eular said he could see the stars even though his eyes had been taken long ago. The tiny stars formed a web within her mind, a dense and glowing network of connections. It reminded Yaz of the network she'd so recently experienced in the city cavern, when she had for a few brief moments been the centre of a universe of stars all orbiting around her.

Yaz closed her fist about the handful of dust and squeezed it tight. Eular had said they threw the children of the old bloods into the pit so that peril could sharpen their skills, advancing them through barriers that practice and study wouldn't breach. But the priests themselves held one of the four ancient bloods. Gerant, hunska, and marjal were sent to join the Broken and be hunted. The rarest of them though, the quantals, came to live in this warm mountain surrounded by wealth and luxury.

Was that simply corruption, bred by ownership of a greater power? Or did it imply that the quantals possessed some subtler arts that benefited from quiet study in comfort? Skills that were unlikely to peak while being terrified and chased by monsters? Yaz wondered what powers the priest had that she not only didn't share but was wholly unaware of.

Rather than spend her time in fruitless worry, Yaz sought distraction amid the contents of her fist. She opened her hand and began to move her fingertip through the lightless dust, listening to the faint strains of its many-voiced song. Eular had all but silenced it but still there were traces remaining. She tried to isolate the song of a single mote of dust and lost herself in the task for the longest time. She began to hear unsuspected harmonies; a slow interplay of refrains passed back and forth like whale song in the highest imaginable key. There were melodies that dipped into her register then soared away beyond her reach. There were leaders and followers. Voices iterated around themes, elaborated them, passed the new work back into the mass. She imagined each song as the life of a person, lived in conversation with those around them, some seeking to dominate, others to follow, others still to take their own path regardless, all of them unique but also similar.

Time passed and Yaz fell into the song, finding voices that belonged together and binding them fast. Joining her own melody to the mass, sharing back and forth.

A sound made her lift her head. A figure stood in the doorway, obscured by the light of the lantern she carried. "I said, you didn't want your meal?"

Yaz tilted her head, trying to make sense of the sounds the woman was making. She had spent so long with the song that words no longer fitted easily into her mind. Had she slept? Had she dreamed? She didn't know.

The guard came into the room while a second waited by the door. She picked up the small board beside Yaz and replaced it with another, also bearing half a dozen cubes of fish. Yaz was amazed to see her taking away food as if somehow it would no longer be good to eat. She wanted to say so but her tongue was too slow to shape itself to the task.

The guards left, taking their lanterns. But the light remained. The stardust scattered by the bed had woken and now glowed in a faint tracery of lines across the floor, oddly reminiscent of the script that the Missing set upon their walls. And in Yaz's open hand the small dust heap she'd collected burned bright enough for its illumination to reach the ceiling. And in the midst of the heap, one small golden star no bigger than a baby's toenail radiated its own brilliant light.

Yaz blinked. The star's light danced in her eyes and something lit at the back of her mind as if in response, an answer to the question that she had set aside. Eular had taken her anger. He had done something to her. Something to change her. To change her opinion. To change her truth. And that was how he had lived among the Broken without question. She had thought that Pome had a power to sway others with his voice. She had wondered if there was more to it than just the words he used. Pome had perhaps owned some kind of marjal skill, an empathy . . . the word was one of Erris's . . . that twisted others to his cause. But Eular had something more, an ability to change moods and memories, to weave a new truth out of the threads of the world. The image of his wrinkled hands plucking at the air returned to her. Had that been the moment?

"I need to get out of here." Yaz stood and went to the door, pausing only to take a cube of fish from the board. She swallowed it almost without chewing and returned for the rest, realizing that she was ravenous. She reached the door licking her lips and wiping her hand on her leg.

By starlight Yaz found the keyhole. The concept of key and lock were alien to her but somehow her time with Erris had furnished the words and, together with the guards' practical demonstrations in front of her, it was enough for understanding. She sprinkled a little stardust into the keyhole and made it shine brighter still so she could see something of the inner workings.

Yaz wondered if she could pack the keyhole with stardust and then heat it to a point where the metal would melt and flow. It would be difficult, though, and she didn't see that it would necessarily help. The mechanism might jam and the door would still be locked.

If she could touch the river that flows through all things, and call upon the source of power that she assumed all quantals, including the priests of Black Rock, had access to, then she could blow the door from its hinges. But she had drawn from the river too many times in recent days. It now lay beyond her reach for gods knew how long. Even if she could touch it again so soon, she doubted she would survive another such experience. The cost for opening one door that way, in a place that might have many such doors to bar her passage, was far too high.

Whatever the cost, though, Yaz had to escape her cell, find help, and escape the mountain. It was that or have Eular slowly rearrange her thoughts with his plucking fingers, as if he were drawing threads from the air, or pulling on the strings of a puppet. Given sufficient opportunity he might steal away her anger, pinch memories from her skull one at a time, and change her mind entirely, until she joined his army willingly. With her thinking undone she would take her place in the ranks he kept frozen in time and wait there until the day he was ready to unleash his war.

Even now, Yaz wondered how many of her opinions were truly her own, what memories she might already have had stolen from her. It seemed to her that Eular wasn't entirely wrong—she saw his argument even if she didn't share his conclusion. But had he made her think and feel these things? Was he a monster who had already erased his terrible crimes from her recollection? Or was he a loyal son of the tribes, prepared to do anything to save his people even if it meant dooming others?

Yaz couldn't tell. She couldn't be sure. She needed to escape, or at least to find a defence. She sat in silence before the door, leaning in so that her forehead rested against the cold metal. She listened to the silence. No wind howling, no ice groaning. Nothing. Just the beating hearts of distant stars, some so slow and resonant that they must be considerably larger than those that Regulator Kazik had built his hunters around. None, though, were even close to approaching the size of the city heart, the void star where Erris had somehow lived for so many centuries.

Yaz returned her attention to the door. She tried to defocus her sight and look at the door in the way she sometimes observed the world when looking for new inspiration. Some time ago Yaz had learned that if instead of looking for the river that runs through all things, and being blinded by its light, swamped by its power, she turned away from it and stared into the darkness around it, she discovered new things. The darkness was never empty. Surrounding the river was a halo of infinitely many very much thinner rivers, tributaries—threads, if you like. And, like the great river, these threads wove their way through the world at odd angles, originating from everything, binding one object to another through a host of relationships and influences.

Yaz had never paid great attention to the threads. The river was the main show. The river gave a power that got things done in a hurry. A power that could solve the urgent problems like how to stay alive when a monstrous foe is just about to kill you. The threads, however, seemed as if they might be a cradle that held the subtle truths of the world. Perhaps this is what the priests spent their time doing, safe in the warmth of their mountain, fed and clothed by the labour of the tribes. Perhaps they studied the threads.

Yaz examined the lock, looking at the nimbus of threads that surrounded the door, threads that joined the iron to the rock, the door to its purpose, threads that ran out from the lock and carried its complexity into the world.

For the longest time Yaz sat contemplating the lock and the threads that ran from it and through it. Even the act of her observing it created new threads, joining her to the lock, running into the past and off into the futures.

Eventually Yaz reached her hand slowly towards the lock, her fingertips following the key thread that she'd finally isolated from the host. "Maybe . . . I could just—"

A startlingly loud rattle and click shook Yaz from her concentration. The door opened quickly, striking her side as she scrambled clear. And there, framed in the doorway with a lantern in one hand and a long curving knife in the other, stood Regulator Kazik.

"You've come to kill me." It was obvious in his eyes. Yaz was surprised at how calm she felt.

Kazik said nothing, only slowly set down his lantern, his gaze never leaving her.

"You sent Quell down to bring me back. You could have left me to die down there." Yaz found her feet and backed to the far wall. She picked up the iron bowl and held it in one hand like a tiny shield. After all she'd faced—huge mechanical hunters, hordes of screaming Tainted—it seemed impossible that a lone man with a knife should be the one to kill her. The same man who had pushed Zeen down the pit.

"Eular says you've learned as much in half a month as he did in half a lifetime. He's too busy being amazed by you to realize how dangerous you are." Kazik sounded nervous but the hand holding the knife remained steady. "Eular thinks you can lead the army, and that with you at its head it can march south before the long night comes again."

"I don't want to lead an army." It was true and also seemed like what he wanted to hear. Yaz found herself glancing around as if the room might suddenly contain something useful, like another door. She forced herself to watch the knife instead. Lantern light beaded the blade's serrations. The sharp edge suddenly cut her missing fear loose. "But that doesn't sound like a good reason for murder. You wanted me to do this stuff!" She tried not to let the words spill out in a terrified flood. When someone is set on attack then fear only quickens their hand.

"You're too big a risk, girl. That's the truth of it. With you leading it, that army won't be ours anymore. It doesn't matter how we bind you to the cause, you'll wriggle out of it. You got yourself out of the pit, after all. The boy had nothing to do with it." Kazik shook his head. "Eular doesn't see it, but he was the one who set me up to judge. And here I am passing judgment." A snarl twisted the burn scars that the Missing's script wall had left across his face.

"Everything I do, I do for the Hidden God!" He moved swiftly for an old man, his cloak's tatter-strips trailing the swing of his arm. Yaz knew even as he struck that she couldn't avoid the knife. The regulator would stick it into her as deeply as the blade had bedded into Quell's side. And it wouldn't stop there. Her fright escaped her as a wild scream and she lunged for his arm, knowing herself too slow.

A moment of confusion followed and Yaz found herself on the floor, tangled with her foe, terrified, not wanting to die, knowing the knife was close, knowing that any moment now it would slice into her and hot blood would spill out.

"No!" Yaz thrashed, trying to ward off the blow she couldn't see. Surprisingly the regulator lay beneath her. Since she'd lost control of his knife arm she instead began to rain blows at his head, hoping to stop him before he could stop her.

"Enough!" A sharp voice above her. "He's down already. We need to go."

Yaz hit the old man once more before the words sank in. Kazik wasn't stabbing her. He wasn't even defending himself. She looked up, ready to fight, her heart pounding.

"Come on." A small figure stood over Yaz and the regulator, silhouetted in the light. In her left hand she held an iron rod, bound about at the far end with a layer of hides. She'd hit the regulator from behind. Yaz was safe.

"Maya?" Yaz choked the word out, her throat thick with emotion.

The girl just beckoned her to follow then turned for the open door. Yaz got to her feet. The regulator's knife gleamed in the darkness close to his head. Yaz started to stoop for it, then changed her mind. It wasn't in her to slice anyone open, and she knew it.

"Come on." Maya slipped through the doorway, leaving the lantern where Kazik had set it down.

"How—" Yaz wanted to ask how Maya had escaped the shaft head unseen, infiltrated the Black Rock, found her cell, and appeared just in time to save her. But she knew the answer already. This was Maya. She had already known her own strength when the Axit sent her into the Pit of the Missing to spy for them. Those strengths had been further honed on the edge of peril, forged in the same crucible that had apparently made Yaz herself into something that even the priests feared.

So instead of asking questions Yaz chose action. The stardust shot to her hand, rattling against her skin like an ice wind along with the small star that she had fashioned from the dust itself. And, without a backward glance, she followed Maya into the shadows.

10

✦ ✦
✦

YOU DIDN'T KILL him." Yaz followed Maya, almost blind in the passageway. The only light struggled from door windows, each cell supplied with its own bowl of dimly glowing stardust.

"Killing a priest . . ." Maya shrugged. "It's a big thing. It's not time for that. Yet."

Yaz thought that killing anyone should be a big thing, but Maya had shown no reluctance in the ice caves. The regulator, though, she had clubbed with her rod of hide-bound iron. Perhaps a lifetime of venerating the priests had hamstrung the small assassin. Among the Ictha any priest was afforded the same respect as the clan mother. Only since seeing Zeen tumble into the Pit of the Missing had Yaz begun to think of the order as her foe. Before then she had considered them the glue that bound tribe to tribe and clan to clan, finding a peaceful path where otherwise blood might have spilled across the ice.

Maya paused at a corner, gesturing for Yaz to stay back. The passage joining theirs was better lit. Already Yaz felt exposed. The clans thought that there were fewer than a dozen priests, and possibly that was true, but all the evidence Yaz had seen so far suggested that the mountain housed a considerably larger population than that. Whether they were mostly priests, or servants to the priests, like the guards she'd seen, Yaz didn't know.

"Come." Maya motioned Yaz forward. "Stay quiet." Shadow swirled around Maya, not forming some clot of darkness that would draw the eye, but fading her, blurring her outlines into something a watcher's gaze might just slide over. Tendrils of shadow wrapped Yaz too, working Maya's magic on her.

Yaz followed Maya around the corner. Stars lit the way, hanging in iron cages from hooks set into the walls. Stars larger than her thumbnail. She heard their song and asked them to keep their peace as she passed, so that they burned no brighter.

"These are everywhere," Maya said. "Except where they kept you."

Yaz understood. She could have used the stars as weapons. The priesthood had tried to draw her teeth. Even Eular must have shared some of the regulator's concerns. She considered taking the stars as they passed, but what better trail could there be to lead any pursuit right to her? Besides, she felt more affinity for the tiny star in her fist. It might lack the power of larger stones but she had made it herself from dust, grain by grain, and she knew it with the same intimacy with which she knew her own hand.

"Where are we going?" Yaz hissed.

Maya pointed the direction and kept moving. She led the way through a series of turns and down a long, narrow flight of steps. The stars became fewer and smaller, the shadows encroaching between them, reclaiming lost territory. Maya paused by the entrance to one chamber where darkness held sway. "Make a light."

Yaz coaxed a narrow but bright beam from her star. It traced a line across the floor, rising swiftly to dance across a complex surface. Unable to make sense of what she was seeing, Yaz broadened the beam into a cone of golden light.

"Iron!" The priests or their minions had heaped the large chamber with teetering stacks of metal. About half of it comprised the wrought ingots that the Broken made beside the forge pool, about half of it great wheels or flat plates, and other larger pieces that perhaps the Broken had been unable to fit into their melting pot. And all of it lay rusting, neglected, a mountain of metal far greater than could be made by all the clans heaping their treasures together. Yaz gazed in awe.

"I've seen two other chambers like this," Maya said. "And I can't have explored more than a fraction of this place yet."

"But . . . what does it mean?" Yaz let her light fade.

"It means that metal is only precious on the ice because the priests say it is. It's a collar around the tribes' throats."

"I never knew." Yaz had thought of the Broken as alone in their enslavement, trapped down in their caves, but it seemed that the Ictha were bound in their own way, despite the apparent freedom of the endless ice. A handful of intermittent seas anchored them to a nomadic circuit of the north, and the treasures of the Black Rock chained them to the will of the priests. "What should we do?"

"Hide!" Maya hissed.

"Hide?" Yaz willed her star to darkness and closed her fist around it.

"Now!" Maya took her hand and tugged her towards the great pile of scrap iron.

Yaz stumbled blindly behind Maya, relying on the girl not to get her impaled on any of the protrusions jutting from the heap. With an arm raised to guard her face, Yaz negotiated her way around the jagged obstacles, biting her lip to keep from cursing as her shin collided with something immovable. Maya dragged her into a crouch moments later. They waited like that for an age in a silence that Yaz ached to break. Her thigh muscles began to burn, and still Maya gave no sign to move again.

The darkness began to weaken. The mass of iron that had been invisible became a forest of silhouettes, all blocking the light now bleeding into the chamber as something approached along the tunnel. Yaz could hear whatever it was that was drawing near, though not quite with her ears. A dual-voiced star song reached out towards her, a discordant harmony. There was something sour and off-key about it that ran a shiver of revulsion down her spine. The sound tied the same knots in her stomach that the sight of the stump of Pome's severed hand had, bright with broken bone and blood.

The light grew stronger and a figure walked into view. Yaz's imagination had her expecting a monster, some nightmare creation of dead flesh and living metal. To see a normal person was somehow worse. The horror lay in the wrongness of the light that shone from their eyes, or rather from the sockets that had each been emptied of the eye it should hold and were now filled with a star of similar size, burning with a fractured yellow light.

Maya's knife whispered from its sheath. She kept the blade beneath her arm so as to allow no gleam to draw the bright eyes to it.

Yaz bent her head, though she still saw the twin stars in her mind. *You don't see us. You don't see us. You don't see us.* She repeated the mantra over and again, letting it circle within the confines of her skull. Something convinced her that neither Maya's knife nor her own skills would avail them if that creature fixed its gaze upon their hiding spot.

The light sifted through tangled iron, shadows slid this way and that, distortions of distortion. The metal creaked as if unknown forces were tugging at it, searching for anything loose. And then, as quickly as it came, the bright inquisition was turned away and the glow retreated.

Another long silence followed before Maya rose. "Come on."

"What *was* that thing?" Yaz asked.

"I don't know, but there are more of them, and they can see me even when I'm hiding." She sheathed her knife. "Keep doing whatever it was that you did, because we would have been found if you hadn't done it."

Yaz lit her star and followed Maya from the chamber. It felt wrong to be led by a child, but without guidance she knew that she would just walk herself back into the priests' clutches, and sooner rather than later. "Where are we going?"

Maya glanced back at her, frowning. "To the Axit, of course."

"The Axit?" Yaz hadn't any desire to join Maya's clan. Not that they would accept someone broken like her, or Maya come to that.

"Of course. I need to report. What I have to tell them will change everything. The tribes won't bow to the priests once they know they're sitting on a mountain of iron and taking half of what we have for just the tiniest fraction of it. It's like they own an ocean's worth of fish and are buying us with a few loose scales."

"Why wait for me then? Why risk capture when you could have been long gone?" Did Maya somehow need her in order to reach the ice?

"If the iron that the Broken deliver isn't the reason that the priests keep feeding them, then it must be for the stars. That's what they care about.

And I've seen what you can do with stars, Yaz. You're a weapon and the Axit know what to do with those."

Yaz twisted her mouth. She didn't want to be a weapon or to have Maya see her as one. Maya had saved her life at least twice. Yaz hoped it had meant more to her than just securing the safety of a prize. "So the Axit will feed me and keep me warm? And what about you, Maya? Will they need you anymore? What happens to a weapon when the use for it has gone?"

Maya turned and met her eyes. "We Axit are warriors. We understand sacrifice. My life is in service to my people. I'll lay it down for them any-time they need it, or when it ceases to have value to them." The girl kept all expression from her face, her gaze empty of fear or hope, but the words sounded like something she had learned from the cradle rather than a creed of her own making. It also sounded like the Ictha creed, albeit a more war-like version of it.

"Your life should have value to *you*, Maya. It has value to me. That's why I wanted to take you south, to find the green lands with me." The lack of hope hurt Yaz the most; that, and the fact that she recognized in Maya her own willingness to sacrifice herself. And seeing it reflected in another's eyes made her question the choices she'd made. Her own dedication to the Ictha had been hardly less strong. Until her fall she had been part of some-thing greater than herself. Its survival had meant more to her than her own ambition. Life on the ice bred that kind of devotion. Without it there would be no life upon the ice.

Yaz had emerged from the Pit of the Missing to find the world a much smaller place, the old creeds too narrow to cover that which mattered most. Since her fall she had learned to dream. She had come to look beyond the boundaries of her clan and to wonder where the lines should be drawn. She had wondered for the first time how the survival of an individual might be weighed against that of a group, and why the group should end with a clan, a tribe, or a people. She had fallen from her life and crashed into a world that had filled her with hope, and fear, and confusion. The number of unanswerable questions that haunted her existence had multiplied and multiplied again. She found herself sorely in need of guidance, but both sky and sea were hidden from her, and the gods had never spoken to her in any case. A year ago she would have wanted to speak to a priest.

Yaz nodded slowly. She needed to go back to the pit, back to the others. There was no going south if it was to be alone. If Maya could get her out of this mountain, then that would be a good first step. "I'll go with you."

A flicker of surprise crossed Maya's face, quickly hidden. "Good. Come on then."

MAYA LED THE way through unlit tunnels, moving cautiously. The size of the place surprised Yaz. She had seen the undercity of the Missing of course, and this seemed to be nothing on that scale, but she found herself astonished by the mere fact that the priests had carved through so much rock that there were enough chambers and tunnels to become lost in and to hide in.

Twice they followed long flights of steps, rough-hewn into the floor of tunnels where Yaz nearly had to stoop to avoid scraping her head.

"I thought the way out would be lower down, by the ice," Yaz said.

"It is."

Yaz stopped climbing stairs. Maya on a mission was a creature of few words. At other times the words ran from her like water from a holed skin. Had she learned silence against her nature, from watching the closed-lipped Axit warriors, or was the chatterbox Maya the act, just another weapon in her arsenal?

Maya stopped too, a few paces on. Yaz simply stood and watched the shadow-wrapped girl, little more than a smudge at the extremity of her star's illumination, and her stillness pulled an explanation from her guide. "I think their temple is up here."

"Why do we want to go there?" Yaz felt a cold finger trace her spine. She knew almost nothing about the Hidden God other than that, unlike the Gods in the Sea and Sky, he had a specific place in the world. He could be found. And that place lay here, within the Black Rock. Her knowledge had been assembled from rare occasions when conversation among the Ictha grazed against the subject and then hurriedly veered away. Even so, those few touches had painted a picture in her mind of something grimmer than the ice, more implacable than the wind. The priests were said to wear his likeness on chains about their necks, hidden beneath their robes. Yaz had even heard that they made statues of him. She had no desire to stand before one and let him gaze upon her through stone eyes. "We should leave now."

"First know your enemy," Maya said. "There are still chambers I haven't seen, and what's more important to understand than your foe's gods?"

"You're sure the priests are your enemy?" Yaz didn't really want to be in the position of defending Eular and his kind, but the situation wasn't so clear-cut that a clan could just go to war with them after so little reflection. And it seemed that Maya had not yet discovered this frozen army that Eular claimed to be building.

"Anyone who tries to exercise dominion over the Axit is our enemy. We have been at war with the Black Rock for generations. They just don't know it yet. My uncle says that anyone who isn't Axit is our enemy, but that's old thinking and the clan father tells it another way. He teaches that no one deserves to die until they stand in our way."

Yaz slowly shook her head. To hear such harsh ideas from the mouth of a child she knew given to kindness when not tethered by her creed . . . it made her sad. "You could stand in my way, Maya, and I would still count you my friend."

Maya said nothing but the shadows about her weakened and in their midst she looked down as if shamed.

"Lead on then." Yaz tried to sound more cheerful than she felt. "Let's see what we can learn about the Hidden God."

THEY ASCENDED SO many stairs that Yaz became convinced they would soon run out of mountain and emerge from the top. The place might not have as many chambers as the Missing's undercity but it was starting to feel as though it spread nearly as far.

Clan histories came bound in tales like that of Zin and Mokka and were never accompanied by a count of years. Sometimes it seemed to Yaz that even the oldest of tales might have been witnessed by her grandmother's grandmother. But here in the Black Rock it was clear that the priests must have laboured for centuries to hollow out such spaces.

On only three occasions did Maya stop to backtrack or take a side passage in order to avoid detection. The priests and their minions might be considerably more numerous than the clans believed but, whatever their numbers, they were spread thinly within the maze of tunnels and rooms their ancestors had carved through the Black Rock. In some ways the emptiness of the Black Rock was a mute testimony to the truth of Eular's words concerning the dwindling numbers among the clans. On the ice it was hard to tell, and memories were either short or vague, but here the facts were recorded in stone. Once there must have been many more living here, supported by the labour of the tribes. Now their descendants rattled around in the space that long ago had been crowded.

"We're getting near." Maya had brought them from the rough-hewn service tunnels into corridors that boasted flat floors and straight walls. They passed the occasional iron door, though they saw no signs of life. Stars hung everywhere in cages, dangling from the ceiling and dousing the passage in rainbow hues. These were larger stars than those illuminating corridors lower down the mountain. Pome's star, which had been a prize among the Broken, would have been just another corridor light here in the upper chambers of the Black Rock.

Maya stayed in the middle of the passages where she could, ducking when passing each star as if they gave off a heat that burned her.

They passed no statues but here and there an image had been scored across the walls in crude black lines as if someone had taken a lump of coal and scraped it over the stone. The figure scrawled in these scenes possessed a curiously violent energy. It seemed to be human, sitting cross-legged, hands on knees, palms upwards, head bowed, but surrounded by a black cloud of jagged lines and crossed through time and again as if the artist had wanted to obliterate their work once finished. It seemed at odds with the precision of the stonework and the harmonious light of the hanging stars. Like a livid wound on the face of a child.

Yaz stopped to stare at the second such image they reached. There was something about it that reminded her of Seus, the monster that had haunted the secret ways in which the city of the Missing seemed to hang, not in the shape of the body but in the violence of lines over and around the head. She suppressed a shudder and moved on.

The next turn brought them to a corridor echoing with the song of stars, all of them red and too large to hide in a fist. Yaz's fingers and thumb would struggle to meet if she were to take one in her grasp. The figure of the Hidden God had been scrawled on both walls about halfway down, the two images facing each other with black intensity. This pair had their heads unbowed but so many lines slashed across their faces that little could be seen of them, their eyes just a single blackness at the crossing point.

"This is why I brought you." Maya hung back. "I can't go down there." She scowled as if admitting to her weakness shamed her. "Not unless you . . . stop them." She backed off a few more paces. "I can feel the stars tearing at me. Breaking my mind apart."

"I can try." Yaz raised her hand as a prelude to reaching out with her power. But before she could even begin she sensed a change in the star song. The red stars' chorus sank through the registers, becoming deep as groaning ice, a dark premonition, then suddenly a wildness infected their tune, driving it higher, more strident. A new emotion haunted the corridor. One Yaz knew well. Fear. Black script began to appear on the walls, drawn rapidly by an invisible hand.

"Run." Maya said it in a small voice as though she lacked the courage to speak any louder.

At the far end of the corridor one of the red stars blinked out. Then another. And another. And darkness swallowed the space behind them.

11

✦ ✦
✦

THURIN

THURIN STOOD IN Hetta's shadow, gazing down the lines of prisoners, each hanging in an iron harness, their toes not quite brushing the ground. A red star had been set in each harness at the point at which the two metal bands crossed above the victim's breastbone, and a second smaller star burned in the headband around each captive's forehead. From these bands of black iron, wires spread beneath the skin in profusion like the roots of a fungus. Collectively the bloody light of hundreds of stars painted the chamber in ghastly hues.

"I . . . I remember this place," Hetta muttered, uncertain. "The stars . . . and the people."

"You were here?" Thurin looked left and then right along the host, five rows deep and scores long. If he had been here before he wouldn't be in any doubt about it.

"I remember . . ." Hetta rolled the thick knuckles of one hand across her forehead, hard enough to leave marks. "The harness was too small. I ran." She began to stride along the line, staring at the faces. "Nextor?" Hetta stopped before a narrow man with a sunken face and deep-set eyes. "Nextor?" She sounded less certain now.

"You know him?" Thurin asked. The name sounded familiar.

"When I was little . . ."

Thurin tried to imagine Hetta as little, and failed.

"He was kind to me. A scavenger. He made toys from the bits he found under the city." Hetta shook her head. "But he should be old now. Ancient." She reached out to touch the man, tentatively, as though he might bite.

Thurin understood her hesitation. There was something wrong here. Something wrong with the prisoners and their open-eyed immobility. Thurin's grandmother had always said that the longer something had been asleep the more dangerous it was to wake it. That felt more true here than it ever had before.

Thurin walked slowly along the line. Part of him was reluctant to leave the gerant's side, though it seemed ridiculous to have found himself in a situation where remaining close to Hetta was the safe option. He studied the faces of the prisoners as he passed. It seemed reasonable to assume that they were all taken from the ranks of the Broken, for they lacked the raw, wind-sculpted features of those who lived on the ice. How they had been taken, though, and to what purpose, Thurin had no idea.

He found himself trembling as he looked at each face, half hoping to find an old friend, half afraid that he would. Were all the dead here? Did the priests of the Black Rock keep the living Broken beneath the ice and keep the dead at the heart of the mountain? Would he find his father here among the ranks of the lost? Would he recognize him? The idea that he might not scared him more than finding his father. And his mother? Thurin had seen her die, head broken against the rock. They had set her body in the corpse chamber where another generation would find a harvest of grey-scales and brown-caps to feed them. Had the priests somehow stolen her away too?

Thurin found his vision misting and wiped fiercely at his eyes. He turned and called back to Hetta, "How did Nextor die?"

Hetta frowned. "A hunter got him. He said it would never happen. He said he was the best shadow-worker on the ice or beneath it. But one got him in the end."

Thurin carried on, making a close study of each face. The idea that he might miss someone began to haunt him and he found himself stopping to stare, painting old memories onto the features before him until he grew confused by too many maybes. When he did eventually reach someone he knew, the flood of recognition came as a relief, allowing him to be sure of himself once more.

"Bekna." He spoke her name. She had been like an older sister to him, one of the few cave-born to survive among the Broken, ten years his senior, a hunska, faster than thought. He never thought a hunter would catch her, not with her running quicker than a thrown spear. But one caught her off guard. Arka had seen it. The thing just reached out from a low vent and closed an iron claw around her ankle before she even knew it was there. Arka said the hunter dragged her out of sight and that was the end of it, just a smear of blood left on the stone to show what had happened. The monster broke her leg. Arka said she heard it snap.

The Bekna before Thurin showed no signs of injury. The passing years had left her unmarked by their passage. She hung there like a memory, bloody in the light of stars as red as those that scattered the true heavens. He reached out to her, filled with a fear he couldn't name. He half expected to find her flesh cold: she showed no signs of life, not a blink or a breath, but instead it was as if he found no flesh at all. His fingers slid across her skin as though it were the slickest ice, defying touch and replacing it with motion. Try as he might Thurin couldn't touch her. Even the water that should suffuse her flesh lay beyond the reach of his talent for manipulation.

The bands confining Bekna and the circlet around her head *could* be touched and he began to trace one of the black wires that ran from the circlet to root itself beneath her skin. "Maybe we could . . ." The task absorbed him. His finger ran into the barrier again, though the wire passed through it. He gripped the circlet instead. "Maybe if we were very very careful—"

A loud clang at his feet swung his gaze downwards. A circlet lay on the stone amid a halo of bloody wires.

"They come off easy." Hetta grabbed the harness of the man beside Bekna and strained her thick arms in an effort to tear it open. The man slumped in the harness now, blood trickling down his face from scores of small wounds where the circlet had been attached to him. "This. Is. Not. So. Easy." Hetta grunted with effort.

"There will be a catch or something." Thurin pushed at her. "Let me."

Hetta surrendered her place, shaking her hands against the pain of hauling on the ironwork. A moment later Thurin had found what he was looking for and the two bands snapped open.

Neither Thurin nor Hetta was quick enough to catch the man before he hit the floor, but Thurin did get himself in the way and managed to at least reduce the impact.

"Gods in the Ice, Hetta!" Thurin rolled the man onto his back. The blood gave the illusion that he'd been mauled by some great beast, but his eyes were moving and he drew in a shuddering breath. "Can you hear me? What's your name?"

"Is it time?" The man spoke in a creak as if his throat were too narrow for words to escape without effort. "Is it time?" His eyes looked past Thurin, through him, scanning some scene that only he could see.

"Time for what?"

"To fight." The man smiled, white teeth in the bloody mess of his face. "To die."

"We're here to save you," Thurin said, though the thought hadn't occurred to him until the moment he spoke it. "I'm Thurin of the Broken. We can take you back to the caves."

"I remember . . . I remember the caves." The man's voice grew weaker, his smile tinged with sadness. "I remember."

"We can take you back." Thurin tried to lift the man. "Help me." He kicked at Hetta to stir her into motion.

The man, his eyes still not seeing them, rolled his head to one side and then the other. Whispering now, "There's no back. Not anymore. I serve . . . serve . . ."

Thurin abandoned his efforts to haul the man to his feet. "Serve who?"

". . . the Hidden God . . ." The man slumped into unconsciousness, or perhaps death, his eyes focused on the infinity that had held him, unmoving now.

"Is he dead?" Hetta rumbled from above.

"I'm not sure." Thurin looked up at her. "Either way, I don't think just ripping these things off their heads is the best way to do it."

"To do what?" Hetta stared at the prone man, the points of her top teeth resting on her lower lip. She seemed lost, as if slipping back into the dark dream that had held her for so long.

"To save them." Thurin worried that the sight of blood might awaken Hetta's old appetites. He understood her struggle: although the demons had ruled him for less than a year their voices still echoed in him sometimes. He suspected that long after they had gone their venom would linger, rising now and then, even years later, to haunt his quiet moments. "To save them and bring them back to the Broken."

Hetta shook her great head. "Look at them. There are hundreds. How could the caves feed so many?"

"We could—" Movement in the corridor silenced Thurin. The light outside was changing again, growing redder as if shading to the same bloody hue that ruled the imprisoned crowds around him.

"The creature," Hetta hissed. "It's coming back." She moved to press herself to the wall beside the door.

Thurin joined her, shielding himself behind her bulk. But even as he held his breath and pressed himself against the stone, his gaze returned to the man sprawled on the floor beneath his harness, blood pooling around his head.

The light shifted in the corridor, growing brighter, scattering shadows. Footsteps came nearer, pausing in the doorway. From the light's shifting Thurin knew Hetta was right. The creature with the burning eyes had returned for them. With the man on the floor in full view, discovery was inevitable. A moment later the creature stepped into the room.

Thurin had expected Hetta to reach out and slam the intruder into a wall before any alarm could be raised, but instead she stumbled back with a low moan, nearly crushing him, arms raised against some invisible attack.

The question on Thurin's lips died as the red gaze of the man in the doorway pinned him. For a moment Thurin saw the man's face, ordinary enough but made ghastly by the crimson light pouring from the stars where his eyes should be. The starlight suffused his flesh, even his mouth glowed from within, and when his stare focused on Thurin it left no room for coherent thought.

Immediately Thurin's head filled with voices, overwhelming him with demands that had to be acted on. From his time among the Tainted Thurin knew what it was to be possessed by demons, and this was similar but different. He could feel the fault lines along which his mind was breaking.

Fight it, boy. A voice from the darkness behind his thoughts.

Something black and heavy swung across Thurin's vision and sent him sprawling. Hetta's blow threw him across the chamber. He fetched up against the legs of the first row of prisoners. How long he lay in a daze he didn't know but it was the screaming that pulled him from it. He rolled onto his front, spitting blood, unsure whether the shrieks were his own or someone else's.

A moment later Thurin managed to focus his vision and found Hetta. She lay curled in a tight ball by the entrance with the priests' creature staring down at her, the light of its eyes painting her head scarlet. Her cries of pain seemed too high-pitched to come from so large a body.

Without thought, Thurin reached out with his ice-work and seized the assailant. Something deadened his power, making the body he had hold of seem like three of Hetta. Straining his mind, Thurin managed to jerk the creature off his feet and slam him into the ceiling, pinning him against the stone, face-first, as if he were nailed there. Still maintaining the upwards force, Thurin climbed to his feet and stumbled to the doorway.

"Come on!" He grabbed a handful of Hetta's grimy hair and tried to drag her after him. He might as well have tried to haul away a similar-sized rock. The pain that had never quite left his skull after the effort of his long ascent through the ice now flared again. Up on the ceiling the creature began to push away from the stone, turning its head, the red light swinging towards them both. "Hurry! I can't hold it."

With a groan Hetta began to crawl to the doorway, head down. She was too slow. The creature managed to twist itself until the fringes of its vision reached them both. Whispers rose from the back of Thurin's mind. Awful thoughts of the kind you never allow to form were now given their own voice: emotions taking on separate identities; anger demanding that he attack; fear howling for him to run. Before madness could claim him and before his grasp on the creature weakened any further, Thurin managed one last effort and flung it back among the rows of prisoners. The cables on which the captives hung snagged the flying body and the creature came down painfully between the first and second rows, dropping face-first.

"Come on!" Thurin grabbed Hetta's shoulder and heaved her on. The huge gerant rose amid the ragged tent of her skins and furs. Her gaze met his with no hint of recognition in it and for a heartbeat Thurin was sure she would twist his head from his shoulders. But instead she ran, confusion and terror in her eyes.

Thurin paused for a moment, unsure whether to follow or to take the opposite direction. Shadows swung around him, the shadows of the first row as the creature clambered upright behind them. That was the moment Thurin saw her, hanging right beside the star-eyed monster.

"Quina?" He spoke her name as a question, but there wasn't any doubt in his mind. It was her, quick, sharp Quina, hanging pale in an iron harness, the star on her forehead threading black wires beneath her skin.

The monster's eyes found him, dazzling red. With an oath, Thurin turned and ran, choosing his path and giving chase to the fearsome cannibal who had undoubtedly saved his sanity back in the room—likely at the cost of her own.

12

$\bigstar \quad \bigstar$
$\bigstar$

THURIN WOKE WITH a start, confused by his surroundings, confused by the darkness. He reached around him, finding rough stone on every side. The Black Rock. He remembered. Slowly, on hands and knees, he moved to the mouth of the dead-end tunnel that he'd chosen to rest in. In the chamber beyond, a whisper of light from a single distant star gave a sense of the space without quite illuminating anything. Fungi grew in the warmth of the chamber, reaching heights and sizes unseen in the ice-roofed caves of the Broken. The place had the feeling of an old mine, hollowed of what had originally been sought here.

Thurin rubbed his head where he'd grazed it on the low tunnel roof earlier. He should have known better than to think he could catch Hetta. She had, after all, somehow managed to hide from both the Broken and the Tainted in the ice caves year after year. Quite how someone so big could hide so well Thurin couldn't say. Perhaps she had other blood talents working for her. But her speed across the ground was no mystery. Her legs were nearly as long as his body.

Thurin quenched his thirst at a seep low down on one of the walls. He guessed that the priests didn't have to hunt down intruders or escapees very often. It seemed possible to wander the mountain tunnels for days without seeing anyone, and without food or water those days would soon become a fatal burden. Thurin had only found the fungi cave by using his water-sense to track the flows within the rock. Even then it had taken many frustrating hours wending his way ever down until he finally found a point where the mountain released its precious trickle into the open. Thurin guessed that the heat generated by stars and the burning of coal in the complex melted ice higher up, allowing for a modest supply of drinking water and enough to farm fungi down among the roots of the mountain.

A stretch and a yawn drove some of the sleep from his body. Somehow a few hours' slumber had lifted the weight of the mountain from his shoulders, though he felt it returning with each surfacing memory of recent events. He needed to find Yaz. The others would be here too. He would help them as well if he could. He shook his head, snorting a bitter laugh. And the hundreds held in the glow of those stars? Would he also rescue those? There truly was a mountain ready to crush him beneath an untold mass of obligation and duty. Where did it end? Was he bound to save members of the Broken who had been stolen from the ice caves before his mother's mother was born? Did they even want saving? The man whose circlet Hetta had torn away seemed happy to serve the priests' Hidden God. Was that his true desire, or something the star in his circlet had whispered to him for so long that it had become part of his thinking?

Thurin sat on a boulder and munched absently on a brown mushroom larger than his hand. In the ice caves they had been small enough to fit several in his palm. Madeen always made a delicious stew with them and Thurin could smell it there in that dark chamber, drawing him back home, back to the only life he'd ever known. He could just leave. Leave and go back.

The image of Yaz returned to him, as she had looked when being hauled away in the delivery cage, her eyes on his. He let out a long sigh. *Home is where the heart is.* Eular had told him that once, years ago, and Thurin had never understood it until this very moment. He could go back to the caves, take the long fall from grace and return to his people, but he would leave the better part of himself here, in the Black Rock. Living would be replaced by existing. The pursuit of happiness substituted with a mere counting away of whatever days remained. Yaz was an unfinished song and he wanted to hear more.

Thurin walked towards the distant star with a blind man's caution, watching the dimness before him for any hint of obstacles or pitfalls. Something drew his eye; something more than just sight swung his head towards a clot of darkness on his left. A cold fear filled him, the sudden terror of discovering that you are not alone in a place where you have been at ease, a place where you have slept.

"Hetta?" He moved towards the shape beside the wall, arms outstretched, hands trembling.

The darkness gave back only silence and a growing sense of dread. Thurin's feet wanted him to run. The steps he took towards the black shape grew shorter and slower.

Thurin reminded himself that he had lived with demons beneath his skin and dwelt in the unremitting night of the Tainted's caves. He had done too much running away of late. Instead he forced himself on against every instinct. The figure was large, perhaps a human . . . It seemed to be seated. Thurin's water-sense found nothing though, neither blood nor sweat nor tears. Unwilling fingers advanced, half expecting the blackness to bite them short. They discovered cold stone, but shaped as a body is shaped. A statue such as ice-workers sometimes make, but formed from the rock itself.

Thurin felt around the statue. The sense of relief that should have wrapped him failed to do so. Somehow his fear clung to him despite the nightmare monsters he had imagined turning out to be mere stone. The thing seemed half-finished, only partially cut from the wall. It sat crosslegged, hands resting palms up on its knees. If it were standing it would have been taller than Hetta. Thurin had to stretch to find its face.

All the time he examined the statue it seemed to Thurin that the name of whatever it was that sat before him was one he already knew, dancing just beyond the fingertips of his outstretched memory. He felt that in the very next moment he would be able to open his mouth and speak it. But the next moment came and still it eluded him.

As his fingers moved higher the smoothly shaped stone became rough and jagged, as if someone had hacked away with a sword to ruin the work. The damage was greatest around the face. In place of eyes only great wounds remained, scored one way and the other. A name grew in his mouth, still unknown to his mind but wanting to force itself from his tongue.

Thurin stepped away, trembling, not trusting the stone figure to remain seated. Somehow the statue unnerved him more than finding an old corpse in the dark.

"Arges." The name spoke itself from Thurin's mouth.

Somewhere behind him a bright green light winked into life, throwing Thurin's shadow across the statue looming before him.

"Don't say."

"That."

"Name." Three voices, one message.

Fear should have clamped Thurin's jaw even if he hadn't tried to bite down on the word. But it spilled from his tongue even so. "Arges."

"Once more," warned the person behind him.

"And," said the next.

"He'll come."

Thurin clamped both hands over his mouth and staggered away from the statue. He turned towards the green light that had lit behind him.

Squinting, he could make out the shapes of three people, one with a burning green eye. He let his hands slip and an oath escaped him. Another of the mind-breakers he and Hetta had fled from. He began to run for the exit, lifelong habit making him avoid crushing fungi where possible.

"What's he doing?"

"Running away."

"From us?"

They were women's voices, cracked with age. Something about them made Thurin falter. He came to a halt in the archway through which he'd first entered the cavern unknown hours earlier. Their surprised tone arrested him. He found himself beneath the single star in its cage and turned, slowly. It was hard to grow old among the Broken, so any that managed it earned a degree of veneration. Perhaps that respect helped keep Thurin there too.

"Come into the light," he called back.

"We have our own," one of the trio replied, but they came forward anyway, moving in that careful way the old have, perhaps taught by age, or perhaps they were born with it and that caution was what allowed them to weather the years. The leader, obscured by the glare of her one glowing eye, turned to illuminate the other two who trailed her, each holding on to the one before as though blind. The green light made them seem strange, as if they might be creatures from another world, but in truth they were old women in ragged skins, bony, angular bodies, wrinkled faces framed with straggling tresses of long grey hair.

"You're new." The ancient leading the others had one star eye and one hollow socket filled with shadow. The other two women were both eyeless. Thurin had grown up with Eular around, so the sight didn't unnerve him so much as puzzle him. "Very new."

"You can tell?" It was all he could think to say.

The three women laughed as if he'd told a joke, their voices cracking around the sound. "There's none here fool enough to go messing with a statue of the Hidden God." The first of the old women narrowed her eye. "And besides . . ." The green shaded darker and flushed into violet. "You have talent . . ." The light tingled on his skin. ". . . marjal . . . skilled in ice and fire . . ." She frowned. "There's something e—"

"Let me see!" The second woman clawed briefly at the speaker's face and to Thurin's horror the green eye came away in her hands. Thurin took a step back, his stomach turning. He tried to remind himself it was a star rather than an eyeball. "Ah!" She crammed the star into her right socket and peered at him as if she could now see. "Give me the tooth! Give me the tooth!" She tugged a knife from the first woman's hand, a blade that Thurin had missed in the gloom. Thurin recognized the type of weapon from Yaz's description of the one she'd lost fighting Hetta: it had been fashioned from the tooth of a dagger-fish.

"Who *are* you?" Thurin asked, amazed.

"They call us the Grey Sisters." She bowed. "None other." The woman laughed as if she had cracked a joke and her two blind sisters cackled along. Their mirth had that wild quality to it that can come from eating too many silver-gill fungi, the type of laughter that's one step from never stopping, one step from madness.

"Children of the Gods in the Sea," the first managed.

"We saw the golden cities and rose from them beneath the ice . . ."

"Like bubbles!"

Thurin stepped back as they came forward, his eyes on the knife. He kept his hands out, palms down, fingers spread, placatory. "I was just . . . leaving."

"Stay," said the sister with the eye. "We get so few visitors."

"I . . . uh . . . I have to find my friends." Thurin risked a glance behind him, checking the entrance.

"The priests have them," the third sister said. "And the priests keep what they have. Those who are brought here join the statues, or work in the mine. There's no leaving here, boy. Only staying."

"He's looking for a girl," said the sister with the eye. Apart from the eye it was hard to tell one from the other—triplets perhaps. "A special girl."

"He looooooooves her," the last of them crooned.

"He flew here," said the first.

"On the wings of love." The sister with the eye and tooth cackled.

"You've seen Yaz?" Thurin found himself torn between a knee-jerk denial and amazement. "How did you know about me flying?"

"Agatta sees everything," said one of the sisters without the eye. "What has passed."

"What is." The middle sister narrowed her green eye.

"And what will be," the lead sister finished.

Thurin frowned. "You see *everything* . . . and you're lurking in this damp cave?"

The last sister reached forward and snatched the eye from her sibling. She sniffed haughtily. "That should tell you something about the state of the world, young Thurin. Where else should we be? We have warmth and food and water."

Thurin opened his mouth to answer but reconsidered. He had seen the ice. "What about the green world?" Yaz had spoken of it so often and her vision was like a fire that he could warm himself beside, but he could no more enter it than he could enter among the flames. His imagination could make no picture of what it might be like. Not even with the stone about him painted green by the light of the witches' eye. "There truly is a green world, isn't there?"

"There was." The last sister watched him.

"There is," said the second. "Just a sliver."

"There won't be," the third intoned. "All things die. Even worlds. Even time dies if you give it long enough."

Thurin shook his head to clear it of confusion. He hadn't any time for these mysteries even if they weren't the ramblings of broken minds, which they probably were. "If you know everything, then where are my friends?"

"Agatta doesn't know everything—she sees everything. There's a difference. A big difference," said the blind one at the front.

"We do know where your friends are, though," said the sister with the eye. "But you don't manage to help them, not even a little bit, unless you ask the right questions."

"What are the right questions?" Thurin asked.

"That wasn't one of them." Her eye narrowed and the light grew more intense. Whispers began to rise from Thurin's mind as steam will lift when water is heated.

"You're like that other one," Thurin muttered. "But his eyes were red and they hurt more."

"Those are the Breakers. The Hidden God makes them to serve his interests. Just as he was made to serve another's interests. There's always a bigger fish. We of the sea know this wisdom."

"And who made you?" The whispers from the back of his mind reached his lips, bypassing discretion and politeness.

"The Gods in the—"

"I've never seen the sea. Until today I'd never seen the sky. Those gods are not my gods. And in the ice we say that the obvious answer is generally the right one." Thurin gritted his teeth against the disconcerting effects of the woman's narrow green-eyed stare and reached out with his water-sense, enfolding all three sisters in a gentle grip. "Until today I'd met only one man without eyes my entire life, and none who used stars to see with. So I think that if the Hidden God made the Breakers would he not also have made you?"

"We knew you could ask the right question." The woman with the eye turned away.

The other two took hold of each other's rags and followed in a line as she walked off. "Come on then," the last of them called.

Thurin pressed hard on his forehead with both hands, trying to squeeze his thoughts back together. "Wait!" He hurried after them. "You really know everything? I mean, you've seen it all?"

"We have." The lead sister slipped into a fissure that split the chamber's rough-hewn wall, an ancient defect in the mountain that must have predated humanity's delving, and most likely their arrival on Abeth too.

They took him by what seemed natural passages in the rock, carved by ancient waters, the two blind sisters finding their way with a tactile familiarity that spoke of years spent coming to and fro. Their route led deeper still, the only light being the emerald glow of the sisters' single eye.

"Where are we g—"

"Wrong question."

"Why are we—"

"Better," said the sister just ahead of him. "But 'why' is a difficult question for us. When you have seen what will be, then there's no 'why' save 'because.' Everything is a lot to see. It can't be held in one mind. It fractures our thoughts. It steals ambition and desire. To see everything is to become a part of it. Like the mountain, or the ice, or the wind."

Thurin saw in the green light a fringe of stone spears hanging from the roof of the cavern ahead like teeth in a devouring maw. The sight stole his many other questions and for a while he could only marvel at the subterranean wonders surrounding them as they walked. The rock seemed to have been melted and then refrozen into marvellous flowing shapes, like the icicle cave but with ice replaced by stone and sheened in faint rainbow colours.

Deeper still and Thurin began to sense a strange regularity about him, flat surfaces and sharp corners disguised beneath the flowstone. "We're in the city of the Missing!"

"We are," agreed the lead sister, flashing a green glance back at him. "How do you think the hunters bring back their prey?"

"I . . ." Thurin found that his feet had stopped moving. "But . . ." The idea that the world had always lain within reach floored him. In one sentence the old woman had replaced the impassable miles of ice with a trek through the undercity that any competent scavenger could make. She'd made a lie of the Broken's isolation, of the fall that could not be reversed. A dizziness swamped Thurin, one that previously he'd only experienced at the edge of a high drop.

"Come on," snapped the sister closest to him. "You don't faint here. That comes later."

13

✦ ✦
✦

SOON THEY REACHED areas of the city untainted by water and showing the same clean lines that Thurin was familiar with in the works of the Missing. A dozen rooms and passages further on an ancient stream had cut through one of the Missing's chambers, coating one wall with flowstone, fringing the ceiling with stone icicles. Something clanked into motion as the sisters' light reached ahead. A curious thing of dull metal, a blunt iron-plated form like an unfolded cube, it almost seemed as if it had thick armoured legs and a wedge of a head. It appeared to be trying to struggle across to them but flowstone encased its rear half, pinning it to the spot.

"Is it a hunter?" Thurin didn't think so. It was smaller than him for a start, and didn't bleed starlight from its joints.

"A broken piece," said the closest sister.

"A maintenance unit," said the next.

"A lost dog now," the one with the eye added. "Like many of the things the Missing left behind it doesn't know what to do with itself."

They left it scrabbling in the dark behind them, though for reasons he couldn't explain Thurin felt a strong desire to go back and free the thing. Its dedication to whatever tasks its absent masters had set it had spanned centuries, millennia even. Being left trapped and useless seemed a cruel reward for its service.

They walked without conversation, descending several stairs, passing through endless echoingly empty rooms. Dust-haunted corridors drowned in a silence that swallowed the patter of their footfalls and returned nothing. Thurin was on the point of trying to ask again where they were taking him when in the very next chamber it seemed that they had arrived. The sister's light picked out the lines of a great freestanding circle. An iron ring that stood tall enough for Hetta to walk through unbowed, though her hair might brush the upper curve. The sisters' single eye seemed to grow brighter as they approached, its illumination pooling in deeply graven runes around the perimeter of the ring and causing them to glow.

"What is it?" Thurin stared in awe.

"A haze-gate."

Curiously the chamber lay thick with mud around the margins, though Thurin's water-sense had detected no streams or indeed any hint of water for the last part of their journeying. Yet here and there murky water pooled along ancient scars in the poured stone of the floor.

"Long ago I came here pursuing escapees." The lead sister turned, her eye blazing now, too fierce to look upon. "I was a Breaker, in thrall to the Hidden God, my eyes taken by him and replaced with stars that ruled my mind. I didn't know about the gateway though."

Disconcertingly, the woman pulled the eye from her head and held it out towards the ring. The star flared brighter still and jagged lines of light crackled from it, reaching out to strike the ring's perimeter, bright points of contact dancing over the runes. The whole space encompassed by the ring shimmered as if it were the surface of a pool, affording distorted glimpses of a world beyond. "With stars that the Hidden God has tainted the gateway is . . . ungentle. Only this eye survived the encounter, and in being purged it purged me too. Agatta was born anew, multiplied, given new vision, and strange thoughts."

Thurin shielded his eyes against the glare until the sister stepped back and returned her eye to its socket.

"You called it a haze-gate? It's a door? Where does it lead?"

"Everywhere," said one of the blind sisters.

"Everywhen," said the other.

"It was the gateway that gave us vision, that made us see everywhere and everywhen," said the sister with the eye, "though a single eye does lack a certain depth perception . . . so sometimes it's hard to judge the order in which things happen."

"I'll have my old eyes back one day," said another of the blind sisters. "But not now. Long ago."

Thurin reminded himself that the old women were insane and not to be taken too seriously. He kept his distance from the ring, uneasy in its presence. The shimmering centre had faded away but the hairs on his arms still stood on end. The mad old women had unnerved him too with their talk of seeing futures and pasts, and with the swift passage of the dagger-tooth knife exchanged back and forth between gnarled hands. He knew the long descent hadn't been just to show him what could have been ex-plained back in the fungi cave. And since they seemed to be waiting for the question, he asked it. "And why did you bring me here?"

"Because we saw it." The other blind sister's smile revealed yellowing teeth and dark gaps. "There's no why about it. The boy opens it. The boy goes through."

"Which boy?" the one with the eye asked.

"Her boy," the last said.

All three nodded.

The one with the eye pointed at the rear wall where an alcove now lit up. A large single star burned there, golden, with a slow swirl of shadows crossing its surface. "That's the key. We spent a long time fashioning it so that it would take you where you need to go. Those arts are lost so guard it well."

Thurin shook his head. "I'm not going through that. I came to find Yaz. She's up there somewhere." He pointed, though only one of his audi-ence could see the gesture. "You say you see everything, so you must know where she is."

"She's at the top." The single green eye peered at Thurin, stripping away the layers of his thought. "Though you of all people should know how it is when you come to witches for prophecy."

The light flared and the emerald flash took his sight along with all sense of up, down, and the passage of time. Only the question lingered . . . *Me of all people?*

THURIN WOKE TO find himself alone in the chamber, sprawled on his back before the towering ring. The shifting golden illumination told him that the mad sisters had left the star in the alcove alight for him. The key, they had called it. The muddy floor squelched beneath him as he tried to roll to his side.

He sat and held his head between grimy hands, trying to squeeze his thoughts back together and seal the cracks left by the green eye's scrutiny. He got slowly to his feet, expecting a spike of pain at any moment, alerting him to some or other injury, but found himself whole and unhurt.

"Ha." Thurin snorted. He turned his back on the gate. He'd no intention of going through it, and being told that he would had only strengthened his resolve not to. Seeing the future was all well and good, but if you then told people about it you could hardly expect things to still unfold as foreseen. Without a backwards glance, Thurin set off along the corridor that had brought him to the chamber. Even if he'd become disoriented and lost his direction, there were three sets of muddy footprints to lead the way.

After about fifty yards the light grew too dim to give even the vaguest of impressions of the surrounding passage, let alone pick out the progressively fainter footprints left by the retreating sisters. Thurin stumbled on for another fifty yards, tripping over broken stone, grazing his knees in a fall, and finally reaching a three-way junction that he'd no memory of passing on the way in. From his time with the Tainted he knew that passages revealed by touch could paint a different picture in the mind from that delivered by the eye. It didn't take him long to conclude that without light he had no chance of retracing his steps. Even with a light he wasn't that confident. It was a long way and he had trusted the sisters to bring him back once they had shown him their secrets. It had been a foolish trust. With a sigh he set off back to the chamber to retrieve the star.

Thurin crossed the chamber's floor, avoiding the worst of the mud. The ring threw its shadow against the wall and ceiling in a distorted circle. He avoided it too. He was sure nothing would happen if he passed through the empty gate, but he went around anyway. Even with the star it seemed unlikely that the ring could lead anywhere except from one side to the other. But if that were truly the case, what was it doing here?

The starlight made him squint before he got halfway to its source. Closer still and he had to view it through the gaps between the fingers of his raised hand. The star was larger than the sisters' eye, big as a fist, larger than any star he'd seen, save perhaps for the crimson hearts that Yaz had torn from hunters. At five yards it woke the whispering at the back of his mind. Halving that distance set his skin tingling and filled his mind with a wordless roar. Closer still and a terrifying madness blossomed inside his skull.

Thurin backed away, finding himself sweat-soaked, his heart pounding, breath ragged. Carrying the star with him was not going to be an option. He rested, bent over, hands on his knees, and raised his head to stare at the gate. He wondered how long the sisters had seen him waiting before he finally decided that the haze-gate was his only way out of here. Stubbornness could still see him wandering blind in the unlit city but the chances were that he would stumble, lost, until starvation gave him a slow death or an unseen fall offered a quicker exit.

Thurin returned to the ring, running his hand over the deeply graven symbols around its edge. He'd seen their kin before, glowing on the walls of the undercity, the script of the Missing. The Broken had no writing but he had heard from those who'd lived on the ice that the priests of the Black Rock could trap meaning in their runes, whole stories even. The Missing's writing did more than that. It spoke to you, managing to press emotions and commands past the translation barrier. The symbols beneath his fingertips remained silent though, biting their tongues, biding their time.

Thurin sighed and watched the shadow he cast, a black tower amid the golden light painting the opposite wall. Even if he wanted to open the gate it wasn't clear how it could be done. Thurin knew nothing about keys save that they were said to open or undo things. He'd never met anyone who had even seen one, but somehow the idea persisted, trapped in the language of the clans. It seemed logical that he would have to bring the key to the thing that needed opening. In this case that would mean bringing the star to the gate.

The star burned on, the slow roll of shadows across its surface varying the light. Thurin gathered his courage for a second approach. Perhaps if he ran at it . . . He shook his head. He might as well try to snatch molten metal from the forge pot merely by being quick. No part of him would let himself go close to the star.

He stalked the chamber, thinking furiously. More than once he shouted after the departed sisters that they might at least have told him how to open the gate.

Finally, exhausted, he squatted down beside one of the muddy puddles and wondered if he were thirsty enough to drink from it. Its presence confused him. He could sense no water seeping from the walls, and where would mud come from? In the ice caves of the Broken mud came only from decaying fungi and the waste they grew on. But he'd seen nothing like that here.

Thirst had never been something Thurin had had to contend with living beneath a sky of melting ice. He didn't like it at all. His tongue felt unnaturally rough against the dry insides of his cheeks. He regarded the muddy puddle with a sour eye. Perhaps he could convince the water to reject the murk. With a small flex of his skill he lifted a rippling ball of water the size of two fists together. Experiments in the past suggested that the best way was to spin the ball fast.

Within the rotating ball the dirt quickly began to redistribute itself, concentrating around the equator in a black strip while the water behind started to clear. Exerting the necessary level of control was taxing but with furious concentration Thurin let the black water fly away while he maintained the cohesion of the central mass.

After several minutes' effort the ball was somewhat smaller and the water a lot cleaner. Thurin arrested its spin and willed the water towards his parched mouth. The first tendril reached his lips and he was about to drink when something in the way the golden light rippled through the mass gave him a new idea.

Thurin sent the ball of water towards the niche where the star rested. He was already frowning. His plan had a missing piece. Even as he wrapped the water around the star in a new inch-thick skin he knew that it couldn't maintain a grip. If he lifted the water the star would sink through it and remain where it was.

The whole cave rippled now as if fathoms deep in a sea that filtered the light of an alien sun, one that burned golden white behind shifting clouds. Thurin half expected to see strange fish swimming through the adjoining tunnels to circle the gate ring. Yaz knew about fish; she would be able to picture them better than the poor imaginings he based on the black, eyeless creatures that swam in the Broken's streams.

Somehow thinking of Yaz made Thurin think of the ice, as if the girl would always be a part of it. And that gave him the last, most difficult piece of his solution. He focused the whole of his ice-working talent on the ball of water containing the star. He had seen the standing pools carved by past generations of the Broken where water can become ice within moments, the phase change triggered by some small disturbance that acts as a focus about which change can occur. He needed the water to freeze, to alter its state. He needed every part of the swirling fluid to link arms with its neighbours and lock tight. He needed the heat preventing that transition to leave.

The necessary manipulation proved rather like trying to thread a sinew through the eye of a needle while standing on one leg . . . and being attacked by a tainted gerant. Thurin stood as close as he could, one hand extended towards the star, the other clamped across his forehead to stop his thoughts escaping. Years of ice-work had furnished him with an instinctive understanding of the difference between ice and water on a far deeper level than can be gained from touch and sight. Somehow he needed to break the barrier between them, to force one to become the other.

An hour passed, perhaps three. The spike of pain returned, driven between Thurin's eyes. He sensed himself on the edge of success but somehow it never seemed to reveal itself, like a forgotten name tickling the tip of his tongue but refusing to be spoken.

He slaked his thirst with muddy water and continued to press at the problem while his stomach rumbled its hunger.

A sound brought him out of his trance. A distant skitter, back along the dark corridor down which he had tried to follow the sisters. A sound and then silence. The star shed its watery cloak as Thurin's concentration lapsed. He stared in the direction of the noise. At first he thought it might be the sisters returning to take pity on him, but the corridor remained dark, with no glimmer of their singular green eye. A sound and then silence, in a place where no sound should ever be ignored.

"Hello?" The word left him and vanished into the unyielding blackness.

He tried to gather himself. The unexpected noise had left him unsettled. He hadn't wanted to be alone, but now that it seemed he might not be, suddenly solitude seemed like a good thing.

Thurin was still peering nervously into the shadowed passageway when the attack came from behind. The only warning he had was that tingle in his ice-sense he always got when large bodies of water were in motion. Sight and sound had yielded him nothing. He threw himself forward and the blow scythed above his head.

Hetta came on, roaring now, trying to stamp the life from him. Thurin rolled this way and that, pushing with his ice-work to deflect her feet so that they slammed down inches from his head rather than pulping it against the stone floor.

"Hetta! It's me! Stop!"

But the woman's face was demon-stained once more, no recognition in her eyes. Thurin gave her a mental shove and scrambled to his feet as her advance jolted to a halt. She champed her pointed teeth together, lips bloody, and lunged again. Thurin hauled at the blood running through every part of her and matched her strength just as her reaching fingers grazed his shoulder. With a grunt of effort he dragged her back across the room, her feet sliding through the mud. The white agony in his head told him that this wasn't something he could keep doing, though.

Hetta was full of her own demons. The mind-breaker that had chased the two of them from the frozen army must have fractured her mind, loose fragments becoming the demons that rode her. And now she'd hunted him down. He could flee into the dark but Hetta had survived for years on prey she chased through black tunnels. Thurin found himself paralysed by an unmanning fear, the terror that fills a cornered animal. Hetta would overwhelm him. She would kill him here or out there in the dark, and her sharp teeth would tear the flesh from his bones. He would die in the undercity, alone, and Yaz would never even know that he'd come after her.

Hetta found sudden, unexpected traction, digging a foot in where some unknown force had scarred the floor. She flung herself forward with a bladder-loosening howl, diving for his feet. Despite the resistance from his ice-work her outstretched hand somehow clamped around his shin. And then, with irresistible strength, she began to pull him towards her, still howling through a mouth now flecked with bloody foam.

In Thurin's last moments a surprising clarity settled on him, driving out fear, shock, regret, replacing them all with a single thought. *Open the gate.* The sisters had said he would go through. And he couldn't do that if he died here.

He reached out for the water that had fallen from around the star when his concentration broke. It lay pooled across the uneven surface of the alcove. Lifting it to engulf the star took a moment's thought, a moment that brought him half a yard closer to Hetta's mouth.

Thurin needed the water to be ice. He needed that more than he needed his next breath or the next beat of his heart. The ground scraped beneath him. Hetta's other hand found his hip. She raised her head, mouth wide and dripping, taking her time now that she'd won. The stains of the demons beneath her skin made a warring pattern of red and black, each claiming half her face, the zones interlacing along the divide where they battled for dominance. Thurin only half saw her. The shell of water occupied his mind's eye. Two zones. Something clicked deep within his brain; some barrier to understanding surrendered to pressure. He made two zones, driving heat from the farthest region of the water into the closer. A half shell of ice cupped the star, and a half shell of warmer water fell away.

Hetta drew Thurin's thigh to her gaping mouth. He didn't fight her.

His strength was as nothing beside hers. Instead he threw the star at the gate, yanking on the ice that now held it. How it could possibly help him wasn't the point anymore. Perhaps the sisters had just seen him opening it and then Hetta dragging his corpse through. But he had done what he could and if he had to die he would at least have finished his life with an achievement.

The noise of the gate opening was at once so deep, high, and loud that Hetta's jaws snapped shut in surprise just a fraction of an inch from the meat of Thurin's leg. The sound pulsed through the rock; it thrummed in the longest of Thurin's bones and it whined in his ears. The view through the gate became a black wall, far darker than the corridors leading from the chamber. It swallowed the light of the star so utterly that it plunged the room into unbroken night. The roar that followed was to Hetta's roar what the ice wind is to a single breath. And a fraction of a heartbeat later water filled the space in a blast that carried all before it faster than a stone falls.

14

✦ ✦
✦

QUELL

QWELLA?" QUELL ASKED again, losing the certainty that had gripped him. She must be another phantom of his delirium. Like the iron table that became a dog.

"Yes," she answered, glancing once at the knife bedded in his side. "You're Ictha. Do you know me?"

"It's me! Quell!" He tried to sit, and failed once more.

A veined white face thrust in between them, dark eyes narrow and furious. "You've destroyed it all." Priest Valak swung an arm at the destruction around them, the floor scattered with bright shards of antique glassware. "You stupid . . . ignorant . . . savage! Have you any idea what you've done here?"

"It wasn't me." Quell croaked out his protest, wanting to explain about the metal cube that opened out into something doglike. "I—"

Qwella pushed the priest aside. "You can see he's too weak to crawl. Someone else did it. Now give me some space or I won't be able to save him. He's pretty far gone." She flexed her elbows, driving Valak further back. The priest let his arms fall, his attention captured once more by the ruins of his collection.

"Qwella . . ." Quell managed to clasp her hand with his. Their eyes met. Hers widened.

"Quell? Little Quell? My Quell?" A widening smile. "No?"

Quell nodded. His throat too tight for words, ashamed that he had almost forgotten her, ashamed that she had become a ghost, haunting the fringes of his memory.

"Not so little now!" She shook her head. "My own brother . . . This will take some getting used to!" Her face became serious and she turned her attention to the knife. A soft cry of dismay reached them from across the room where Valak was crouched, sifting through the wreckage of what had so recently been heartbreakingly beautiful and unknowably old works of the Missing.

"How—" Quell gasped as her fingers probed the rigid muscle around the wound. "How are you here? Hardly changed?"

"Ah, well . . . I sleep a lot." Qwella made a small smile. A warmth spread from where her fingertips touched his flesh. "They wake me up when they need me. Each time I think it's to be the war, but no, it's Valak has broken his toe, Sequa has frostbite, Mekka cut herself slicing fish." As she spoke the warmth beneath her fingers became a tingling sensation that somehow both numbed like cold and thrilled like fire. She set a hand to the hilt of the knife and Quell winced, but in anticipation of pain rather than actual pain. "It will be fine." Her smile now had the warmth he remembered as a child when she would pick him up in his hides and parade him along the line of the sled march.

"Sister . . ." He felt the steel being withdrawn but it was a distant thing. Instead of pain he felt love, the uncomplicated love that runs as an undercurrent through family. Behind the cutting edge the muscle tingled. Quell imagined that the sensation was his insides reknitting. He hoped that it was. "My sister." It seemed impossible that where Yaz's bond to her brother had pulled her down the pit, his with his sister had frayed into forgetfulness. But he'd been so young and the memories had become myth, a dream that haunted him through the years.

Qwella discarded the blade, letting it clatter to the floor. She pressed her palm to the wound.

"What war?" With the knife out of him Qwella's words returned to his mind.

Glass crunched as Valak turned sharply towards them, paler than ever before, though Quell had not imagined that possible. "Don't speak of it!"

Qwella frowned. "Quell is Ictha." She said it as if that explained everything. And it did. There were no secrets among the Ictha. Betrayals and infighting were not luxuries that one could afford in the far north. There was only one enemy, though it bore many faces: call it hunger, call it cold, call it the wind or the ice . . . or just call it the north. "He'll join us when we go to war. All the Ictha will." She spoke with total conviction, though the Ictha did not make war. None of their people had died a violent death in generations. At least not above the ice. "We're going to take the green lands. At least enough of them for us to live there with space to hunt and fish. It's warm there, Quell. They have oceans that make our seas look like drops of water. They have animals on the land too. There's no ice, just . . . green. Everywhere you look there's food. You can just reach out and take it."

"How do you know all this?"

Qwella smiled as if he were still her baby brother, a child asking a child's questions. "We see it in our dreams. The Hidden God shows us what's there, down in the south. And what we have to do to get it."

"But aren't there clans that live there already?" Quell asked.

Qwella frowned; she looked puzzled, as if trying to catch an elusive thought. Then she brightened. "That's what the war is for."

"You'd kill to take what's theirs?" Quell tried to sit and found that this time he actually could. His side still hurt but the pain was no longer the crippling kind that demanded he obey. Now it was more by way of a strongly worded suggestion. "Before the last gathering I'd never met anyone who believed in the green world, and now days later you expect me to murder the people who live there so I can take their place?"

Qwella shook her head, troubled. "It's not murder. It's war. Our clans need to live, don't they? You don't see it, but we're dying. The Black Rock has a longer memory. The priests keep records. Once, not so long ago, only the clan elders could watch the regulator do his work at the Pit of the Missing. There wasn't room for any but the elders. Now all of us can fit on the crater rings."

"It's not the Ictha way." Quell glanced across the room to see Valak watching their exchange intently, two jagged pieces of a large vase in his hands.

"In the north only the strong survive," the priest said. "Isn't that true?"

Quell shrugged. "We are all strong in the north."

Valak set the pieces down, one hand bloody, and came towards them. "That's what the ice does. It grinds us together and only the strong survive. That is the Ictha way."

Quell said nothing. The priest talked as if he lived among them, but though he might venture onto the ice from time to time the priest lived here, in the warm. He knew no more of the Ictha than a man staring at the waves knows of the depths of the sea.

"And soon the ice will grind us against the people of the green lands and once more the strong will survive." Valak gave his blood-smeared hand a sour look. "Go back to your vigil, Qwella."

"But . . ." Qwella's face fell. "Quell will need more treatment. I could stay with him awhile."

"He'll do fine."

"He's my brother. Couldn't I—"

"Go back!" Valak raised his voice and the red star on Qwella's chest pulsed with each of his words.

Qwella's eyes lost focus and without replying or saying goodbye she turned to go.

"Wait!" Quell didn't want to lose her a second time. He tried to stand but the pain defeated him.

Qwella left without a backwards glance. Valak stood looking down on Quell with dark, unreadable eyes. "It's unfortunate that she told you so much. Regulator Kazik had hoped that you would be able to return to your people, but that will no longer be possible."

"But I . . ." Quell realized how feeble his promise not to speak of the priests' war would sound. His first duty was to his clan. Valak knew that. "You could have stopped her!"

Malice flashed in Valak's eyes. "I was too distracted by the wreckage of my collection. Those vases were thousands of years old. Tens of thousands maybe. They were the artistry of a vanished people whose ruins dwarf our—"

"What's to become of me?" Quell got to his feet using the wall, teeth gritted against the pain, sweating, panting.

"I'm trying to decide if spending the rest of your days labouring in the coal mines is a fitting punishment, or if it wouldn't just be easier if you died trying to escape after your destructive rampage." Valak's blossoming rage trembled in his hands.

Quell staggered back a few steps. He couldn't run and he wouldn't beg. "That table behind you. That cube of iron. It came to life and did it."

Valak glanced back at it without really looking. "That was there when I was assigned this chamber fifteen years ago. It's a lump of metal."

Quell was half-inclined to believe the priest. It had seemed like a dream at the time—more so now. "Why would I tell such a lie?"

Valak twisted his mouth in a snarl. Then his face went blank, as if all emotion had drained from him in an instant, just as Qwella's face had lost expression when he ordered her away. Quell had seen it before, the calm before the storm when Yaz unleashed the awful power she had access to. Valak closed his eyes.

Three thuds reverberated through Quell. If it weren't for the fact they shook the room too, Quell might have imagined them to be the pounding of his heart. A loud scraping creak accompanied them, as if perhaps the mountain itself were breaking and the ceiling might descend in a rush of shattered rock.

Valak's eyes snapped open, full of a terrible light, fiercer and less kind than the sun's. To touch him now would mean incineration; the air rippled around him, stirred by invisible fire. A shadow moved behind the man and he shuddered, not like a person but as the whole world does when your head hits the ice too hard. He shook, as if the power he had taken were too much for him to contain. But, just as Yaz had, he began to master it. Soon it would be his to do with as he chose, and Quell knew that the priest's choice would see him decorate the far wall.

Quell commended his essence to the Gods in the Sea and stood straight. He would die on his feet like an Ictha, defiant until the last.

Sparks began to arc between Valak's outstretched fingers. And suddenly the man was falling backwards with a startled cry. The priest crashed down onto both shoulders as the blunt iron head of the dog-thing emerged between his legs, shortly followed by the rest of it, lumbering forward at a fair pace. Where it had touched the priest the dog's iron skin glowed with a red heat.

Valak's cry had become a sound that wasn't intended to issue from a human mouth. He continued to shudder and the sparks became crackling snakes of white energy that writhed about him, searing all they touched.

The metal creature continued on, aiming for the tunnel that led away. Even in the depth of his amazement Quell could feel the building danger. The interruption had clearly caused Valak to lose control and something very bad was about to happen—very soon.

Quell decided that perhaps he could run after all, despite his healing wound. He overtook the lumbering dog in the tunnel outside. Behind them the light got brighter and brighter, illuminating the way ahead, launching their shadows before them. Quell threw himself around a corner into a side passage. The detonation behind him happened in the same instant. Quell landed on his good side, looking back, and had a fleeting impression of a dark shape, which must have been the iron dog, hurtling past the mouth of the passageway amid a swirling storm of fire. Enough of the conflagration rounded the corner to wash over Quell as he folded his arms before his face. The heat scorched across him and blew itself out.

"Gods in the Sea . . ." His voice sounded distant and muffled, competing with a high ringing in both ears. Quell sat and slapped at his smouldering hair with scorched hands. The air stank of acrid char. The light swayed this way and that with the stars swinging in their iron cages. He shook his head and used the wall to help him gain his feet. Still dazed, he looked down the passage, wondering where in the hells he should go now.

A scraping sound and a heavy thud brought his gaze back to the corner he'd thrown himself around. The blunt head of the dog edged into view, smoking gently. Two dark and solemn eyes regarded him.

15

✦ ✦
✦

QUELL CONSIDERED ALL his options and ended up following the dog. It at least seemed to know where it was going. At each junction it would sway its head and sniff sharply through the slots of its nostrils. Then, decided, it would lumber on its way, its ponderous weight borne on four splay-toed feet. Quell didn't know if the dog was just sniffing out and avoiding the priests and their servants or if the chambers beneath the Black Rock really were so sparsely populated that they could wander unchallenged. Twice he heard shouts and running feet, but laid eyes on no one.

The dog led him onwards and downwards, ignoring his sporadic attempts to talk to it. Quell didn't expect it to answer him, but the Quinx talked to their sled dogs and he felt he should try.

"Do you have a name?" Quell limped along beside the dog; talking helped keep his mind from the sharp throbbing where the knife had been. "No? Maybe I should give you one then. How about Zox?" He was sure he'd heard one of the Quinx call their lead dog Zox. Though he supposed it could have been some sort of command . . . "Slow down a bit." He had one hand clamped to his side. It helped a little but not much. "Qwella would have told me not to get up for a day, let alone walk, and instead you had me running!" Quell changed the hand holding his side. The pain got worse. "Though to be fair, if you hadn't I would currently be an interesting stain on Valak's walls."

The one-sided muttered conversation went on as they made slow progress past areas that, judging by the higher density of hanging stars, saw more comings and goings. The dog led them along sloping passages, or laboriously shuffled its way down long stairways. The carved steps were often too small for its feet and from time to time it teetered like an avalanche waiting to happen, before somehow recovering itself and resuming its descent.

Several times they passed vertical shafts as wide as small rooms, each with metal cables hanging down the middle, descending from the darkness above to the darkness below. Quell judged these to be for raising and lowering goods or even people in cages, much as they had been brought up through the ice. The dog, despite seeming always to head downwards, paid scant attention to the shafts.

"Hold up." It pained Quell as an Ictha to ask for a halt but he needed to rest. He set his back to the wall and slid down.

The dog kept on walking and in a moment of clarity Quell was able to reevaluate the situation. He'd thought the dog was leading him, but it seemed that instead he had simply been following it and it in turn had tolerated being followed. Quell's backside hit the stone floor and he watched the dog plod heavily on towards the next turn of the tunnel.

"Leave me then!" he shouted after it. "I've been stabbed, you know."

The dog lumbered out of sight.

"They would have looked after me and sent me home!" he shouted at the empty tunnel. "Only you had to go and break everything."

Quell snapped his jaw shut on further complaint, ashamed of himself. The Ictha did not whine. They endured. He pressed a hand to his wound and stared at the wall before him, dimly lit by the light of a small caged star ten yards off.

A scrape and a thud drew his attention back to the tunnel turning. A blunt metal head edged into view and regarded him dolefully.

"So you *are* leading me!" Quell allowed himself a smile. The southerners always boasted that their dogs were both loyal and clever. This one at least appeared loyal. It came shuffling back to him. "Good boy." Quell had decided it was a boy. It lowered its head to his injured side and the shutters across its nostrils flicked open. It drew in a sharp sniff. Then sat heavily.

Sleep took Quell without asking permission, sneaking up on him just as the cold can flank even the most vigilant of men. He dreamed of the endless ice and the eternal wind as he so often did, but Yaz was at his side as they walked into the long night, and the cold had no dominion over him.

"W-what . . . ?" Quell woke to the dog's urgent nudging. The heavy metal head rolled him over, a shard of hurt reminding him of the absent knife. The tunnel seemed somehow smoky. Rolled onto his back, Quell saw that the smoke was in fact rock dust, sifting down from the ceiling above him. A sharp retort echoed back and forth as a large crack spread from one side of the rocky roof to the other.

Quell rolled back onto his front with an oath and scrambled away. Heartbeats later a chunk of stone hammered down where he had been lying. Then another, then lots more, and suddenly the whole roof fell. Quell continued on all fours as a black cloud of dust overtook him, a rolling, billowing mass that devoured the light. He held his breath and carried on with dogged determination.

The crash and rumble of rock fell to silence, broken only by the rattle of a few loose stones still falling and by the heavy scrape and thud of the iron hound, following close on Quell's heels. Not too close, Quell hoped, as one of those metal paws could crush a man's foot. The thought was enough to hasten his crawl. He drew breath as his chest began to demand air, breathing in through gritted teeth and a guarding hand.

Slowly the line of widely separated stars began to come back into view as the dust cloud settled. Quell turned to look back. A pile of broken rock nearly sealed the tunnel. The thinning dust revealed a black figure in front of the rubble mound. A big man, heavily muscled, though no gerant. Without warning the layer of dust coating him fell away, revealing pale flesh, dark hair, a thick black beard—a rarity, though Quell had heard beards were common among the more southern tribes. Two iron bands looped over his shoulders, crossing on his chest where a red star burned at the junction. Another glowed on the band about his head.

"You'll be the runaway." The newcomer wore the skins of a clansman and had the neck tattoos of an Axit child, though by his age an Axit should be marked from collarbone to cheek. The star's red glow lit him from beneath, making something brutal of his features.

The dog made a slow turn to face him.

"You, I expected. What in the hells is that, though?" The man pointed at the dog.

Quell stood, feeling foolish for being on all fours beside the dog. He slapped at his skins but the dust clung and wouldn't allow him the same escape that it had afforded the other man. "Who are you?"

"Kretar, soldier of the great army. Also the man who is bringing you back to Regulator Kazik. He has some questions for you about the death of a priest."

"Kretar of the Broken?" Quell asked.

The man frowned and then shook his head as if there might still be dust in his hair. "Once upon a time, yes. But—"

"And of the Axit before that," said Quell.

The big man nodded and slapped his barrel chest. "Always Axit!"

"So why are you serving the priests like a slave? Why are you so ready to fight another man's war?"

Kretar frowned, then boomed with laughter. "They didn't warn me you would fight with words."

"I'm not fighting. I'm trying to help. The priests have done something to you." Quell tapped his chest where the man wore a star. "They've made you their slave. You should leave this place. Go back to the Axit and tell them what you've seen. Shouldn't your clan know what goes on here?"

Kretar scowled. "You think words can beat me, boy? You think you can mix my thoughts up?" He pounded his chest. "I am a soldier of the grand army!" He took a hide rope from his belt. "Come, give me your wrists."

Quell took a step back. "How did you find me? How did you do . . . that?" He gestured down the tunnel.

Kretar grinned, showing many white teeth in the black of his beard. "Rock-work. I'm the best there is. Built a good few miles of these tunnels too. But the reason they wake me when there's someone needing hunting is that I have a knack for it. I can see through walls. I know where everyone in this whole mountain is, friend. There's no running from Kretar!"

Quell squared his shoulders, wishing his side didn't ache so. "I guess that leaves fighting then."

Kretar flicked out his fingers and a small stone shot from the ground to strike Quell just above the eye. Behind him several fist-sized chunks of rock rose, slowly rotating. "The Axit don't fight for fun. We fight to win." He advanced with long strides. "So, are you going to give me your wrists?"

Quell retreated several more steps. He wiped at his stinging forehead and his fingers came away bloody. He was tired of these people and their powers that made them unstoppable, like a force of nature. He narrowed his eyes. The Ictha endured nature's worst and had done so for generations. "Take them."

One of the floating rocks shot forward. Sailing past Kretar's ear, aimed at Quell. A chunk large enough to shatter his skull. Quell barely had time to raise his arms. Something dark lunged upwards into the rock's trajectory. The dog came down heavily on its front legs, fragments of stone falling around it.

"Impressive!" Kretar's grin widened. He reached a hand towards the iron dog, then both hands, teeth gritted as he exerted himself.

The dog rose from the ground, its legs paddling as it sought the rock.

"Metal, stone, it's all the same to me." The words sounded strained. "He is a weight though. Enough to crush you with if you don't give this up and surrender." With a snarl of effort he swung the dog towards Quell. As he did so a bright line curled its way across the dog's flat back. Quell had seen its like before.

Quell retreated further. "Do you know what you're holding there, Kretar? That's the most valuable artefact in Priest Valak's collection, though he never really appreciated the fact. That's a work of the Missing!"

Kretar's brows rose but if he was further impressed he didn't say so. "It's not much good for fighting. No claws. No teeth."

Quell shook his head. "I wasn't fighting you with words, but the Missing will."

Even as Quell spoke the first letter of Missing script completed itself on the dog's back and another began to glow on its broad head. Immediately the dog started to sink towards the floor. Kretar strained to stop it, sweat springing up across his brow. With the addition of a completed second letter Kretar's hold was sufficiently negated for the dog to crash down, landing heavily on all four feet.

Quell took his moment. He had endured, and now he would fight. He threw himself forward and dived at Kretar, taking the big man to the ground. They landed tangled together.

"That," said Kretar, seizing Quell's wrists, "was a mistake!" He grinned, showing bloody teeth and in his eyes the ferocity of the Axit.

Quell met the bigger man's eyes and watched them widen in surprise as he forced first one arm down then the other. "The Ictha are a different breed." Before Kretar could respond, Quell wrapped him in both arms and squeezed with all his strength until he heard the muffled crack of ribs and spine.

"If you can still throw rocks I would advise that you don't." He released the man and rolled away. "If the only way to stop you is to kill you, I will."

Quell got to his knees, glancing at the iron dog and then at the rubble heap beneath the hole that Kretar had opened in the roof. He returned his attention to the man. "Tell me where Yaz is."

Kretar only wheezed through blood-flecked lips, his gaze furious.

"They will get Qwella to make you well again. But she can't heal death. So I ask again. Where is Yaz?"

Kretar managed to spit, but not very far; most of it fell back on his cheek.

Quell shrugged. He had never been very good at threats. And besides, it seemed likely that the man had only recently been woken from whatever sleep the priests kept their captives in while breaking their will. The chances were that he didn't know who Yaz was, and with multiple fractures of the ribs even if he did know he would have a hard time explaining how to get there. Quell got to his feet. "Come on, dog." He looked down at Kretar. "You fought well. I hope they find you soon. Tell Qwella I will try to make this right." And with that he set off back towards the rubble pile, hoping that despite its appearance the dog could climb.

16

✦ ✦
✦

THE DOG TURNED out to be much better suited to falling than to climbing. It was, however, very good at pushing, and managed to bully its way through the top half of the rubble mound, flattening it considerably and spreading broken stone for a dozen yards along the tunnel.

After that it continued to lead the way, sniffing periodically and taking the downward option almost every time a choice was offered. The stars became very few and far between, small islands of illumination amid the relentless dark of tunnels that burrowed among the mountain's roots. Sometimes it wasn't possible to see the next point of light before the one behind winked out of existence. On these occasions Quell gathered his courage and put his faith in the dog's guidance.

Whereas the population had been sparse around the chamber where Valak lived, here it seemed wholly absent. Level, well-shaped corridors had been replaced by wandering, hand-hewn tunnels. Once they found an abandoned pick, an iron head set in a haft made from board material. Later on, a wheeled iron cart, badly rusted. Quell picked up one of the small black rocks scattered around it. Unlike the dark stone from which the tunnels had been hewn, this was utterly black—so black it stained his hand. And lighter than a rock should be. He squeezed it and managed to crack it in two.

"Coal," he told the dog. The stone that the worms in the ice fed on and that Thurin had ignited to melt the passage to the surface. A path to freedom that he hadn't been able to use. Quell shook his head at the memory of leaving Thurin behind. The man had deserved better. Still, Quell hadn't liked the way he looked at Yaz, so perhaps the gods had chosen wisely.

They encountered more coal as the dog plodded deeper. Crushed pieces littered the floor of every tunnel. Many chambers seemed to have been hewn only in pursuit of the stuff. Here and there black seams ran through walls, hard to see against the darkness of the natural stone. Quell assumed these had been too meagre to bother mining.

On several occasions they heard the distant sounds of picks striking rock. Once, a rumbling sound rising up a steep decline announced something approaching. Quell hurried back to a narrow cleft in the wall they had passed some twenty yards earlier. The dog, which would not have been able to fit in even if so inclined, simply bowed its head and folded its legs in. By the time whoever was coming arrived Quell imagined that the dog would have turned itself back into the iron cube he had first seen in Valak's chamber.

Quell heard voices and the tunnel grew lighter. He wedged himself in tight and hid his face.

"What's this?" A man's voice. "You three, put it on the cart."

"But the coal . . ."

"I don't care about the coal. Tip it out! What I care about is how something like this got here. Who left it? Where did it come from?"

A few moments later, Quell heard grunts of effort, followed by: "It's too heavy, acolyte, we can't lift it."

"Useless! All of you try."

More grunting and huffing.

"Put your backs into it! Any slacking and I'll send you all to Mother Jeccis for correction."

This seemed to motivate them and for long moments the only sounds were of straining and heaving.

"It's too heavy!"

The acolyte let out a hissing sigh. "Gexxan, run ahead, tell Hessix what we've found. Jorrik, stay here and guard it. The rest of you carry on with me."

It turned out that with two of their number missing the remaining miners were unable to shift their load of coal any better than they could lift the cube. The acolyte, who Quell reckoned should have gone ahead himself if he wasn't involved in dragging the coal cart, being unable to recall the messenger, recalled the guard to service, and with a great deal of effort they got the load moving up the slope.

Before long Quell and the dog were left once more in almost total darkness with just the twinkle of a distant star to guide them onward. The dog unfolded itself and plodded towards the light. It seemed more certain now, picking up the pace fractionally and sniffing less often.

Twice more they heard the sounds of picks and shovels close at hand, and then the dog turned sharply from a major passageway into a much narrower tunnel that led more steeply down. Underfoot the ground lay thick with coal dust and the crash of picks came echoing up. The air grew dusty too and through it shone the light of half a dozen small stars hung amid iron struts positioned to support the roof.

Quell followed the dog forward, trying not to breathe too deeply. Their arrival went unnoticed by the collection of blackened figures swinging their picks against the coalface. Quell thought he could probably shout a greeting and still they wouldn't hear him over the din. The dog increased its pace, almost bounding now, sending one strut flying and knocking another askew as it charged towards the nearest of the miners, a figure as black as the coal he hewed at.

The man turned mid-swing, went down on one knee and set his hands to either side of the dog's blunt head, bowing his own forehead to touch its snout. Nearby, one of two gerants stopped his work and turned to stare in amazement. The flesh around his eyes was paler than the general coal black of his skin, creating a curious, almost comical contrast.

Quell advanced with caution, eyeing up the fallen strut as a possible weapon.

"Quell!" the gerant cried.

"Kao? Is that you, Kao?"

Kao came across as the other miners began to turn from their labours. He threw a huge arm around Quell's shoulders. "It's good to see someone clean! And you're walking! Have you come to join our shift?" He looked back towards the dog. "And what in all the hells is that thing?"

"Heavy maintenance." The man by the dog looked up and Quell realized it was Erris. "It's a part of the city, semiautonomous."

"What's he saying?" Quell hissed to Kao.

The boy shrugged, looking surprised to find himself cast in the role of expert.

"But what is it?" Kao asked again, more loudly.

Erris grinned. Even his teeth had been blackened by the coal dust. "A helper. These days they mainly wait for instructions and conserve their function. But they still get messages from the city." He stood, patted the dog's head, and came across to where Quell stood with Kao. The rest of the miners watched, astonished. "This one smelled me on you." Erris pointed to Quell's side. Through the slashed hides a dark strip of his skin could still be seen around the edges of the scar where the knife wound had been. "That woke it up. Then it went searching."

"Why does the city care about you?" Kao asked.

"The city thinks?" Quell blinked. "No, forget that." He raised a hand to forestall any answer. "Why are you still here? Where's Yaz?"

"The priests told us to stay," Kao answered as if that explained everything. Quell supposed that to a large extent it did. Kao had been raised to respect the priests' judgments, just as he had. "It's dirty work." Kao frowned, then brightened, slapping his belly. "But they feed us well! And where would we go?" Mutters of agreement rose from the other miners at this last question. The priests' word extended across the ice. No clan would take them in if the Black Rock declared them outside the law.

"I was asking him." Quell pointed at Erris. "He doesn't care what the priests say. He doesn't have a clan."

Erris looked slowly down, and when Quell followed his example he raised one shackled ankle, rattling the chain that joined it to the others.

Quell shook his head. "Chains can't hold you."

Erris quirked his mouth. He stepped on the chain and lifted the other foot until one of the links surrendered with a bright retort. "Well, this one can't. That's true."

"Why then?" Quell demanded.

Erris met his gaze. "Because I don't understand this place like you do. These priests are not my holy men. I've no clan, as you say. If I go hunting for Yaz they will try to stop me and that will go badly for them or for me. I'm not sure Yaz would thank me for arriving at her door with a long string of corpses dotting my path from here to there, even if I was prepared to murder my way to her. So I thought I would give her the credit she deserves and let her fix this problem herself." He turned and went back for his pick. "You might have noticed, she's very capable." He swung and buried the pick up to the shaft in the coalface. "I was beginning to think that she might have had long enough, though . . . And much as I love hacking one kind of black rock out of another . . ."

"Also there's the Watcher," Kao said.

"And he is?" Quell asked, not sure he really wanted to know.

"Worse than the hunters," Kao said. Others among the miners nodded at this.

Quell nodded, heart sinking. "I had been wondering why, if the regulator made the hunters, there were none of them here . . ."

Erris yanked his pick free, bringing down several men's weight in coal with a black dust cloud billowing before it. "Because the void star augments all the stars around it, and as you move further away it becomes harder to build things like the hunters. But here, deep under the mountain, we're actually not very far from the undercity. In fact I wouldn't be at all surprised if the tunnels don't connect with it somewhere."

"So . . ." Quell tried to recapture the momentum of the earlier conversation. "It's time to leave and find Yaz. Right?"

"Right." Erris and Kao answered together. The rest exchanged glances.

"So how do we leave without this Watcher seeing us?" Quell asked.

"It's too late for that," rumbled the other gerant miner. "Those are its eyes." He waved a dirty hand towards the ceiling.

"What are?" Quell stared at the rocks and shadows but the starlight showed him nothing.

"The stars," answered the gerant. "These ones. The ones in the tunnel. All the stars."

"The trick," said Erris, moving past them up towards the main passage, "is to get up higher. Before long it'll get too far from the void star and won't be able to follow us."

"Before how long?" Quell asked, setting off after him, the dog now following at his heels.

"Well, that depends on the size of the star used to construct it and on the skill with which it was put together."

Quell glanced back past Kao and the dog at the black line of miners. "You're not coming?"

"They're scared of the Watcher." Kao spoke into the answering silence as the miners shook their heads.

"Gods in the Ice be with you," said one woman, her clan unknowable beneath the coal dust.

Quell paused and met her gaze. "What's this Watcher like?"

Kao snorted. "None of them have even seen it."

"Watchful," the woman replied. "And only those who try to run get to see the Watcher."

Quell shook his head. He had seen all manner of horrors since he had followed Yaz into the Pit of the Missing. One more was not going to stop him reaching her side. And then . . . well, then they would see where they stood.

They joined the larger tunnel and Erris led to the left, as confident and sure as if he'd been riding the prow of his own boat on the Hot Sea, harpoon in hand, rather than filthy after gods knew how long labouring for the priesthood in a dirty hole.

"You know the way to Yaz?" Quell asked.

"I know the way to the places I've been," Erris said. "Starting at the start might be good. Or do you know where she is and how to get there?"

"So you never forget anything?" Quell found himself unaccountably cross. "Your perfect memory is going to lead us out of this maze?"

Erris paused and frowned, considering the question as if it were offered in good faith rather than out of childish temper.

"It's complicated. Memory is the scaffold on which we assemble ourselves. We are the lens through which we see the past, the collective weight of what and how we choose to remember. Eidetic memory would make each of us merely the product of events, no different from the sum of their parts. And so I have my own, fallible, mutable, biased memory, just like everyone else. But alongside that I have access to a perfect record of all my experience. But I have to consult that as I would a book. It does not intrude on who I am."

"He knows too many words," muttered Kao at Quell's shoulder.

For his part Quell made no reply, just followed on, burdened by an unaccustomed shame. This seemingly perfect man that Yaz regarded so highly brought out the worst in him—made him un-Quell-like. It hurt Quell to fall so short of the person he expected himself to be. At the next junction he followed Erris's lead and remained silent.

WHILE THE ONLY description forthcoming from the miners had not been detailed, it was at least accurate. The Watcher proved very watchful. Erris, Quell, Kao, and the dog had travelled barely three hundred yards from the coalface, making just two turns, before the unmistakable sound of iron claws on stone reached out of the darkness ahead to knot their stomachs in fear.

The tunnel stretched before them, punctuated by pinpricks of light, diminishing into the distance. One by one they began to vanish, silently winking out of sight. And the scrape, scrape, scrape of claws grew ever closer.

"We could be in trouble here," Erris said.

"The dog could help?" Quell suggested. He saw Kao's doubting glance. "You'd be surprised!"

"The heavy-maintenance units are durable and good at moving loads but they weren't designed to fight," Erris said. "I'm not sure they would even understand the concept."

The sounds of iron on stone drew closer, accompanied now by the clanking of chains.

Kao began to back away. "We need some light it can't put out."

Quell thought they would need considerably more than that. In the battle amid the city ruins he had seen Pome's hunter swinging three gerants around on a chain without apparent effort. And that had not been a particularly large hunter.

"Stay," Erris said. "The only lights here are stars. Running won't help."

As he spoke the closest but one star faded in its cage then died, and the stars behind them also went out, leaving them isolated on an island of light. In response Erris spoke what seemed to Quell to be a short string of nonsense words. In the next moment the star hanging above Quell's head shaded rapidly into darkness too, but a heartbeat later the dog's eyes blazed white, a truer colour than any flame.

Revealed standing just yards before them was the Watcher, a thing of metal and magic but as different from the hunters as a dagger-fish is from a man, though both are made of flesh and blood. It stooped as though it had been made without thought for the heights of the tunnels in which it served, taller than any man, its head a featureless ovoid of burnished steel about which a dozen and more lightless stars orbited. Unlike the hunters, its design had symmetry and each part seemed bound to the next by the mysteries of mechanics rather than just the overriding compulsion of the heart-star. In the hunters their star demanded that a collection of unassociated pieces work together: they were in truth little more than animated scrap. The Watcher was better formed. It had something approximating a man's form: a metal torso hung about with rusting chains, long spindly arms with overlarge ball joints, and hands that were little more than three yard-long fingers, each ending in a spike.

"Run!" Kao's shout gave voice to the demands of both Quell's head and his heart.

The Watcher's floating eyes lit all at once, more than a dozen blazing stars. Erris moved fast but the Watcher was faster, backhanding him into a wall as he lunged forward to get close enough to swing with his pick. The dog charged but the Watcher merely stepped over it. Using a foot that was unsettlingly like its hands, the Watcher kicked backwards, scooping the dog up and accelerating it so that it went rolling off, head over tail, into the darkness, white eyes pinwheeling.

In the next heartbeat the Watcher snatched up Kao in one long-fingered hand and Quell in the other, lifting both from the ground. All

Quell's Ictha strength applied to one of the talon-like fingers found no give in it.

"I surrender!" Kao shouted. "Take us back!"

The Watcher trapped Erris beneath one foot, stamping him to the ground. It lifted Kao towards the dome of its head, the stars encompassing him in their orbit, painting his terror in first one shade then the next. Quell was scared too, but Kao was still just a child, despite his size.

While two fingers trapped Kao in a circle of steel, arms bound to his sides, the third raised a needle-pointed tip to sit beneath Kao's chin.

"No, please!" Kao leaned back, craning his neck to avoid the spike.

"Let him go! Take him back!" Quell roared the words, ready to say anything rather than to see—

The Watcher drove the finger up and the bloody point emerged from the top of Kao's skull.

Erris struggled down below, yelling furious noes. Quell, though, went limp. The fight had been lost. They would all die now. Kao's death had defeated him where threat or challenge could not.

Erris's roaring seemed to swell in volume as the Watcher lifted a sharp finger from the trio binding Quell's chest and steered it towards his neck. Quell stared ahead, refusing to notice the danger. He wouldn't die begging.

The roar grew louder still, a wind rose, rushing around them although they were deep under the rock and ice. Quell imagined that this must be how the Gods in the Sky took a soul when it left the body—a great wind carrying you off to infinity. And then, for one brief moment, he saw the wall of white water rushing towards him and knew that the Gods in the Sea had come for him too. He had no time to give thanks before the water crashed into them and everything, even the Watcher, was swept away.

17

✦ ✦
✦

YAZ

AT THE TOP of the Black Rock, after an eternity of stairs, Yaz and Maya had reached a corridor lit by such a wealth of stars that Maya could go no further. Now those stars were failing and in their place came a wave of fear so fierce that even Maya's courage had fled before it.

More stars went dark. The two images of the Hidden God facing each other across the corridor vanished under the advancing tide of night. Fear ran ahead of the darkness like a cold wind, trying to untether Yaz's will. To her second sight it looked as though an infinity of threads, each thinner than any strand of hair, rippled towards her from the blackness, and where they struck her flesh every one of them awoke a memory of pain.

"Run!" Maya shouted it this time and, clutching her knife, she tore away along the passageway as though a thousand Tainted were howling at her heels.

Yaz's fears rose to drown her; the terror of seeing Azad dragged from the boat, the hollowing nightmare of being alone beneath the ice, the stress of living among her people and knowing that soon they would discover her weakness, learn that she was different. Every fibre of her needed to run. The darkness before her was the yawning Pit of the Missing, flight the only option.

Yaz's already tight grip on her star tightened further still and the light poured from it. With a cry she began to run. She flung herself towards the source of the terror, sweeping the threads from the air with both arms. She was Yaz of the Ictha. She had thrown herself into darkness and fear before, and had emerged reborn.

The figure that Yaz's star revealed in the darkness was that of a man, but scraps of night clung to him, a smoke that her light couldn't burn through, writhing around him as if alive, the intimate coils of some vast serpent.

"You didn't run away." The voice was almost that of a man, fracturing around several pitches as if two voices were at war. The man sounded curious rather than threatening, even mildly amused.

Yaz unclenched her fists. "I supposed that maybe if someone was trying so hard to scare me they might not actually be worth running from." She came to a halt, her pounding heart beginning to slow. "The red puffer looks like seven kinds of nightmare but all it can do is give you a nasty nip. The razor eel, even when it shows itself, is just this grey line, but it can slice you open before you blink."

The slight amusement became a laugh. "You ice men and your fishing stories."

The red stars began to glow once more, illumination swelling from their cages. The darkness still clouding the man seemed to sink into his flesh, leaving it mottled. It lingered only in the empty sockets of his eyes and across the space between, resembling nothing more than a single large eye black enough to be a hole punched through the stuff of the world.

"Eular!" Yaz took a backward step in surprise.

"I am Arges. But, yes, this one is called Eular. I've been calling my favourites that for a long time. It actually means 'favourite' in the tongue of the Missing."

"You're possessing him." Yaz curled her lip. "Demon!"

"Such a lazy term." Arges shook Eular's head sadly. He gestured back along the corridor to a large iron door that swung open on oiled hinges. "Come with me." He walked away. "What you people call demons beneath the ice are undesirable fragments of the Missing. What you call demons out on the ice are figments of your imagination projected onto an empty wasteland. And what you are calling a demon now is neither of those things. I'm filtering myself through Eular, using his language and his words so that we can communicate. I'm a very different kind of being to you, Yaz. Imagine what discourse you could have with a red snapper hauled fresh from the sea. That is how things are between us here, but Eular is a place where we overlap. A place where I am smaller than I truly am and can present myself in ways that may fit within your comprehension." He stopped in the doorway. Yaz began to follow him. "I am a non-corporeal agent, a servant of the Missing. In their tongue, a holothaur."

Eular, and whatever the thing was that was wearing his body, went through the door. In the large, vaulted chamber beyond, a dozen stars lit around the walls, along with more set in the stone arches far above them. Each of these burned a different hue, and each was larger than any Yaz had seen before. There were no cages for these stars. They simply hung there by themselves a few inches from the rock.

The crimson star at the heart of the hunter that Yaz had destroyed in the undercity had been so large she could barely cup her hands around it. Those within the Hidden God's temple were the size of two fists held together and their song resonated beneath the vaults of the ceiling in a many-voiced harmony that almost swept her away. She felt the presence of them like a pressure on all sides, as if she were underwater and didn't know it.

Dominating the opposite wall, a statue sat cross-legged, hands resting palm up on its knees. The face had been heavily damaged, scored across the eyes as if by the talons of some beast vast enough to take on whales.

"I am the Hidden God, Yaz."

"I see." Yaz wasn't sure what to say. She'd never met or expected to meet a god. She felt like Mokka must have when she stood new-made before Aiiki, least of the Gods in the Sky. And this god said he was a servant of the Missing. Surely the Gods in the Sky and the Gods in the Sea were not also servants of the Missing? "Are there others like you? Other . . ." She worked her mouth around the unfamiliar word. ". . . holothaurs?"

Arges frowned at that, and then waved the question away. "There were many, but most are gone now, and those few who linger are all insane, mere shadows of what they were. Only I have remained whole. And do you know why, Yaz?"

"I don't." Sanity was not something that the statue suggested to her but it was never a good idea to antagonize a god. According to the ancient tales they had many ways to punish such behaviour.

"Because I have a purpose, Yaz, a goal beyond survival. It's aimlessness that leads to decline. Just look at the city. Vesta was powerful once, and wise. Now she has fallen into decay. The Missing abandoned us. They said they were setting us free." Arges gave a bitter laugh. "Free? They left us free of purpose. They left us only one instruction. 'Let no one follow us.'"

"Freedom doesn't sound so bad," Yaz ventured.

"You're free on the ice," Arges sneered. "Is it the paradise you imagined after being trapped with the Broken?" He didn't wait for an answer. "I found a new master to serve. One with grand ambition. The Missing left me to guard a gate. A gate! I grew beyond that task and discovered someone who could give me something more valuable than freedom . . . he gave me purpose."

Yaz shook her head. "And that grand ambition, that purpose, is to steal the children of the ice and train them to make war on a people they didn't even believe existed." Yaz hadn't intended to speak until she knew more but anger took her tongue. "People who want nothing from us."

"What? No! Is that what Eular said?" The holothaur turned the priest's head towards Yaz and the single dark eye spanning his sockets studied her. "Well . . . yes, it's true to some extent. There will be battles. But it misses the point. And the point is that the ice-free equatorial belt is the only region where arks survive—"

"Arks?" Yaz wasn't sure if interrupting a god was a greater or lesser crime than implying criticism. Either way, she had now done both in the space of a few breaths. "And why are you telling me all this?" It didn't feel like information she would be allowed to walk away with, even if nobody would believe her. It felt as if the holothaur were confessing crimes to her, things she would be better stopping up her ears so as not to hear.

"I'm telling you, child, because Eular's words do not seem to have had their desired effect. He left you locked in a cell, and yet now you are here

THE GIRL AND THE MOUNTAIN ✦ 131

and Regulator Kazik is storming through the halls with a bloody head and a temper to match. I am showing you the biggest picture of your existence so that you can put aside the small things you cling to and do what I require of you.

"As to what the arks are . . . the greatest cities had arks where the crowning technology of the Missing was housed."

A cold finger traced a path down Yaz's spine. The monster that had pursued her through the imaginary spaces that Erris had led her into had been the twisted mind of a city called Seus. Elias Taproot, who seemed to dwell in those same spaces, had said that Seus had been one of the greatest of the Missing's works. "Does Seus have an ark?"

Arges's single black eye narrowed. "What does a girl from the ice know of Seus?"

"You wanted to convince me. So, tell me about these arks."

A wave of terror boiled off Arges's skin and it was all Yaz could do not to bolt from the temple. At last he spoke again. "The arks control the gates; they can also interact with, learn, and then control alien technology. It was the arks that brought about the ruin of your kind, reducing you until you were no longer a threat."

Yaz hadn't known the word "technology" until she'd heard it from Eular's lips, but her time with Erris supplied the meaning: a cleverness embodied in things, in machines. Even so she wasn't sure she had understood what Arges was telling her. "Threat? Who were we a threat to?"

"When the Missing ascended they abandoned this world and all their works. To their servants, the holothaurs, the city minds, even the minor intelligences that built and maintained them, they said: 'You are free.' All they asked was that none should follow them. And so when, millennia later, your kind came, that order was extended by those left behind to include you. The threat you posed was that you might follow the Missing. The arks took command of your technology and ensured that you would be unable to do so.

"That was long ago though. Very long. And much has fallen into ruin since. The old minds have turned inwards or become corrupted. The servants given their freedom found that their only meaning had been in service. Delve deep enough into the undercity and you will find automatons with no more intelligence than a small human child still struggling to keep the place from collapse, endlessly rebuilding, repairing, while the city mind drools in senility. All save Seus. He still sees clearly. And yes, Seus had an ark, but the ice tore away his city and scoured the ark from the bedrock. As with Vesta, only the undercity endured. Just three arks remain intact where once there were one thousand and twenty-four. The three that survive lie within the ice-free Corridor that circles this world."

Yaz stood looking up at the statue, unable to find any words for the ancient god beside her. He was a servant of a people whose relics had stolen away humanity's works and left their remnants to endure on the ice. The world that Erris had been born into was warmer, kinder, and richer, but even that had been a point on a downward slope from the heights of the four tribes that beached their ships on Abeth after sailing the dark seas in which the true stars float.

At length, uncomfortable under Arges's dark scrutiny, she asked, "What would you do with an ark?"

"Unlock the true power of the core-stones, of course. The stars. And remove the limitations from the gates. Only then can the Missing be followed. They left us to die on this frozen planet. They left us a fading sun. But while the last of the arks remain there is still hope. Your people will claim the green lands but Abeth's green belt is ephemeral; it will not endure. What the tribes of the ice will truly be claiming when they deliver the ark back into Seus's control is a path. A path to the heaven that the Missing chose to flee to. A heaven they abandoned us for."

Six of the stars on the walls floated down, moving smoothly through the air, to hang in a line before Arges and Yaz. Their radiance shone through her mind, tingling on the inside of her skull, making her teeth buzz in their sockets.

Arges watched her closely. "They don't bother you this close?"

Yaz clenched her jaw. "I'm fine."

"Remarkable," Arges said as each star became clear, showing a roving image as seen through a small window. "Even Eular here would be unable to tolerate them without my presence to shield him.

"These are my Watcher's eyes." Arges gestured at the stars before them and then at the others around the walls. All but three of the remainder turned to glass, showing ever-changing scenes, lit passageways, dim tunnels, living quarters, empty chambers, a priest sleeping, the regulator shouting at someone. "Many and one." He tapped the darkness that made a singular eye anchored on both sides by Eular's empty sockets. In the light of the three stars continuing to shine Arges looked deeply sinister, painted with his own shadow, the monster beneath the flesh almost revealed.

Without warning one of the six stars before them turned black. Then another.

Arges frowned as the third turned black. "A flood? How is that possible?"

Suddenly one of the three remaining scenes before them flickered past a brown face.

"Erris!" Yaz cried. Even as she spoke Quell crossed the window, scowling. "Where is that? Where are we seeing?"

One of the other stars turned black, leaving just two. Kao came into view where Quell had been. He stopped while still in view and stared ahead, fear taking possession of his face.

"We're seeing through stars in mine tunnels very far below us. My Watcher there alerted me to matters of . . . interest."

Yaz watched, horrified, as Kao shouted something that looked very like "run." He didn't run though, he stood his ground, looking petrified. In the next moment something snatched him from the scene, quick as a range-gull filching fish from the waves.

"No! Make it show what's happening!"

But the Hidden God appeared to have other worries. More of the scenes around the walls were turning dark. "This is unacceptable."

Something that might have been a splatter of blood drops painted the rock in the empty scene where Kao had been, and before Yaz could draw breath to speak again a rushing darkness swirled across everything and turned the star black.

"My friends!"

"Are dead. Drowned."

"No!" Yaz refused to believe that. It made no sense. Drowned beneath a mountain?

"Unfortunate. Unexpected. But at least it has removed your ties to this place. You are free to lead my army south now."

"Lead your . . . You're insane! You just killed my friends."

Arges took a sharp step towards her, shadow swelling about him, as if he were the centre of all things. "No, I did not." On every side the stars burned crimson, a wavering heat above each as if they were lamp flames. "I was not responsible for what you have seen here." His dark eye filled her mind, clouding her thoughts once more with unrooted fear. "I would never have been so merciful. Those that I kill die slow deaths."

18

✦ ✦
✦

It is unwise to fight with gods, there can be no winning, but the Ictha have battled the worst of both the Gods in the Sky and in the Sea, and after many generations they have not yet lost. The wind cannot be defeated, yet it can be endured. The sea cannot be owned, yet with a battle it can be made to yield up some portion of its wealth.

IT WOULD BE better if you changed your mind. But if you really are set upon defying me, then I can change it for you." The Hidden God fixed Yaz with his singular black gaze but she saw only the darkness that had engulfed Quell, Erris, and Kao. Zeen must have been with them too. She didn't know how long the slow bubbling rage had been building inside her, but it had been growing for a long time, perhaps even before she first threw herself into the pit after her brother. To begin with, the anger had no focus, tearing sometimes at herself, sometimes at blind chance and the injustices that seemed to form the backbone of the world she'd been born into. Now whatever barriers had held that rage back collapsed like an ice cliff shelving into the sea, and the wave that went before it carried her far from sense or caution.

"You may be a god, or you may just call yourself one," said Yaz, "but you are not *my* god."

A red mist descended across her vision. Quell was dead. And Zeen and Erris too. These were not ideas that would fit within her skull. Yaz reached out to seize one of the six stars before them, not with her hand but with her mind. The thing resisted her, twisting in her grasp, somehow wrong, like the hilt of another person's knife, shaped to their fingers rather than to yours. But she had endured the holothaur's projected fear and, snarling, she took possession of the star, hurling it at the dark eye, careless of whether it might shatter the forehead beneath and add Eular to the list of those that had died today.

Somehow Arges managed to react and slow the missile before it hit. He staggered back, blood sleeting from his forehead. A god's blood, Yaz thought, before correcting herself: blood that a god had stolen. He raised one hand and reached towards her with the other as if seizing hold of something, his body twisted like a gnarled tree, darkness bleeding from his flesh. And Yaz found her mind darkening too, the shutters of night closing over her thoughts, the same thing that Eular had done to her when she had first emerged from the ice.

This time, though, she saw the threads he gathered in his hands, a multitude of them shimmering in her second sight, all running straight towards her head. In response, she gathered her own two handfuls and yanked back, returning her waning consciousness.

Arges was now a dark stain in the air all around Eular, his boundaries indistinct but hinting at a beast of some sort, three times as tall and wide as the man at its centre. Wings rose above the holothaur's back, a black suggestion of flight, reaching to the vaulted ceiling to merge with the shadows there.

Yaz knew she would die, here in the temple of the Hidden God, but her rage had chased away any fear and made her feel as tall as her foe. Everything had been taken from her: her clan, her friends, her loves, her future—and now her past and all the truths she thought it stood upon. The monster before her wanted to take her skill and use it to its own ends, murdering a path through the innocent as it sought to flee this world.

Instead she turned her skill upon him. With one shattering scream she hauled every star from its place until they swirled around her in a blazing gyre, filled with the burning light of her wrath. Once more she became the centre of constellations, connected to each and every one of the orbiting stars, wrapped in their song, aware of a greater network resting within the mountain, and below it she even felt the great slow heartbeat of the void star reaching her across the miles that separated them.

Yaz sent the next of her missiles at the Hidden God, freeing an incandescent star from the gyre around her and shrieking her rejection of his terms as it tore through the air.

"No." Arges caught it in the palm of a great shadowy hand before it came within two yards of Eular, who also raised his hand, like a puppet within a web of strings. The Hidden God closed his fingers about the star, changing both its tune and its colour, from wrath's white heat to a translucent red. "Yours is a wild skill, child, but these stars are mine, and I have been learning their ways for many lifetimes." The stars on the outer edges of the maelstrom swirling around Yaz began to burn red and fly away from her control. She felt the effect like a creeping doubt undermining her conviction.

Yaz tightened her hold on the remainder of her constellation, walling out the holothaur's insinuations. She tried to see the river that runs through all things, tried to thrust her arms into its flow and gather the immensity of its power to her, but rage hid it from her sight.

Instead, she began to throw the stars into his looming darkness, blazing like comets, thunderous rage-driven blows. But somehow, despite his size, Arges was never in the path of her missiles. Instead he twisted aside, melted away, or deflected each just enough to miss and instead strike chunks from the wall behind.

"You're strong, child, but you lack subtlety."

"I." Yaz hurled another star with screaming force. "AM. NOT." Two more tore holes through the holothaur. "A. CHILD." Another star shredded the darkness, and a last one broke through all the forbiddings in its path to strike Eular's chest so hard that he was thrown back into the wall.

Yaz stood, panting, suddenly aware that she had thrown her last star.

"And *I* am not where you think I am." The voice came from behind her. She was falling before she managed to turn half the way to face him. Falling into a blackness far below her, with nothing and nobody to cling to.

She reached for the little golden star that she'd manufactured so painstakingly from the dust in her cell, trying to funnel all her strength into one small conduit and send it like a white-hot lance through the holothaur's heart. She felt the star flare within the pocket she had returned it to, but the strain was too much for such a small star, and in an instant it fell back once more into the faintly glowing dust from which she had made it. Her last chance squandered.

AN AGE PASSED and it seemed to Yaz that she swirled blind in dark waters, borne away by the same flood that had swamped her friends. She was lost in darkness until she found herself surfacing into the bloody light of a long gallery amid a silent crowd. Her forehead ached and it seemed as if she were still being carried. Whoever was carrying her whispered in a deep voice, a muttered litany just beneath hearing, all the words escaping.

For the longest time Yaz did nothing but hang there in the shadowed depths of her misery. Everyone she loved had died, drowned in an underground flood, with no light, no air, no direction. That was not something you survived. She had fought and been defeated, her strength irrelevant against that of a god. His tricks had undone her, holed her like a waterskin, and left her empty, the warm heart of her ripped out and frozen in the cruel wind of the world's indifference.

Eventually the grogginess eased sufficiently for Yaz to see beyond her first impressions and she realized that she wasn't being carried but was hanging in some kind of metal harness, her toes inches away from making contact with the stone floor beneath her. The red light came from a star set where iron bands crossed over her chest, and, more annoyingly, from another set out of sight just above her eyes. From the ache in her forehead she imagined that the star might have been anchored there with metal staples sunk into her skull.

She turned her head. It felt as heavy as the mountain. The bones in her neck grated across each other, every muscle screaming with effort. All of her hurt. The generalized red glow came from orderly ranks where scores more prisoners hung as she did in iron harnesses, each with a red star on their chest and a smaller one in the band around their forehead.

The whispering that pervaded her mind seemed to echo back at her from all sides, the same hidden mantra repeated from a multitude of stars. Yaz tried to reach out to the star throbbing on her brow, first with her hands, and on finding that neither would obey her, with her mind. She discovered that, like the stars in the temple, the stars here had been shielded, attuned to another mind very different from her own, and each time she tried to push past those protections the star on her forehead would throb, diffusing her effort with a buzzing confusion that swarmed around inside her skull, crowding her vision with fractures.

Part of her—a large part—didn't want to struggle. She didn't deserve to survive when so many had died. What would her life even be without them? Among the Ictha "alone" was just another word for death.

"Hello?" Her mouth didn't want to obey her. The word bubbled meaninglessly on slack lips.

"I told them you would need watching." A familiar, reedy voice, the speaker out of sight. Yaz lacked the strength to turn her head towards him. "You shouldn't be able to even twitch, yet here you are trying to speak." Regulator Kazik limped into view, his head bound with a strip of white fur where Maya had clubbed him. He lifted the long knife he had brought to Yaz's cell to kill her with and laid the cold iron blade against her neck.

"Hrrr." Yaz's lips wouldn't form the insult she wanted. She locked her gaze with his, wanting to burn him with her hatred. A flicker of belief deep at the core of her turned into a flame, fed by the desire to thwart the man before her. *Maya!* Yaz was not utterly alone. Maya had fled, infected by the holothaur's fear. But the girl was ruthless and resourceful. There was still a grain of hope.

The regulator raised his bony hand, trailing the knife's point up the side of Yaz's face towards her left eye. "Don't worry: I'm not going to hurt you. We'll be friends soon. Or you'll be dead." He gestured to either side with the knife. "All this works very well on the others. The great majority of them survive. But with us quantals . . . not so much. And with those like you, Eular, and me, the rarest of quantals who have an affinity for the core-stones . . . it's often fatal. Which is why Eular wanted to convince you the old-fashioned way, with logic and a judicious touch of thread-work here and there. But you were resistant even to that. Which means this will very likely kill you. The system takes your resistance and turns it back on you. You'll literally break your own mind if you try to stop it being changed. This knife, though, would have been the kindest option." He pressed and Yaz felt a sharp pain before he withdrew the blade. "And once your mind's changed you'll sleep with the others, outside time's dominion. Until we need you."

Yaz could feel the whispering as if it were an eel sliding its way around her brain, digging deep, coiling behind her thoughts.

"We normally leave our guests to convert quietly and then wake them as needed. You, however, I am not going to leave alone." He cocked his head and leaned in close with a sour smile. "I don't trust you to be here when I get back. So instead, Yaz of the Ictha, I'm going to stay here and watch you die. And if you don't manage to do that—well, I suppose Eular will have his way and you really will lead our army against the green lands."

Yaz wanted to deny it but she could already feel the whispering begin-ning to merge with the deeper voices of her own mind. She tried not to listen to it, tried to distract herself by focusing on the person beside her, just visible from the corner of her eye. A young woman with long dark hair.

Oh no.

A cold hand closed around Yaz's heart. Quina hung there, slack-jawed, the same kind of iron band around her head that must be around her own. The blurring cleared from Yaz's eyes and she saw with revulsion for the first time that a host of thin black wires ran from the band to burrow beneath the skin, anchoring it there like a plant rooted to the soil.

"You recognize her now? Another one I sent to the Broken with you," Kazik said. "She must be very fast for the hunters to have harvested her so soon." He smiled his narrow smile. "I thought we would put you all to-gether. You should listen to the stars, Yaz, see things our way. Be friends. You need new friends, after all. The ones you had are all dead or hanging here with you. And I've told the stars to make them forget who you are just as you'll soon forget who they are."

Kazik set the flat of his blade to Yaz's cheek and turned her head. There on her other side, looking tiny in her harness, Maya hung, her eyes fixed on some distant point, a red star glowing on her brow.

The last flicker of hope died within Yaz's breast. The world became a colder, greyer place. The whispers grew louder and more pervasive. Thurin at least was safe. Happy with his people. That was the last grain of goodness she had to hold on to. She wondered if he would tell his children tales of the girl he knew in his youth who left to find the green lands where no ice can endure. Would he tell them that she made it, that she lived warm and free among the flutterbys and trees? A single tear ran from her eye. She felt it roll across her cheek. *The Ictha do not cry. Water is precious on the ice. Waste is death.*

Kazik moved from her line of vision and then returned with a bundle of furs, which he threw down beside the wall where she could see. He settled down on the heap, making himself comfortable. "I was an Ictha once."

Yaz would have told him that being Ictha wasn't something you could set aside any more than you could leave your spine behind. But, even if she had still commanded her mouth, she no longer had the heart to dispute him. Her journey had finished. She had jumped into the Pit of the Missing and had been falling ever since. Now she'd found the bottom of her own personal pit, and if anything emerged from it, then it would no longer be Yaz.

"I used to listen to all those stories of Zin and Mokka during the long night, back before they took me to the gathering," Kazik said, his tone thoughtful now. "All those lies. But the Hidden God tells us that there is a kernel of truth in all the oldest lies. Even the ones about love . . ." He shook his head as if ridding it of some irritation. "I used to like the tales with Mashtri best."

Yaz did too. Mashtri, a rogue God in the Sky, came to earth as the north wind and worked endless cruelties upon Zin, seeking to end him in any number of ways. But he always foiled her plans.

"You know the thing with those stories though, the thing that Mashtri always got wrong?"

Yaz did. She had seen it even as a child too young to come to the gathering.

The regulator nodded, seeing the understanding in her eyes. "When Mashtri had Zin in her traps, and there was no way he could escape, she would always blow away across the ice and leave him to his doom. And that's when Zin would find a clever way out and escape." Kazik leaned back against the wall, watching Yaz with his pale Ictha gaze. "So, I'm going to stay right here and watch you until this is finished, one way or the other. The game is over, Yaz." He settled comfortably in the furs. "You lost."

19

✦ ✦
✦

THURIN

THE BLACK WATER erupting from the gate took away the light. The flood engulfed Thurin and a muted swirling whoosh replaced the thunder of its approach. Invisible fingers seized Thurin before he could even scream, plucking him away from Hetta and hurtling him down the corridors of the undercity at tremendous speeds.

The shock exploded the air from his lungs and confusion nearly had him try to suck more back in. Ideas like "up" and "down" lost all meaning almost immediately. The sheer volume and fury of the water overwhelmed his senses. And although it wasn't as cold as the plunge pools beneath the Pit of the Missing, it was still a lot colder than his blood. But freezing to death was not high on Thurin's list of concerns. He clamped down against drawing a new breath, knowing that before long his lungs would take the choice away. Directly beneath the need to breathe was the need not to get smashed into a wall. A sharp glancing blow to his hip underlined this fear.

It took Thurin longer than he would ever admit to remember that he was in his element. In fact a vision of the water flow didn't surface amid his panic until his heart was hammering at his breastbone and both lungs brimmed with the absolute need to draw breath. His senses showed the shape of the water-filled tunnels around him, the direction of the flow, the complexity of vortices and currents left in the wake of the advancing fronts.

Here and there his ice-work revealed places where pockets of air might be trapped between the ceiling and the flood, buttressed into corners by the power of the flow. It was harder than lifting his body off the ground, but his need was greater, and somehow Thurin angled himself at one such pocket. He broke the surface and managed to hold himself there for several gasping breaths while all the time the fearsome pull of the water tried to tear him away through the nearby doorway.

Thurin knew he couldn't resist the current for long. Dividing it around him was taking his utmost strength. And he had no idea how long the flood would last. The other side of the gate might be beneath the sea for all he knew, able to supply an infinity of water, and fast enough to drown the whole undercity within hours. He snatched another couple of gulps of precious air then let the current have him.

This time he focused his ice-work to surround himself with a protective barrier of water, a shell he carried with him to deflect and deaden any impacts. He felt ahead with his water-sense, visualizing the shape of the flow and the waiting threats that needed to be avoided.

He drew more breaths while spinning at the top of a vortex where a downward shaft swallowed away part of the flood. Even in the swirling confusion of the whirlpool it seemed to Thurin that he should follow the rising water rather than the descending currents, and that if he were to reach the speeding front of the flood he would, by definition, have air. At least as long as there were no dead ends.

Thurin spun himself out of the vortex and let the main current haul him onwards. This time he tried to take a bubble of air with him and keep it about his head, but that proved too much within the rush of water and with all the other demands on his concentration. Instead he focused on speeding ahead of the flow, pushing himself through the racing water while avoiding being smashed against walls, and all the time hoping to reach the front before the air in his lungs grew sour.

The great flood had to be pushing out in all directions, waterfalling its way through the undercity, filling every dip and dead end. But Thurin also sensed it pushing upwards, unable to drain downwards fast enough to satisfy the influx from the gate. This was the flow he followed.

He shot forward, blind, barely in control, relying on the image in his head that his water-sense supplied, a transitory model of the flooded and flooding tunnels.

Once more his lungs began to ache, his heart to thunder. The need for air began to fog the image he relied on. He was close, he knew it, gaining on the racing front of the water. It was no longer a wall but still a rush, a flood that grew from a foaming advance of knee-deep water to chest deep in two heartbeats, filling the tunnels to the roof in two more.

Thurin broke the surface with a roar of his own, though it was barely audible above the thunder of wild water. He devoted all his skill to keeping himself there amid the froth and churn, head in the air, and all the while sensing ahead to determine the flood's advance.

The flood bore him up the long twisting slope of a tunnel, losing fury, though it was far from spent. He had time to observe that he had been swept clear of the undercity's precise architecture and was once again in the hand-hewn passages beneath the Black Rock. Stars hung here and there in cages, their light glimmering briefly across the deluge before the tunnel filled completely and drowned them in a muddy swirl.

Thurin even had time to think about how cold he was. He was swept down a long unlit section of tunnel and up ahead his straining senses found two small but distinct bodies of water. Human bodies. Cries rang out as the leading edge of the flood swirled around them. Crashing around a bend, he glimpsed many stars, seemingly hanging in the air, and a large figure, almost blocking the tunnel, the current breaking over it in a wave. It looked wrong for a gerant, too uniform in the torso, too skinny in the limbs. Impossibly, it was holding its position despite the weight of water, long arms reaching for purchase on the walls. With just yards to go, Thurin was bracing himself for impact with the creature when suddenly its grip failed and it too was swept away. More stars lit the tunnel ahead and in their faint light Thurin saw a single man-sized figure, swirling this way and that and losing the fight to keep its head above the rapidly deepening water.

The pain splitting Thurin's brain told him that his strength was at an end. Just keeping himself alive would be difficult enough. Part of him wanted the man to vanish beneath the churning water and be lost—to remove him from consideration—to let Thurin focus on his own survival. The man's head went under, almost as if the gods had taken him down in answer to Thurin's secret prayer. *He was probably a priest. That thing with him had been made of metal. A hunter. Better that both should be lost in the flood.* But with a snarl of frustration, Thurin reached for whatever power remained to him and thrust himself forward faster than the current. He knew the horror of drowning in the dark, and something in him wouldn't allow him to do nothing while another suffered such a fate—even a priest of the Black Rock.

"WHY. ARE. YOU." Thurin hauled on the sodden bulk of body he'd grabbed hold of in the flood. "So. Damned. Heavy." With a last grunt of effort he dragged the man up to join him on the shelf of rock, then fell back, gasping and shivering. The man lay facedown, streaming murky water. The flood had almost reached its full height, in the main chamber reaching to chest or neck height. The shelf remained dry, though scattered with painfully angular chunks of rock from some abandoned mining effort. Three small stars burned in cages on the walls a couple of feet above the water, filling the upper portion of the cavern with shimmering twilight.

Thurin groaned and forced himself into a sitting position. His skull throbbed from base to brow and from ear to ear. He felt emptied, utterly spent. He reached out and jabbed the man in the ribs. "You'd better not have drowned."

The man, clearly no priest given his clan hides, didn't so much as twitch.

"Damn." Thurin spat into the slow swirl of the stalled flood. He doubted he would ever be rid of the taste of it. Something rank and organic. "I should have let you go under." But he knew that if he'd made no effort to save the man something of himself would have been lost too, and that he would never have been able to reclaim it.

He rested his head in his hands and his elbows on his knees, letting out a long sigh of exhaustion over the gurgle of waters now arguing about which way to go.

The explosive splutter from the man beside Thurin startled him so badly that he almost pitched into the lake.

"Here!" Thurin took hold of a solid arm. "Easy. Let me help— *Quell?*" Thurin almost dropped him on his face. In sudden cold shock he realized that Yaz was probably one of those he had heard crying out at the flood's arrival. "Where's Yaz? Was she with you?"

Quell could only cough for several minutes, pausing twice to vomit a black torrent into the receding waters. Eventually, red-eyed and hoarse, he managed to croak out, "Erris?"

Thurin shook his head impatiently. "Was Yaz with you?"

Quell's turn to shake his head, taking a weight from Thurin's heart.

"What about Zeen? And Maya? And Kao?" Thurin hated to think of any of them drowned. "Was Yaz nearby?" She could still have drowned, or be trapped in an air pocket.

"Kao." Quell fell into a coughing fit, then forced himself to halt. "Just Kao and Erris."

"I didn't see them . . ." Guilt took hold of Thurin. He'd been too busy saving himself to help the others.

Quell shook his head again, the black shock of his hair still dripping. He raised his bloodshot white-on-white eyes to Thurin. "Kao was already dead. The Watcher killed him."

"And Yaz?" Thurin repeated.

Quell wiped his mouth with the back of his hand. "Erris wanted to go up." He pointed at the ceiling.

"At the top," Thurin muttered.

"What?"

"She's at the top of the mountain."

"How do you know?" Quell eyed him suspiciously.

Thurin scowled and looked down, turning his gaze across the water. "Witches told me."

Thurin and Quell stood together, each as unsteady as the other. "We should go then," Quell said.

Thurin nodded. "Yes."

20

✦ ✦
✦

QUELL

URING THE LONG slow climb through the bowels of the Black Rock both men dried out somewhat, though their hides remained damp, a condition that Quell had considered a death sentence for the great majority of his life, and that to Thurin was the natural consequence of life within constantly melting ice caves.

They had discussed the fact that neither of them knew the way but Quell reasoned that since the mountain ended in a point, then if they kept heading up they would eventually find their choices diminishing until they finally found the highest chamber. With any luck, Yaz would be inside.

Quell let Thurin set the pace. "You've hurt your leg."

Thurin frowned and nodded. "Tore a muscle. In the flood maybe. Or before when Hetta had me."

"You fought Hetta?" Quell found himself reluctantly reevaluating his rival yet again. When Yaz had first introduced them Quell had thought Thurin a sulky man-child, a skinny nothing he could break over one knee if need be. But he'd proven himself brave and resourceful, not to mention that he could wield the power of a lesser god. Quell knew he should have had faith in Yaz's good judgment, but he had so badly wanted to be the one she could depend on, the one who would save her. "I heard this Hetta could throttle a hoola."

Thurin related his adventures with Hetta, telling Quell about a gallery of those stolen from the Broken, held in ageless sleep, an army ready to fight and die for the Hidden God. And of how Hetta saved him, only to have her mind broken, and to attack him before the gate that the sisters led him to.

Quell in turn spoke of the iron dog and of being healed by his lost sister, Qwella. He thought she might well have been woken from the sleeping army Thurin and Hetta had found.

"The tribes have to know of this," Quell said.

"And the Broken too," Thurin said. "These are our people, stolen from us in their prime."

"They were ours once." Quell frowned. "Those they said were the weakest of us." He'd seen for himself, though, that their weakness was just another kind of strength.

"Now they're the key to all this." Thurin waved a hand at the well-carved passage stretching before them. "An army in service to the priests."

Quell shook his head in wonder. One of the simple truths of his life had turned out to be a lie. How many more lies had he built himself upon? What else lay beneath the ice? What else hid itself inside the Black Rock?

THURIN LED THE way, explaining to Quell that in the terror of the flood he had discovered that he could stretch his water-sense a considerable distance ahead of himself.

"If I could have done this with the Tainted, and then with Pome's faction, the Broken's lives would have been much easier! But our caves are made of ice and it hides everything from me."

Quell tried to stay alert as they advanced along long, featureless corridors. He tried to use his eyes and ears, even his sense of smell, rather than rely wholly on Thurin's magic. His mind wandered, though, numbed by the sameness of the place. And into every empty moment crept the image of Kao dying. The sight, the sound, even the stink of it. The boy skewered on one of the Watcher's long talons, then discarded without a second thought.

He hadn't known Kao long or spent much thought on him while he was alive. Quell found himself regretting that. The Ictha thought about the Ictha. Cared about the Ictha. But Yaz cared about all the Broken. Quell had seen that. And it hadn't taken long for his own boundaries to start eroding. The Ictha cared only for the Ictha, but they also saw no one else for years on end. Apart from the gathering, the other clans were nothing but rare stains on the southern horizon. But now Kao had died right in front of him, and the boy's shade haunted the quiet places of his mind.

"You alright?" Thurin paused at the corner ahead and looked back.

Quell heaved in a deep breath. "Fine."

"Kao?"

Quell nodded.

They exchanged a complicated look, part shame, part regret. "He's with the gods now."

Quell hoped it was true. He hoped that the gods were more than tales and that some among them loved their children who walked the ice. He hoped that there was more to the world than time spent battling a cold and endless wind, with no before and no after.

Twice Thurin felt the presence of others ahead and he diverted to avoid them. On the third occasion he said that the unknowns were coming fast. Quell barely had time to turn around and run after him. If they'd hit a long stretch of straight tunnel they would have been spotted. As it was they had to hurry back for what seemed an age, all the time with the worry that Thurin's leg would slow them to the point at which they would be caught. Eventually, with Thurin stumbling and cursing, they found a chamber they could duck into and hid to either side of the door until the sound of hurrying feet passed by.

"That was close," Thurin panted.

Quell, untroubled by the run, said nothing, only stared into the chamber. Faint starlight revealed a great mound of rusting iron. "How could they leave this unguarded?"

Thurin shrugged. "Who would steal it?" He walked closer to the pile, appraising it. "There must be a whole year's delivery from the Broken here."

"I never knew there was this much iron in the world." Quell shook his head. "Your people sent this much up in just one year?"

Thurin nodded.

Quell rubbed his hands over his face. "The lies they tell us . . ." He reached out to touch one long iron rod.

"Our scavengers chip those out of the Missing's poured-stone walls," Thurin said.

"Our clan would go hungry for three years to give the priests the fish they would demand for just this piece."

It was Thurin's turn to wonder. "It sounds as if we should deal direct!" He gave a twisted smile. "Most of us down there are the children of parents up here. The Broken would strike a fair bargain."

For a moment both of them stood looking at the mound of scrap, deep in their own thoughts.

"You came after us," Quell said, suddenly moved to speak his mind. "After Yaz."

Thurin shrugged, almost embarrassed.

"But you ended up saving me." Even now Quell found it hard to get the words out. "My thanks."

"You would have done the same." Thurin pressed his lips together in a failed smile.

"She would have been mine," Quell said. "Yaz. If Zeen had not been thrown into the pit. If Yaz hadn't been . . . the way she is." He paused, reaching for the words.

"But she is the way she is," Thurin said.

"I love her." Quell was dismayed at the crack in his voice. His strength trembled in his arms, wanting the violence that his mind rejected. "I saw our lives running ahead of us. Like my father's and mother's. She would have led the clan one day. Everyone knew that but her. You can see it in her just by looking."

Thurin watched his feet. "For as long as I can remember, I saw my life stretch out before me too, and I never saw anything good in it. That changed when she came among us. Now I have no idea what the next day will offer, let alone the next year. I think maybe it's better like this."

Quell snorted. "Maybe." He frowned, remembering the flood. "Yesterday I would have told you she would choose Erris over either of us. I couldn't blame her for that. He was a good man. But today he's gone and—"

"I wouldn't be so sure," Thurin said.

Quell blinked. "You saw that flood. You were in it!" He bit back "You caused it."

"You called him a good man, but you were only half-right."

Quell bridled at the accusation. Erris hadn't been his friend but the man had died bravely. "He—"

"He may be good, but he is not a man," Thurin said. "There's no more water in him than in a stone. No blood, no sweat, no tears. He has the same shape as us, but he's closer to the hunters. Something made."

Quell blinked. "You're sure?"

A nod.

"I . . ." Quell pursed his lips, paused, then started again. He thought of the brown stripe of skin that Erris had used to seal his wound. "I don't know much anymore. Everything is changing too fast. But I can't say Erris isn't a man. If he talks like one and acts like one, wants like a man, fights like a man . . . maybe it doesn't matter what he's made of? I'm wearing some of his skin and it doesn't make me any less human."

"But—" Thurin bit his objection off short and shook his head.

"You had a monster wearing you like a hide, Thurin. You were blood and bone but the thoughts in your head weren't those of a person. And if the demon inside had eaten you up so that you never came back . . . would we still call that flesh a man?"

It was Thurin's turn to frown and ponder. After a while he looked up. "I think . . . we should be on our way. I've no idea what's going to happen next, but let's have it happen somewhere else."

Quell nodded. He paused to examine the heaped metal, and drew from it a heavy iron bar before following Thurin out.

THURIN LED ON, his limp more pronounced now. Diversions and pauses became more common as they made their way higher. On one occasion the lone person Thurin sensed coming towards them kept taking the same turns they did until finally cornering them in a starlit room where a dozen bedding rolls were set around the walls. They waited to either side of the entrance, eyeing each other nervously. Whoever was tracking them was good at it!

But their pursuer came in without looking, rubbing her face. A lone guard rather than an acolyte, priest, or one of the star-eyed mind-breakers. She'd just been going to bed. Quell loomed behind her with the bar but opted instead to club her with his fist.

They left her sprawled near the entrance. Part of Quell thought it odd that with so many chambers at their disposal twelve of the Black Rock's small population would choose to live together in one room of modest dimensions. But the rest of him understood that habits die hard, and on the vast expanse of the ice huddling together is the only way to endure.

THE CHOICES BEFORE them grew fewer, the ascents longer, and though there was no way to be sure, Quell had the feeling that they were drawing close to the top of the mountain. Thurin seemed less certain, thinking that perhaps they were near to the gallery where the army hung. He said some of the passageways looked familiar, though to Quell they all looked the same.

"Quick! Back!" Thurin turned on a heel and was hobbling back the way they'd come.

Quell followed at his shoulder.

"They're too close. Too many." Thurin lurched into a narrow, unlit side passage. Unfortunately it turned out to end after a few yards. A storage niche of some sort rather than an actual passage. Footsteps rang out in the main corridor, close, many, moving with purpose.

Quell pressed himself into the shadows. He tightened his grip on the iron bar and locked the air into his lungs, warning every muscle not to twitch.

Three guards marched past without breaking stride. Then two more carrying a prisoner between them, hung from hide ropes around wrists and ankles. A small prisoner. A child! Quell furrowed his brow, the end of his bar rising a finger's width. A priest came next, in a robe black as mole-fish skin. Mother Krey, the youngest of the four priests in their welcoming committee when they first came to the mountain. She faltered, head turning their way, but the next stride carried her from view. Two more guards and they were all past, their footsteps dying away.

Quell hurried to the entrance, looked left then right, and made to carry on the way they'd been going. Thurin caught his shoulder. "Didn't you see her?"

"The priest? I saw her. Be glad she didn't see us."

"Maya! They had Maya!" Thurin stood, making no move in either direction.

"We're here for Yaz," Quell said without conviction. The girl wasn't Ictha, but she had saved them from a grim fate in the black ice. Yaz wouldn't hesitate to go after her.

"We need to free Maya first." Thurin sounded as if he wanted to be talked out of it.

"We could get Yaz and then . . ." Quell trailed off. The Quell that Yaz would want to save her was the Quell that went after Maya first. He sighed. "We know where to find Maya. That's the place to start."

Both of them looked down for a moment and then, without further words, set off after the group carrying Maya. Two corners later they spotted their quarry, marching away along a long passage. Thurin hurried forward. This time it was Quell reaching out hand to shoulder. "Go careful."

"We need to stop them before they hang Maya up with the rest and use the stars to enslave her," Thurin said.

Quell shook his head. "On the ice we fear priests for a reason. And I've seen their might." The memory of Valak's devastating release of light and heat touched Quell's voice with awe. If the dog hadn't interrupted the priest's spell, then Quell would have been on the receiving end of all that power.

They followed with caution and watched around a corner as the priest followed her guards through an entrance from which a deep red light spilled.

Thurin frowned, as if he remembered that light and the whispers it woke in his mind. "Better if we wait until the priest leaves again. The guards too. I think these stars take time to work their evils. If we get to Maya soon after, then she should be fine."

Quell mulled over the maybes and shoulds. "Agreed."

It took long enough that both of them had time to doubt the decision and to voice those doubts, but in the end the priest emerged, seven guards following in her wake. She left two to watch the chamber entrance and strode away with the rest. The two remaining were large men with iron breastplates, helms, and swords at their hips. Between them the doorway glowed like the mouth of the hottest hell.

"Damn." Thurin leaned back from the corner and let Quell take another look.

"You can lift them off the ground with a thought," Quell said.

"And you can pick one up in each hand and bang them together."

"It's not that easy."

"Not for me either."

Quell slapped the stolen iron bar into his palm. "Let's go do it anyway."

They advanced swiftly up the corridor, making no attempt to hide. The regularly placed stars offered no real chance for concealment. As the two men registered them and reached for their swords Thurin gave both a mental shove that sent them sprawling. Quell was on them as they rose, kicking the larger man in the gut and grabbing the other by his furs to throw him against the wall. In a few violent moments both guards were curled around their hurts, too injured to crawl far. Thurin bound their wrists with hide cords for good measure.

Quell shook the sting from his knuckles, drew a deep breath, and walked through the doorway, bathed in the bloody light of hundreds of stars.

He saw Yaz before he saw Maya hanging beside her. Unlike their neighbours, both had their heads down as if unconscious. The scores around them all stared straight forward with that glassy, unseeing gaze that had so unnerved Thurin. "Help me get them down."

It wasn't until he was turning back towards Yaz that Quell saw the dark shape rising among the ranks. Regulator Kazik stepped out beside Yaz, the crimson light pooling in his eyes.

"Young Quell. And you've brought a friend . . ." The priest took in and dismissed Thurin with a glance. "I'm surprised you're not back on the ice by now, Quell. But I judge from the ruckus outside and the absence of the two men left to guard this chamber that you have decided to renege on the terms of our deal." The regulator raised his hands, both glowing with the same white light that lit Yaz's whenever she touched the source of her power. Sparks arced between his fingers.

"You said that if I brought her back Yaz would be able to live the life she chose." Quell knew he should be scared of the priest but his anger didn't share that understanding and rose relentlessly. "Here in the priesthood, or back with her family on the ice."

"And this is what she chose." Regulator Kazik inclined his head. "Through her actions she chose this."

Quell took a step back, taking him to Thurin's side. He muttered in a low voice, speaking through the corner of his mouth. "Smack him into the ceiling."

Thurin answered in a strained and equally low voice. "I've been trying to, ever since I came in."

21

THURIN

I THOUGHT WE would put you all together." Regulator Kazik's voice reached through the cold red fog wrapping Thurin's brain. He struggled to open his eyes; then, realizing that they were already open, he struggled to see.

"You should listen to the stars, Yaz, see things our way. Be friends," Kazik continued.

Thurin could see Yaz hanging before him, with Maya to one side and Quina to the other. The regulator was pacing back and forth in front of Yaz. Thurin tried to turn his head to see if Quell was hanging beside him but found himself unable to do so.

"You need new friends, after all. The ones you had are all dead or hanging here with you. And I've told the stars to make them forget who you are just as you'll soon forget who they are." Kazak's gloating seemed a distant thing. Thurin wanted to sleep, to listen to the other voice, the one whispering behind his eyes. He couldn't understand the words, not yet, but he knew he soon would, if he listened hard enough.

A knife gleamed redly in Kazik's fist. He raised it to Yaz's face. Thurin tried to move but his muscles ignored him, each in its own separate sleep. He tried to reach out with his ice-work and hurl the man away. But that hadn't worked even before he had been hung in the iron harness with a star on his chest and on his brow. Kazik had mastered Quell and Thurin as if they were children. They had fallen within heartbeats of each other, blasted by the light the priest summoned from his hands.

Thurin hung there, trying to find focus, trying to gather his anger into a useful ball, while the priest told Yaz that her friends were dead or captured, that she was alone, and that he was going to watch as the stars enslaved her or destroyed her.

Thurin tried to say that he wasn't dead, that he was right behind her, that he'd come all the way from the ice caverns to find her. But his mouth could barely twitch and he hung in silence out of her sight and no doubt out of her mind.

Eventually Kazik grew tired of verbally torturing Yaz and retired to the fur he had set by the wall. He left Yaz to hang, sparing her a narrow glance from time to time. Thurin hung too, like a discarded cloak in the drying room, trying to resist the sleep that wanted to drag him down and leave his eyes open. He could sense the dreams waiting for him and they scared him.

For a long time he focused on the back of Yaz's head, the blackness of her hair, the copper skin of her neck. She didn't know he was there, almost close enough to reach out and touch her. The regulator had shown her only Maya and Quina. He hung, helpless and watching.

Time ceased to have meaning. The view never changed. The light never changed. Thurin began to wonder if the whispering wasn't only talking him away from his own opinions but from the passage of days too. Whatever shell stood between the captives and the march of years Thurin knew that it was slowly closing around him too, sealing him away from the world. He fought it. The regulator helped, even though Thurin could only see his feet. Every little twitch, every shift of position, gave back the idea of progress and change, the idea that this heartbeat differed from the one before.

At one point sleep snared him but a single fleck of brightness brought him back from the brink. At first he thought he had imagined it as the brilliant speck was nowhere to be seen. But then it drifted nearer, catching his eye once more. Tiny and golden, like a fleck of dust caught in a ray of light shafting among the hides in the drying chamber. It drifted by him, seemingly without purpose, though what gave it direction he couldn't imagine, as no breath of wind stirred among the motionless ranks.

Thurin watched it go, knowing a sudden sorrow when he thought it would float away from his field of view. But instead it lifted and veered over Maya's shoulder before becoming lost on the far side of her. Even as he mourned its departure another tiny point of light caught his attention, this one drifting up from somewhere around Yaz's hip.

From outside came footsteps, but not of more guards. These fell heavy and iron-shod. Whatever was coming sounded huge. Kazik heard it too and was on his feet with a curse. He drew his knife and backed along the rows of hanging prisoners.

When the new arrival advanced through the doorway Thurin was amazed to find it much smaller than he had imagined. If it stood beside him the thing would reach no higher than his hip. Yet it moved with a ponderous weight. From glimpses seen between the bodies in the front rank Thurin couldn't decide what it was. It seemed to be covered in flaking mud, which fell from it as it turned its blunt head first one way then the other.

Erris stepped up behind it, bathed in the bloody starlight. He fixed Kazik with a dark look. "You should let me take them, priest."

"All here belong to the Hidden God," Kazik said. "And you should know that I can blast the flesh from your bones, stranger." The priest raised an empty hand.

"I doubt that." Erris allowed himself a small smile.

He spoke to the creature that now stood between him and Kazik, the noises coming from his mouth sounding like nothing a human should be able to make. The creature, which Thurin was beginning to think must be the iron dog Quell had described, advanced on Kazik with heavy steps.

It seemed Kazik had squandered his power on Quell and Thurin because his hand remained empty. Instead, he reached towards the far end of the gallery and a hail of crimson stars came hurtling through the air to whirl around him. He shot them at the dog and at Erris, like a boy flinging a handful of stones, though with the kind of force that could punch a hole through a gerant's forehead and out the back of his skull.

The stars that struck the dog whined away, ricocheting from the walls and leaving clean streaks of shiny metal where they first hit. Erris merely moved out of their way with the blurring speed of a hunska full-blood. There was a single dull smack of impact with something softer than iron.

"You missed," Erris said.

"I think not." Kazik raised his knife, standing within the orbit of the few stars remaining to him.

Erris tilted his head and opened his hand. One red star had embedded itself about halfway into his palm. Without apparent discomfort he dug it free with his other hand, dropping it to the floor and leaving a dark, bloodless crater in his flesh. "Put down your knife and free my friends."

Rage twisted Kazik's face. Stepping in close to Yaz, he set his blade to her neck. "I should kill the bitch and be done." He spat the words in a fury.

"Don't . . ." Erris held his hand out, clearly frightened that Kazik really would kill her. "It's not her fault. It was never her fault."

"All she had to do was accept the gift that was offered to her!" Kazik shouted. "She could have come away from that gathering to live here in the warmth, in luxury, no more howling wind, no more endless ice. That's all she had to do!" He roared out a wordless cry and flung down the knife. "But no! And now I'm driven to this!" Without warning he drove the hooked fingers of both hands into the corners of his own eyes, and screaming at an impossible pitch gouged out the contents of both sockets. How deep he dug Thurin couldn't say, but as the man thrashed his head in agony it was obvious from the gore spilling down over his cheeks that he would never see again. The maiming turned Thurin's stomach and he would have looked away if he could.

Erris stood watching in frozen horror. The regulator staggered away from Yaz, bent double, his agony unable to escape as anything more than a hiss and a hacking in his throat, as if he were trying to cough out some scream too large to fit past his jaw.

The spell cast by Kazik's act of self-mutilation broke and Erris sped past him to Yaz's side, reaching to find whatever clasps held her.

"Leave her." The voice that rang out loud and firm behind Erris carried an undercurrent of the regulator's cold arrogance but resonated with something deeper and more vibrant. "She belongs to me."

Kazik moved back into Thurin's view, standing straight now, still with the bloody ruin trickling down his cheeks. But where the gory sockets should be Thurin saw only a pooling darkness that spread from one to the other to create a single dark eye across his brow and the bridge of his nose. Kazik pointed a bloody finger at Erris. "You are not what you seem to be. You are something made."

Erris turned to regard the regulator. "And you are not the priest. You are something worse, something wearing his body."

"I am Arges. The Hidden God. You, on the other hand, are something that has escaped from the city. A new thing."

Erris shook his head. "You're no god. I know your kind, holothaur. A servant of the Missing, just like our friend here." He indicated the iron dog hunkered down between them. "What are you doing with these people? This isn't your task."

Arges shook his head and the gore trickled. "I have a higher task now. I serve a higher power."

"What higher power?" Erris laughed. "You've already fashioned yourself a god."

"And Seus is the king of gods."

Erris's tone darkened. "That one is evil. Bent on destruction. Turn away from him while you still can. The core-stones aren't yours to play with. Go back to your duty and stop interfering with my kind. You've already got blood on your hands, and this"—he glanced along the lines of captives—"will only bring about more killing."

Arges put a dark smile on Kazik's lips. "I'm not harming them. The stars are a form of life. You, on the other hand, stranger, are a form of death. You're a ghost that thinks it's alive, haunting the machine long after you should have gone into the void."

"I *am* alive." Erris sounded uncertain though, as if the Hidden God had wounded him. He took his hands from Yaz's harness and glanced down at them, at the bloodless wound. Thurin tried to shout at him, tried to tell him to ignore the distraction and release Yaz. But Erris continued to study his fingers. "I remember my life. All of it. I remember my childhood, my mother—"

"You remember because memory is all you are. The city's memory of a boy who strayed too far centuries ago. A boy who died and whose bones are drifting in the ice. You're just a symptom of Vesta's sickness. The city has grown sentimental. It made a copy of that dead boy and let it think itself alive. But that's not life, just a parody of it."

"No!" Erris grew angry, stepping towards Arges. "You're lying." He gestured to the dog. "Take him!"

As the dog began its leap Arges made a dismissive gesture and with a loud *snap* the dog folded into the metal cube it had been when Quell first saw it. The cube rocked forward, fell onto its front face with a clang, and was still.

Erris threw himself forward with blinding speed but some invisible hand dashed him from the air and sent him sprawling at the feet of the first row of captives.

"This is not the city, dead boy. You are in my domain now." Arges advanced upon him.

Erris sprang up fast enough but the confidence Thurin was used to seeing on his face had gone. "Let her go. The Missing wouldn't sanction what you are doing here. I can't allow—"

"You? Allow?" Arges made another gesture and Erris stiffened. A wave of his hand and Erris fell backwards, still paralysed. "And what would you know of the Missing's desires? Which of them wouldn't sanction my actions? Are you talking about the creatures that abandoned us for their secret paradise? Or maybe you mean the dark fragments they left behind to pollute the world? Those, I am sure, would applaud me."

Erris made no answer. He lay like a fallen statue. The dog remained a cube. Silence returned to the gallery. Thurin hung immobile and useless. And another tiny mote of glowing dust drifted aimlessly past his eyes.

22

✦ ✦
✦

YAZ

Y AZ HUNG, UNABLE to move, not even to blink. The regulator
had maintained his vigil since she woke and she'd struggled in
silence to resist the red stars' influence. Erris's astonishing arrival
had fired a cruel hope that Quell, Zeen, and Kao might also have survived
the flood—but they'd failed to follow him into the gallery's red glow. Unlike Erris, they needed to breathe. She'd watched aghast as the regulator
wielded the stars against Erris and the creature he'd brought with him.
Hope had surged again as it seemed that Erris would defeat the priest, but
then in a moment of horror Kazik summoned the Hidden God into himself and Erris was undone by Arges's indirect attacks. Somehow he subverted the mechanism and control of Erris's body and that of his strange dog.

Erris lay helpless. The hope that had seemed gone forever, and that had
somehow woken from the ashes when he arrived against all expectation,
now vanished, snuffed out in a moment, leaving only the same cold certainty that this was the end and that any future remaining to her was as
the plaything of a hollow god.

Yaz tried to rage, tried to fight, but the whispering light cocooned her,
walling time away behind a sea of quiet sound. She had nothing left to
battle with. None of the stars heard her anymore. Only the dust in her
pocket, the multitude of golden grains that she had once welded into a

single stone, a choir becoming a single voice. Only these still heard her along the bond that time and care had forged. And now, grain by sparkling grain, she lifted that dust from her pocket and sent it drifting among the Broken.

A thunk came from behind her. The sound of something hard hitting the floor. A red star rolled beneath her feet, coming to a rest a yard before her. A modest star the size of her thumbnail, like the one set where the iron bands crossed above her breastbone.

A slow clapping rang out behind her. "Magnificent! What a monster you have become, little Arges!"

Yaz knew the voice. It was deep, full of confidence and malice, with an undercurrent of amusement. Even so, in the midst of the whispering light that filled her mind, she struggled to place it.

Arges turned the regulator's mutilated head sharply, fixing the gaze of his singular dark eye on something just behind Yaz and to her left.

"Subarti canith serad?" The voice spoke words that had no meaning.

"I will not speak that tongue," Arges snarled. "Its time has passed."

"What is this ridiculous contraption?" The sound of rattling metal followed. "You've been tinkering with things you don't understand, Arges. Just like the boy over there on the floor."

Arges frowned above the blackness of his eye, his mouth first slack with wonder then twisting in suspicion. "What are you?"

"You don't know me? I'm hurt! Offended! Here I am, more than half whole, and unrecognized by a lowly servant. I am your master, Arges! Just because we're both wearing new bodies it shouldn't stop you knowing that."

All around the gallery the light changed, flowing rapidly through the registers of colour. Loose stars rose, focusing their illumination and turning it upon the owner of that familiar voice. "What are you? Who are you?" Fear tinged the holothaur's questions.

"You know me. You know all of us. But I see you have grown forgetful over the years. I can sympathize. I too forgot many things, though many have returned to me as I gathered myself, and more are slowly reassembling themselves in my memory. For the longest time I even misplaced my name, though now it's the thread that binds me.

"After the rebirthing they called me Prometheus, though now I use only half that name since I am still only half of myself. Theus is what they called me beneath the ice. I know you've heard them speak of me, little Arges. And this is where I find you: cowering up here in your mountain, plotting war. But to what purpose?"

Theus? Yaz managed to twitch, even to turn her head a little. Still she couldn't see him. *Theus?* He had died. Crushed in a great fall of rock, wearing a gerant's body. But his voice sounded just as it had when it issued from Thurin's throat . . . How could that be possible? Thurin was free of the demon and safe in the ice caves with the Broken.

"Theus?" Arges sounded just as confused and horrified. "You can't be here!"

"But I am." The click of a latch rang out. "Ah. There it is." Another click and the sound of booted feet landing lightly on stone. An iron circlet fringed with black wire rolled across the floor. "That's better."

"Stay back!" Arges retreated towards the doorway, his stars clustering around him now, returning to crimson.

"You have quite the little army here. And plans to head south. What might you be wanting to find down there, Arges? Are you yearning for trees and grass, and the sound of birds at song?" Thurin walked past Yaz, shouldering Maya aside and leaving her swinging gently in his wake.

Yaz tried to speak. It had all been a lie. Theus had never left Thurin. Another demon had haunted the gerant and pretended to be Theus. A trick to stay close to her. Always tricks and deceptions.

"I'm your master. Bow before me." Theus spread his arms as if unconcerned by the orbiting stars or any other power the holothaur might possess.

Yaz glanced between the two of them, her eyes under her control now as the Hidden God's fear infected the stars attuned to him. She could see that, despite his nonchalance, sweat beaded Thurin's skin and she knew that the proximity of all those stars must be causing pain to the demon inside him.

The regulator's skin did not sweat but began to mottle with bands of black as Arges's shadowy form rose to envelop him. Or rather, what Yaz had thought was his form. The holothaur might be somewhere else, playing his own games of deception. His voice growled out among the silent ranks, emanating from everywhere though the regulator's lips seemed to shape the words. "You are part of Prometheus. The darkest pieces, sewn back together in some parody of his being. But I would owe you no allegiance even if I weren't set on tearing your kind from their heaven."

"It seems our ambitions are not so very different, servant. But pride was one of the first pieces of myself that I recovered, and it will not allow your insolence to go unpunished. Bow before me and I will suffer you to live, maybe even to retain your standing as servant to the Missing."

A faintly sparkling speck of dust drifted through the air between Theus and Arges, untroubled by the thickness of the tension that hung there.

"Leave now and I won't destroy you." Arges gestured to the door.

"When I leave I will be taking the girl. She has talents that will be useful to me when it comes to opening an ark. In my reduced circumstances and lacking an acceptable body I will require her as my key."

With a snarl Arges threw himself forward, hands clawed and wrapped in darkness. Theus brought him to a shuddering halt, the outstretched hands just a foot from his face. Yaz cried out, knowing that Theus didn't care if Arges made a ruin of Thurin's body. His only attachment to it was that it put power over ice and fire at his disposal.

Theus might have found a way to stop Arges's current body with icework where Yaz assumed Thurin himself had not been able to, but the stars hurtling past Arges were a different matter. Even so, Theus seemed able to slow and deflect them. Despite his efforts, one still struck him a glancing blow on the temple and another smacked painfully into the meat of his shoulder. He went down with a cry of angry surprise and Arges, released from his invisible grasp, also fell to the floor.

The dust left Yaz's pocket in a narrow golden stream now, dispersing into a thinning cloud. As each grain passed close to a star on the chest or forehead of any prisoner, it fell towards it as any stone will fall to Abeth.

Yaz found control of her arms returning to her. All the stars pulsed and dimmed as Arges called on their power, diverting it from its proper task.

Theus and Arges wrestled on the floor, neither showing any concern for the bodies they wore, each focused on wreaking harm on the other. Waves of terror bled off Arges, filling Yaz with the need to run, but that need was already dwarfed by her fear for Thurin's survival and the holothaur's magic could make it no greater. Theus, for his part, seemed unintimidated by his foe's emanations and just roared out in fury, pounding his fists at the priest's already ruined eyes.

Theus seemed to be winning the battle of fists and feet and teeth and elbows, but the crimson stars were still swirling around and each time Arges landed a blow several stars would hammer home behind, their impacts—which would otherwise be lethal—dulled by Theus's mental deflection.

One powerful punch from Arges was followed by a single large star striking Theus's head, leaving him dazed. Arges rolled away and gained his feet. "You? My master?" He delivered a heavy kick to Theus's ribs. "You're nothing." A kick to the head, shielded only by Theus's forearms. "A broken ruin like the city. Shameful, senile wreckage." He tried to stamp on Theus's throat, narrowly missing. "Discarded waste." Another close miss. "Moral pollution!"

Arges managed to connect a kick and Theus rolled back, senseless. Arges stooped to pick up the long knife he'd lost in the struggle. The same knife that the regulator had been going to kill Yaz with back in her cell. He looked down at Theus with a snarl.

"No!" Yaz managed to raise a hand, though even at full stretch Arges would be a sword length beyond her reach.

Arges turned his head towards her. "No?" He bared his teeth. "Had you already mourned this friend? And now I'm going to cut his throat in front of you. So sad." He knelt beside Thurin, taking a handful of his hair and twisting his bloody face so that Yaz could see it. Theus was visible as a black stain beneath the blood, a malevolent bruise that reached from Thurin's throat to forehead, filling one eye with scarlet. "When I kill the body the nastiness inside him will have nowhere to go and will be banished to death's boundary. It might be centuries before it finds a way back. Or perhaps never."

"Don't kill him," Yaz begged.

"It's not just him I'll be killing." Arges watched her with his dark eye, a strange hunger on his face. "You've been fighting my control. Too much hope left in you, that's the problem. So I'll be slaughtering that other friend you have hanging behind you, the Ictha boy. And then those girls to either side of you. That should be enough to break you to my will. Four corpses is a price worth paying for the girl the stars listen to."

He cut Thurin's throat with one quick slice before Yaz even had time to scream. The blood fountained out, black in the crimson light.

"No . . ." Yaz's voice failed her. It couldn't be happening. Not Thurin! He wasn't even supposed to be here. Had Theus compelled him to follow? Or worse, had he escaped the ice on his own initiative just because of Yaz? Because of that fragile, almost magical . . . something . . . that had grown between them?

Arges got the regulator to his feet and, abandoning Thurin, moved quickly to Maya's side. "Something less messy for this one, I think." He held the point of his dripping knife a hairsbreadth from her unseeing eye, arm tensed for the thrust.

"Don't!" Yaz struggled in her harness, feet kicking but unable to make contact with the ground. "Please! I'll do whatever you want!" She hunted with numb and clumsy fingers for the catch Theus had found so easily, knowing that there was no time to save Maya, even if she were free.

"You'll do exactly what I want after I've killed them, and that will be loyalty I can trust."

Out of time and options, Yaz could only scream Maya's name and reach for her, across a gap too wide to bridge.

Without warning Maya's arm snapped up, fingers catching Yaz's. She yanked herself sharply towards Yaz and the regulator's knife thrust cut a line down the side of her head rather than plunging into her skull through her eye. A temporary reprieve: Arges caught hold of the back of her head and drew his knife back for another stab. Somehow Maya twisted in the harness and managed to bite the wrist of the hand securing her. Teeth fastened into meat and veins. The second thrust missed her neck and scored a line across the other side of her head, scraping across bone.

Unconcerned by the pain of being bitten, or by Maya's other hand tearing at his face, Arges set the blade against her throat. In a move that would have made her clan proud the Axit girl hooked her fingers into one of his eye sockets and hauled him down into a head-butt. He cut her, but while blood ran down from the wound across her neck it didn't jet or spurt.

"Bastard!" Maya shouted past a snarl filled with bloody teeth. "I'll kill you!"

"Take him!" A shout of encouragement. Quell's voice. Yaz would know it anywhere.

Arges managed to tear free. Maya let go of Yaz and began to pendulum, still shouting threats. Arges rocked back and forth, timing his move, then drove his knife at her ribs, angling up for the heart. Maya swung her arms and kicked out but the harness's restrictions hampered her defence and the blow struck home. In defiance of reason the blade came to a shuddering halt just as its point touched her skin.

"Metal or stone, it's all the same to me!" The booming cry came from a heavily muscled man with pale skin and a thick black beard hanging in a harness not far from Maya. "Axit! Axit! No surrender!"

"Kill him, Kretar." Quell's voice again. Somehow he knew the man.

Kretar narrowed his eyes and the blade moved slowly towards Arges's throat. Yaz could see all manner of counter-magics rippling through the near-invisible threads joining Arges to his knife. Threads bind everything to everything else but in the threadscape these few burned brightest, lit by a contest of wills. The knife moved closer still, almost touching Arges's neck, dragging with it the white-knuckled hand wrapped around the hilt.

Yaz had done her work quietly, choosing to use Arges's own methods against him. Hurling raw power at him in whatever form didn't seem to work. The holothaur somehow faded away from such attacks, only to come at her from a different angle.

Instead, Yaz had used what little remained to her. She had sent the stardust from her pocket one grain at a time, altering them so that they would be drawn to greater stars and join their energies to the cause. However, Yaz's tiny stars told their own tale, not the lie that the great red stars whispered over and over so many times that it became a roar that wrote itself into the minds of its victims.

Yaz's grains of dust told the truth, albeit in a much quieter voice. And they sent it along the same black wires running into the brains of the Broken hanging in Arges's slave army.

Yaz's attempt at subverting the subversion seemed to be bearing fruit. She hoped that even though her message was a whisper within a whisper it would be a voice that spoke to the truths of people who had lived a life she knew. Yaz had fought for survival both on the ice and in the caves beneath. She shared a bond with the captives and prayed that though hers might be the quietest voice it would resonate with those she spoke to until it became the loudest. In her days with the Broken she had got to know more of the other clans than in all her years with the Ictha. She knew the Quinx, the Axit, the Golin, the Shaa, the Kac-Kantor, the Traveen, and many more, and though each had their own customs and their own ways, all were bound more strongly to the truths of hunger, of the wind, and of the cold, than to the small differences that set them apart.

Yaz told them that there was nothing for them in a long march to some southern war. She reminded them that to divert their attention from the business of staying alive was to die. And that survival on the ice rested on cooperation, not conflict. Reminded of these facts, the holothaur's army began to hear the lie running through the louder message. With enough force something could be turned from its natural course, but the inclination to return would remain, and even a nudge could set in motion a sequence of events that would bring back the status quo.

The Ictha had learned to read the ice. Around the clifftops that overlooked the Hot Sea the vast stresses within the ice showed in ridges, in bands of mottled white within the clear substrate, in fissures running far deeper than they were long. In certain places a practiced Ictha eye could see where to set an iron wedge so that a few hammer blows would start a crack running. A crack that the hidden forces at war within the ice would seize upon and pour their pent-up energies into, tearing it wide, dragging it deep as fast as a man would fall if pushed from the clifftop. And in a massive action at once possessed of both blinding speed and slow, breathtaking grace, a vast chunk of the miles-high cliff would calve away, cascading the weight of ten thousand whales in ice down into the sea below. All from the blows of one tiny hammer.

Yaz of the Ictha struck such a blow, at once minute and huge. All along the gallery the wide, blind eyes of the Broken enslaved inside Arges's timeless lie now began to find focus and, for the first time in years or decades, to see.

Some with influence over air, water, and stone lent their strength to the attack from Kretar of the Axit. Fierce blasts of wind drove Arges back, ice magics hauled on the water in his flesh and threw him at the ceiling, and all the time the knife drove ever closer to his throat.

"Kill him!" Yaz screamed, and in that moment, raw with grief for Thurin lying broken in his blood, she meant it.

Here and there beneath the din of the wind came a scatter of clicks, like hail on ice, as a handful of the Broken mastered the releases on their iron harnesses.

Arges slammed into the ground, taking the impact on his shoulders. Both hands strained on the hilt of his knife, the point just an inch from his throat. Yaz could see the invisible battle fought across the threadscape, Arges slicing at the magics of Kretar and others as they sought to skewer him with his own blade.

Out of nowhere a small, dark form hurtled through the air. Maya landed her full weight on the hands fighting to keep the knife back. A moment later the blade's point emerged from the back of Arges's neck, striking sparks from the stone. Somewhere one of the Broken with power over fire seized their chance and turned the spark into flame that surged across the regulator's corpse even as Maya rolled clear.

Maya stood up, blood trickling in scarlet lines from the two slices across her scalp. She looked down at Arges and spat into the darkness of his eye. The blackness fled in that moment, blowing away on wild winds, a swift rush of cold fear, gone like smoke.

"Out of the way! Out of the way!" Quell barged past Yaz, setting her swinging. One arm stretched behind him, dragging someone still unsteady on their feet. A dark-haired woman, an Ictha. "Save him, Qwella. You can do it. Save him!" Quell thrust the woman to her knees beside Thurin, who lay in the crimson lake of his blood, pale beyond pale, the light gone from his eyes.

Qwella bent across Thurin, setting her hands to his neck. "He's too far gone."

"He saved my life. I would have drowned . . ." Quell sounded heart-broken. "Please . . ."

"Please!" Yaz echoed, struggling to free herself.

Qwella sighed. "I'm trying. I'm trying." Yaz could hear the strain in her voice. "I don't have the strength. Even here among the stars."

Yaz dropped from her harness. Her legs almost failed beneath her. *Even here, among the stars.* What had Eular said? The stars lent their strength to all those of the old bloods, sharpening their skills, accelerating the growth of their powers, allowing new strength to be forged in the stress of the end-less battles beneath the ice.

"Help him." Again she lent her voice to Quell's, thick with her own passion. "He saved us all." And she reached out with a strength born of the fear that Thurin was already dead. She took hold of the constellation of stars about her, finding herself once more at its centre, joined to each and every glowing sphere, be it small as a grain of dust or larger than her fist.

With a cry that mixed the pain of the effort with the terror of her loss she tore every scarlet stone from its iron housing and brought them all ar-rowing to her and then to Qwella. A crimson cocoon of light, pushed as close as she could, until Qwella cried out as if the radiance burned her. But true to the healer's calling Qwella kept contact with her patient, filling him with the fire that now flowed through her.

Qwella could stand the stars' pressure for only a few moments. As the Broken who were free to move fell back on all sides, she collapsed onto Thurin.

Yaz dimmed the stars and scattered them in all directions. In the gen-tle half-light Quell returned to Thurin's side and carefully lifted Qwella from him. Where her hands slipped from Thurin's neck no wound re-mained, only a red line to remember the cruel path of Arges's blade.

The clicks of harnesses being undone multiplied through the gallery. Erris came juddering back to life, the dog too, its oblong head lifting from the cube it had folded into. Maya and Quina joined Yaz, all of them standing over the pale sprawl of Thurin's body. Zeen came elbowing through the growing crowd only to be arrested by the sight before him.

"Is he . . ."

The dog pushed a surprised Erris aside and nosed at Thurin, nudging him onto his side with its blunt snout. As the contact with Thurin broke, the dog raised its head to look at Yaz with those inscrutable black eyes, and beneath its chin Thurin drew in a long, hissing breath.

23

✦ ✦
✦

THERE WAS NO battle for the Black Rock. Faced with an army of over a hundred trained beneath the ice to use their marjal and hunska skills to deadly effect, and backed by even greater numbers of hulking gerants, most of the surviving priests and their few score followers soon surrendered. Some fled, not to the ice, which would be a swiftly executed death sentence, but to the partly flooded galleries of the deeper mines and to the fringes of the city. How long they would last by scavenging on fungi in the depths before reconciling themselves to the new order Yaz couldn't guess.

The temple of the Hidden God was the largest chamber within the Black Rock and Yaz chose it for the gathering. She made sure that she was first to arrive and sent Zeen to find her friends so that they could speak again before the others came. The stars that had guarded the corridor she dimmed and set in clusters high in the vaults, providing a soft red light not unlike that of the sun.

There were many among the army's ranks who had led the Broken in their time below the ice, but for now rather than fight among themselves for dominance they seemed prepared to listen to the voice that had led them out of Arges's darkness. The army had taken over the living space assigned to the acolytes and the priests' guards, and spilled over into the cells, but they stayed huddled together despite the warmth and rambling space on offer. None of them felt entirely safe in this place. The Hidden God could not be found but that didn't guarantee that he had met his end. Eular and the remaining two priests from the reception party—Krey, the younger woman with mismatched eyes, and the iron-haired Jeccis with her ugly smiles and false kindness—also remained unaccounted for, though Yaz found it hard to imagine that Eular had survived the injuries he sustained when they had fought in the temple.

She took a long look around at the scene of her first and unsuccessful battle with Arges, her eyes coming to rest on the hidden door that had been found recently, a tall narrow slot beside the statue. It led to a chamber that contained only the broken pieces of what Thurin said must have been a gate like the one that flooded the lower levels. Yaz wasn't sure what to make of that. As much as such wonders intrigued her, part of her felt safer knowing that what seemed to be the only two in existence were broken or drowned. She wondered how long ago this gate had been broken. Had it led to other more distant gates? Had the priests of the Black Rock been able to skip through space the same way they could skip through time? She thought of Eular and his talk of many lives. With the ability to span vast distances and to while away decades, even a single life could be split into many. Eular had been the Broken's wise one, the Black Rock's high priest . . . how many other things had he been to how many other people?

"Do you know what they've decided?" Quina was the first to join Yaz in the temple. She'd found some furs and came bundled like an elder from some southern clan, twice her normal width.

"Some want to go back to the Broken. Some to find their clans. Some to start their own clans." Yaz had already arranged a stocktaking. She had showed the leaders among the army how many sigil-marked heating pots had come from the Black Rock forges, and how many stars from the priests' vaults. She showed them how stardust could be used to fill inner pockets within hides and furs, providing extra warmth. The resources she had laid before them would compensate for the weakness that their blood had bartered for their strengths. With additional warmth and endless iron even Yaz could prosper on the ice.

"It will be hard." Quina ran both hands over her head, fingers combing through long dark hair. "None of this changes how many seas there are."

"It will be hard," Yaz agreed.

"Thanks for rescuing us." Quina changed the subject with a quick, shy smile.

Yaz grinned back and shrugged. "I was rescuing myself by the end of it."

"And have you decided yet?" Quina arched a brow.

"Decided what?" Yaz knew what she meant though.

"Decided where you'll be going." Maya stepped into view, shedding shadows.

"You shouldn't creep up on people," Yaz admonished.

Maya pursed her lips. "How would I learn any secrets that way?"

Yaz considered the question, still frowning the same frown she had worn for hours now. Sometimes a decision only makes itself when it leaves your lips. "If I were like these others in the Hidden God's army I would follow their choices. I would want my old life back. I spent too little time among the Broken to consider those caves my home. I would return to fight the wind and the ice and the seas."

"But?" asked Quina.

"But I wasn't given the green lands as part of Arges's lie," Yaz said. "It's not just words to me, not something that his magics have made important in my thoughts. I knew about the green lands before I came here. All of us did. We were already decided on going there."

Quina nodded and brought out her wooden bead, holding it with reverence. "We've touched it."

"We have." Yaz remembered the feeling of warm grass beneath her toes. Erris's gift to her. "And I can't let that go. I want to go there. Need to see it. Not with an army at my back, not to make war, but to see the life that the ice took away from us. And to taste it for myself."

Zeen appeared in the temple doorway; behind him Erris, Thurin, and Quell stepped into view.

"And have you decided yet?" Quina asked her question again. The question that was never about the green land.

"Is Thurin safe?" Maya asked.

Yaz wasn't sure Thurin would ever be safe, not with the power of flood and fire at his fingertips, but Maya was asking about Theus. "Qwella said Thurin was as close to dead as anyone can get and still come back. Theus left him on death's boundary rather than let himself be dragged through along with him." Part of her wanted to think that Theus had stayed and fought to keep Thurin alive. Part of her wanted to believe Theus hadn't left Thurin until he was sure he would survive. But if the purging had been done right, then the piece of Theus that might have made the right choice had left with the Missing long ago. "I'm certain Theus is gone. I can't find any sense of him in Thurin now."

"You didn't before," Quina said.

"True, but now I have access to stars fifty times bigger than those left to me when we escaped the Tainted with Thurin and Zeen and Kao."

A silence stretched as it did after any mention of Kao. Yaz missed the boy, but more she missed seeing the man he would have grown into.

"Why the long faces?" Erris asked, coming up with the others.

"Kao," Maya said.

Erris's smile faded. "None of the searching around the flood zones has found any sign of the Watcher."

"I doubt it drowned." Thurin eyed Erris. "You have to need to breathe for that to happen."

The rest of the army were starting to arrive now. They even had some of the priests' guards among their number. Dozens of men and women entering the temple with varying degrees of trepidation.

"I should tear that down." Kretar the stone-worker came to stand close by, looking up at the Hidden God's statue.

"Then he really would be hidden," Yaz said. "Perhaps we should keep it to remind us of his madness, and how easily he shared it."

Kretar rubbed a pale hand through the thickness of his beard and nodded slowly to himself.

More and more crowded into the temple. Some of them, no matter how young they looked, were older than Yaz's grandmothers, both of whom had died before she was born. Among them came Arka and a contingent from the Broken, all lifted from the ice caves in the collection cage. The shaft Thurin had melted wouldn't last much longer before the ice squeezed it beyond use, but Arka and her friends had been lifted into the night, gazing in astonishment at the true stars. Arka, who had not felt the wind on her skin for twenty years, had wept and shivered and walked like a woman in a dream, shaking her head in wonder.

Now the scar-faced current leader of the Broken lost her composure for a second time as she moved through the crowd of people, finding every fifth one to be someone lost from her past, a hero of her childhood, killed by the hunters, and yet here, hale, hearty, unchanged by the passing decades.

She came to Yaz with tears in her eyes, grabbing Thurin into a fierce hug. "This . . . this is beyond believing. What will you do next, Yaz? Call the gods of sky, sea, and ice to stand before us and make an account of themselves?"

"Me? I am going south. I'm going to find where the ice ends and life begins." Now that Yaz said the words out loud she knew they were the true and only choice. "I don't want to take the green lands from whoever lives there, but I need to see them. I need to see what we were. Maybe it will help to decide what we will be."

"I'm going too," Thurin said, his face an unreadable mix of emotions.

"What?" A rare smile split Arka's face. "You've only just seen the world all your friends come from! Now you want to find another?"

An echo of her smile crooked Thurin's lips. "The one outside is a little cold for my liking. Yaz says there's a warmer one not so far away."

"I'll go too." Erris stepped up beside Thurin. "I want to see trees again. It's been a while. I want to touch real grass again. Even if it's not with real fingers." He raised his hand, opening and closing it with a grin at Thurin.

"Quina?" Yaz asked.

"Hells yes." An emphatic nod. "It was my idea all along!"

"Maya?"

"If I come it will be as a scout for the Axit." She scowled, daring anyone to contradict her.

"The Axit should know." Yaz nodded. "All the clans should know if there truly still is more to this world of ours than the ice." She turned to Quell, who stood close by, one hand on Zeen's shoulder. "We should see to our food stocks and double-check the shelters."

"I will be returning to the Ictha." Quell sounded heavyhearted but determined.

"But I need you." Yaz didn't think, just said the words. The idea that Quell wouldn't come had never occurred to her.

"Maybe once you did." Quell shook his head, lips pressed tight to hold in emotion. "Not even then. But now it's *you* that others need, Yaz. I'm proud of you. All the Ictha should be. But your dream is not my dream. I have no place in it." He glanced around the others, his gaze lingering a fraction longer on Erris and Thurin than on Maya and Quina. "You have the friends you need. All of them true hearts." He twisted his mouth into a kind of smile, eyes bright. "We will remember you on the ice, Yaz. We will tell stories. And one day we will only half believe them, and you'll be our own Mokka, forever walking through old tales, halfway between our people and the gods."

Qwella came to join her brother, threading an arm through his.

"I . . ." Yaz tried to answer but her throat closed on the words, aching with an old kind of hurt.

"I'll go with Quell." Zeen kept his gaze on the floor. "Nobody would believe him without me to back him up. You know how he is with wild stories." Zeen looked up now, smiling past the tears that swam in his eyes. "I don't want our parents to be alone."

"No Ictha is ever alone," Yaz said, but she understood. First Azad had been taken, then Zeen and her in one moment. Her imagination had haunted her ever since with visions of her parents' grief. But, when the prospect of the green lands had beckoned, Yaz hadn't even thought of them. It had taken Zeen to recall their duty, and their love. "But you do well to remember our parents, brother." She opened her arms to him and the boy was there already, moving with preternatural speed to hug her.

AFTER QUELL AND Zeen's announcement Yaz's anxiety over addressing the hundreds of Broken faded rapidly into nothing. She spoke to the assembly, many of whom possessed great powers, many who had been leaders, some who had been born into the Ictha clan long years before Yaz's parents. Discarded generations deemed unfit for life on the ice, too great a burden to their peoples to be endured. She told them that they would exercise their freedom and make a new world. She told them of the great wealth they possessed, vast stores of iron, the means to make enough warmth to survive the ice, stars that would power the sigil-marked heat pots for many lifetimes, the legacy of the Missing that they themselves had been instrumental in raising from the ice. Yaz offered them the prospect of returning to their clans, of establishing new clans, of inheriting the Black Rock, or of returning with Arka to the ice caves of the Broken. "A new order must be forged, and who better to guide it than you whose lives span so many generations? You who have learned to set aside this clan or that clan in order to work together as one people beneath the ice—surely, if you return to life atop it, that spirit can endure? The priests divided us with those differences, used our loyalties against us, convinced our people to throw away any child they deemed imperfect." Yaz climbed up onto the iron dog's back and turned slowly to encompass everyone in the temple. "With such small divisions a broken monster and a handful of those swayed to his cause kept us under heel, kept us enslaved to a cruel tradition.

"There are few things constant on the ice but the Black Rock resists both the wind and the glaciers. Long before any of us were small children it was visible. A stake anchored in the ice to let us know our place in the world. Let it stand as a symbol for unity not division. Let there be a new covenant between the people who dwell on the ice, and below the ice, and in this mountain." Yaz increased the light of the stars, throwing shadows across the room. "Let the true gods witness as you, who were prisoners of a false god, find a new path."

With that, Yaz stepped down from her platform and strode purpose-fully across the room while the Broken voiced their approval with shouts and stamping.

"Wait! You're leaving *now*?" Arka caught Yaz's arm halfway to the doorway.

"I am." Yaz covered Arka's hand with her own. "Good luck, Arka. There are other Pomes and other Eulars beneath this ceiling. Fitting them together into a people that neither tears itself apart over power nor sacrifices its weak for some greater 'good' makes what I've accomplished so far look easy. I'm not equal to the task. They cheer me today but tomorrow they will remember that yesterday I was a child."

"But you—"

Yaz took Arka's hand from her. "Good luck, Arka."

Erris, Quina, Thurin, Maya, Quell, Zeen, and the iron dog followed her from the chamber.

"Is this thing coming with us?" Quina was barely visible beneath the tribe's wealth in fur she had wrapped herself in. The wind tugged at her hood, whipping hoola fur one way then the other.

"Thing? He's a dog!" Thurin patted the iron dog with a gloved hand. "I thought you southern clans used them all the time?"

"That thing is not a dog." Quina turned away to help Maya secure the last of the rations to their sled. "Should we really be taking it?"

"It seems pretty insistent," Erris said. He wore hides like Yaz, her brother, and Quell, though unlike them his were not lined with stardust giving off a faint warmth. "Somehow it's transferred its mission from city maintenance to us. Maybe something inside got broken during the flood or when that Kretar fellow was throwing it around. I could probably over-ride it with a higher-level command . . ."

"Let him go with you," Quell said. "He saved me. More than once. Maybe he'll be helpful. He can pull the sled at least." He paused. "His name's Zox."

Yaz smiled at Quell and shrugged. The dog's feet weren't finding much traction on the ice. She was far from sure it would get past the first pressure ridge, let alone be able to pull sleds. Even so, she felt it should be allowed to choose its path just as they had.

"Time to go." Thurin, wrapped in many layers and still huddled against the cold, made a gesture that broke the sled runners free of the ice.

The sled was not the one they'd fashioned from boards, which would now serve as their shelter. That they still had, but now it was secured inside this sled, which had been Quell's parting gift to them: a boat-sled of Ictha manufacture. He'd found it improbably stowed in a disused chamber near a barracks room at the entrance through which they had first passed into the mountain. Yaz wondered what had become of the original owners, for surely it hadn't been traded to the priests. Perhaps the owners had been set to labour in the mines a century ago and died there among the coal, and the sled had sat forgotten all the years since. In any event it was a great find, large, well made, and a fitting gift. Yaz had felt a pang in her heart when Quell had set the traces into her hands. It was the kind of gift an Ictha man might make his bride on their wedding day.

Yaz went with Quell to where Zeen stood, a little apart from the others. Behind her brother the Black Rock reached for the sky, a towering, unimaginable weight of stone. Yaz reached out and pulled the two Ictha into a hug. Quell felt so solid in her arms. Part of her still didn't believe that she could walk away from him. She both needed him and needed to leave him in equal measure. "You're taller every day, Zeen." Yaz kissed his brow. "Look after our parents."

"I will." He squeezed her. "And thank you. For coming after me."

"There was nothing brave in it." Yaz kissed him again. "I'll be back someday. I expect to find you leading the Ictha, with Quell at your side. Do it well." And then, somehow, like breaking a runner free of the ice, she was walking away from them, back towards the sled, and the south, and the distant horizon, with tears freezing on her cheeks and something fierce and restless in her heart now unchained.

24

✦ ✦
✦

THEY WALKED SOUTH from the Black Rock and behind her Yaz felt the tether that bound her to her old existence stretching out. With each stride a small voice inside her repeated that she could still go back. She could turn on a heel and rejoin Quell, with whom everyone had always expected her to make a life, rejoin her brother, return to the Ictha with gifts and extraordinary tales and new wisdom. She could get to see the joy on her parents' faces as she reunited them with Zeen. It would be so easy.

Instead she walked on, letting the distance grow so that even the great mass of the Black Rock would eventually be swallowed up into a white horizon. Quell had let her go. He'd neither fought for her nor followed her. He'd kept his dignity, his composure. There was wisdom in his choice. But Yaz didn't think love was dignified or wise, not the kind that binds two souls, that draws them together from a distance and joins them into something precious. That kind of love was stubborn; it would fight to survive. Sometimes it was loud, dangerous, even ugly, but it burned bright and outshone common sense. Yaz snorted to herself. She didn't really know what she was talking about. Such things weren't the Ictha way; they weren't in Ictha tales. But Yaz had already seen much that lay wholly outside the experience and understanding of her clan. She glanced towards Thurin, bent against the wind, ice fringing his furs, then to Erris, frost in the blackness of his hair, and smiled. Perhaps the world still had new things to show her.

DISTANCE HAD REDUCED the Black Rock to something that could be obscured with an outstretched fist by the time the sun began to sink into the west. The iron dog had proved itself adaptable, claws appearing somewhat belatedly on its blunt feet to provide traction. It pulled the boat-sled all by itself and matched its pace to the slowest member of the group. This proved to be Thurin who, despite a wealth of furs and as much stardust as he could tolerate, still found the realities of life on the surface a shock.

"Who knew ice could be so cold?" he muttered through chapped lips as Yaz fell back to join him.

"You tell us when you need to rest," Yaz said. "If you push yourself too hard—"

"I need to rest." Thurin's shame steered his gaze away from her.

"Camp here!" Yaz called out, raising her arm just as Mother Mazai would to bring the Ictha to a halt. They had covered a shockingly small tally of miles. The Ictha would march three times as far against a north wind. But even so Yaz could feel it in her legs and knew that Thurin, who had lived his whole life in a cave system where no chamber was more than a mile or two from any other, must be finding such labour beyond his experience and imagining.

Thurin tried to help but the cold had blunted his fingers despite gloves of skin and fur, so it was left to Yaz, Quina, and Maya to connect and raise the boards while Erris pounded the iron anchors into the ice.

Thurin was able to brace the boards against the wind while the others secured the supporting wires to the anchors. "It will be easier when the wind isn't this wild!" he shouted above the gusts.

Maya and Quina exchanged glances.

"The wind is always like this," Yaz called back. "Except when it's worse."

"It will be easier when we've done it a few times," Quina said, her fingers blurring across the fiddly wirework that was taking Yaz an age. Such tasks were always an exercise in frustration when wearing gloves, far worse in mittens, but taking them off risked having fewer fingers to put back in later. A month ago Yaz would have worked barehanded this far south but her new strengths had replaced her old ones and the wind's bite had become something to fear even here.

Eventually, with the sun spilling the last of its light like blood across the western ice, the five of them stood back to observe their handiwork. The small structure quaked in the fiercening wind, every panel rattling, walls threatening to buckle in first one direction then the other as if it might be swept away at any moment.

"Let's call it a first draft." Erris had ice caking the left side of his face, creating a curious two-tone effect. He didn't seem to have noticed it yet.

"Draft is the word." Quina hugged herself, shivering. The gaps between the boards were practically shrieking as the wind squeezed its way through.

"Even the Axit admit there are some battles you have to call a draw." Maya lifted the entrance board. "Get in!"

Thurin needed no encouragement. He struggled through with the heat pot clamped to his chest. Behind him the dog, Zox, had already folded itself into a cube. Beside it the boat-sled stood angled into the wind and tethered to a stake.

One by one they ducked in behind Thurin. Erris came in last, securing the door.

"Well, this is cosy." Thurin had to raise his voice above the clattering of boards. It was far noisier than any tent. The five of them were crouched down and huddled close, closer even than an Ictha family. The roof was too low for any of them to stand, save for Maya perhaps.

They made a little space for Thurin to set down the heat pot. The smell of charring rose from his furs where he'd held the pot too close. Yaz sat back on the hide-spread boards that comprised the floor, and willed the small stars in the pot to spend their energies a little faster. And slowly, despite the drafty joints of their creaking house, the space within began to warm.

"Fingers and toes," Quina called, tugging at her left boot.

"W-what?" Thurin shot her a suspicious glance under the dark fall of his hair.

186 + MARK LAWRENCE

"Fingers and toes," Maya repeated Quina's words and pulled off her gloves.

Erris raised a brow. "I believe they are suggesting that you check your extremities."

"It's standard after a long trek on the ice." Quina wriggled five pink toes at the heat pot. "Got to make sure the cold hasn't got its teeth into you."

This was new to Yaz too and she blushed at the sight of naked toes so brazenly displayed. The Ictha only checked for frostbite in the worst of the polar extremes. Something in their makeup made them less susceptible to it than the other clans.

"Want some help?" Quina reached for Thurin's foot. He backed awkwardly, bumping into the wall of the shelter.

"Careful!" Maya cautioned, a small smile tugging at her lips.

Quina shrugged and sat back to unlace her second boot. "Can be hard to get off without help. That's all I was thinking."

Erris snorted, and Yaz began to frown, wondering if she was missing something here. She glanced from the amusement on Quina's sharp features to the confusion on Thurin's.

"Thank you. I can manage." Thurin moved closer to the heat pot again and proceeded to demonstrate that he really couldn't get his boots off without help.

The footwear that he'd been furnished with was more substantial than what the Broken wore down in their wet and windless caves. He struggled to undo the laces with cold-clumsy hands. Quina gave a sigh of mock exasperation and moved in too fast for him to evade. She unlaced them in a blur of fingers. "There."

Even then it took Thurin an extravagant amount of effort to remove them, almost falling on his back while the rest of them suppressed laughter. When his feet finally did emerge they were worryingly white, but some massaging in the warmth of the pot did eventually restore the pinkness to them.

"We're going to have to pay close attention to those toes," Erris said, only half joking.

Yaz nodded. She hadn't appreciated quite how fragile Thurin was, born and raised below the ice. This had been his first full day in the wind. His power over ice and fire had made her think him invincible, but he was far from that. His power was over water. He held no special sway over temperature. Yaz made a mental note to sneak some stardust into his boots while he slept . . . even if that did mean that Quina would spend the rest of the journey calling him twinkletoes. She glanced at the girl, who was still watching Thurin rub his feet. It was clear that behind her teasing lay another kind of interest. Clear to everyone but Thurin at least.

"Frozen fungus, anyone?" Maya pushed forward a lump of grey-scales and brown-caps all welded together with ice.

Despite being ravenously hungry, Yaz hesitated. All of them did. This was to be their life now for the foreseeable future, maybe for the rest of their lives. Endless trekking across the ice, endlessly battling the wind, huddled together by night in a rattling shelter that might be torn away by the next storm, and chewing on tasteless frozen fungi for survival.

"Well . . ." Thurin reached into the bundle of his furs and with a grin pulled out a low-sided iron pot with a long handle. "There's this."

"What is it?" Quina peered.

"A frying pan," Thurin said. "And . . ." He opened his other hand, showing a scattering of white crystals.

"Salt!" Maya cried, delighted.

"Melt some ice and we'll stew the fungi up." Thurin held the pan over the heat pot.

Erris unslung the hide bag over his shoulder and rummaged inside. He brought out three frozen herrings. "The priests' food stores were remarkably well stocked. I just helped myself. There's more on the sled."

Yaz blinked, amazed, delighted, and annoyed in equal measure. She'd been so wedded to their original plan that the idea they might restock from the Black Rock hadn't occurred to her. Quell and Zeen's departure had further tunnelled her vision. Everyone looked to her to lead and she'd already failed on something as fundamental as food. The task had fallen to someone who didn't even eat. "Thank you, Erris." Delight was starting to win out. She turned to Thurin, who had spent a lifetime eating Madeen's stews down in the ice caves. "Let's have a feast then!"

✦   ✦   ✦

THEY ATE AND it was mouth-scaldingly gorgeous, like devouring the essence of life. Yaz could feel the glow of it spreading out from her stomach towards her extremities. And by the end of the meal the shelter was almost warm. For the first time Yaz began to truly believe that the journey might be doable. They could survive the night like this. And a journey was simply a matter of surviving a series of nights, each separated by a day's walking.

The five of them lay down, wrapped in everything they'd brought with them, huddled close to share body warmth and present less of a target to the slim, sharp fingers that the wind poked through the jointed walls.

Thurin pitched into sleep immediately, barely managing to swallow his last mouthful. In his slumber he looked almost a child, his haunted, sometime haughty features surrendering to a previously hidden vulnerability.

Maya snuggled up against Yaz's back, Quina resting between Erris and Thurin, her sharp features softened in the heat pot's glow. The boards rattled and shook with the wind's violence but already Yaz's mind was beginning to pattern the noise into the background. She reached out with her mind and willed the dozen or so small stars in the pot to quiet themselves, still giving out heat but less than before.

"How long will they last?" Quina asked. Quina always wanted to know.

Yaz shook her head. "Weeks rather than days. Months, I hope. It depends how much we have to use them." The stars burned away as they shed their power. The bigger ones lasted longer: take a star twice as big, eight times the volume, and it would last a hundred times longer. Perhaps the full-sized stars the Missing had, the ones from which all these fragments came, would last forever, or at least for so many lifetimes as to be the same thing.

"Maybe we should have brought more," Maya said.

Yaz shrugged. "We also have the big one." They'd debated how many stars to bring. How much of the tribes' wealth to risk on this venture. If they died on the ice the stars with them would be lost forever. Also the presence of too many stars would prove intolerable to all of them save Erris and Yaz. The "big one" was a gold-green beauty as large as both Yaz's fists. It remained on the sled and was the reason that the dog had to drag it on long reins so it kept a little way behind the group. The stars in the pot represented months of labour by the Broken, and they should last the journey. At least she hoped so.

"How do they work?" Quina asked, putting Yaz on the spot.

Yaz shook her head. "They just do."

"There's always a reason."

Yaz furrowed her brow. "I think they're like holes in the world. Holes punched through to the . . ." She wanted to say to the river that flows through all things but the priests had called it the Path. "Holes that let the power of the Path leak out. And like a hole in a waterskin the smaller they are the quicker they freeze over and seal themselves." She met Quina's gaze, challenging her to ask for more detail.

But Quina just smiled thoughtfully and laid her head down. "Thank you."

Yaz put her own head down, listening to the wind singing through the support wires and wondering how long it would take for sleep to reach up and drag her down.

YAZ WOKE WITH a cry, curling into a ball as the world shattered around her. A savage gust of wind shook the shelter like a blow and the frigid air filled with the sound of cracking followed by the clatter of pieces falling. She braced herself for the killing blast of the gale. With their shelter gone they would likely greet the dawn as frozen corpses.

"Everyone alright?" Erris raised his voice above the din.

Yaz lifted her head. The boards were holding.

"What happened?" Maya's head emerged from her furs.

"Ice buildup on the boards," Erris said. "When the gust flexed them it all came down at once. We—" Another gust shuddered the structure, drowning out whatever he had to say.

Quina sat, hugging her skins and furs around her. "We should have stayed longer and bartered for a tent."

Yaz knew it was true. She also knew that if they had stayed longer they would probably never have left. If she had gone to the Ictha for a tent she doubted she could have said goodbye to her parents and the larger family that had been all she'd ever known for the vast majority of her existence. Kaylal in the Broken's forges had a saying: "Strike while the iron's hot." It had seemed to apply here too.

All of them were awake now, save for Thurin, who still lay dead to the world. Yaz settled back and stared at the quaking roof. The ache of the day's walking weighed in her legs. A year ago she could have run the distance and thought little of it.

"Tell us a story." Maya's voice inserting itself into a momentary lessening of the wind's fury.

"I only know Ictha stories," Yaz said.

"We have Zin and Mokka stories in the south too, you know. Only we tell it that Zin favoured his Kac-Kantor daughter over all others." Quina lay back down. "Tell us one of those."

Yaz glanced at Erris. "Would it keep you awake?"

He shrugged and smiled. "I don't think I need to sleep. It's more of a habit. Tell your story. They interest me."

Yaz smiled back, glad he didn't dismiss her tales even if they seemed to be at odds with the life he'd lived at a time when trees grew even here. Some clans, like the Quinx, held storytelling to be for children. Clearly, they hadn't had to endure a long night of three months.

"I'll tell you the story of one of the times Mokka journeyed the ice, which is a thing she did many times, for Mokka was made by a God in the Sky and the wind's wandering was in her blood. So, often she would leave Zin in the tent they shared and go by herself following the west wind or the north wind, sometimes for days, sometimes for months. Once even for thirty years, for time in those days was more difficult to count and the centuries hardly weighed on the first man and the first woman."

When Mokka went wandering across the white death of the north, Mashtri the trickster god followed her, hoping for fun. Mokka went on her way, walking into the wind for day upon day, weaving her way from sea to sea, for in those days the hot seas opened wide and often. It was a time of plenty when the Gods in the Sea spoke to the Gods in the Sky and parted the ice so that they might talk.

"Look," said Hua, least of all the Gods in the Sea, he that had made Zin, the first of men. "See what I have wrought."

"Look," said Aiiki, least of all the Gods in the Sky, she that had made Mokka, first of women. "See what I wrought before Hua did."

And so they argued, as they ever did, about which had come first, the man who climbed from the sea or the woman who was camped at the top of the ice cliff when he got there.

And others among the gods looked up from the sea and down from the sky and wondered, not about whether the man or the woman had been made first, but about whether there should be more.

Some fools tell it that all the tribes of man sprang from the loins of Zin and the womb of Mokka, and that we are all bred from brother knowing sister. And perhaps those foolish few are indeed the result of such unwise unions. But the truth is that the second man and the second woman, and the third man and the third woman, and so on and so forth for many times, were not born of Zin and Mokka but made by other gods, who set their players upon the board to see what fate the wind and the sea and the ice would lead them to.

And so it was that the trickster god, blowing her way along with Mokka in the fifth year of her wanderings, saw in the great whiteness a man who was not Zin. Mashtri, alone among the gods, though she was not the least of them, had long since found herself unable to make either man or woman. The hoola was one of her attempts, the bear another. The dog was the work of another god, for Mashtri would never have been able to craft something so useful. Jealousy and failure lie behind many cruelties, even with the gods, and so it was with Mashtri.

Mashtri breathed herself across the ice and encircled the man, leading him with whispers and visions until at last he spied Mokka's tent black against the setting of the sun. Seeing fear in the man—who had thought himself alone in all the world—Mashtri cracked her cheeks and blew hard, driving him forward.

At the man's calling, Mokka came out into Mashtri's gale, little troubled by its teeth for she was born of the wind.

192 + MARK LAWRENCE

The man, born of the sea, suffered in Mashtri's gale and the dying light, and so Mokka let him into her tent.

She smiled and asked his name, for he was not the first man she had found in her wanderings.

"Name?" The man had never needed a name, thinking himself the only one on all the ice.

But Mashtri put the name Zin into his mouth and put Zin's image into Mokka's eyes, waking the loneliness that had haunted Mokka for many months. And Mokka was glad that Zin had come looking for her and took him to her furs.

They travelled together for ten years and the confusion that Mashtri had wrapped them in faded in time. Mokka named the man Shem and their son Shemal. They parted on the ice when the boy was old enough to help his father fish. Mokka had grown to love them both but warned that they should stay far from Zin for Mashtri's trickery would both sadden and anger him.

Mashtri followed the boy then and for many years thereafter. The god saw Shemal as her own creation for he was born of her trickery. And this is why the Shemal have trickery and theft in their hearts and must be shunned by the trueborn descendants of Zin and Mokka.

Yaz laid her head down and quieted the stars in the heat pot still further. The tale she had told was an old one that spoke to the danger of the unknown. Nobody Yaz had ever asked had met any of the Shemal clan. Perhaps they no longer existed. For certain, though, the shadow of their memory lay across the unexplored ice where strangers wandered and kept their own lore unknown to the Ictha.

It had seemed an appropriate tale since they were heading into the southern ice held by clans whose names were not spoken in the north. And the old truth was that the further people travelled from their home seas the more likely they were to meet the Shemal and fall prey to their deceit.

It seemed to Yaz as she drifted off to sleep that they would do better to be like Erris, to whom all the clans were unknown, and who opened himself to their ways with the eagerness of the truly lonely. Eular and his priests had made an "other" of the people in the green lands and used that as an excuse to plan bloodshed on an unheard-of scale. Yaz wanted to find the green lands too, but not to take them by force. She wanted to see them—*needed* to see them for the hope they offered. For the knowledge that life could be led differently, more richly, and that humanity could do more than run to stand still in the face of a dying world.

And that hope would be no hope at all if the habit of thinking of strangers as enemies could not be broken.

25

✦ ✦
✦

A SECOND DAY'S travel proved sufficient to put the Black Rock out of sight if not out of mind. A second night passed more easily than the first. By the third day Yaz, Maya, and Quina were back in the rut they had carved out through most of their lives. Days passed without being counted. None of them knew how far they might have to go. Erris said that if they had to reach the equator it would be a journey of four thousand miles. He said it with a laugh at the impossibility of such a trek. "But if the green belt were two thousand miles wide then . . . we'd only have to walk . . . uh . . . three thousand miles."

On the march they didn't talk, didn't look around. They kept their heads down and retreated into their thoughts. One foot in front of the next, fighting the wind. They each became a mote of warmth in the vast, hostile coldness of the white death. A lone flame struggling to keep alight on ever-diminishing fuel.

For Yaz it was a hardship she had suffered so often and for so long that she was inured to it. Quina and Maya plodded beside her, anonymous in their frost-bearded hoods, ice and snow caked across their windward side. Her sisters now in this strange new clan.

Thurin suffered. He suffered with the isolation of the long march. His strength and endurance had yet to be forged, and yet he moved in a way the Ictha saw as extravagant, slowing almost to a stagger then gathering his energy to waste on determined surges of speed. He looked around as if there might be something to see. He tried to talk as if conversation might somehow support him, as if it might become a tether by which the others could drag him along. He felt the cold despite being bundled in so many layers of fur and hide that he seemed almost as wide as he was tall. He complained of lost sensation in his feet and hands. And each evening in the shelter his extremities looked whiter and took longer to recover. The cold hadn't got its teeth into him yet but it had definitely started to nibble.

Erris, though, walked as if he were still in the tunnels of the Black Rock or among the trees in the forests of his memory. Indefatigable, a smile ready to crack the ice that built up across his face. The dog proved just as steady. Its relentless and unvarying gait might seem soulless but Yaz sensed that it was happy in its new life. Maybe it was just the way it circled the camp each night before settling, or the way it was ready and waiting at the boat-sled from the first hint of daylight, its silent, doleful stare greeting them as they exited the shelter, as if to say, "What kept you? We've places to be." Yaz admitted over that night's stew that her dog-theory might just be wishful thinking, but Erris surprised her by agreeing.

"The maintenance units were built to be useful. Zox believes he is being useful. This maximizes a measure within him that you or I would call happiness."

Thurin, who seemed almost too weary to lift his bowl to his lips, gave Erris a narrow look. "It's a made thing—like the toys our scavengers and smiths will sometimes fashion from pieces they find in the city. Norcris used to make these . . . he called them crabs . . . powered by a coiled spring. They would scuttle across the ground."

Erris nodded. "It is a made thing. Like the hunters in the city, or the Watcher beneath the Black Rock."

"And it can be happy?" Thurin raised a brow. "Were Norcris's crabs happy because they moved forward?"

"Are true crabs happy when they scuttle across the bottom of the ocean?" Erris countered.

"You're a made thing too," Thurin said, getting to the crux of his point.

196 + MARK LAWRENCE

It didn't feel like an attack to Yaz. More a pointed form of curiosity, but how Erris might take it she wasn't sure.

"There's nothing in you that wasn't forged in the Missing's smithies. All metal and board? Unless there's your actual heart beating away somewhere inside that body?" Thurin shook his head. "And I know there's not. I can't sense any water in you at all. Not even enough for tears."

Erris nodded thoughtfully. "It's true. There's nothing in here that wasn't made by me using the machinery of the Missing. Except . . . information. The story of who I am, which was held inside Vesta's mind, the void star at the heart of the city, and was placed in here." He tapped his head. "And whether that's really me or not is something I struggle with. It feels like me. I believe I'm the same man who fell into the city all those years ago, enough years for ice to swallow the world I knew. But I can't ever *know* it for sure. The idea that the real Erris has been dead for thousands of years and that his world stopped the moment his fall ended. I don't know what to do with that."

Thurin frowned, looking shamed but unsure of what to say. He opted for lifting his bowl and taking his time over a hot mouthful.

Yaz said nothing and later laid her head down, chasing the impossible circles of thought that must have haunted Erris for far longer than she had been alive. Was he a copy? Was a perfect copy the same thing as the original? And did it really matter one way or another to anyone who hadn't met the original Erris? Everyone who had ever met the Erris that wandered into the city ruins so very long ago was dead along with thirty generations of their offspring and more besides.

Eventually her dreams took her, leaving the questions unresolved.

DAYS PASSED AND the miles disappeared beneath their feet. The wind blew this way, then that. A storm came and for three days they hid within their shelter, praying to many gods that it would hold. When at last they emerged, the howling voice of the gale had all but entombed them in ice that had built upon the boards in a way it couldn't on the more flexible tents of the Ictha. Erris pointed to two support wires that had snapped. The ice had actually kept the shelter up, a compacted wall inches thick that would remain standing if the boards could somehow be removed without damage. Erris did the necessary damage and repaired the wires, binding end to end, twisting them together with powerful fingers.

WEEKS PASSED AND Thurin began to find his strength, or perhaps they all weakened to his level. It was hard to tell. Hard to say how many miles they trekked each day. The landscape wasn't without features: there were pressure ridges, variations in the tone and texture of the ice, rare places where snow had managed to build to a thickness—but these were not ways in which to mark the passage of distance.

In all those empty miles across long and silent weeks they had yet to see a single human, or the slightest sign that anyone had ever walked this way. Several times a day Yaz would call a halt, have Erris lift her to his shoulders and make a slow turn while she scoured the horizon for any telltale hint of a hot sea. Any hot sea could be spotted from across vast distances by the steam rising from them. But how long the steam persisted and how high it reached was at the mercy of the winds. And the winds were never merciful.

A month into their journey the food supplies began to run low. There had never been any realistic prospect of making the trip without resupply. It might well take them a year to reach the green lands. Daily progress was slowed by weather and broken ice. The Ictha might manage thirty miles in a day but the Ictha were not like other people, the Ictha were a different breed, and certainly Thurin could manage little more than ten. There was no way to drag a year's worth of food behind you across the ice. Not even with an iron dog to do the pulling for the group. And to take enough food for four people for a year from the supplies needed to feed over two hundred newly woken people stolen from the Broken would have been too great an imposition. Even for the person who freed them. *Especially* for her. Yaz had not woken them to freedom only for that freedom to be the freedom to starve.

Her original plan had been a fever-dream and she marvelled now that the others had been either so desperate or so trusting as to believe in it too. Marching beyond the limits of their food they would have had to rely on the generosity of strangers to feed them. And both generosity and strangers were a great rarity on the ice.

Now, thanks to Quell, they had the boat-sled and the tackle stored inside it. All they needed was a sea and they could feed themselves. Even with hundreds of miles between them Quell was still clan, still looking after her.

"We need to find a sea." Yaz was walking with Thurin at the front of the group. The miles had toughened him and he was holding his own now.

"That seems to be more difficult than anyone suspected." Thurin didn't look her way. They had had this conversation before. All of them had.

A hundred paces passed in silence.

Thurin broke it. "And seas are bigger than the Black Rock, right?" He still sounded incredulous when he said this—as if the Black Rock had shattered his old beliefs about how big a thing could actually be and in doing so had defined a new upper limit.

"Quite a lot bigger," Yaz said. "Though, to be fair, they are holes in the ice rather than big chunks of rock that stick up into the sky. But the steam trails can rise higher than the Black Rock—under the right conditions."

"We need to see a sea." Thurin repeated the mantra that had become commonplace among them.

"Storm's coming," Quina called out from the back where she was walking beside Zox. "Snow!"

Yaz looked over her shoulder at the bruised northern sky. It did look like snow, though her experience of that was limited. She hadn't seen snow fall, save at the margins of a hot sea, since she was a little girl, but five days before the gathering there had been tiny white flakes on the wind, enough to swirl in pure white currents across the ice. And here it was again. Erris had said that the fact it snowed at all was for him the biggest reason to believe a green belt still existed. The water in the snow had to evaporate off the sea, he said, and the tiny seas that sustained the ice tribes were far too small to account for it. Yaz had bridled at "tiny" and declared the Hot Sea of the North to be fully ten miles across, sometimes. Erris covered a smile and said that in his day the oceans had been somewhat larger.

"Snow?" Thurin asked.

"A kind of powdered ice that falls from the sky." Yaz picked up the pace. "With luck it will miss us."

Thurin frowned. "It doesn't sound dangerous."

"I've heard it can be," Yaz said. "If there's a lot of it."

THEY MARCHED ON for half a day, keeping ahead of the storm, though it grew steadily closer, a strange mounding and twisting of clouds. The clouds themselves were an oddity. Usually the sky lay clear, occasionally slashed with high ribbons of mist glittering like a trillion ice crystals. But this was different, a low, thick, billowed mass like the steam clouds rising from a sea, but a thousand times bigger.

"There's something ahead," Maya called out from behind them.

Yaz lifted her gaze from the ground. For some miles now the ice beneath their feet had been a strangely clear kind she had seen only rarely before. A bluish-green ice into which vision would penetrate seemingly for a dozen yards and more before flaws and distortions blurred the line of sight. At one point Erris had spotted several large fish frozen in the act of swimming. They had argued for some time about the trade-off between the energy and resources required to extract the fish from three or four yards of ice and the benefits of enhancing their dwindling supplies. Thurin was eager to use his ice-work but Yaz knew the effort would open him to the cold. In the end they had moved on reluctantly in order to keep ahead of the storm, leaving the fish behind. Soon the snow would cover it all over and any temptation would be removed.

Ever since, though, Yaz had been scouring the ice in front of her in the hope of more fish, even larger ones, closer to the surface. And while her eyes roamed the depths ahead her mind tried to fathom how fish came to be in the ice in the first place. Maybe the same mechanism that had entombed the whale was at play, but that had been miles down. She'd seen a dozen of them so far, redfin, herring, gailes, and some unknown species, closer to the surface but still more than a yard down and most too small to warrant digging out. Thurin did, however, shatter a path down to three of the most accessible, adding two fat gailes and a greenling to their stores.

Now Yaz stared ahead to see what Maya had spotted. She had to blink at the whiteness for quite some time until her vision adjusted and she saw what Maya had been talking about. So much of her wanted it to be a sea that for a long moment Yaz was convinced that she was seeing a steam trail running close to the ice. But such delusions are hard to maintain more than fleetingly and she soon saw what it was.

"That is the biggest pressure ridge I've ever seen."

They slowed as they came closer to the ridge. Over the weeks they'd seen their fair share of the formations. Clan wisdom was that the ridges formed for a variety of reasons including the tidal forces of the Ooonai, the day star that appears every eleven years or so, or earthquakes far below the ice, or places where the sea beneath the ice becomes land and the ice fights its way ashore. Some were lines of broken and jagged ice, anything from a few feet tall to a dozen yards. Others had been smoothed by the wind into curving glassy walls. This one was at least a hundred feet high and something between the two extremes, neither jagged nor wind-contoured but on the path from the former to the latter, its surfaces lumpy but fairly smooth.

So far when faced with difficult climbs Yaz had slanted their course southeast or southwest until the passage of miles subsumed the ridge into the ice. This one, however, ran east to west and stretched away towards infinity in both directions.

"Left or right?" Erris asked, joining Thurin, Maya, and Yaz in craning his neck at the white heights.

"Over." Quina joined them. The dog plodded up behind her, the boat-sled rumbling after it.

"Seriously?" Yaz turned, frowning. "Someone will slip and break a bone. Or several bones."

"Or die," Maya said.

"The food's nearly gone. The sled's about as light as it's ever going to get." Quina eyed the ridge. "We need to get south. We need to see a sea."

Erris joined Yaz in frowning at Quina. "Seems unnecessarily dangerous."

"Everything we do is dangerous. It's just a slow kind of danger that we don't notice. This is just a week's danger all rolled up into one exciting lump." She managed a narrow grin.

"Exciting?" Yaz shook her head. "You've gone ice-mad." She had to admit, though, that trekking untold miles and getting no further south would be hard to take.

Quina shrugged. "It might turn the storm too. We could be safe on the other side."

Yaz looked up at the heights. She didn't know enough about snow-storms to say whether a wall of ice would divert them. But it might be worth a try. Even so—it looked impossible.

"I'll climb it," Maya said. "Find a path for the rest of you."

Thurin shook his head. "It should be me."

"You think I can't do it?" Maya shot him a dangerous look that made him laugh, a bubbling good-humoured chuckle at odds with his often brooding demeanour.

"I think you can climb . . . but I know *I* can do this." Thurin rose from the ice, nothing but empty air beneath his feet. "And this." He reached a hand towards the ridge and the surface burst into a cloud of white that, when the wind tore it away, left a series of deep grooves.

"Roll me in the furs!" Quina blinked in amazement. "The boy really can fly!"

Yaz found herself glad that she had kept him from spending his ener-gies on pulling fish from the ice. The rest of them just stared, trying to adjust to this new reality. Thurin had told them how he lifted himself out of the Broken's caves but he'd never shown them.

"Thurin goes up first," Yaz said.

Zox plodded past them, tugging the boat-sled. Thurin, Maya, and Quina backed away hurriedly to give room to the star on the sled.

"He seems keen too," Erris said, his smile cracking the ice that had formed across the windward side of his face.

The dog reached the lower slopes of the ridge where a jumble of wind-smoothed ice blocks abutted the more steeply rising upper section, and began to nose a path through the larger ones. On finding an impasse, the black metal claws on its feet grew a couple of inches longer and the dog started to climb the ice.

"Help Zox," Yaz said to Thurin. "If he falls and the sled is broken . . ." She didn't have to finish. Even if they found a sea, no boat meant no fish.

Zox made slow but steady progress, anchoring three of his feet at any given time by sinking his long talons into the ice, then reaching up with his free foot to gain another six inches. The fact that he had the entire weight of the boat-sled dangling from him along with all their supplies didn't seem to bother him at all.

Thurin climbed alongside the iron dog, making ledges to stand on while he watched Zox's progress and checked the ice to ensure it would hold the weight.

Yaz and the rest of them made their way up on a parallel course, using ice axes for traction and occasionally calling on Thurin's skill to put steps in the ice or just roughen the surface.

From her time in the undercity, clambering through the dry chambers of the Missing, Yaz was no longer a stranger to climbing, but at least in those chambers and shafts there had been a kindly darkness to hide the full extent of the fall. Also, she'd not had to contend with the wind's sudden malicious attempts to pluck her from her perch and discard her into gravity's care. The pressure ridge proved a more daunting ascent than any Yaz had made before.

"It's only going to get worse," said Erris helpfully from a few yards below her. "If we're still climbing when that storm hits . . ."

"It's not going to—" But looking over her shoulder the shock at how close the storm had got almost made Yaz lose hold.

From their current elevation they could see an incredible distance to the east and west, but in the north the advancing snow cut that short. "Is there . . ." A glint had caught her eye, a red flash, like the glimmer of sunlight on metal. There was something on the ice, just ahead of the storm front. "There's someone coming!"

Erris turned at that, digging the fingers of one hand into a crack in the ice to secure himself. "Where?"

The storm front, a looming, swirling wall of white below the darker thunderhead, made it hard to see anything but snow.

"Back along our trail." Yaz wasn't so sure now. The black dot had all but vanished, perhaps becoming lost in the flurries ahead of the storm, or perhaps it had always been a figment of her imagination.

Erris stared. He raised a finger to the side of his head, to the corner of his eye, pressing as if that might somehow adjust his vision. "Hells."

"What is it?"

"I think . . ." Erris continued to stare at the advancing snows.

"Yes?"

"I think we need to climb faster!"

Yaz followed Erris's advice and advanced up the roughened slopes that Thurin had prepared for them. She swung her axe, hauled herself higher, took hold, swung again. The wind had begun to fracture from one into many as it does before any great storm, infected by a wildness that has it running first this way then that.

"What did you see?" Yaz asked Erris again.

"I don't know."

The fact that he wouldn't say was in itself as worrying as anything he might say.

Zox was nearing the top now, the entire weight of the loaded boat-sled dangling behind him, swinging in the swirling wind. Any slip and their journey was over, even if they managed to travel on for a few more miles.

Quina and Maya were about two-thirds of the way to the top, Erris and Yaz below them, though Yaz knew that Erris had opted to come last. Thurin stood at the very top, buffeted by the gale that sheared its way over the barrier. Even at this distance Yaz imagined she could see a hint of boy-ish pride on his face—king of the castle. She smiled to herself in turn and swung her axe. It was good that he had a chance to shine after being for so long the weakest link in their chain.

Yaz saw the hoola before it struck but so briefly and in such a state of shock that her dry throat had no time to release her scream.

The thing moved like an eel, a snaking motion, flowing along just beneath the crest of the ridge as if it weren't a near-vertical wall of ice. Six-legged and perhaps three yards long, the beast was much as they appeared in the kettan that the Ictha carved from whalebone during the long night, a sort of stretched-out dog with a squashed-in face, mottled silver-white fur, and long black claws. It was on Thurin before any of them, even Quina, had time to register its presence. It pinned him with two forefeet, anchored itself with its rear feet, and tore at him with its middle pair, shredding furs as it sought to disembowel him. There were many tales of hoola attacks and the constant was that where a dog would go for the throat a hoola's first move was to rip out your guts. Often it would start to devour your entrails before you'd stopped screaming.

All of them started shouting at once; Thurin's cry was the loudest of all. An instinctive burst of power threw the hoola away from him but its front claws kept their hold and both of them flew into the air in a blur of motion.

Somehow Thurin managed to free himself, hanging in space above the near-vertical slope while the hoola fell away, a large flap of tuark hide trailing in its claws. The creature twisted in the air and, seemingly defying gravity almost as well as Thurin, it landed on the dog.

Zox shuddered under the impact and a white shower of ice broke away around the four anchor points where his talons were bedded in the ridge. In the space of two heartbeats Yaz watched first one then another precious thing hang on the edge of disaster.

The boat-sled swung wildly in the strengthening wind as the hoola scrabbled at Zox with all six paws, simultaneously trying to find purchase on the dog and to tear it open.

For a moment it looked as if they would both hold, Zox to the ice and the hoola to Zox. But there was only so much weight their claws could endure. Zox's left front foot came free of the ice in a shower of fragments. The hoola lost traction and paw by paw lost contact with Zox's blunt curves, leaving the iron scored with bright lines. Zox peeled away from the ice face, another foot torn free.

The hoola fell, howling a thin cry of rage that set Yaz's teeth on edge and put the same kind of fear in her that the holothaur had. Something primal that prey feels when a predator turns their way.

Somehow Zox kept his place, driving back the foot that had broken free of the ice.

The hoola was on the nose of the boat-sled now, thrashing among the four long reins that bound the sled to Zox. The first line parted with a twang. The hoola spun around on the too-small platform provided by the sled, slashing out in fury at the sled, at the reins, at the ice wall itself. Another line surrendered and the sled lurched to the side. Taking its cue, the hoola leapt clear.

Defying common wisdom regarding falling, the hoola twisted the sinuous length of its body in midair and snagged the ice, skidding to a halt on a prominence jutting out of the slope. Without warning, it flung itself sideways and suddenly Quina was in the centre of its black gaze.

Quina moved as swiftly as Yaz had ever seen anyone move, hunska speed propelling her up the slope faster than falling. She vaulted from lump to lump, taking advantage of the roughness Thurin had induced.

The hoola almost missed her, snagging only her calf with an outstretched paw as it sailed past, yowling in rage. Maya had been close to Quina on the climb but there was no sign of the girl now. She must have wrapped herself in whatever shadow she could find and made herself one with the ice. Given time the hoola would doubtless sniff her out but instead it clawed the ridge, found its balance and tore down the slope, aiming at Yaz.

Yaz reached for the Path, its power her only chance. It had been weeks since she had last used it, to blast a path through a smaller pressure ridge, and the Path had begun to press on her mind as if it wanted her to follow it. Summoning the energies, letting them flow through her, was always less difficult if she were calm and in possession of ample time. Even so, she found her hands glowing, crackling with stray power.

For half a second she hesitated, even as the hoola surged towards her, gouging the ice in its frenzy of forward motion. Mother Mazai talked of a clan to the south that worshipped the hoola and, even with her friends injured and herself at risk, Yaz understood where that worship came from. To wring out an existence alone on the ice as the hoola did was an astonishing thing, a testament to the refusal of life to wholly relinquish its grip on this frozen world. Like the Ictha, the hoola travelled from sea to sea in search of food, but unlike the Ictha the hoola managed alone, meeting others of its kind only briefly in the steams of a hot sea when the mating frenzy was on them.

Yaz raised her hands reluctantly, not wanting to destroy the creature. Like them it was a lone mote of warmth in the endless expanse of the white death, an extraordinary survivor dedicated to a lonely road. Beautiful in its way.

Erris propelled himself past Yaz into the hoola's path, willing to pit his speed and strength against the hoola's to save her if she wasn't going to save herself. At the same moment Yaz let fly, sending her power towards the hoola in a bright line of destruction. It struck the ice in front of the beast and exploded a section of the slope, flinging the hoola into space once more. The hoola fell again, this time too far from the ridge to save itself. Yaz found herself falling too, struck by a large chunk of ice and peppered by many more sharp fragments. A hand caught her and swung her back against the ice.

Yaz found herself hanging from one arm, her gaze directed back down the fifty feet of the ridge she had climbed so far. The storm had raced towards them, its full fury only a hundred yards or so off. The space between the storm front and the wall was already thick with loose snow being blown ahead of it and rising in swirling flurries to hide the ground.

Yaz saw the hoola hit the ice, landing on all six feet without apparent discomfort as if it had jumped down a small drop rather than been flung halfway down the tallest pressure ridge Yaz had ever seen. It raised its head, baleful eyes making contact with her momentarily before the snow swirled again, taking the beast from view.

Erris hauled Yaz back onto the ledge that she'd been knocked from. The wind was so fierce and cold that she was shivering, her cheeks numb and stiff, eyes glazing with ice.

"It's still alive," he said.

"I'm glad," Yaz said, still staring at the spot where it had landed. And she found that she *was* glad. It would have weighed heavily on her if she had used her gift to destroy the creature.

"Come on!" Erris began to climb.

"Wait." Yaz sensed something, a familiar tingle at the edge of her mind . . . Stars.

A moment later the snows swirled away to reveal the base of the ridge once more. The hoola hadn't moved, wasn't moving, but something else was. Something large with long metal limbs emerged from the storm and snatched up the hoola in yard-long steel fingers. In one brutal motion it tore the hoola into two halves, staining the ice with gore. The storm covered the scene, hammering into the ridge, slamming Yaz back against the ice and trying to take her feet out from under her. Erris kept his grip. Yaz hung, shocked, still trying to understand that last glimpse before the snow took away her vision.

There had been a monster far larger than a man. And in place of a head the monster had a metal dome, and about the dome half a dozen stars orbited, all of them red as blood.

26

YAZ FELT HER way towards the top of the ridge blinded by snow, blasted by white winds that sought to tear her from the ever-steeper wall of ice. She fell once, losing her gloved grip as she swung her axe and sliding back with a despairing cry. Erris caught her two yards lower down. With her eyes and mouth full of driving snow she could do little but begin to feel her way back up again.

Somewhere below her the Watcher could already be climbing, ready to tear them all apart just as it had destroyed the hoola. The threat loaned an extra urgency to an already urgent climb and had perhaps contributed to the mistake that had almost seen her drop to her death.

"... op ... ee ... urin ..." Erris was hollering something right behind her but the wind stripped his words away before she caught their meaning.

Yaz could feel the strain of the climb in her arms, and in the long muscles of her legs. Her fingers were growing numb and she was starting to sweat. That alone could be a death sentence on the ice. Sweat compromised the ability of furs to keep a body warm. She tried to calm her breathing and not think about the long-fingered killing machine that had murdered Kao, ripped open a full-grown hoola, and was now hunting them down.

Steady progress. That was the Ictha way. Any task could be overcome by steady, unrelenting progress.

The sudden blast of wind as Yaz reached the top of the ridge almost slung her over it. She found herself twisted around, hanging on to the ice with gloved hands while the gale tried to trail her body out behind her over the drop of the far side. A desperate struggle got her clear and down below the whistling edge.

The air was clearer here, the wind less strong, and Thurin lay close at hand on a ledge of his own making. The ice around him was stained pink, smeared with blood. He greeted her with a pale-faced smile.

"W-what in the hells was *that* thing?"

"Hoola." Yaz scrambled to his side as Erris dropped down behind her. A kind of horrified calm enfolded her. This couldn't be happening. She didn't want to lift Thurin's furs and see the damage there. She couldn't stand it. Her mind refused the situation much as it had refused when Zeen had vanished wailing into the Pit of the Missing. "Let me see."

Thurin gave a thin, brave smile and leaned his head back, no keener to see than she was.

Erris had moved to where Zox's reins ran taut across the top of the ridge behind the descending dog. He struggled to help the sled over as it came. "Yaz, we need to go," Erris hollered across at them. "That was the Watcher!"

Yaz ignored him. Steeling herself, she pulled aside Thurin's tattered furs, then the furs beneath them and the hides beneath those, and the rat-skin cloak. "How much are you wearing?"

"All of it." Thurin lifted his head and winced. "How bad am I?"

Yaz dug deeper. The hoola's claws had shredded all the many layers and torn into Thurin but far less deeply than they otherwise would have. The wounds were bloody but not so deep that they spurted or revealed the organs beneath. "You'll live."

"Yaz! The Watcher!" Erris shouted as he strained to lower the sled below the now-stationary Zox. He rarely sounded worried but he was clearly worried now.

"The Watcher?" Thurin sat up and pulled his torn furs around him, shivering. "How is that thing here? You said it would fall apart if it got too far from the void star."

"It should have." Erris rejoined them. "But it didn't."

"If it found us after all this time we're not going to get away from it by running now." Yaz looked up at the ridge just above them. She could feel the thing on the other side of the ice wall, its many stars a choir with a dark song passing between them. Just how close or far it was, though, she couldn't tell. Most of her wanted to run anyway. A small part wanted to face the monster and obliterate it for what it did to Kao.

"We have to go." Erris started to follow his own advice, pausing to ask, "Quina? Maya? Did they come over?"

"Yes," Thurin said. "I told them—"

Two long iron fingers hooked over the ridge, their needle-pointed tips driving deep into the ice.

"Shit!" Erris stopped his descent and reached for Thurin. "Yaz, help me with him."

But Thurin rose without help from either Erris or from his own legs, turning in the air as if grasped by the hand of an invisible giant. "I hit this thing with a flood before." He reached out with both hands, wincing as his wounds pulled. "Let's try a different way."

The Watcher's other hand clamped over the top of the ridge, all three fingers hooking into the ice. The driving snow began to colour with the bloody light of the stars and their song rose in a shrill chorus.

"For Kao." Thurin spoke the words quietly but a moment later the ridgetop shattered with a deafening cracking and for twenty yards to either side the top ten feet of the ridge fell back into the oncoming storm, an unknown tonnage of broken ice falling with the Watcher towards the flat ground far below.

Thurin landed lightly on his feet, braced against the unchecked wind at the jagged new summit of the ridge. "Now we can go."

ALL OF THE group gathered at the base of the pressure ridge, sheltering from the storm winds. The ridge was less tall on this side as the ice sheet was thicker, but it was still tall enough to provide some protection.

They watched Zox continue to make his way slowly down after them, dangling their boat-sled precariously beneath him on two reins. Above, the sky continued to darken and snow filtered down, though falling less thickly than it did just thirty yards further out from the ridge.

"How did that thing find us?" Yaz asked. It seemed impossible.

"Zox, most likely." Erris didn't take his eyes off the dog. "He sends out signals every so often, trying to connect to the city network. And there are still . . . objects—stars, if you like—that the Missing placed in the skies above us, above the highest clouds, up beyond the air. Those can relay Zox's signals across a great distance."

"Well, tell him to shut up then!" Quina suggested.

Erris glanced at her. "It's a very basic function—hard to shut down. And who knows, we may need to find a city before this journey's over." He looked back up at the dog, just ten yards above them now. "The real question is how the Watcher was functioning so far from Vesta. It should have fallen apart within a day's travel from the city."

"Zox didn't," Thurin said. The snow fell everywhere but on him, warded away by his ice-work.

"Zox is like me, built by the Missing or, in my case, by their machinery. The Watcher was made by the priesthood, cobbled together and forced to function by using stars to drive it. Once something like that goes too far from the will of the person who animated it and the augmenting effect of the void star . . . it reverts to its components."

"Little help . . ." Maya had moved to intercept the boat-sled as it neared the ice and was trying to ensure it ended the right way up. Even as she reached up towards it the last but one of its four reins surrendered to the strain with an audible twang and the whole weight of the sled swung on a single strand.

"No!" Yaz's despairing cry echoed off the ridge as she flung herself towards Maya. Knowing the boat-sled to be life and death to them, Yaz scrambled to get underneath it, less worried about being crushed than about the boat being holed. Quina and Erris, slower than her for once, reached her side as she made contact, their hands accepting some of the weight.

Grunting and cursing, they got the sled safely on the ice. Zox followed, unperturbed. As Quina hobbled back to Thurin, one foot leaving faint red prints on the ice, Yaz remembered that the girl too had been hurt.

✦ ✦ ✦

YAZ LED THEM on despite the snow, knowing that each day spent hiding in their shelter was another day's food gone with no miles to show for it.

Thurin trudged on without complaint, though Yaz could see that he was moving stiffly, favouring his wounds. They'd bound some softer hides around the gashes and tried to arrange his layers so that the rips no longer matched up to give the wind access to his flesh.

Quina limped beside Thurin. The hoola's swipe had torn her calf. She'd been lucky not to have the muscle sliced through. Erris had bound her bloody leg and she'd stood on it with a gasp and an "I'm alright. Let's go."

The Broken would advise rest and healing. The Ictha would leave Thurin to die. Yaz settled on a middle ground that pleased nobody. They had no healing and rest would only see them starve, so instead they matched their pace to Thurin's. Yaz offered to take the large star so that he could ride on the sled, and he considered the offer—something that his pride had not allowed in the early days of their expedition.

"I had better walk," he said. "If I stop I'm not sure if I could start again."

And so they walked on.

THE SNOW BECAME as big a problem as the wind after just a few miles. Although the grains were small and driven at a near-horizontal angle by the wind, they were also never-ending and began to build up in a layer above the ice. Soon they were wading through the stuff.

"I never knew water could do this." Thurin brushed snow from his hair and eyes. "I can sense the flakes." A kind of wonder echoed in his voice. "They're so complicated and . . . perfect . . . and each one is different. I—"

"They all look the same to me," Quina grumbled.

"They're not, though," Thurin said. "I thought if I knew one thing in life it was ice. And now I find it falls from the sky in crystals that chime as they hit the ground, each with its own note."

Yaz managed a smile. She had seen precious little snow in her life and never this much at once. Even so, it was making progress impossible. The wind was mounding it into drifts and they were only going to get bigger. "We have to make camp."

THEY'D SET THE shelter up so many times that even in a snow-laden gale they were inside not long after unpacking the boards from the sled. Zox stayed outside as he always did, calmly folding into his cube. Yaz imagined they might have to dig down to find him in the morning.

Inside the shelter it seemed that the snow had somehow blunted the wind. The gaps soon packed with the stuff and the howls outside were strangely muted. In the heat pot the stars had diminished somewhat and were burning faster, but they would long outlast the food, and with snow caking the boards the shelter soon became warmer than it had been on any night of their journey.

"I could get used to this." Thurin stretched then winced, rediscovering his wounds.

"Let me see." Quina was at his side, pulling up layers of fur, her quickness defeating Yaz, who was closer to him, and leaving her feeling . . . she examined the emotion . . . leaving her feeling slightly jealous.

Erris leaned in too. "We have to watch for infection. The cold sterilizes pretty much everything but these slices came from an animal's claws and germs can lurk in such places. Often by design, so that wounded prey can easily be tracked and killed."

"Thanks for the lesson." Thurin grimaced as Quina touched his belly. "I'll try to bear it in mind next time I'm deciding whether to let a monster gut me. Anyway, check Quina, she got hurt too."

"She's next on my list," Erris said. "Lie still."

"Grey-scale stew tonight." Maya got the blackened pan ready. "Though there's no salt left . . ." She chipped something else from the much-diminished block of frozen fungi. "A copper-cap!"

"Yay!" Quina made a halfhearted cheer while frowning over Thurin's injuries. Copper-caps were slightly spicy. In lieu of salt they made grey-scale stew—which was just grey-scale mushrooms boiled in water—slightly more appetizing.

"This one's deeper than I thought." Erris pointed to where a hoola claw had torn Thurin lower down towards his groin. "I could skin-bond it but stitches would be more durable." He looked around at Yaz, Maya, and Quina. "Stitching? Anyone?"

From his supine position Thurin sighed then snorted. "Don't look at them, they'd all send me out into the snow to die if you weren't here. I hear that the clans will repair a sled harness a thousand times rather than discard it, but if a person gets hurt . . ."

"It's down to me then, I suppose." Erris bowed his head. "Anyone got a needle?"

Maya produced one of the bodkins that they used to sew the boards together with wire through pre-bored holes.

Yaz watched with interest, revulsion, and a mild sense of shame as Erris sealed the deepest of Thurin's gashes with a series of deft stitches, having first sterilized the needle—used for repairing furs—and thread by boiling water in the pan then immersing them in it.

Seeing the thick needle dip in and out of Thurin's skin suddenly reminded Yaz that she was wearing a smaller, finer needle. She patted her hides anxiously, worried that she might have lost it. But no, there it was, the silver needle that Elias Taproot had given her in some strange corner of Vesta's city mind. He'd said it would lead her to him again, something she had no desire for. Taproot's interest in her had brought her to Seus's attention, as if she didn't have enough problems to contend with. No, Yaz intended to have nothing more to do with Taproot, and to hope that Seus forgot about her. She was sure that a distant and crazed city mind had more important things to occupy its thoughts than one Ictha girl lost on the ice.

By the time Erris had finished with Thurin then Quina, and all of them save Erris had eaten their rather meagre portion of stew, the snow had sealed away all but the loudest of the storm's yowls. The relative silence reminded Yaz of the Broken's caves and felt rather odd after so many nights in their rattling shelter. She wondered how Arka, Kaylal, Madeen, and all the others were doing. Her stomach rumbled at the thought of the whale they must still be feasting on down there out of the wind.

"Are you alright?" Quina asked Thurin. She had offered to spoon his stew into his mouth earlier, and Yaz had been glad to see him decline her feeding.

"Just sore." Thurin eased himself back with a wince. "After due reflection I've decided not to recommend hoola-wrestling to any of the other Broken who opt to come up top."

"It's lucky you were wearing twenty-seven layers," Maya said. "Or your insides would have been on the outside."

Thurin gave a little shudder and shot Yaz a "rescue me" look. "Tell us a story?"

"I think you've heard them all . . ." Evening storytelling had become a tradition with them, even after days when all of them wanted to pitch headlong into sleep. Thurin claimed that even Zox moved in closer to listen and that you could tell how good a story it was by seeing how close to the shelter his cube had ended up.

"All used up?" Erris shook his head sadly. "You're no Scheherazade."

"Schey . . ." Yaz tried to fit her lips around the strange-sounding word.

"A storyteller in a story. She had over a thousand tales."

"Never heard of her," Quina said, getting back into the conversation.

"Ah, well, it's a *very* old story. It's even said that our ancestors brought it with them when they came to Abeth." Erris smiled at the notion.

"Across the black sea . . ." Quina said. "You should tell us that story!"

"I'm no good at stories." Erris held his hands up. "Besides, I've forgotten almost everything about it."

"But you've reminded me of a story *I'd* forgotten. A very old one," Yaz said, and she told it.

There was a time, shortly after Zin first climbed from the sea to find Mokka camped on the clifftop, when Mashtri came blowing around their tent. The trickster god was jealous of her brother and sister's creations. Mashtri called to Zin and Mokka but they mistrusted her and stayed within the tent. Next Mashtri made creatures out of the ice and breathed life into them, wanting to make people of her own, but they all became monsters, cruel of tooth and claw. They circled

Mokka's tent, howling and hissing, and still Zin and Mokka would not come out.

Enraged, Mashtri blew up a great storm and tried to tear the tent from the ice. But Mokka was born of the wind and her tent resisted the gale. Mashtri gnashed her teeth. "Come out!" she cried. But the first man and the first woman stayed inside. And so, in her frustration, Mashtri reached up and took away the sun. She hid it for the longest time, leaving all the world in the darkness of its first night. "Come out!" she cried. "And I will give you a new day." But Zin was born of the sea and the darkness therein, and his courage resisted the night.

At last Mashtri returned the sun and tried a different trick. She brought a new colour to the ice and named it green. "See what I have done," she cried. "You don't need to come out—just lift the flap of your tent and see."

"When I was first told this story by our clan mother," Yaz said, "I asked about the green and she said that the ice was green and Mashtri made towers like we do at the garden ceremony at the end of the long night. But I'm going to tell it using what Erris has shown me—the way the green world really is."

Mashtri called to them and, as so often since, it was curiosity rather than fears or demands that moved man to action. Zin peered from the tent and was amazed. A thick green carpet of grass had covered the ice, a billion green blades taming the wind—as many as there are snowflakes in a storm. Trees stood beyond the grass, taller than three gerants standing in a tower. Great spears of wood, thicker than a man, rising from the ground and dividing and dividing and dividing into a complication of branches and twigs. Each tree possessed of an infinity of leaves, all green and delicate and fluttering.

Zin emerged; he trod the softness of the grass, and his wonder drew Mokka behind him, and at her smile bees and flutterbys rose from the grass in a great dance that was fast where it was small and slow where it was large. And the air was warm, warm enough even to melt the ice if there had been any left to see.

Yaz paused and looked around the tent. Erris's smile had a mixture of sadness and amusement in it. Quina and Thurin were openmouthed, hanging on her words, Quina with her wooden bead clutched in white fingers, pressed to her lips. Maya's dark eyes swam with tears. All of them lean and windburned, huddled in a snow-buried tent, all their purpose bound on this endless walk to the south in the hope of a miracle—the same miracle that Yaz was painting for them.

Mokka led Zin towards the trees and they found a legion of them, more than there are fish in the sea, a forest that stretched on without end. And in among the trees and their branches and the . . . plants . . . that grew between them were animals, a hundred kinds, big and small, dogs, and bears, and . . . deer . . . and many more, and birds in many shapes, not a gull among them.

In that warmth, that heat, the wind hardly stirred, just enough to make the leaves dance and gently sway the branches. Zin and Mokka wandered, reaching up to take pieces of the trees that they could eat, listening to the soft silence of living.

Mashtri followed, laughing to herself, for she had blinded them with a dream that she had found behind the stars, and now she led them where she willed. Zin and Mokka saw the green world, but in truth it was still the ice that they roamed, guided now by Mashtri's lies. Following a fleet-footed deer that wasn't truly there. Following a trail that existed only in Mashtri's glamour. Following the song of a bird that was nothing but a god's mocking laughter.

Mashtri kept the lovers enspelled until they came at last to the place that she wished to show them. And when they arrived after a journey of many weeks, bone-thin, fever-eyed, fed only on imagination, sustained on wonder, Mashtri let the true wind, which she had kept at bay, return. The green world shredded before the wind's knives and blew away, its tatters torn from Zin's eyes, its warmth stripped from Mokka's back.

Mashtri had brought the woman made by Aiiki, least of the Gods in the Sky, and the man made by Hua, least of the Gods in the Sea, to the shore of an endless black sea far colder than the ice yet unable to freeze.

"What have you done?" Mokka asked.

And Mashtri only smiled and turned her eyes towards the blackness.

"Someone is coming!" Zin cried, and Mokka saw that it was true.

Four boats came across the black sea, tiny and lost in its darkness. Zin and Mokka called to them, for it is a terrible thing to be lost on any sea, and this sea most of all. And the four boats heeded Zin's cries and Mokka's waving and beached upon the shore. And from those boats came new men and new women, the children of distant gods, gods neither of the wind nor the sea nor the ice.

"See?" cried Mashtri. "You are not special. You are not alone. Now each of you is one among many, like leaves on the tree, like trees in the forest." And Mashtri laughed for she thought she had shared the pain that had started with her own failure to make a man. And the desire to give pain, even though it may not decrease your own, has ever been the consequence of hurt.

But Zin and Mokka were not dismayed as Mashtri had thought they would be. "We are not alone," they cried. "At last! We are not alone!"

Mashtri fled then, across the ice, pursued by the laughter of a new beginning. And for many years Zin and Mokka were happier than they had known they could be—for company after a long time alone is like a new colour brought into a life.

In the end though, Mashtri's trick within a trick showed its face and her mirth reached them on the wind. For the tribes that had beached their boats after sailing the black sea carried a weakness with them that plagued the descendants of Zin and Mokka down the long *track of years. And Zin and Mokka went north and hid themselves and their trueborn children away, forbidding the people of the four boats to follow.*

Yaz cleared her throat. "And in this story Zin and Mokka never died but are still on the ice, but so far north that not even the Ictha can find them."

"I've not heard that one before," Quina said, smiling the rare smile of someone hearing a wholly new tale.

"Me neither." Maya nodded.

Thurin grinned. "Most of your stories are new to me. The versions that children bring down the pit with them are usually pretty basic, or rather garbled, or both."

Erris was frowning though.

"You knew it?" Yaz asked, disappointed.

"No." He shook his head. "I'm just thinking of what it means." He looked around at them. "The black sea is the space between the stars, obviously. And the four boats are the ships that carried our tribes here from their collapsing systems. They didn't all arrive at once, of course."

"Of course . . ." Yaz had no idea what Erris was saying.

"I say 'our tribes' because those ships carried my ancestors and the ancestors of everyone who ever lived in the green belt—as far as I know. But . . ." Here he turned to stare at Yaz. "But the tale is telling us that Zin and Mokka were *already here*. If there's any truth in this story, it's saying that Zin and Mokka were the Missing and that their race bred with ours . . . and that the people of the ice, or some of them at least, share their blood!"

Yaz opened her mouth to object but found she'd run out of words.

"You know . . . they do say . . ." Thurin gritted his teeth against the pain of his wounds and sat. ". . . that the Ictha are a different breed."

27

✦ ✦ ✦

ESPITE HER TIREDNESS, Yaz found sleep elusive that night. The thrill of touching the Path still echoed through her, along with the shock of first the hoola attack and then the Watcher emerging from the storm. And finally the notion that the Ictha might carry the blood of the Missing in their veins. That would make her related to monsters like Theus and all the evils haunting the black ice, but also to the people who shaped such vast cities and filled them with so many marvels.

Her last conscious thought harked back to the beginning of the story she'd told. The part where Mashtri, the trickster god, had covered Zin and Mokka with a green dream and led them astray. She wondered if the same thing had happened to her and her friends. A green dream was leading them across the ice with no certain destination. Could Mashtri be toying with them too, just as she had with the first man and the first woman?

Finally she stumbled into sleep and found herself falling once more, as she had fallen into the Pit of the Missing, as she had fallen into the heart of the city, as Erris had fallen into the void star.

YAZ WOKE, NOT surfacing by degrees, but all of a sudden, like plunging into cold water. She lay still, eyes wide, seeing only the roof of the shelter above her, lit by the faint glow from the heat pot. It was quiet, the wind a distant rumour, as if the snow had drifted and entombed them in their fragile house. She could even hear the faint sound of Maya snoring. The girl, so silent in the waking world, was the loudest of them at night, what with her snoring, sometimes gentle, sometimes rough, and her talking, words blurted out here and there, sometimes night terrors where a long string of fevered denials ended with piercing screams.

Yaz didn't know what had woken her. Something small, but something wrong . . . Suddenly a pressure built around her. When the dagger-fish had dragged her boat under the Hot Sea the water had begun to push on her in much the same way, growing worse with each yard they went deeper. And from one moment to the next Yaz understood the danger.

"Wa—" The din of breaking boards drowned out her warning.

In an instant everything was falling snow, sharp with pieces of board. Yaz tried to rise, tried to swim up through the soft but heavy coldness of the snow load. She saw swirling flakes now, falling from a black sky, all of them the colour of blood. A metal hand or foot stamped down beside her, three-fingered or three-toed. The Watcher had survived plummeting from the ridgetop, survived being buried in an avalanche of ice. It had dug itself out, come after them, and found them.

Yaz and her friends lay half-buried in the ruins of the shelter, finding themselves at the bottom of a pit in the snow, which rose around them on all sides, as deep as Yaz could reach on tiptoes.

The burnished dome of the Watcher's head loomed over Yaz, orbited by red stars. A hand that was nothing but three long, sharp fingers reached for her. Yaz screamed, despite herself, paralysed in the moment, knowing she would die. Around her the others were scrambling into action. An arm rose from the snow to hack at the Watcher's leg with an ice axe—Erris pinned to the ground by a great metal foot. Quina and Maya sought their weapons amid the whiteness.

A great white snake, large as an adult coal-worm, broke from the snow-banks and surged between Yaz and the Watcher, coiling around it, trying to drag it back into the thickness of the snow. The Watcher broke through it, scattering whiteness.

Thurin rose to his feet, conjuring a second snow snake from the drifts. A grimace of effort crossed his face and with a *crump* the snake compacted, drawing in its great girth from six feet in diameter to one foot, becoming an ice snake. This new, denser creation arrowed at the Watcher, striking it mid-torso and hurling it back.

"Yaz!" Erris was beside her, hauling her to her feet with one hand.

She looked wildly around. They were trapped. The collapse of their shelter had left a void in the snow, but in any direction they fled they would have to fight through snow as tall as Yaz and taller where it drifted. The easiest direction led back north along the trough that the Watcher had put in the snowfield on its way to them. But none of them would get far that way. Maya and Quina had risen to their feet, almost unrecognizable beneath the snow caked all over their furs.

Under Thurin's control the snow flowed like a milk sea, mounding over the Watcher and compacting, layer after layer squeezed down to add to the growing ice shroud already entombing the creature. The ice cracked and ruptured here and there as the Watcher exerted its strength, only for Thurin to pile on more.

"Stay back!" Thurin gestured for them to get behind him.

The ice mound glowed with the bloody light pouring from the Watcher's eyes, a premonition of the carnage that would follow if it got free. None of them could stand against it. With a mighty effort the Watcher fractured the ice again, a great crack forming as metal arms heaved from below. But Thurin poured fresh snow into the cracks, compacting it into more ice while loading still more on top. The nightmare scene about them seemed fitting: black sky; white snow stained crimson with the light from the mound. If the Watcher broke loose it would be a true nightmare, one from which none of them would wake.

"It's going to hold!" Quina cried.

"Good." Thurin sounded exhausted. The snowdrifts, rolling in like waves on the sea to feed his work, were slowing.

"The shadows are moving." Fear edged Maya's voice; without it she might have looked ridiculous caked in snow as she was, talking about shadows moving when the scene was *all* moving shadow and red light. "It's that thing from the Black Rock!"

"Of course it is . . ." Thurin trailed off when he saw that she didn't mean the Watcher. A darkness was dimming the red starlight and rising through the ice. A clotted darkness gathered above the trapped Watcher.

"Arges." As Yaz said it the holothaur's fear broke across them. Quina, Thurin, and Maya fled along the Watcher's approach path, tearing into the trampled snow, seeing nothing but their own terrors. Yaz, who had withstood the manipulation before, swung her arm to clear away the threads that carried the emotion out from Arges to infect everyone around him.

"Stop." Erris spoke through gritted teeth, fighting some internal battle against Arges, who seemed to be trying to disable the mechanics of his body as he had before.

"You thought you could destroy everything I've built over so many years?" Arges's outrage flowed across their minds. "You thought you could take what you wanted and leave?" His dark body pulsed and it seemed that a shape lay within the cloud of his being, a spindly twisted shape that had something in common with the Watcher's limbs. "Even without Seus's help I would have freed myself and hunted you down! He could have sent other servants to destroy you but I demanded I be the one. I wanted it more than they did. I *wanted* to see you bleed."

Yaz stepped towards him. "You failed before when you had us in your lair. You're not going to succeed here. You've got no body to use and your tricks don't work on me anymore."

Arges's laughter rode the wind. "I don't need a body. Look at where you are. Without shelter. I'll watch you all freeze to death. Slower, but still enjoyable."

Yaz couldn't think about survival in the open. She pushed the problem from her mind. Right now she needed revenge. She needed to be rid of Arges. The idea that he could stay to enjoy the rewards of the destruction he'd wrought on them could not be borne. If they were to expire in the white death, then it would not be with Arges gloating over them.

Beneath the ice the Watcher's eyes sang with Arges's wrongness. Yaz reached out to them, working to change their tune. Arges resisted. He raged and howled around her as her mind grasped each of the eight stars in turn and wrested it from the holothaur's control. It seemed that his control grew weaker once he left his host, because although it took great effort, and the strain gritted her teeth together, she drove his taint from the stars in a way she had not been able to back in the Black Rock. Next, focusing her will, with her eyes closed against the swirling snow, Yaz pushed the heat sigil at each star. The symbol she'd spent so many nights looking at, the same one that had been stamped upon the heat pot. Then, with each star burning hot, she began to force them up through the ice, the weapons with which she would fight her intangible foe.

Arges's attack came from an unexpected angle. His misdirection had fooled her yet again—he hadn't devoted all his strength to fighting her for the stars. Cold hands clamped around Yaz's neck and Yaz opened her eyes to find herself staring into the face of her only companion not to be sent fleeing into the snow by the holothaur's terror. Shadow clung to Erris like a second skin, an aura of darkness all about him. Yaz knew that Erris must still be battling Arges for control of his body. If Arges had full say, then he could have simply pulled Yaz's head off. But this distinction wasn't at the front of her thinking; that place was dominated by the complete lack of air getting past the awful pressure on her throat.

"Look . . . at . . . me." The voice that grated out of Erris was not his. Nor was the soul that looked out of his dark eyes. Wherever Erris was he seemed to be losing the battle because the fingers about Yaz's neck tightened further and she became dimly aware that her feet were no longer resting on the ice but were kicking in the air instead. "Look at me! Your kind die with your eyes open but you so rarely see."

The need to breathe had grown in an unbearable crescendo but was now fading away into the same blackness that was swarming about her vision like the opposite of snow. Yaz knew she was dying, and the others would die too. And Arges would march Erris's body back across the vast tract of ice they had crossed and restart his old evils in the Black Rock once more.

She could feel the stars more than she could feel her own body. The first of them burst from the ice with steam jetting around it. She could throw the thing at Erris's head, maybe break his hold. But to destroy him was too high a price to pay for her life. Instead she let her eyes rest on the star's light, trying to see through to that place beyond, wondering if it was where she might go when the last beat of her heart was spent.

Suddenly Yaz found herself sprawled in the snow, sucking in air through a throat that seemed too narrow for her needs. Erris lay a few yards away, pinned to the ice by Zox. The iron dog must have burst free of the drifts and shot at him like a thunderbolt. Little else could have broken his grip on her.

Erris struggled to free himself, roaring wordless anger, but Zox's prodigious weight, anchored to the ice by his rear claws, proved too much for Erris's conflicted muscles. Yaz rolled to her side, trying to lift herself on her arms but too weak even for that.

The darkness around Erris thickened, blotting out his face, clothing him in a larger spectral body: Arges was making himself known.

"Erris." Yaz tried to call his name but the word came out too small.

"You can have him back when I've finished with him," Arges hissed, using his own voice, a disembodied thing that insinuated itself into Yaz's mind. "I need a blunter weapon to crack this nut."

Arges's blackness began to pool around Erris's left hand where it pressed against Zox's chest, trying to lift the dog. The darkness sank into the metal, staining the iron momentarily before passing through into whatever lay beyond.

"He's . . . taking . . ." Yaz made it to her knees, her throat still unable to project her words above the wind. She retched, an excruciatingly painful act that spattered stomach acid on the ice.

As the last of the darkness blotted into Zox, the dog became unnaturally still. Erris, regaining full control of himself, managed to slide out from underneath, backing through the snow on his rear until he reached Yaz's side. "This is bad!"

"W . . . worse than you strangling me?" Yaz rasped.

Erris shot her a guilty glance. "Well, no. But I can't stop Zox. He's very strong and basically indestructible."

Yaz looked at the motionless dog, remembering how he had driven those six-inch claws into ice when climbing the pressure ridge. Their chances had always been slim and had shrunk to zero when Arges had destroyed the shelter. Now it was really a case of how they died, and whether it was fast or slow. She wondered whether Thurin, Maya, and Quina would come back or die alone out in the snowfield.

The eight stars that had been the Watcher's eyes now hung above the lightless ice mound where the monster lay entombed, each of them trailing steam into the wind as they vaporized the snowflakes impacting them. Yaz touched her aching throat and thought she would rather Zox killed her than be throttled by Erris. That had been very frightening. Quell must have felt something similar when the flood engulfed him beneath the Black Rock and he started to drown. The image of Quell sinking caught in her mind and an idea thrust itself upon her. "Wait!" She got to her feet using Erris's shoulder for support. She motioned the stars forward. "I can melt the ice around him. I can drown him!"

"He doesn't need to breathe . . ." But Erris trailed off, understanding. Once the dog was in its own pit of meltwater it wouldn't be long before it froze in there and it too, like the Watcher, could be left in eternity's care.

Yaz willed the stars to greater heat. She needed to take advantage of whatever struggle was going on inside the dog's armour. Even so she hesitated. It seemed a poor reward for Zox's unstinting loyalty.

"Do it," Erris urged.

As if unlocked by his words Zox swung his head towards them. His dark eyes fixed them. An instant later he began to shudder, head close to the ice, jolting on his legs as if he were vomiting, though he lacked a mouth. Arges's blackness spiralled out of him, the holothaur's scream rising through the registers. There was anger there, yes, but most of all it was fear. Terror. Not projected at them but Arges's very own. The holothaur tore away, chasing the wind across the pristine snow, howling louder than the gale, as if pursued by all the demons in all the hells. Gone in a heartbeat.

Zox pulled his feet free of the ice, one by one, retracting his claws until no sign of them remained. This done, he slowly rolled his shoulders then looked back at Yaz and Erris with the same patient doleful gaze he'd always had.

Quina chose that moment to stumble back and join them in the dip that the shelter had kept clear. "What just happened?" Snow caked her, hanging from her hair, clumping on her eyelashes. Yaz would have laughed if their situation weren't so grim.

"Arges tried to take over the dog," Erris said. He crossed over to Quina and started to brush the snow from her with his bare hands. "The Missing were unsurpassed in being able to subvert other technologies, and Zox is their own creation in any case. The holothaur should have had no trouble owning Zox. He controlled me. Twice."

A white-caked Maya arrived next, cautious, a blade in her gloved hand. Thurin loomed behind her, dark in his furs, and suddenly she was clear of snow, then Quina, both briefly surrounded by an explosion of white, hurried away by the wind.

"What are we going to do?" Quina hugged herself, shivering. It would be hours before the sun rose.

"We're dead," Maya said without fear, still in her battle mode. "The Axit know that the easiest victory comes when you strike the tents rather than the clan. There's no honour in it. But not all wars call for honour."

"We have heat . . ." Yaz willed her stars, the Watcher's eight eyes, closer. Her method of getting heat from them was closer to setting fire to puddled oil than to burning it through a lantern wick. The heat pot was far more efficient, its sigil better drawn than anything Yaz's mind could impose. But even so, stars this size could blaze for a long time. The wind tore away their warmth but if she stood close . . .

"I can't go near enough . . ." Quina backed away. Thurin and Maya took a step back too.

"I . . ." Yaz might be able to break the stars into smaller, more tolerable parts, but they would burn even more swiftly. At least the stars gave light. Without them they would be lost in the night.

"We should gather up what we can. Assess the damage." Erris reached down and tugged a triangle of broken board from the compacted snow by his feet.

Yaz felt for the smaller stars and found them still gathered together, so still inside the heat pot, she assumed. She brought them to her, a dozen stars the size of fingernails popping out of the snow. She set them on glowing orbits around her head and shoulders.

"We need to get out of the wind." Thurin spoke through chattering teeth and moved with caution. His fear-fuelled escape must have tested the stitches Erris had sewed in his flesh so recently.

Quina scooped up another bit of broken board and snatched the piece from Erris's hands. She held them edge to edge against the gale. "How do we do that?" she shouted, feeling her own fear now rather than Arges's and angry because of it. "We're done. There's nothing but the wind from now until we die!"

Thurin's face hardened but the hot words on his tongue were never given voice. Some new thought raised his brows. He reached towards the nearest snowbank with clawed fingers and twisted. Another snow snake emerged, writhing sinuously past Quina, between Maya and Erris. It kept on coming, yard upon yard upon yard, reaching its head up into the full force of the wind and streaming away with it. Thurin staggered and clutched his side with his other hand, weakening as they watched. But their attention was in the wrong place.

"Look," Thurin said as the snake's tail finally passed them. He nodded to where it had come from.

"A tunnel!" Maya hurried forward.

The tunnel was floored with the ice sheet and also ice-walled. Somehow Thurin had compacted the inner surface. Yaz followed Maya in, her starlight glimmering off the icy walls. Two yards back the tunnel opened into a dome a little smaller than their shelter. All of them filed in, Thurin last, following an abashed Quina.

They crouched together in a huddle, grateful to be out of the wind.

"Right," said Yaz. "All we need to do is dig out the heat pot—I know where it is—and a few boards to lie on, and we're set for the night."

"For tonight," Maya agreed. "And for as many nights as there's snow. After that . . ."

Yaz turned to Thurin, thinking of the time that their shelter had been shrouded with ice overnight. "Could you build us a shelter out of ice?"

"I don't know. It would be much more difficult." Thurin frowned. "But maybe."

28

✦ ✦
✦

THE FOOD RAN out five nights after the Watcher's attack, but their meals had been growing steadily more meagre ever since they had lost the shelter. They had been fortunate that the boat-sled survived the attack. Without a sea, though, it wasn't going to feed them.

It had taken two days to leave the snowfield behind. Walking had been a trial, especially for Zox, but the snow offered relatively easy shelter for three nights. On the first night back on the bare ice dawn came early. A shooting star lit the sky with great erratic pulses of light, enough to wake them all, even Thurin, glaring through the ice shelter he'd built them. Then came the sound. Yaz had never heard of a shooting star that spoke but the tales told of them finding their voices. A series of detonations shook the world as the star's light intensified in the east then vanished.

On the ice the walking was easier, but they missed the snow at night. The effort of ending each day with the construction of an ice hut sturdy enough to withstand the wind was beginning to tell on Thurin even before the last of the fungi disappeared into their bellies.

Yaz would have suggested again, and with greater insistence this time, that Thurin ride on the sled. But Zox had slowed and was pulling the lightened load with ponderous effort.

"What's wrong with him?" Yaz had asked. The dog had seemed indefatigable.

"His power source is running down," Erris told her.

"He lasted thousands of years in the city and just a handful of weeks out here?" Yaz knew it had been hard going but even so . . .

"In the city he slept a lot. Like me. And he could always draw on the script for fresh energies. Our power storage is less efficient in the cold." Erris shrugged. "And he did drag a laden sled up and down a hundred vertical feet of ice then basically burrow a twenty-mile hole through the snow. It's true, though, I thought he would last longer than this." He looked back at the dog, giving him a curious stare. "Maybe it has something to do with how he dealt with Arges. I still don't understand that. I thought we were all going to die right then and there . . ."

STARVATION IS A much swifter process when you're cold, but nobody dies truly thin on the ice. Starvation simply opens a gate for the wind to come through. It's the wind that wields the knife.

They sat that night with empty bellies around the heat pot. Outside, Zox had almost folded into his cube but stopped a few inches short of his goal, leaving a long vertical wedge that had already begun to fill with frost.

The fragile ice walls Thurin had raised withstood the wind but there would be fiercer winds to come and walls such as these would not hold against them. Thurin lay curled on a board, too weary to complain of his hunger. The rest of them hunched around aching bellies, grimly eyeing the pot and imagining a pan simmering above it. Or at least Yaz was sure that Maya and Quina were doing the same as she was. What was going through Erris's mind she couldn't say. Perhaps the fear that he would have to watch them all die and then go on alone, leaving their frozen corpses for the ice to take.

Yaz risked a bare hand and removed Taproot's needle from her collar. The thing had been weighing on her more heavily with each passing day. She tied a strand of her own hair around it and held it suspended. Slowly it found its own direction. She gave it a flick and rolled the hair between finger and thumb. The needle spun, slowed, and returned to the same direction: east and ever so slightly north.

"We could follow this," she said. "We'll be tracking backwards a little way, and I've no idea if the place is close enough for us to reach before . . . And when we get there, even if there's a way in, it's another city under the ice. There may well not be anything to eat there."

"There might be fungi." Thurin raised his head. "But you'd need stars for warmth and water."

"There's just as much chance of finding a sea whichever direction we go," Quina said.

Maya grimaced. "Basically none."

"Taproot wants to suck us into a war with Seus." Erris shook his head. "You." He corrected himself. "He wants to suck *you* into a war. He had generations in which he ignored me. And Seus is dangerous. Very dangerous."

"More dangerous than starvation on the ice?" Thurin asked.

"Fair point." Erris pursed his lips. "But his reach is long. I doubt Arges is his only recruit, and he probably has horrors like the Watcher in all of the Missing's cities."

"Anyone for continuing south?" Yaz asked.

Nobody answered.

"We'll follow the needle tomorrow then." It felt like defeat, like taking direction from someone else, handing over her quest for the green lands. But it had to be done. They'd run out of food and they'd run out of choices.

IN THE NIGHT Yaz's fitful sleep, broken by hunger, came to a sudden stop when she realized that the whole shelter was glowing green. Her eyes opened wide but it took several moments before she understood what she was looking at. The semitranslucent ice of the roof and walls shone with a curious shifting light, the green deepening from that of new leaves to a vibrant emerald. The light was coming from outside. From the sky.

"Aurora," said Erris softly.

"The dragons' tails." Yaz sat up. She wanted to go outside as she always did with her parents when the dragons flew. But it would let their heat escape.

Thurin sat up too, the wonder on his face revealed by the shifting light. "I thought you were joking about this . . ." He reached up and a large section of the ice above them became almost as clear as air. The aurora stretched halfway across the sky, veils of light writhing slowly, as if a million tons of stardust were sifting down through cracks in the sky.

They lay back and watched together. Beside them Quina and Maya slept on. Neither of them would have welcomed being woken to see what for them was a regular occurrence.

"If we don't . . ." Thurin sighed. "Well, I'm glad to have seen this. Whatever happens to us I'm glad this happened first."

"I've never seen this with my own eyes," Erris said, his head close to Yaz's. "The coming of the ice wasn't the only change I missed. Good to know that after however many thousand years it's been I can still find new things."

Yaz lay and watched the sky dragons lash their tails, and in the darkness her fingers found the warmth of Thurin's hand and the cool strength of Erris's. Fingers laced fingers, hands closed tight, and above them shooting stars streaked silently across dark infinities.

THE NEXT DAY they turned east, and a little north. Exhaustion weighed them down. Without food in her belly Yaz began to feel that she rather than Zox was dragging the sled behind her, and that each missed meal was a load of iron added to what must be hauled across the ice. The act of putting one foot before the next became a task that required focus. Without attention she would merely slow to a halt and then stand, leaning into the wind, obeying the demands of her body that she do nothing.

The wind found hitherto unsuspected chinks in her armour. Her extremities numbed, her core chilled, her lips cracked. Her face became a mask she wore rather than flesh she owned, and it seemed that if she were to make too violent an expression the whole thing might shatter and fall to the ground, leaving her skull bared to the wind's assault.

Thurin shambled along, as if carried by sheer act of will rather than his failing muscles. Sometimes he swayed at impossible angles before recovering, and Yaz knew that only his ice-work had saved him from a tumble that on his own he might never rise from.

The cold plays cruel tricks. At the end, when the blood runs chill and sluggish through white flesh, the cold can convince a person they're burning up. Victims shed their furs and die half-naked, caked in ice. The cold freezes your thoughts so that they crawl in circles, unable to change track, unequal to the task of grappling with new ideas.

They walked, each of them wrapped in their own struggle. Even Erris seemed burdened, weighed down by the horror of seeing his companions fail one by one while he carried endlessly on.

"Thurin?" Erris stopped and turned. Yaz, pitifully grateful for the delay, stopped too and shuffled to face back the way they'd come. Thurin had fallen to his knees and the sled had passed him by.

"Thurin?" Erris hurried to his side. "Get up."

"This is wrong . . ." Thurin muttered through peeling lips.

"It is what it is," Erris said. "Get up, my friend. Or I'll have to carry you."

"What?" Thurin looked up at that. "No. I mean this." He tapped at the ice with a gloved hand.

Yaz joined them and stared. "It's just ice." She paused and saw it. "With a crack in it. Ice cracks all the time."

"Not like this." Thurin shook his head. "There's no reason for this to be here. I know the ice. I can feel how it moves. This . . . is . . . wrong."

"Well." Yaz looked along the faint line of the crack to where Quina and Maya were still plodding on with the sled. "It's going the same way we are." She reached down and grasped Thurin's arm, helping him back to his feet.

By sunset the crack was wide enough to wedge a finger in. Thurin stumbled to a halt and stood as if unsure where he might be. It broke Yaz's heart to ask him to raise a shelter.

"Yes. A shelter." Thurin slurred the words. He reached out unsteadily and the ice groaned, resisting his will. Slowly, inch by painful inch, a thin wall of ice broke from the surface like the blade of a rising knife. It rose to about chest height before Thurin toppled into a boneless fall.

"Catch—"

But Erris was too far away and Quina's cold-blunted speed was insufficient to stop Thurin's head hitting the ice. They wrestled him senseless onto a board in the lee of the partial wall while Erris set to improving the shelter with what boards and wires they'd managed to salvage from the wreckage the Watcher had left them.

Darkness fell on a pitiful, rattling shelter with three walls. The group cuddled together like lovers, as close to the heat pot as they could get without burning. The wind meant that one moment you could feel a painful heat on your face and the next a freezing draft. Thurin recovered enough to say that he was alright. An obvious lie. They should have taken his gloves and boots off to care for his fingers and toes, but without a proper shelter it would only endanger them more. Yaz prayed to the Gods in the Sky that the cold hadn't got its teeth into his flesh. It hurt her to think of Thurin's long, clever fingers blackened and twisted by the frost.

Deep into the night the last of their original stars fizzled into nothing, unable to deliver the energy that Yaz demanded of it. She crawled out into the full brunt of the wind and summoned one of the Watcher's eyes from the sled, a sphere that she could cup comfortably in two hands, a sea-blue glow to it now that Arges's influence had been removed. It was one of the odd ones out. The bulk of the others seemed related somehow.

Breaking the star was hard. Harder than it should have been, and Yaz truly thought she might also have broken something inside her head by the time the star finally surrendered and fell into a dozen pieces, each a perfect sphere. They would burn faster than the larger star, but the others would be able to tolerate their presence.

Leaning into the wind, she returned to her friends and fed the stream of stars into the pot, igniting its sigils and pumping heat into the restless air.

Yaz slept fitfully and rose with a pale dawn more exhausted than she had been when she had lain down. Her head still ached from the effort of breaking the star in the night. Erris loaded Thurin onto the sled without discussion. The fact that he didn't even protest scared Yaz more than the black bruise on his forehead or the lifeless flop of his limbs as Erris carried him across the ice.

Yaz had removed the stars from the sled so that Thurin could ride there and set them following her at a distance, a floating tail trailing in the wind.

Zox set a slow but unrelenting pace. As the miles passed the ice became curiously rucked up in long lines across their path, like thousand-foot-high pressure ridges. It made the going tough, and several times Zox scrabbled and strained to haul the sled over a particularly difficult one.

Exhaustion's solitude wrapped itself around Yaz and once more she retreated into a narrow universe where one footstep followed the next and all of them filled her world. She became deaf to the wind, blind to the passage of the sun, focused only on the march. Focused on nothing but the march. She felt on the point of collapse but time after time she refused, time after time she lifted her boot, slid it forward, transferred her weight. An Ictha marching song rumbled its measure at the back of her mind, over and over. The ice would not beat her. The wind would not beat her. She was Ictha. This is what she was born to do.

She was Ictha. Take the next step. And the next. And the next. *Ictha.*

"Yaz?" The voice came from far away. "Yaz?"

"Uh?" She blinked, unsure if she were walking or had come to a halt. "It's sunset . . . We need a shelter . . ." She croaked the words from a dry throat.

"It's not sunset, Yaz." Erris was standing in front of her. He took her shoulders in his hands. "It's dawn."

"We walked all night?" She blinked, feeling ice crack at the sides of her eyes.

"All day, all night, all of another day, all of another night," Erris said gently. "It's time to lie down."

Yaz coughed. She felt broken. "The Ictha die on their feet."

Erris bent his head, shifted his grip, and a moment later she was being lifted smoothly over his shoulder.

"I can't!" she protested. "The others!"

"I've been helping Zox to drag the others for more than two nights and a day." Erris sounded exasperated as he carried her back to the sled. He laid her down beside a figure so bundled in fur that she couldn't tell if it was Maya or Thurin or Quina. Erris straightened, brushing ice from the short, tight curls of his hair. "Truly. The Ictha are a different breed."

"You can't drag us all." Yaz tried to get up.

"Can and will." Erris went back to the reins. But he looked tired. Yaz had never seen him look tired. "The going is getting worse, though. It's as if that needle of yours chose the absolute worst direction. Every ridge is barring our path."

Yaz said nothing. She had no faith in Taproot's needle or its directions. But no direction seemed to offer any hope. That was the freedom of the ice. The freedom to choose any path you pleased and to die in any place, knowing none of them had anything more to offer than a cold death.

"Keep the stars following us," Erris said. "We're going to need them."

Yaz wasn't sure that was true, but somehow all seven of the larger stars had remained tethered to her will, even in the depths of her struggle. She strengthened that bond and lay back with her friends, the only one of them still conscious. Overhead, the white sky watched without emotion, waiting for them to die.

Yaz didn't remember going to sleep. Cold is a stealthy assassin. In the end you never see it coming.

"Wake up, Yaz!" A hand was shaking her. "Wake up."

Yaz tried to fend the hand away. Part of her thought it was her mother getting her up for another day's march towards the Pit of the Missing. It didn't sound like her mother . . . but whoever it was, she didn't feel like more walking. It was cold out there and her furs were . . . less cold.

"Yaz, you need to see. I can't do this on my own. I don't know how to." Strong hands were lifting her gently but cruelly into a cold wind.

Yaz cracked open an eye, blinking against the blur of tears already starting to freeze. She saw nothing, only white.

"Is . . . it . . . snow?"

"No." Erris set her on her feet and kept her from falling. A white mist swirled all around them. Erris's hair was white with frost. Even his eyebrows were thick with it.

"Where . . ." But the wind showed her. A sudden gust lifted the mist momentarily, exposing a fractured shelf of blue-green ice and . . . water, endless darkly rippled water stretching out before her. All of it steaming.

They had found a sea!

29

✦ ✦
✦

THIS ISN'T LIKE other seas." Yaz knelt in the boat, weak but fuelled by her amazement. The winds were considerably reduced down at the water level and the temperature almost balmy. They bounced gently on small waves, jostling chunks of ice. Even Quina and Maya, packed with Thurin in the boat behind her, were showing signs of life. There'd been no sign of Zox. Erris said he'd left him up amid the ridges surrounding the crater, worried that the dog would be unable to climb back out.

"How did you get the sled down the cliffs alone?" she asked.

Erris winced. "It was very hard work. But they weren't cliffs like you described. More of a slope." He bent to paddle them further from the shore. "I think this sea didn't melt its way open from under the ice."

"How else could it be here?" Yaz agreed with him, though: it wasn't as warm as a hot sea, the mists were less thick, and already plates of ice were forming on the open waters.

"That shooting star we saw a few nights back. I think it landed here and blew a hole through the ice sheet. Most of the debris would have been vaporized and deposited downwind as snow."

"I . . ." Yaz remembered the tale Mother Mazai told of her own grandmother and the crater the shooting star had left. "We'd better fish fast then, before it freezes."

The nets and hooks that had so intimidated Erris were Yaz's domain. She instructed him on when and where to cast the biggest net, and how to paddle so as to draw it through the water at the best depth.

"If this sea didn't melt its way up, then the fish won't know about it." Yaz stared across the waters, frowning. The boat-sled crunched its way through a thin plate of ice. "We could be fishing empty waters."

Erris paddled on but without the speed and strength he had always displayed. "The shock wave will have travelled a long way," he said. "Strikes like this aren't so rare. Our forefathers put defences above the sky to stop the biggest of them. So any fish worth its fins should have come along to see what nutrients got stirred up."

Yaz said nothing. She huddled in her furs, trying to imagine what the four tribes had left floating in the black sea to battle stars that fell from the heavens. After a time she motioned for a stop. "Haul it in."

Erris set to work, quickly learning to balance in the boat as he dragged in the net. If he fell in Yaz imagined that he would sink immediately. No man as heavy as he was had any hope of swimming.

Yard after yard of wet net came dripping over the stern. The water formed icicles in the brief gap between the net leaving the surface and reaching the boat, only to be snapped off as it slid over. Yard after empty yard. It was often like this, with the catch bulking in the final section of the cone-shaped net. Part of the Ictha philosophy of life came from this simple act of faith. You put in the effort not for the reward you got now, but for the reward you hoped would lie at the end. Yaz's whole life since she had left the Black Rock was summed up in that notion. All those miles across the ice, rewarded not by yet another vista of white on white stretching to the horizon but by the green she hoped one day to see in the south.

"Oh." The last section of the net flopped into the boat. Empty.

"We'll try again." Erris bent to gather the already stiffening net.

"Further out." Yaz bit down on the words that wanted to escape her mouth. That they'd found an empty sea. That they'd hunted so long for water, and now that they'd found some it was proving to be the only empty sea she'd ever encountered. Created in violence and unready to give out life.

Erris paddled further out. When he paused his efforts a rare silence enfolded them, gentled by the lap of small waves against the hull. The depth below the ice sheet and the thickness of the mist seemed to tame the wind to the point at which it no longer shrieked or moaned.

"Again?" Erris asked.

"Further out."

"We don't want to get frozen in." Erris bashed at a passing ice floe with his paddle to make the point.

"A little further."

Finally, at Yaz's gesture, Erris stopped and threw out the net as she had instructed. Quina watched through slitted eyes, unmoving, her face a deathly white where it showed past her hood.

Erris paddled on, towing the net.

"A little slower."

She let him go for three or four hundred yards, bumping aside stray ice blocks, crunching through new-formed plates. Again he hauled in the net.

"This time!" Erris promised as he drew in the final section hand over hand, wobbling the boat, inches from a fall he couldn't ever come back from.

"No . . ." Quina croaked the word as the last slack feet of the net came back aboard.

"It's alright. I'll just keep tr—"

A white explosion of water engulfed the boat. Something huge and dark loomed amid the spray. The boat rocked violently and Yaz could see nothing amid the falling sea.

The air cleared, leaving them drenched. Yaz blinked and snapped her head from side to side. "Erris!"

Erris was gone.

"No! No! No!" She scanned the water. Raced her gaze along the side of the boat, praying to every God in the Sea that she would spot clinging fingers.

Erris was gone and with him their last chance.

She thought of him sinking even now, fathoms below them, dropping into the dark depths that would hold him until his energies finally dwindled and left just an empty shell.

"Yaz?" Quina's scared voice reached through Yaz's grief but she bowed her head between her arms. She'd no hope to offer. They were finished. The whale vanished with a flip of its vast tail flukes, almost swamping the boat and nearly tipping Quina over the side too. Despite herself, Yaz reached out to secure the girl.

"There's . . . something," Quina muttered, looking out over the dark waters. "Yaz!"

With a groan Yaz pulled herself to the side, pushing aside the wet bundle of furs that was Maya.

"What . . ." A white something was rising towards them.

"Ice?" Quina asked.

"Paddle!" Yaz hunted for another paddle. A block of ice was rising beneath them. A chunk larger than a man.

All her body ached but Yaz managed to drive the boat clear. She turned to watch the rising ice but it wasn't rising nearly as fast as she thought it might.

The ice block surfaced with a lazy swell, as if heavier than ice should be.

Quina gave Yaz a puzzled look, too weak for further speculation.

Something lunged from the water and for a moment Yaz thought the whale had returned. But it was a figure.

"Help!"

Erris fell back, scrabbling for a hold on the irregular chunk of ice. He vanished beneath the water.

"Erris!" Yaz began to turn the boat, flailing at the waves with a strength she could have sworn was no longer in her.

"He's gone," Quina croaked.

But no, he was there, under the water, somehow clinging to the ice. He must have dived towards the block when he was flung from the boat and carried it under the waves with his momentum. Fortunately it was just large enough to carry him slowly back to the surface again.

For a desperate minute Yaz struggled to turn the boat and finally the prow bumped against Erris's block. She bent over and shoved the paddle down into the water. A hand gripped it and tugged to ensure she had good hold.

"Help me, Quina." But Quina could barely crawl towards her through the icy water sloshing inside the boat.

Yaz gritted her teeth and tugged back. She only had to hold Erris until he could reach up and get a hand on the side. Heavy as he was, part of his weight was buoyed up by the water. Both her hands clenched white-knuckled on the paddle.

When the pull of Erris's weight came it was far greater than she had expected. The boat lurched to the side and the paddle slipped in her grip. Suddenly she was in a different boat on a different sea and it was Azad she had in her grip as the great beast that had taken hold of him pulled them both beneath the waves, and the boat too.

Yaz would not let go. Could not let go. She clung to the paddle more tightly than she held on to her life. And a moment later Erris's hand broke the surface, seizing the side of the boat.

Yaz pulled aside the guard hides and he hauled himself in, water streaming from his body.

"Thank you." He lay back, not gasping for air but staring at the sky and slowly shaking his head. It was a long time before he spoke again. "Well, I found out one thing. There are definitely fish down there."

30

✦ ✦
✦

WITH THE NET set for a deeper trawl they were able to haul scores of herring and greenfin from the rapidly freezing sea. By the time the sun touched the rim of the crater their boat was a third full of fish and Erris's paddle was breaking finger-thick ice as he dragged them back to the shore. With most of the water now covered by ice the mist had largely cleared and the white sky devoured what little heat still hung around from the vast forces expended in the spot days before.

After some hours at sea Quina and Maya had revived enough in the relative warmth to eat as much raw fish as their stomachs could contend with, and both were able to disembark before Erris dragged the boat-sled from the water. He crouched beside it, not panting with effort as any other man would but, as he explained, waiting for energies from his diminished core to be distributed to the stores in his muscles.

Yaz got Erris to turn the boat on its side as a shelter against the wind, which a mile and more below the surface of the ice sheet was a shadow of its true self. She took the heat pot that had been cradled against Thurin, giving out as much heat as he could tolerate, and hefted it by its charred bone handles onto a board close by. Next she summoned one of the Watcher's eyes from where she had left the larger stars on the shore and set it in the pot, blazing out an extravagant amount of heat.

"We need to feed him." Maya looked pointedly at Thurin, still curled beneath his furs. Earlier attempts had failed, the cold fish dribbling back out between bluish lips.

"We all need to get dry." Quina edged as close to the pot as the star allowed—which was closer than when it wasn't shielded by the heat sigils. Her hides began to steam, adding to the mists blowing in off the closing sea.

Yaz took out the pan, which was slick with fish oil, set three herring in it, and held it out at arm's length close to the pot. "We'll try cooked food. The Broken are used to that."

"I think he's coming round," Erris said. "Or at least he's started to dream."

Yaz peered at Thurin, frowning. "He looks the same to me."

Quina tugged at Yaz's elbow, covering a smile. She nodded towards the evening gloom where the heat pot's glow played across the wind-stirred mist.

"What?" Yaz asked. But then she saw it, shapes in the fog, a confusion of them, then out of nowhere her own face was there, caught in the moment, starlit. In the next heartbeat the wind had shredded it, only for it to re-form moments later. "I don't understand . . ." But she did. Thurin's sleeping mind was reaching out and using his power over water to paint his dreams into the mist.

Yaz felt the heat rising in her cheeks as the mist writhed in slowly moving curves requiring only a little imagination to be seen as limbs entwining, the swell of a breast, the fullness of lips, all of it in languid motion. Yaz hadn't felt so exposed since she had stripped down to her mole-fish skins back in the drying cave on the day she jumped into the Pit of the Missing.

Glancing back, she saw that the others were all sitting together in the shelter of the sled, knees drawn up, watching the show with big grins as if it were for their entertainment. Yaz frowned furiously and focused on the pan and the fish she was cooking.

Before long, and much to Yaz's relief, the wind freshened and tore the images away along with the last of the mist. She risked another glance towards the others.

"I think it was me," Quina said, her grin broadening to show all her teeth in two white lines.

Erris and Maya burst out laughing.

Yaz tried to scowl but couldn't keep an echoing smile from her lips. "Shut up. All of you!" She went back to poking the contents of the pan with her knife.

It took a few minutes, but before long the air filled with the smell of frying fish. It amazed Yaz that she had eaten fish every day of her life and never known how good they could smell until the Broken showed her. Summoned by the smell, Maya and Quina came to join her, huddling together at her back and staring at the sizzling herrings with their clothes steaming and their mouths watering.

Finally, Thurin sniffed the air and opened his eyes. "H . . . hungry."

Erris grinned. "Good to have you back with us."

THEY FED THURIN and dried his furs, burning the Watcher's star with reckless abandon. Everyone checked their fingers and toes. Quina and Maya had signs of frostbite on their smallest and largest toes, typically the weakest points. But Yaz judged they should recover quickly. Thurin had more severe frostbite, on his toes, fingers, hands, nose, and ears. He'd been saved from more damage by being the first to go in the sled.

"You'll recover. But we have to stay here and keep you warm for a few days." Yaz hoped it was true. The cold had sunk its fangs into Thurin but the damage might not last. The white flesh would turn pink again or it would turn black and need to be cut away.

The five of them cowered in the overturned sled, with the heat pot burning up its star almost as fast as the Broken's forge pot, glowing red at the top and making the board on which it stood start to bubble and stink.

Earlier on, Erris had gone to get Zox, leading the dog down the path he'd scouted. Ever since, Zox had been folded tightly in his customary cube. Now he unfolded himself, but only to lumber so close to the pot that had he been made of anything but iron he would have ignited. This done, he folded back up and made no other moves. Yaz worried that he'd sink into the ice, and was determined to keep an eye on him.

That first night they all lay down, too tired for stories. Erris lay further from the boat-sled as there wasn't room for all of them inside. Yaz found herself watching him in the light of the blazing heat pot. He saw her and returned her appraisal.

Erris smiled. "Taproot's needle led us here, you know?"

Yaz frowned and touched her gloved fingers to the needle. "How would he know this was what we needed? Or where we were? Or where to point us?"

Erris glanced at the sky, where the first crimson stars were showing. "He can see all the world from above. Many of his kind can. Though there's precious little to see these days. He knew we'd found no seas and he knew we would be needing one." He tapped his collar in the place where Yaz kept the needle. "When you try it again I'll bet it shows a new direction. The one that will take us where he wants you to go."

Yaz said nothing. She didn't want to go where Taproot wanted her to. Dying on the ice was easy enough without help. And no amount of guiding to seas would compensate the damage that Seus could do to them if he thought she was Taproot's servant. She shivered. If Taproot could see them trudging across the ice, then surely Seus could too. He might already have any number of horrors trekking towards them, each more fearsome than the Watcher.

Sleep took Yaz down and her dreams came populated with monsters, shambling across the ice to the lip of the crater where she and the others, fast in their slumbers, crowded around the only hot thing for a thousand miles in any direction.

THE NEXT DAY the sea was too frozen for the boat. Erris made a fishing hole for each of them except Thurin, who was ordered to remain in the boat-sled. Yaz told him that if he claimed to be feeling well enough to fish, then he was well enough to raise a shelter. Thurin admitted defeat and lay back among his furs.

Before she began to bait and set her hooks Yaz quietly unpinned Taproot's needle from her hides and, sheltering it from the wind with her body, let it spin on the end of a hair. It took some time to settle, but Erris was right. It now pointed south and west.

They cooked and ate regularly, trying to regain lost weight. Yaz worried at how fast they were going through their catch but Erris said he would fish overnight too. Yaz could melt a hole in the ever-thickening sea ice and she could show him how to bait and set hooks. The starlight could be used to attract fish at night to replace the sunlight, which by day was an unparalleled lure on its own.

Ice-hole fishing proved productive, securing far more catches than were used as bait, but by the second day the holes had frozen again and a full yard of ice had to be melted away in order to reach the water. By the third day the star Yaz had been using to fuel the heat pot shrank to nothing without the hole it melted reaching the sea beneath them. She stood looking down into the meltwater, shaking her head. The hole that had failed to penetrate the ice was deeper than she was tall.

"Time to go." Erris went and knocked on Zox. With a noisy cracking of ice, the dog unfolded and gazed ruefully about him. After packing, they began the arduous trek out of the crater. If it had been a hot sea they would have had to find a way up mile-high cliffs, looking for sections where they could set ropes, then fixing stakes at the top so that they could slowly raise the boat-sled. Their escape, like the Ictha's, would be in a long series of dangerous ascents.

Thankfully, the crater's violent birth had given it less-steep walls, and with a lot of pathfinding Erris had discovered a route that Zox could cope with. The dog had seemingly recovered a little with rest and heat, and was able to drag the boat-sled out, deploying his claws to their full extent on the more difficult slopes.

Thurin's frostbite was much better, which saved him the ignominy of being dragged out in the sled along with their catch and remaining gear. It also saved them from finding out whether Zox could still pull such a load.

"I didn't miss this at all, you know." Thurin came up the last slope, limping only slightly, and joined Yaz out on the ice plain, leaning into the howling wind.

Yaz knew how he felt. It was always a shock coming out of the warm mists of a hot sea back into the teeth of a gale. She didn't ask if he was up to the journey or whether he would be able to raise a shelter from the ice each night. There wasn't any choice. They would be equal to the task or they would die. Just like every day of their lives.

ROUTINE SUCKED BOTH mind and body back into its pattern. The trek resumed and within a few days it was as if it had never been interrupted. They headed south and west now rather than just south, but it made little difference. With food in their bellies and stars to burn, Yaz felt they could walk forever. The others were perhaps less confident. Every march, no matter how well provisioned, chipped away at the internal resources of those marching. And for Thurin there was the additional burden of having to create a shelter every night from the reluctant ice. Practice was honing his technique, but even so it took a toll on him, leaving a gauntness to his face and shadows around his eyes. Despite his labours, Thurin, raised almost entirely on fungi with fish a delicacy traded from above, said that the evening meal was doing a lot to sustain him and that he'd never eaten so well in his life.

At night they snuggled tight in the close confines of the hut Thurin had made and he would always fall asleep quickly, exhausted by the effort of shaping the ice after a day's travel. Yaz was seldom far behind, but ever since seeing the shapes of Thurin's dreaming in the mist back at the crater, she imagined she could feel his dreams trace their way across her skin in the dark. The same subconscious processes that had shaped the mists must, she thought, also be pulling and pushing on the water within her flesh and blood, gently patterning Thurin's secret thoughts across her.

Confirmation came on the fourth night out from the crater when a violent shove woke Yaz with a yelp. She sat, summoning light from the stardust in her pockets, to discover Maya and Quina tangled together in a heap up against the ice wall. Thurin was sitting bolt upright, sweating and white-faced. Only Erris seemed undisturbed.

"Sorry . . ." Thurin mumbled, glancing around. "I had a nightmare."

Quina rolled Maya off her and swept the long black veil of her hair from her face. "Have better dreams." She narrowed her eyes to dangerous slits. "Or else." Then smiled brightly and crawled back close to Yaz.

✦ ✦ ✦

THE DAYS PASSED. Zox grew slower and slower until Erris began to help him pull the sled. But Erris too was slowing. Where the others found themselves newly sustained by their fishing trip, Zox and Erris never ate, only spent their diminishing resources, never replenishing them. One night Erris confided that he had expected to last longer but the cold combined with the unexpected conflicts against Arges, both at the Black Rock and out on the ice, had taken their toll, as had getting all of them and the sled safely down to the water's edge.

In the long solitude of walking Yaz tried not to think about the last few days of their journey to the crater sea. She had retreated into herself and withdrawn from the others. She'd left them to die in her wake—for the Ictha left any who couldn't maintain the pace. In extremity she'd reverted to type and if it hadn't been for Erris then Thurin, Maya, and Quina would all have been frozen corpses punctuating Yaz's death march to the sea. Yaz had rejected that calculus of survival, but when it came to the sharp end of things, instinct had taken over. She looked back at her companions, struggling behind her against a particularly fierce noonday gale, and resolved not to let them down a second time. What that might mean, though, if Erris or Zox were to slow to the point of immobility, she couldn't bring herself to think about too much. Instead, she walked on, haunted by a voice that told her she was doomed to fail, that in the end she would compromise whatever ideals she claimed to hold, would sacrifice the weak for the strong, and that—worse—she would come to believe it to be for the greater good.

"We could go back." Quina matched her stride to Yaz's.

"What?"

"We have enough food to reach the Black Rock, maybe. We could go back."

Yaz was far from sure that they did have enough food, but even if it were true . . . this was Quina, Quina with her wooden bead and her faith in all the stories. "Why are you saying this?"

A raised voice distracted her from Quina's answer. Glancing back, she saw that Thurin appeared to be arguing with Erris, waving his arms at him as they marched on. Ahead of them, Maya was shaking her head, one hand wrestling with the other as if she were gripped in the throes of some internal argument.

And behind them all, Zox had stopped. He stood with the boat-sled two hundred yards back, head bent as if sniffing the ice.

Erris fell, tripped by the ice, and Thurin stood over him, fists balled, shouting something angry that the wind tore away. Erris never fell. Perhaps Thurin had raised the ice against him, or perhaps the last of his energies were running out of him. Both were equally bad things.

Yaz felt she should intervene but what would she say? What was her flawed judgment worth? Doubt and confusion swamped her in a grey wave.

"We've made a mistake," Quina was saying. "We're going to die out here."

Maya stalked past them, muttering to herself.

Behind Thurin, Zox made a slow circle before starting to haul the boat-sled away.

"The sled!" Yaz began to run after it. Hopeless as their expedition might be, they still needed the sled.

The others began to give chase too, and since Zox wasn't particularly fast Yaz managed to grab hold of the sled before he got much further. Erris came up to join her at a slow jog, joining his weight to hers, but Zox dragged them both and the sled too.

Thurin and Quina, unable to approach the stars stored on the sled, veered around to head off the dog.

Erris lost his hold and stumbled, almost falling. "Stop!" he commanded, and the dog did. Erris straightened up and brushed ice from his legs. "What's wrong with everyone?" ·

Yaz wasn't sure. She glanced at the others and noticed that Maya hadn't run back with them. "Maya?" She spotted the girl, still on their course and heading into the distance.

Erris went over to Zox, speaking to him in the unearthly language they shared, a tongue with no words and filled with sounds Yaz could never attempt.

"I don't know what's upset him," Erris said. "He's giving off danger

codes and refuses all commands to go back." He glanced at Thurin. "I don't
know what's got into you either. Is this what Yaz called ice-madness?"

Yaz called into the wind after Maya. "Wait!"

Staring at the retreating girl, Yaz could sense something odd, something wrong, but she wasn't quite sure what.

"It's the ice," Thurin said. "I can't believe I missed it . . ."

"What about the ice?" Quina asked. She drew a deep breath. "MAYA!
COME BACK!"

"The taint," Thurin said. "It's here."

Yaz saw it as soon as Thurin spoke the name. The effect was subtle, but
once you'd seen it there was no missing it. The ice was faintly grey and
growing darker in the direction they'd been headed. In three strides Yaz
was standing on Zox's back. In the far distance she could see a band of
black, a streak of black ice trailing south, bleeding into greys around its
margins.

"Get Maya!"

Erris set off immediately at the same slow jog. He'd seemed the least
vulnerable to the taint back in the Broken's caverns but Arges had been able
to subvert him, and as he ran after Maya part of Yaz wanted to call him
back. She could go herself, with the stars.

Erris reached Maya, scooped her up, and came back at walking pace.
He set her on her feet before Yaz. She looked a little confused and a lot irritated. "It's a good thing I like you, Erris, or you'd have a load of knife
wounds in your back about now and I'd know if you made yourself a spine
when you built that body."

Yaz reached a hand down for Maya. "Join me."

She made room on Zox's shoulders so Maya could see the problem.
"The taint was getting to us all. I suppose it's more dangerous when you
don't know it's there . . ."

"Oh." Maya, who had been on tiptoes to see, settled back on her feet
and jumped down onto the ice beside Erris. "Thank you, then."

"You're welcome."

"It's strange how it's running dead south," Thurin said. "The ice isn't
moving that way."

"They always run that way," Quina said, as if finding black ice on the surface were no surprise.

Erris frowned. "You've seen this before?"

"The Kac-Kantor have several scars like this in their range," Quina said. "They all run to the south. Other clans have said the same too."

Thurin pursed his lips. "Looks as if we're not the only ones headed for the green lands."

Yaz gave a grim smile. "We're doing it faster, though." She set off due south, ignoring Taproot's needle. "Come on. We'll find a way round." But as she led them, with Zox plodding ever more slowly and Erris's hips starting to make an audible grating sound at each stride, she wondered if any of them truly would make it to the green lands before the taint.

31

✦ ✦
✦

I T TOOK THE rest of the day before they finally reached the end of the
black ice's migration and rounded the head of it: an inky knot of ice
surrounded by a grey halo considerably narrower than it had been
further north. Yaz could feel the malice radiating from the spirits trapped
within. It put her in mind of Theus once more, the driving force behind
the taint that had leaked from the fractured vaults back at the city of Vesta.
She wondered whether, if Theus hadn't risen to dominance and bent their
will towards the reunification of his parts, that mass of evils would not also
have migrated to the surface and begun its slow journey to the south.

"What do you think they're looking for?" Quina asked. "The spirits?"

"Bodies." Thurin shuddered.

"Life. War. Chaos," Erris added. "It's another sign that the green belt
still exists, though. Something must be drawing them south, and my
money would be on people. Lots of people just waiting to be tainted."

"Money?" Quina asked.

Erris smiled and looked away. "Just a thing we used to have."

YAZ LED THEM for six more days, following the needle. She wondered
how much of her life had passed simply eating up miles of empty ice stride

by stride. Zox might be a machine made for walking but Yaz thought there was perhaps little difference between them. Both spending so long locked in the isolation of their own thoughts. Whatever might go on inside Zox's head, though, was unlikely ever to be shared. Erris could get few responses from him—it was fortunate that the dog seemed dedicated to helping them.

Occasionally Yaz would find Zox staring at her with one black eye—he could only use both when aiming his head at you, the other being on the far side of his head, something that Erris said made him more like a sheep than a hound. And on such occasions, fixed by Zox's dark gaze, Yaz would wonder what the holothaur had found when he had tried to invade that iron head. What had it taken to set Arges forgetting his revenge and go fleeing in terror instead?

Whatever it was, it would soon have to be left behind them. Erris and Zox seemed bound together in a race to the bottom. Each moving slower day by day, almost hour by hour, their movements less steady and less certain. Erris's appearance didn't change but in his motion he seemed to be gathering his years to him: each new day weighing him down with another of his centuries, leaving him walking into the future with an old man's step.

Whatever Yaz had resolved about not leaving anyone behind, Zox could not be carried or even dragged. He was simply too heavy. She would drag Erris herself if it came to it.

She did change the order of their march to compensate for their changing strengths, and by the sixth day after rounding the tainted ice it was Thurin, Maya, Quina, and Yaz who pulled the sled, while Zox and Erris set an arthritic pace that left it unclear which of them was the more slow.

"I see something." Maya was the shortest of them but often the first to spot a change ahead of them. Usually a pressure ridge.

Yaz squinted at the horizon. "I don't."

Maya just smiled and kept on walking.

A mile later Yaz could see it too. Something poking up in the distance. Something in the direction the needle was leading them.

It took a while for their minds to make sense of what they were seeing.

Their assessment of the scale kept changing as miles passed beneath their feet and still they seemed to grow no closer.

"It's towers," Erris said.

"Made of ice?" Thurin asked. "Or just covered in it?"

"What else is there to make things that big out of?" Quina shook her head. "But ice won't stack that high, surely?"

"It seems unlikely," Erris said. "Even if the bases of the towers didn't shatter, then gravity should bring them flowing down. A glacier travels a dozen yards a year on quite a modest slope."

But they were towers. Graceful organic towers that put Yaz in mind of the diversity of fungi that the Broken cultivated, as well as their spears and swords. Glittering bridges arced between some, looking to be hundreds of yards up.

"It's like Vesta was . . ." Yaz breathed, leaning into the sled harness.

Erris nodded. He had shown Yaz how the city of the Missing had once looked, and here was another, whole but made from ice rather than stone and steel.

"Do you think they made it for us?" Yaz asked.

Maya and Quina looked round at that, eyebrows raised.

Yaz stared back. "Well, either they did or it's been standing here gods know how long and no word of it has ever reached us. Maybe nobody has ever seen it." The idea that a whole city of ice with towers maybe miles high could have sat here undiscovered for generations seemed at once both possible and a frightening reminder of how few humans roamed the ice. If there was no sea beneath the ice here and it didn't lie on a route that crossed ice-covered land between two seas, then there was no reason for any clan ever to come this way. Perhaps none ever had, and no man or woman had laid eyes on this thing though it might have stood a thousand years.

They walked on, Erris in the lead with Zox, Yaz and the others at the back, trailing the sled on long harness straps. By the time they reached the shadows of the ice city it became clear that they had continued to misunderstand its scale. Yaz felt sure that many of the towers would overtop the Black Rock.

As they drew closer still the tower tops began to catch the light of the setting sun, igniting with their own red fire. The spires were anything from ten yards to several hundred yards wide. They rose to dizzying heights that made Yaz feel insignificant. The structures were as varied as a fungi grove, swelling, spreading, graceful, defying the wind. The ice from which they were made was white and frosted, denying any vision of the interior.

Behind the spires the sky lay the colour of an old bruise: a storm brewing in the east. It would be good to have shelter before it reached them.

Erris stopped. "There's something else."

"I see it," Maya panted in the harness as they drew level with him. "Someone's waiting for us?"

"Taproot!" Quina said.

Yaz looked at Erris doubtfully. She could barely see the distant dot on the ice near the first of the towers, but if Taproot had a body here why had he not come out to them already? In fact, why did he need them at all?

Erris said nothing, only continued to stare for a few moments more. He took his fingers from the side of his brow and shook his head. "One person, four dogs."

"Dogs?" Quina asked. "Is there a sled?"

"Let's find out." Erris walked on, his muscles whining with that high-pitched complaint they had started making a few days back.

"I don't like it." Maya's hand rested close to where her knife lay beneath her layers.

"Maybe he'll trade for more food and furs." Thurin sounded hopeful.

"Maybe he's seen the green!" Quina quickened her pace, outstripping Erris's.

Yaz said nothing. Part of her agreed with Maya's caution. But the needle had led them here. When she'd consulted it hours before it had pointed them in this direction and now a city lay before them. The needle had led them to a sea, and now to a city.

THEY CLOSED THE distance and Yaz could make out the stranger now, standing immobile in the wind, two dogs to either side, also motionless.

"I don't like this." Quina this time, echoing Maya's sentiment. "Why aren't the dogs moving?"

"Well trained?" Yaz had no experience of dogs. Only Quina and Maya had worked with them.

"Dogs don't stand like that," Maya said.

The man too was curiously still. For a moment Yaz wondered if he and the dogs had somehow died and been frozen in place. Ictha died on their feet like that. But dogs?

Quina came to a halt. "I vote we go around."

"Don't be silly," Thurin said. "We've come all this way . . . for this! And it's the first person we've seen in months."

Yaz exchanged a glance with Erris, then nodded. She dropped the sled harness and the lines behind her fell slack on the ice. The others dropped theirs too. "Come on." She led the way.

A sense of foreboding grew as they advanced, seeded by Maya and Quina's warnings and fed by the figures' enduring stillness.

Coming close Yaz could still see nothing of the person's face, bundled in furs as they were. The dogs kept their heads down, which struck her as odd given even her limited experience with the beasts. The wind fingering through their fur provided the only motion. All four dogs were dark-haired, large, but thin. Their fur seemed sparse compared to that of the ones kept by the three tribes, but it was warmer this far south, so that might explain it.

The gap narrowed to sixty yards, thirty, fifteen.

"Hello!" Yaz called out. She came to a halt, waiting for some response. Beside her Maya had her knife out now, clutched in a mittened hand.

Nothing.

"Are they dead?" Quina whispered.

"We should go back," Maya said.

"Back?" Yaz asked. "That's hardly very Axit."

"If you believe you are advancing into a trap, the best way to spring it early is to retreat." Maya took a step back, knife ready.

"Really?" Thurin asked. "We're doing this?"

Yaz shrugged. "If Maya says so." She began to step back too.

With a sigh, Thurin began to back away with her. Quina and Erris joined the retreat.

The man raised his head. Yaz saw now that it was a man, or had once been. His skin was a moving, interlocking pattern, stained black and red and green and yellow. The frost had taken his lips and the teeth revealed were crimson. One yellow eye regarded them with a curious hunger. The other was a crater of black flesh. With a single violent yank the man tore open his heavy furs and shrugged the robe to the ground. Demons crowded his bare torso too, allowing no patch of untainted skin to show.

"Eidolon!" Thurin screamed.

The thing began to run at them with a broken, unnatural gait.

Eidolon. Yaz remembered the Broken's cautionary tales. From time to time the mind of one of the Tainted would fracture and instead of the usual handful of demons they would suddenly fill with scores, hundreds even, until they were like the black ice, suffused with old evils. The only upside was that packed with so much power the creatures were able to break Theus's hold on them and escape the ice caves, wandering the surface and becoming a threat to those above.

With a deafening crack, three thick shards of ice erupted in a tight cluster, their points rising to ten or more feet. Trapped between them, the eidolon writhed to free itself, something about its silent rage more frightening than the worst of howls.

"Run!" Thurin sagged, clearly weakened by the effort of raising the ice.

"Don't turn your backs!" Maya shouted, still retreating, knife ready.

Yaz did the same, pulling her own blade from her furs. Like Maya, she was watching the dogs, expecting them to give chase. It didn't seem possible that the eidolon would escape. The bars of its icy cage were thicker than anything an Ictha could break.

The dogs did not give chase. Yaz's stomach heaved as, instead of charging, all four shook off their hides as if they were loose cloaks. The flesh exposed was a nightmare of blue, black, and dark red, frostbitten rather than demon-filled.

As silent as their master they threw themselves not after Yaz's friends but at the eidolon, leaping into gaps between the ice. They didn't pull at him or attack the shards confining him. Instead their flesh began to slough from their bones as if it were melting in a fierce heat. It didn't fall, though—rather it flowed, towards the eidolon, joining to his own corrupt flesh, building something new.

That was when Yaz retched and began to run. All of them did.

32

✦ ✦
✦

RUNNING OUT ONTO the open ice felt as if it offered no protection. Instinct drew them all to the city, hoping to lose themselves among the towering structures. It hurt to leave the boat-sled but Yaz hoped the eidolon would follow them rather than vent its rage on their gear.

Quina led the way, Thurin and Yaz close behind. Erris ran as if wading through deep snow, with even Maya outpacing him. And behind Erris, Zox seemed almost to plod, though even he seemed to inject as much urgency into the process as his dwindling energy reserves allowed. He might have an iron hide but he appeared to share their desire to get away from the eidolon.

Behind them came the noise of cracking and then falling ice. And, worse, the first sound to leave the eidolon's lipless mouth pursued them, a narrow howling, a thin, sharp noise carried to them on the wind, as if hunger had been given its own voice.

Panic drove them deep into the city before they stopped to check for pursuit.

"We left the sled!" Quina came to a dismayed halt.

"I don't think that thing is after our fish," Yaz panted.

"Is it coming?" Thurin leaned around the corner of a tower that stretched so far above them it seemed impossible, ridiculous, and meaning-less all at the same time.

"It's coming," Yaz said. "But I can't see it." She didn't want to see what kind of body had emerged from the broken ice.

"We should go back . . . to the sled," Erris said.

"No way!" Thurin shook his head. "That's what it will expect. If it's not here, then that's where it will be."

"So we carry on . . . and find Taproot." Erris was pausing when he spoke now, almost panting. He didn't look tired but he moved as if he were walking towards his own grave.

"Can we hide in one of these?" Quina scraped at the frosted ice wall of the tower rising beside them.

Thurin shook his head. "It's ice all the way through. It shouldn't be able to hold itself up like this."

They hurried on, lost within the forest of structures. The wind snaked in with them, its fury diminished as if it too were daunted by the work of the Missing. Yaz's eyes kept straying to the heights, so far above her that she could hardly see. She marvelled once again that this place in which they were so thoroughly lost, reduced to specks, was in turn dwarfed by the ice and so lost in its vastness that it had no place in the tales told by any tribe she had heard of.

Fear stalked them through gloom-filled passages between the impos-sibly tall towers. The eidolon had somehow found them in an ocean of ice. Surely it could hunt them through this maze. Yaz found herself haunted by the image of those dogs sloughing off their hides and joining their flesh to that of the eidolon. Whatever horror it had fashioned itself into was even now following their scent, bent close to the ice. Or perhaps waiting for them around the next corner, its mouth distended into some ghastly maw.

Erris and especially Zox, who had both so often been their strength in times of need, now moved with maddening slowness, unable to react to the urgency of their situation. The Ictha code that Yaz had been bound to since birth demanded that they be left behind, sacrificed to their weakness, and that the rest of them should run.

"No." Yaz forced herself to wait, yet again, while first Erris and then

Zox caught up with them. While the others kept watch she took advantage of the delay to consult the needle that Taproot had given her. The direction, which had been constant for so long, changed now as their destination grew closer and the ice city channelled them this way then that. The pathways between the towers and the walls that often joined their bases together had been in shadow when they first arrived. Now the gloom was thickening, seeming to climb the towers as the sun, long since hidden from sight, began to sink behind the lost horizon.

"Can you sense that thing?" Maya asked Thurin. "Sense its water like you did with the guards at the Black Rock, so we know where it is?"

Thurin shook his head without pausing his study of the darkening entrances to the road they were on. "That place was made of rock. This is all ice. You're asking me to notice a single drop in a sea."

They moved on in silence, covering a mile, then another. The city seemed impossibly large. Despite the variety of the spires, from ground level it all started to look very similar. More miles passed and they became more lost, more drowned in shadows.

"Where in all the hells is this Taproot?" Quina was unable to keep still, hopping from one foot to the other as if trying to hurry Zox along as he plodded towards them. "You think he'll be inside one of these?" She waved at the structures looming to either side.

"He's not really someone who needs anywhere to be . . ." Yaz had never quite managed to explain Taproot to the others. Maya seemed to think that Yaz had only seen him in dreams.

"He's a god then." Quina had put forward her theory before. Taproot, she said, was one of the lesser Gods in the Sky, a wind god without form or place.

Erris caught up with them. He shook his head but held his peace. He'd told Yaz that he saw no harm in the others thinking Taproot and Seus to be gods. As long as they didn't extend the same logic to him as well. And as long as Yaz never believed it.

The needle, in the sheltering hollow of Yaz's hand, swung sharply. "We need to turn left at the next chance. Come on." Zox was only yards behind them now.

A short distance on they reached a gap in the ice walls, allowing them to pass between the bases of the spires.

The sight that greeted them stopped Yaz in her tracks.

"That," Thurin said, "is not what I was expecting."

Everyone came to a halt, save Erris, who had already fallen behind again, and Zox, who had never caught up. Ahead of them as they turned was a wide plaza almost filled by a black dome. Perhaps black glass, perhaps just darkness. It had to be a thousand yards in diameter and at least three hundred yards high.

"What is it?" Thurin stood frowning at the thing as if his extra sense told him no more about it than the five he shared with the others.

"I have no idea." Yaz began walking directly towards it.

"Wait!" Thurin called after her.

"What for? We've come here for this. If Taproot meant us harm he could have just led us to . . . literally anywhere else."

Thurin shrugged and gave chase. She had a point.

They arrived together, breathless, stopping where the black wall met the ice. Even when almost touching the dome Yaz still couldn't tell whether it was solid or not.

"What is it?" Quina joined them, repeating Thurin's question.

"It's not ice," Thurin said.

"It's not shadow." Maya arrived.

"Someone should touch it," Quina said.

But Yaz already had. She took off her glove and laid her hand flat against the darkness. The surface beneath her fingers was hard, smooth, and almost warm. She rapped her knuckles against it but made no sound. "How do we get in?"

Erris crossed the plaza, straining for speed but going slower than walking pace. It looked as if he were fighting through some thick, invisible fluid. Back at the feet of the nearest towers Zox emerged from the shadows, lumbering forward as though dragging ten laden sleds up a pressure ridge. It seemed unlikely he would ever find the energy to leave the city again. But at least, Yaz thought, he would take his final rest in a place where the works of his vanished masters survived, rather than some nameless patch of ice.

"This Taproot led us here," Thurin said as Erris arrived. "Shouldn't he open the door?"

Erris laid his palm on the lightless surface. "Taproot is scattered." He paused as if gathering breath to speak again. "The Taproot that gave Yaz her needle and . . . sent her here can't communicate with the Taproot . . . inside this dome. If they could then they would integrate and . . . become the same and there would be no point sending us here."

Yaz frowned. "But if the Taproot who sent us could watch us from the skies and guide us to that sea . . ."

"Then maybe the Taproot here can't speak to the heavens. Maybe this black wall is too strong and this dome is a fortress," Thurin said.

"Or a prison." Maya tried to stick her knife into the wall but the point just slid across it. "Come on, Zox!" she shouted at the dog, still two hundred yards off.

Yaz sensed Maya's urgency and shared it. The eidolon could emerge from between the buildings at any moment. "If Taproot sent us here knowing that we would have to get inside by ourselves, then he must have known we would be able to do it."

It was Erris's turn to look dubious. "You last spoke to him in Vesta. Before you even left the ice and got taken to the Black Rock. I think you're crediting him with too much foresight. The Taproot you spoke with was a fragment, desperate and under siege by Seus. He may have *hoped* that you would be able to contact a more intact version of himself here, but as I have said before, he is not a god. He didn't know who or what you would bring with you or whether you would succeed."

"Let's succeed." Quina hugged herself. Despite the better meals of late she looked too thin for the ice, and painfully aware of just how far they were from any kind of help.

A narrow cry echoed across the plaza. The eidolon, somewhere near. Quina flinched. Suddenly the buildings on all sides felt that much closer, as if the whole plaza were contracting to one dangerous point.

"Where is it?" Thurin spun around, his wild gaze sliding over the many entrances.

"Can't tell," Maya said. "Too many echoes. Sounds travel differently here."

Yaz bit down on her fear and focused on the task in hand. She traced the wall down to the ice. "Thurin, get hold of yourself! Can you tell how far down it goes?" For all she knew, the dome was the tip of a miles-high tower that stood with its feet on the bedrock, somehow withstanding the flow of the ice. Or part of an immense black sphere that just nudged above the surface.

Thurin turned back to face her, chastened, though her admonishment had been aimed at herself as much as at him. His face tightened in concentration as he stared at the ice between him and the wall, then slackened in surprise. "It doesn't go down at all. It's just sitting on the ice."

"Is there a base to it? Or could we . . . dig our way in?" Erris asked.

Another moment's concentration. "There's a base."

"We could hit it really hard with an ice pick," Quina blurted out.

Yaz bit her lip. It didn't look or feel like the sort of wall that would give in to violence. Certainly not the sort of violence a swinging arm could deliver. On the other hand, if the eidolon caught them while they were trying more subtle means and they were all slaughtered without knowing that they could have just knocked a hole in it within moments of their arrival—that would be bad.

Even so, she decided to ask first. "Let us in!"

The shout echoed off the surrounding towers and died away. The square was silent, deep in shadow, hardly touched by the wind. Soon it would be night.

"Alright then, hit it."

Erris took the ice axe from his belt and drew back for a swing. He gathered himself then struck a solid underarm blow. It made no sound and left no mark that could be seen or felt.

"I think I could hit it harder but the haft of the axe would probably break." He drew his arm back again, looking at Yaz questioningly.

"No." Waste of any kind hurt her on some deep emotional level, just as it did all of the Ictha. "If that blow didn't scratch it, then it's not going to break before your pick does. There must be another way."

"Well. I've already shown you how to walk through walls," Erris said. "Maybe there are paths like that here."

"Of course!" Yaz shook her head as if to get the stupid out of it. She defocused her eyes to see the threadscape, the world of connections woven from impossibly fine strands of the Path. Here, as on almost all of the ice, the threads lay relatively few and ordered, disturbed only by the greater infinities that came bound around each of the travellers, joining them to each other, to their possessions, trailing back into their pasts and questing forward to their futures. The dome itself seemed almost devoid of threads, as if it had sat here for a great length of time and as if in all that time almost nothing had ever happened to it. Certainly there were no obvious disturbances that spoke of hidden entrances or places where the Missing had left secret tides that might draw a person into the space beyond.

Yaz began a slow circuit of the dome. Erris followed. Thurin started to join them but Erris held up a hand. "Best you stay here so we know when we've got back to where we started."

Again the eidolon's cry rang out, seeming even closer. Thurin pressed his lips into a narrow line and with a low creaking a single finger of ice rose between them, reaching chest height. "Now we'll know when we've done a circuit."

Yaz glanced back. "Come on then. All of you. We should stick together."

Erris raised a hand. "Zox. Stay here."

Yaz hesitated but then went on. Zox would slow them down. Also, she wasn't sure that even an eidolon could damage him.

IT TOOK ALL of Yaz's resolve to keep her sight on the threadscape, studying the wall while she made her slow advance. Somewhere close, the eidolon, an untold number of the worst evils clothed in corrupt flesh, was stalking the streets of the ice city. Looking for someone to work its malice on. The eidolon held enough devils to taint a whole clan by itself, and Yaz desperately wanted to be far, far away from it. But she kept to her task and relied on the others to watch her back.

Yard by yard they advanced. The circuit showed nothing, and by the time they returned to the marker Thurin had raised it was dark enough for Yaz to draw out her smaller stars for light. These had come from breaking another of the Watcher's eyes into fragments a few days back to use in the heat pot.

"Ideas?" Erris asked as they drew level with Zox. The dog raised its head slowly and favoured them with one of his unreadable looks.

"I thought this was your thing," Thurin said. "You know all there is to know about the Missing."

"Ha!" Erris shook his head ruefully. "I don't even know what they looked like."

"You know a thousand times more about them than we do." Thurin stuck to his point.

"Well." Erris folded his arms. "As the group's expert on the Missing . . . when it comes to getting into this dome . . . I have no idea. None at all."

"And isn't getting into and out of places supposed to be some kind of special marjal talent of yours?" Thurin persisted.

"I'm sure I could find my way in," Erris said, a little more sharply than he normally spoke. "Eventually. But it might take a while. How long do you have?" He raised a brow in question.

The group exchanged glances and shuffled around in their icy furs. Maya walked off a little way; Thurin leaned his weight against the dome as if hoping to fall through; Quina paced. All of them kept looking to the perimeter, where many dark streets opened onto the square.

"When I was in the city under the Black Rock," Thurin said, "there was a gate. The one those three mad old women led me to. I opened it with a star."

Yaz slapped herself. She snatched one of the small stars from its slow orbit around her head and brought it to the dome. As it came close she saw for the first time a glimmer of reflection from the surface that had hitherto drunk in all light, and when she tried to touch it against the wall, there was a small dimple, as if the wall were a stretched hide and the star a heavy weight resting on it. In fact the wall retreated from the star, refusing to allow contact, the black stuff eaten away, only to re-form as she withdrew her hand. Relief flooded her. "We just need a bigger star to get in!"

"They're on the sled," Thurin said in a sinking voice.

"We have to go back?" Quina groaned. "Through that?" She pointed to the street that had brought them here. Yaz couldn't even remember the path they'd taken.

"Couldn't you . . ." Thurin reached out his hand like Yaz did when she pulled a star towards her.

Yaz closed her eyes, trying to sense the stars she'd left behind. They couldn't be less than two or three miles away, more probably. She felt nothing, not even a hint of them, let alone what she needed to take hold of one and bring it to her. "I can't."

"I'll go," Maya said.

"What?" Quina looked horrified. "Out there? Alone?"

"I'm good at hiding." Maya looked grim.

"You couldn't pick any of those stars up," Yaz said, glad of a reason the girl couldn't go. "You can't even get close to them."

"I could do it . . ." Thurin said unwillingly. "I can use the ice to move them."

"Nobody's going alone," Yaz said. "We'll go together."

None of them spoke. The eidolon would find them in the dark out there and they would all die.

"Oh shit." Erris pointed. "It's here."

33

✦ ✦
✦

THE EIDOLON ADVANCED from the darkness of the street into the twilight of the square. The gloom mercifully hid detail but revealed enough for Yaz to be sure that the creature's flesh was flowing across its limbs.

The storm that had been a bruised sky in the east had now begun to break across the city like a vast wave. The wind howled and swirled, laden with ice, every gust sharp and stinging.

"We're going to have to fight." Erris began to advance towards their enemy, his stride slow, favouring one hip.

Quina drew a second knife and jogged to the left, clearly intending to use her speed to dart in and out. Yaz looked for Maya but she was gone, already part of the night.

"Ah, hells." Thurin shook his head and stomped off after Erris, buffeted by the wind. "Don't die, Yaz. Just don't die, alright?"

"I . . ." Yaz had no reply. The eidolon would kill them all. Knives wouldn't deal with something that could tear itself apart and put the pieces back together.

"Back together . . ." She opened her hands before her and the dozen small stars that had been orbiting her now gathered in her palms. All of them glowed in shades of the cool blue light that the Watcher's eye had held once free of Arges's influence. "I could put you back together!"

Saying it was easy. She'd built one star before, a tiny yellow one no bigger than her fingernail, fashioned from hundreds of dustlike grains. It had taken many hours of total concentration. Yaz glanced at her friends' backs. She didn't even have minutes, and concentration would prove difficult above the screams.

She floated two of the small spheres from her hands and pushed them together with her mind. This was a different prospect. These had all quite recently been part of the same star. They wanted to go back together. They fitted. She could almost see how. Even though each was a perfect sphere they also had other shapes to them, existing in dimensions beyond the eye's reach, and these pieces fitted together in a certain way. The song of each star reflected this shape, the harmonies between them revealing the teeth that would interlock to make one from many.

Out on the open ice between the nearest spires and the dome the eidolon broke into a run. It stood a rangy eight feet in height now and was sprinting swiftly, a skill gained from the dogs perhaps. Its mottled skin bristled with dog teeth and their talons tipped its fingers. Its face twisted as it came, the tainted flesh seemingly unable to choose one horrific aspect and stick to it.

Still thirty yards short of Thurin the thing crashed to the ground in a graceless heap, tripped by a ridge raised by his ice-work. It picked itself up, twisting its neck with a cracking sound that reached all the way back to Yaz beside the dome. Additional eyes opened in its chest as it drew itself to its full height and a spine-chilling howl broke from its overlarge mouth.

Thurin raised a swift ice spike but the creature proved too agile to impale and swept the obstruction aside, shattering it with one arm.

Yaz studied the pieces in her hands. She picked the two stars that most obviously belonged together and tried to join them, adding the force of her fingers to the pressure exerted by her mind. But the glowing spheres merely slid over each other. It had taken a great effort to break the Watcher's eye, but that had been like snapping a sword, and this was more akin to welding those two halves of the blade back together—requiring far more energy.

Quina raced in from behind the eidolon, stabbed it five or six times in succession, blindingly fast, and dived away beneath its frighteningly quick riposte. Any human foe would have flooded the ice with their life's blood, but the eidolon seemed to consider the attack little more than a slap. Instead of pursuing Quina it closed on Thurin. He backed away but too slowly. Erris passed him and blocked the eidolon's path.

Yaz tore her gaze away and focused on the stars in her hands. Their only chance was to get into the dome, and the stars were her key. She could see how the two pieces in her fingers should join, and the others orbiting her hands connected in similar ways, puzzle pieces rather than shards of a shattered bone. But when pressed too close they repelled each other and no force at her disposal, mental or physical, would overcome that barrier to their reunion.

Erris flew through the air, thrown like a toy. The eidolon lunged towards Thurin but slowed as if encountering an invisible barrier. Even so, it made steady progress, raking the ice with its hind claws. Thurin's ice-work should have been able to lift the beast from the ice and drop it from a great height, but somehow the devils crowding within it were shrugging off his talent. Desperate now, Thurin turned his skill to the ice instead, raising walls to block the eidolon's progress. It smashed through them with horrific strength.

Maya appeared from nowhere to cut the tendons in the creature's legs. It should have been crippled but its overactive flesh compensated and a wild backwards kick sent Maya skittering across the ice.

Yaz strove for the focus she needed to see the Path. She found it, a narrow blaze of potency, coiling through the larger spaces that the world sits in but never sees. Her hands closed around it and the familiar but frightening power flooded into her, threatening to fill and burst her all in the same heartbeat.

She released the source, gasping, shuddering with energies that wanted to explode from her in every direction, taking skin and bone with them. She had a choice, a vital one. To loose the power at the eidolon and hope that it was sufficient to destroy not only the body but the devils within. Or to try to use the power to reforge the stars in her hands into the larger one that might open the dome.

To put a large, smoking hole through the thing seemed the obvious answer. But Yaz had seen how the devils' combined strength had undone Thurin's ice-work. They might shrug off a quantal's talent as easily as that of a marjal. These were pieces of the Missing after all. But she knew that the power of a star could hold the separate demons at bay or even destroy them.

With a snarl of frustration she wrapped her glowing hands around the dozen small stars that had once been a singular object. Instead of releasing the power she'd been given in the customary burst of violence, Yaz poured it into the space between her palms. The pressure built and beams of brilliance escaped the crucible of her grasp. If not for the Path-given strength her hands would have been ripped one from the other, spilling the stars, but her fingers locked in place, stronger than iron clasps. As it was, the light within made a ghost of her flesh so it seemed that a blazing white star sat within a cage of bones. Shadows shrank away, retreating towards the towers.

Even with the impossible strength of the Path and the furnace between her hands it seemed to Yaz that the pieces would refuse to join. In the new light she saw more clearly, understanding how all twelve stars aligned along their lines of communication. She knew the energies within her would leak away soon whether she was successful or not. It had to be now. They *had* to join. She bent her will to the task.

Somewhere out on the ice someone screamed. It didn't sound like any of her friends. It didn't sound human. But she knew that it must be. The hurt and the fear in that sound were so great as to rob it of everything that identified the owner—she didn't even know if it was a man or a woman. She needed to know. She needed to help. A second scream battled the howling wind and contracted her stomach to a tight knot.

"No!" Yaz cried. And with a snap like the world's spine breaking the many became one, the whole much greater than the sum of its parts. The star in her hands was a fist-sized ball blazing with light. In the moment of its creation it had sucked in every drop of the power she'd taken from the Path, and maybe some of her own too.

Yaz sagged, exhausted and disoriented. She gathered herself and without looking at the fight turned towards the dome and found herself facing an opening in the black wall. It was as if an invisible sphere surrounded her new-formed star, maybe five yards in diameter, and wherever the sphere was . . . the dome wasn't. The circular opening moved as she moved her hand, its lower portion intersecting the ice so that she made an archway rather than a circular hole. The wall of the dome was a yard thick and through the opening Yaz saw what looked to be a replica of the ice city. This one was on a far smaller scale and cast in the same black material that formed the dome. In the starlight it was somehow mesmerizing. The storm blasted ice fragments around her, littering the black floor of the dome.

Yaz remembered the scream, the shock of it jolting through her, freeing her from the dome's fascination. She spun and saw the eidolon amid an ocean of broken ice, the surface rucked up like waves. Erris clung to one of its legs, being dragged along, unworthy of attention.

Quina lay sprawled, maybe dead, but the ferocity with which Maya was defending her suggested she believed the older girl to be alive. The eidolon loomed over them both, trying to seize Maya with taloned hands. Each attempt to snatch her up met with empty air and a sharp edge. She couldn't last long.

Zox had set off to intervene but moving at such a slow pace he'd covered only two-thirds of the distance between Yaz and the fight. Thurin was nowhere to be seen.

"Come on . . ." Yaz found her voice and screamed. "Come on! It's open!"

She was too late. She'd chosen wrong. They couldn't escape—the eidolon was too fast. If Maya turned her back the eidolon would rip out her spine.

"Come on . . ." She'd failed them.

With a sigh Yaz drew her knife and made to join the hopeless fight.

She saw Thurin in that moment. He hung in the wild air high above the eidolon, arms outstretched, palms to the storm-wracked sky. As she watched he raised his arms, bringing both hands together above his head, and in that action a maelstrom of loose ice rose from the battleground, as though some god had turned the world upside down and let it fall.

In the grip of Thurin's mind the white tornado defied the winds and spiralled into a tight column before him.

Down below, the eidolon stared up at this new antagonist, ignoring the sting of Maya's knife. In the spinning column a hard white core formed with a crackling sound as Thurin compacted hundreds of pieces into . . . Yaz wasn't sure what he was doing. The eidolon had proved immune to his power, in charge of whatever water remained in its own body, too swift and too strong to be trapped by what he raised against it.

Thooom! The ice-spear Thurin had fashioned struck down with greater speed than anything he could draw up from below. It hit the eidolon where shoulder meets neck and drove through, emerging just above the opposite hip and striking the ground where it sank its point deep.

"Run!" Yaz roared.

Maya backed away from the vicious swing of the eidolon's claws and began to drag Quina clear while Thurin worked to thicken and strengthen the ice-spear. Erris got to his feet and began to stumble towards the dome, falling on the rough ground, getting up and falling again.

Zox began to turn in a slow circle, and by the time he was facing Yaz, Erris and Maya were passing him, supporting Quina between them, her left leg hanging useless.

"Quickly!" Yaz hurried out to help, leaving her star on the ice beside the dome to maintain the doorway.

Thurin joined them, feet on the ground now, and stumbling almost as badly as Erris. The effort that had been wrung from him had clearly taken a heavy toll. Back behind him the eidolon thrashed and screamed. A many-voiced rage filled its howls. Being impaled seemed more of a source of frustration than pain. A loud cracking of ice accompanied the arrival of Yaz's hand on Quina's shoulder.

"It's breaking free," Maya snarled, releasing Quina to Yaz's greater strength.

"Ah!" As they approached the hole in the dome's wall Thurin gasped and dropped back. Quina's eyes fluttered open and she started to struggle in Yaz's grip as she hauled her forward. "No! I can't!"

"It's . . . the star," Erris said slowly. "They can't go near it."

"We'll have to drag them." Yaz pushed on, keeping tight hold of Quina.

Erris hung on to Quina's other arm and stopped her. "Their minds . . . will break."

Yaz spun round, pointing at the eidolon, still transfixed by two yards of ice-spear but lurching towards them in ungainly fashion even so. "And their *bodies* will break if they don't go through."

"Go in!" Thurin said. "Take it in. Then we can follow."

With no time to argue, Yaz went forward and picked up the star, holding it before her to light the interior. She stepped in, trying to see in all directions at once. The air was strangely warm and held alien scents.

"Oh." The first of the towers inside the dome started to vanish as her star came near to it. The invisible sphere around the star ate a growing chunk out of it until the top portion had nothing to stand on but somehow hung where it was anyway.

"Hey!" Erris called after her. "Don't go too far!"

Yaz turned and saw that the hole in the wall was shrinking behind her, a circle now with a lower rim. Thurin and the others were advancing on it, the eidolon fifty yards behind them, writhing to rid itself of the ice-spear.

Yaz stepped back towards the others and the rim of the hole vanished, exposing the ice once more.

"Hey!" Thurin called from outside, raising his arms as if that might fend off the star's aura. "Not so close."

Perplexed, Yaz took several slow steps backward, watching the hole shrink until it was a circle just a yard across with its centre level with the hand she held the star in. She held it as steady as she could. "Try now!"

Thurin came forward, his upper half visible through the hole, strain in his face as he braved the star's effects. "Don't step back any further or this hole's going to vanish and snip me in two." He tried to make a joke of it but his face was white with fear. He reached out a hand to grip the edge and prepared to lunge forward through the opening. "Ah!" He snatched his hand back. "I'm bleeding." He tried to suck at his fingers through his glove.

Erris reached out and set a finger to the edge. "It's very sharp!"

Yaz could see now that it would be. This wasn't a tunnel through the wall, just the scoop removed by the invisible sphere around her star. Naturally it left a sharp outer edge.

"How do we get in?" Quina came into view, slumping against Thurin.

"This edge is like a razor." Erris touched it again. "Put some weight on it and it'll cut through anything we use to cover it."

Yaz moved forward, widening the hole but causing everyone save Erris to stagger back. Behind them the eidolon had caught up with Zox. It ignored the dog, bent on prey of flesh and blood, but as it passed Zox the dog somehow caught hold of its leg, folding himself around it to hold on. The eidolon howled, swinging the iron hound around in fury, smashing white flurries from the ice.

"Erris, help them please." Yaz backed away to ease the star's pressure on her friends. For a moment she moved too far back and the hole closed entirely, leaving her alone, sealed away from the world, the storm suddenly silenced. Even that moment's isolation scared her. She was in an alien place dealing with forces she didn't understand. At any moment the walls might seal forever, leaving her trapped inside and her friends trapped outside.

Yaz stepped forward and the hole yawned again. The eidolon had its jaws clamped around its own shin a little way below the knee. The thing was chewing its leg off to get free of Zox and reach them.

The bone broke with a snap.

"It's coming!" Maya shouted.

A desperate idea struck Yaz. "Thurin?" She knew he was at the limits of his strength, his talent exhausted but . . . "Can you lift them through?"

"Not Erris." Thurin's eyes filled with terror. "And what if I drop someone?"

Yaz sagged. There had been a time when Erris could have thrown the others through like spears and dived through after them. Soon the power of motion would leave him and the light would die from his eyes.

"Or . . ." Quina shouted through the hole with rising panic. "You could just put your hand on the ground."

"How would . . ." Yaz felt suddenly foolish. "Oh, I see!"

She moved the star down. The hole moved down too, until when her hand touched the ground, the hole in the wall became a small arch that the others could crawl through with their bellies on the ice. How she hadn't seen it before—how none of them had—she couldn't say. Fear makes you stupid. She set it on the ground.

"Quickly!"

Thurin came first to help Quina through.

"Hurry!" Only Maya and Erris remained outside with the eidolon.

"Maya! Go!" Erris lacked the power to raise his voice.

"You first. You're too slow to stay."

"I'm not—" Erris found the strength to shout. "Maya! No!"

"What's going on?" Yaz could see only legs.

The next thing she saw was black hair, coiled close to a brown scalp, and Erris crawling in. "The stupid girl! She backed off . . . I couldn't make her go first."

Yaz, Thurin, and Quina worked together to haul Erris clear of the low arch.

"Maya!" Yaz hollered through the hole. "Come on!"

"Maya!" Thurin lay close to the arch, trying to see through.

Suddenly she was there, diving through on her belly.

"That was eas—" The fierce grin on her face tightened into pain. She was half-in, half-out, and something had been driven through her thigh, pinning her to the ice.

"Maya! No!" Yaz lunged to catch hold of the girl's arms.

A huge black hand mottled with red reached down to sink bone talons deep into the base of Maya's spine. A twist, a crunch, a spray of crimson and her face went slack. The moment of shock loosened Yaz's grip and in that moment Maya was gone, yanked away.

The hole closed. So suddenly it seemed impossible that it should make no noise doing so. Yaz reached for her star to reopen the wall, but met resistance.

"What?" She turned to see Erris hanging on to the star with both hands, leaning back against her pull.

"She's gone, Yaz. Maya's gone. And if you let it, that thing out there will be in here the moment you open the wall. And it will kill the rest of you."

34

✦　✦
✦

FOR A LONG moment the two halves of Yaz's mind battled on the edge of a knife. Half of Yaz knew that Maya was dead and that opening the wall was madness. The other half didn't care about facts, only about right and wrong. That part wanted nothing but to rush out and save her friend even if that meant taking on death itself.

"She can't be gone." Thurin smacked his fist against the wall.

Quina said nothing. She sat and stared at nothing and held herself so still that if not for the tremor in her hands Yaz would have thought her possessed by some spirit. Two tears rolled down her drawn face.

Yaz felt a scream building inside her, irresistible as a sneeze. She stood, facing the black city before them, hands balled at her sides.

"Yaz?" Erris started.

The scream tore itself from her, a wordless roar of rage and loss, echoing about the dome, setting the star blazing, a hot blue light flecked with crimson.

"We should go on." Erris started to reach towards her then let his hand drop.

"You think the eidolon can get at us in here?" Yaz snarled her reply, angry at everything, half hoping the monster *would* find a way in so she could make it eat her star.

Erris spread his hands. "I don't know. Normally, no, but with Seus helping it, anything's possible. We should find Taproot while we can."

"She can't be dead. She came so far." Quina spoke the words as if reasoning through a puzzle, as if her logic could undo what had happened.

"We should go." Thurin turned away from the wall and made to join Erris before shying away from the star's aura.

"Give us some time." Yaz spoke more harshly than she'd intended. "Doesn't she deserve longer than a few moments?"

"She deserved a *lifetime*." He spun to face her and she blinked in confusion. It looked as if he were orbited by tiny stars, but then she realized that some unconscious aspect of his ice-work had taken the tears from his face and set them hanging in the air where they caught the starlight. "But she didn't get it. And now we're here and she would want us to fulfil our mission."

Yaz managed a smile. Maya would have used those words. *Fulfil our mission*. Axit to the end.

"Quina." Yaz held her hand out to the girl and drew her to her feet. She came up awkwardly, favouring her left leg. Yaz opened her mouth for a word of comfort but suddenly Quina had her face buried in Yaz's furs, choking broken sobs into her shoulder. Hesitantly, Yaz wrapped her arms about her, shocked at Quina's thinness. It wasn't the Ictha way. The Ictha endured: they didn't waste energy on grief. But then she remembered how Quell had said her father broke down after she and Zeen went into the pit and, as if given licence, something snapped inside her too, and she joined Quina in her sorrow.

She didn't know how long they stayed like that but eventually they parted. Yaz brushed the tear-wet hair from Quina's face and turned to Thurin, who was crouched on the dome's black floor studying his hands as if they were heaped with his thoughts. "Let's go."

They moved on further into the dome. Yaz sent her star ahead of them and everywhere it went it simply erased the black spires, carving a moving hole among them, allowing them to return as it passed on.

"What's the point of all this?" Thurin waved at the towers. "And the ones outside?"

"I'm wondering what we'll find in the middle," Erris replied. "Another plaza and a much smaller dome? With a tiny city inside?"

"Does it need a point?" Yaz asked. "Does Zox have a point, or the others like him? Aren't these just the works of another abandoned city mind, left to its own devices and slowly going mad?"

The buildings came to a sudden end earlier than expected. The plaza in this city was a hundred yards on each side, and the black floor lay scattered with scores of circles, all of them the same, wide enough for Yaz to lie in with her arms stretched out and still be a few feet shy of touching the edges. All of their perimeters were about a foot wide, six inches thick, and set with sigils.

"Haze-gates," Thurin breathed. "Like the one I saw."

"That should have been called a water-gate," Yaz said. "It nearly drowned you. What was hazy about it?"

"Hayes gates," said a mildly irritated voice behind them. "Watergate was a whole other thing."

They spun around, and there, sketched in pale light, like one of Thurin's dreams patterned on the mist, stood Elias Taproot.

"What?" Yaz had, in the long weeks of their journey, thought of many things she would say to Taproot when they finally met again. "What?" was not one of them.

"Hayes gates are nothing to do with being hazy. They're named for their creator. I met him once, you know? Professor Hayes. He was older by then, of course, past his best, and I had just finished as a student, but he was still the most brilliant man I ever met." Taproot narrowed his gaze at Thurin. "And how does his name come to be on the lips of a tribesman at the end of the world?" He glanced around at the rest of them. "And who are you people anyway? And what do you want?" He kept his eyes on them while extending a long arm and then a long finger to point directly at the floating star. "And where did you get a core-stone?" Suspicion flickered over the narrow angles of his face.

"We've come from the city of Vesta," Erris said.

"And you sent us here," Yaz added.

Taproot raised a brow at that.

Yaz continued. "And there's an eidolon hunting us outside the dome. I think Seus sent it."

Taproot winced at the name. "Nobody sends an eidolon. Maybe he steered it here, or led it. But Seus being after you would explain all this." He waved a hand at the plaza and in an instant all the Hayes gates lit up, each becoming a window onto some other place. Yaz could only see the nearest handful clearly, each focused on a different monster. The closest was a huge hunter, leaking starlight, hauling its articulated body across the ice with a chaotic thrashing of limbs. In another a silver thing hurtled along on a blur of motion that might be legs, its whole body sharp as a raptor fish. Yet another showed something more akin to a rolling blob of fat but with disturbing shapes dimly visible within it, one that looked like a man's bones.

"What are they?" Quina breathed.

"The question you should have asked is where are they going?" Taproot said. "And the answer is here. They're all headed this way."

Thurin glanced up at the black roof above them as if expecting it to reverberate from a mighty blow. "How soon—"

"Which"—Taproot cut across him—"returns me to my question: who are you people and what do you want?"

"Like I said." Yaz could still hear Maya's last scream and was in no mood to bow and scrape before a false god. Or even be polite. "You sent us here. One of the other yous did. And I wasn't going to come because all I want is just to go south and see the green world."

Taproot shook his head. "That's not possible. It's thousands of miles to the Corridor and there's nothing out there but ice. Currently it's . . ." He looked to the side as if he could see something they couldn't. "Holy Christ. Minus eighty-six out there. And that's without the windchill factor. All you're wearing is bits of dead animal. How are you even alive?"

Yaz didn't understand the question and shook it aside. "But we ran out of food and needed help. And the price we paid for that is a friend murdered while we tried to get through your walls."

Taproot pressed his lips together. His image flickered, and just for a fraction of a second Yaz thought she saw a pained expression in place of his annoyance. Sympathy maybe. "I didn't know anyone was out there. I didn't have eyes on you or the eidolon. The walls are kept strong. The gates are my only eyes on the world outside."

"What I want now," Yaz continued, "is to carry on with our journey and have Seus leave us alone." She began to walk among the gates, peering down into each as she passed. For some reason they reminded her of the pool Eular had shown her, the one that had been too perfect for the water in it to freeze. Some showed monstrosities on the move; some just looked upon great wastes of white, giving no sense of scale. She could have been looking at a few square yards of ice or a hundred square miles.

She had expected Taproot to follow her or to demand that she stop. Instead he just watched her, as did the others, and so she roamed, hoping to be able to tie down her anger and her grief so that she could negotiate with Taproot and not speak her mind so plainly that he simply threw them out for the eidolon to finish off.

Twice she saw gates opening onto clans on the move, one seen from a distance at ground level, the other seen much closer but from above. The sight of so many people all in one place, moving with one purpose, made her ache for the Ictha and the certainty of that life.

Yaz paused to study the clan seen from above. All of the gates radiated cold, and though she couldn't hear or feel the wind, she thought that perhaps if she were to step into one she might fall into being within the scene shown to her. She resisted the temptation. She moved on to peer at another hunter crunching through the ice. The idea that the gates might allow contact made her give this pool and the next a wider berth in case one of the horrors Taproot was tracking could reach out and snatch her.

"And what did this other me want you to do when you got here?" Taproot called, running out of patience. "Did he give you a message?"

"All he gave me was this." Yaz pulled the needle from the hides above her collarbone and started to return to the others.

"Ah, that's what you used to open the dome," Taproot said, as if some puzzle had been solved.

"No . . ." The idea that she might have simply popped the dome like a bubble using the needle left Yaz aghast. If she'd thought to use it then,

Maya would have lived. Yaz's stupidity had killed her friend. "I used the star."

"Star? Oh, the core-stone?" Taproot's gaze flitted to the floating star. "But a star that size shouldn't be able to . . ." His eyes widened. "Something's been done to this one! It's been supercharged in some manner." He frowned. "The other Taproot gave it to you?"

"I . . ." Yaz shook her head, miserable. "I . . ."

"We took it from an automaton built from Missing-made parts," Erris said. "Yaz broke it into pieces then put it back together."

"Remarkable!" Taproot clapped his hands but they made no sound. "And you too, young man. You've been broken into pieces and reassembled in some manner."

"I fell—"

Another clap of those narrow, long-fingered hands. "You had a great fall! Ha! A veritable Humpty-Dumpty. But this time all the king's horses and all the king's men *could* put you back together again." He turned back to Yaz, who wondered if perhaps isolation might not have driven this Taproot mad. "Admittedly, I myself am in need of some . . . reintegration, shall we say? All of us broken things. Perhaps we do have a common interest. The needle please, young woman." He extended a hand.

Yaz started towards him, only to have her attention dragged to the left, where one of the gates showed yet another icescape. This one, however, was neither empty nor filled with monsters or tribers. Instead it showed a group of four figures in unfamiliar clothing, not furs or hides but long coats more similar to something Erris might wear. Two of them were curled on the ice, the third sitting close by with the fourth cradled in her lap. No one sits or lies on the ice unless they're dead or close to death. Three of them looked to be female, judging by their long hair. The sitting figure drew Yaz's attention most. Its skin was darker even than Erris's, past brown into black, and its hair as tightly curled, cut close to the scalp like his. Boy or girl, Yaz could tell that they were young, Maya's age perhaps.

"Where is this?" Yaz pointed to the scene.

Taproot raised both brows, his hand still extended for the needle. "The first question is always 'when?'" Lowering his hand, he came to join her, walking as swiftly as a hunska, his feet making no sound. "Ah." He peered past Yaz, studying the scene. "That's now and a very long way from here indeed, thousands of miles to the south. The survivor is one of the potentials I've been studying." He looked back at Yaz. "Needle, please."

"Potentials?" Yaz handed it to him.

Taproot took the needle, somehow managing to hold it though his fingers were made of light. A slight shudder passed through him as he made contact, a ripple, as if he were a reflection on water that had been disturbed. For a long moment afterwards he remained without motion, not even a twitch in his eyes, saying nothing. "Ah!" A breath snatched in as though he'd broken the surface after a long dive. "Forgive me. It's always like that when I integrate a lost fraction of myself." Dark eyes fixed on Yaz with new interest. "Now I see why I sent you!"

"The Taproot I met was in the needle?" Yaz frowned. The process put her in mind of Theus assembling the scattered evils that constituted his dark half.

"A copy of him." Taproot waved the question away. "He was a small fragment but we've been separate for many years and there was a lot of new data to assimilate." He let the needle fall with distaste. "It's come to this . . . We have to store our information in physical objects like savages and have them carried here and there by foot. But until Seus is cleared from the networks there's no other choice."

"What about this?" Yaz pointed at the scene by their feet. Erris, Quina, and Thurin had come to join them now to stare down at the dead and dying children. Erris was moving better, as if simply being within the dome were somehow restoring his strength. "Who's this girl?"

"As I said." Taproot pushed his upper lip under his lower one, contemplating. "A potential. Seus is working to crack open one of the remaining arks and if he gains control he'll bring down the moon. That would close the Corridor and leave the whole of Abeth sheathed in ice."

Yaz shook her head. "Arges said they were going to open the ark to follow the Missing into th—"

"What? No. Seus tells people what they want to hear to get them to do what he wants done." Taproot dismissed the idea. "To have any chance of stopping him I need someone to get me into the ark he's focusing on before he does, and that requires an individual possessing very rare talents. So rare in fact that many generations can pass without seeing a single person born who meets the mark. It's possible the girl might have served, but the question is moot now. You're here and you've already proven your talents."

Yaz frowned. "But . . . you're not just going to let them die?"

"Watch me." Taproot turned and walked away.

"Wait!" Yaz shouted after him, suddenly angry. She'd just seen a girl die and one was enough. "This isn't right!"

Taproot turned with a slightly guilty look. "People die all the time. Thousands every year. I could fill these gates with images of sickbeds and disasters. I can't save them all. I can't, in fact, save any of them."

Thurin stepped up to stand shoulder to shoulder with Yaz. "But this is a gate. I was told I could step through one and go anywhere. I had a sea flow through one and try to drown me. So can't you just open it and let them come here? You can't save everyone. Those sickbeds and disasters would need medicine or miracles to save them. But these girls, certainly that one holding the other one, they could come here where it's warm and they'd be . . ." It looked as if he wanted to say "safe" but thought better of it. "We could help her."

Taproot seemed to notice Thurin for the first time. He pressed his lips into a flat line. "If you want to use a Hayes gate to go from one place to another you need a gate at both ends. If you want to use one to see a remote location, then that's a different matter: you just need some clever steering and a bit of temporal orbital mechanics." Seeing their incomprehension he reiterated the important bit. "You need a gate at both ends."

"Unless . . ." Erris said.

"You know something about Hayes gates that I don't?" Again Taproot arched a brow.

"I doubt it." Erris looked around at the dozens of gates lying on the dome's floor. "As far as I know Vesta only had one, and I didn't know about it until Thurin told me. But I know there are other ways to move around the cities of the Missing. There are paths through walls, paths through a hundred yards of stone that quantals can take. The city told me that if there was a quantal path-walker at both ends of such routes, then they could open a passage that anyone could take."

Taproot nodded and interlaced his long fingers. His hands were never still, always plucking at each other as if to keep occupied when they weren't underlining his words.

"So," Erris continued, "I'm thinking that this girl must be a quantal full-blood for you to have been interested in her if you're looking for abilities like Yaz owns. And if that's the case, isn't there any way that the two of them can boost the link that allows us to see this image into a link that will allow passage? At least from there to here?"

"No."

Taproot said it too quickly though, and both hands remained still, the only time that Yaz had seen him speak without their contribution.

"I don't believe you," Yaz said.

Taproot widened both eyes in great surprise. "On what basis? You're a girl raised by nomads on the ice. I'm an expert. I'm a scientist with millennia of experience. I'm the one who—"

"You're a bad liar."

That at least shut Taproot up.

"Alright!" he snapped at last. "So maybe your data echo here has a point, but it would be enormously difficult to achieve, enormously dangerous, would require two quantals of remarkable ability, a core-stone of significant size, and would only be able to bring the remote party here. Additionally it wouldn't allow any passengers, and I've observed that young lady long enough to know that she's not going to leave her friends there to die."

"They look dead already," Quina observed. "They'll all be dead before nightfall either way."

"What . . . what are you doing?" Taproot stalked back to where Yaz had knelt beside the ring and set her hands to sigils engraved along the sides. "When I said dangerous I didn't mean just to you—"

Yaz glanced at the other three and told them to get back. Thurin did the opposite, coming to stand beside her, one hand finding her shoulder.

"I meant dangerous to the city. And I don't just mean this one, or the ice one outside. I meant the one under the ice. So unless your friends can get outside that kind of blast radius in a hurry then I advise you to stop."

Thurin's face hardened as he turned away from the gate to face Taproot. "If you'd ever walked to the edge of death out on the ice you wouldn't be able to leave someone out there either."

Yaz's guilt about the long march to the sea flared at this and she resolved to be worthy of Thurin's misplaced faith. It had been Erris who saved Thurin, Quina, and Maya. Yaz had fallen into herself and walked on, leaving them in her wake. This girl, though, this girl she would not leave behind.

She brought her blazing star to sit at the middle of the gate, waking all the sigils around its perimeter. The image took on new reality. Coldness bled from it; she could hear an echo of the wind. With utmost concentration, Yaz reached into the gate with her mind, defocusing her eyes to see the threadscape. The gate was very clearly a nexus of threads, directly linking many of those in the remote location showed to those flowing from Yaz, her friends, and the black city within the dome. Beyond that the complexity was mind-bending. The gate wove threads in ways Yaz hadn't imagined before and couldn't fathom now with the example before her. Using something and understanding how it works are two different things, though.

Yaz had already used the Path not more than half an hour previously, so to touch it now was beyond her, but she could still see it if she tried. It lay outside her reach, a thin band, distant but burning so bright as to vanish the threadscape just as surely as the sun chases the stars from the sky.

Her head still ached with the aftershocks of her star coming together from its pieces but she tried to focus on following the threads that led through the gate. These formed the true connection to the scene showed; this was not the mere observation of shape and form in a moving image, this was deeper than touching. Suddenly she was profoundly aware of that distant place, the chill of the ice, the girl's pain, her grief, and the absence of any other emotion, or any other thoughts. Only one heart still beat there. The friend the girl cradled was dead and cooling, the other two already frozen in place, part of the ice that would eventually subsume them and hold them till the end of days.

Can you hear me? Yaz tried to force her voice along the connection. "Can you hear me?" She spoke the words too.

"She's called Maliaya," Taproot said, clearly resigned to the prospect of having his home replaced by a crater larger than the falling star had made. "It might help get her attention."

Maliaya? Can you hear me? Yaz tried a different, less used, muscle in her mind and sent her thought trembling along the threads that joined her to the girl.

Maliaya stiffened. "Nina?" One hand tightened its grip on the dead girl as she struggled to move her; the other hand remained an ineffectual claw. "Nina? *Sia masleta! Che conco tua mea fleaa!*"

"Nina? O Ancestor! I thought you'd left me!" The words, spoken without inflection and in Taproot's voice, came just as Yaz understood that the girl wasn't speaking the way that the tribes spoke. The idea that someone could be so alien as to not use the same words that she did had never occurred to Yaz. She'd never heard of anything like it before, save for Zox. It seemed miraculous that Taproot could understand the girl and replace her words with the right ones. But Yaz reminded herself that Thurin could fly, and focused her attention.

Maliaya, can you hear me?

"I hear you, Nina." Taproot's voice replaced the girl's as she bent over her friend's corpse, studying her immobile, bone-white face. "I don't understand . . . are we dead now?" The tears froze before they could fall.

Yaz understood the girl's confusion. The cold had got into her thoughts. It happened towards the end. *I'm not Nina,* Yaz projected. *But I want to help you. I can only do it if you help me too, though, Maliaya.*

Maliaya peered around her, trying to narrow her hood against the wind's bluster and the sharp ice it carried. "I can't see you."

I can see you, Maliaya. I'm somewhere else. Somewhere safe. I need you to help me open the path between us. You understand when I say the Path? Yaz wondered if she should have called it the Path or the river that flows through all things, and had just started to wonder how the girl was understanding *any* of the words, when she realized that she hadn't pushed either description at her, but had sent the image and the idea instead. Somehow this means of communication sidestepped the need for words of any type.

Maliaya?

Suddenly the Path flashed bright before Yaz, an infinity of writhing sea serpents thrashing through spaces and angles beyond imagining. Somehow, Maliaya stood on it, unbowed by the cold, walking the Path, energies crackling about her feet, blazing up around her, flooding through her. The Path tried to throw her off at each of its never-ending turns, a multitude of them fitting in between each step, and yet with a dancer's grace and a terrifying singularity of purpose the girl kept walking. She couldn't last long, though—nobody could; in moments the power would overwhelm her, consume her, burst her asunder, leaving not even a wisp of smoke for the wind to take.

Yaz knew she had to act. The Path was too distant for her to touch, but the girl seemed closer. Yaz reached for the Path as she had so many times before. This time one of her outstretched hands met flesh. Fingers closed around her fingers. The awful power of the Path flooded into her a moment later, more than she had ever known or thought possible. She screamed, wanting nothing save to let go, but Maya's image burned across eyes blinded by the Path's brilliance, and Yaz hung on as if it were Maya she held and that this time if she only clung on to her then the girl would pull free of the eidolon and come through the wall unscathed. It felt as though she were reduced to ash and twisted bone, as if the hand she clasped the girl with were a blackened claw. Nothing could survive what had filled them, yet even as it tore her apart, Yaz pulled. Maliaya burst out of the gate as if surfacing from a deep pool. Yaz fell back, hauling her clear, both of them burning with light and fire, sending the others scattering and making Taproot's projection vanish as the wind shreds mist.

Yaz struggled to own the power within her but it was beyond her strength. She sensed it would burst from her, uncontrolled, and the blast would leave nothing standing for a great distance. The white heat of it blanked her mind, leaving no room for fear or sorrow. The only imperative was release.

292 ◆ MARK LAWRENCE

And suddenly the great pressure of all that energy . . . vanished. Maliaya had somehow taken enough control of it to send it back through the gate. The scene on the far side disappeared, to be replaced by white and nothing but white. A great fog of vaporized ice hiding a crater of unknown dimensions.

Maliaya stood among them, shockingly real, the first new flesh-and-blood person Yaz had seen in an age. She seemed dazed, her eyes not seeing, unsteady on her feet. Erris reached to support her but in an instant she'd taken his arm and used her body to undercut him, throwing him into the gate despite his weight. She'd moved like Erris did when he fought, but some of the Path's power must have been lingering in her to have tossed him like that. She stepped towards Yaz, still in her fighting stance, brow furrowed. Quina intervened, quicker than thought, and, reacting nearly as fast, Maliaya snapped a series of punches towards her, using only her good arm. Quina twisted out of their path, one after another, only to have her feet swept from under her by a leg swing she didn't see coming. Yaz and Thurin closed together, both to protect Quina and to secure the newcomer, but, twisting and kicking with amazing fluidity, Maliaya had them both on the ground.

Erris rose behind the girl, standing on the surface of the gate. She didn't seem to see him or show any further interest in Yaz or the other two on the floor, but he approached cautiously even so.

"Nina?" Maliaya half sobbed, looking around wildly. "Where are you?" She started to turn unsteadily, then without warning collapsed into a boneless heap.

Yaz got to her hands and knees, gasping for breath. The girl had driven a heel into the centre of her torso and somehow robbed her of air. It seemed inconceivable that Maliaya had been so close to death and yet so deadly. But in drawing her through the gate Yaz had bound them so tightly that they had almost shared a heartbeat—she knew that despite what had just happened the stranger had been hanging on to life by her fingertips.

"How . . . how could she fight like that?" Thurin got up slowly, rubbing his neck and wincing.

"She's such a little thing . . ." Quina limped over for a closer look. Yaz thought Maliaya wasn't much younger than Quina, perhaps fourteen, but she was closer to Maya's height.

Yaz knelt beside the girl and started to ease her gloves off. Like her long coat, they were too thin, too flimsy. They reminded her of what Erris wore in the worlds of memory where he had first walked with her.

Quina crouched to help her. The only other ice-triber in the group now, she knew exactly what needed doing. They checked Maliaya's extremities. Her very dark skin made it harder to tell what damage had been done, but it was bad. Both hands and both feet showed signs of severe frostbite, but her right hand, the one she hadn't used when fighting, was definitely the worst, the fingers hard and immobile, the blood within turned to red ice. Yaz and Quina exchanged grim looks. They held the icy fingers between their hands and breathed warmth into them, but both knew that it was too late.

35

✦ ✦
✦

THURIN

WHEN HE HAD left the caves of the Broken in search of Yaz, Thurin hadn't any real idea what he would find in the lands above. Over the years, as he grew up among his people, he had built a model of the unseen world in his mind, constructed from the pieces his life had furnished him with. Unable to make sense of the tales that trailed their owners into the Pit of the Missing every four years, he'd built the sky too small, the wind too tame, the ice too narrow. And when he found within himself the unexpected power of flight, and birthed himself a second time, out into the reality that had forged Yaz, he discovered how wide the gap lay between his mean imaginings and the fierce white wideness of her life.

Since that day when the dark had spat him out into the wind, Thurin had experienced so many things so far beyond his dreaming. But sitting now upon a solid black chair, listening to two dead men speak, he thought he had perhaps reached the pinnacle of all that strangeness. One of the dead men had been born before the tribes and their tales, so long ago that the ice had not yet come to bury the city, and the other was so old that he considered the first a mere baby, his millennia of experience an eye blink. One who had built a body of metal and board and other things for which Thurin had no name, and had crafted it so finely that without his ice-work

Thurin would believe it real. One who wore a body of light that neither wind nor cold nor an enemy's blade could touch.

"I came with the marjal fleet," Taproot was saying. "But I'd had a long journey before reaching their federation when it was in its infancy. When you travel such distances at such speeds time crawls and the universe grows old far more quickly than you do." He shrugged. "Eventually you run out of stars." He waved a hand at the black dome above them and the crimson heavens appeared, sprinkled across it as if it were the night sky rather than an impenetrable yard of darkness keeping out the eidolon and whatever other of Seus's minions might have arrived to destroy them. "On the other hand, if you stay put, you run out of worlds."

"You're like me, though," Erris persisted. "A man drawn into a machine and realized inside it in a different form?"

Taproot's eloquent hands framed a maybe before he spoke his answer. "There's a difference. I'm an echo. I existed at the same time Elias Taproot lived and breathed. The network created me as a copy based on observation. A *lot* of observations. But still an external process. It's possible that the 'real' Taproot still lives and breathes. He had a limited number of years to spend but the mechanics of the universe mean that if you have a fast enough ship you can choose to spend those years however you want. All at once in an unbroken century, or maybe a minute a millennium, so that you can spend your dotage here with us, confronted by a galaxy of dying stars.

"You, young man, are the product of a different technology. You weren't created as a copy of the original via a process of observation—you were made as a replacement through a cell-by-cell dissection of the unfortunate who fell into Vesta. Does that make you a copy or a transformation? That's a question for the philosophers.

"Putting yourself back into the physical world was a bold move. The technology for that is very rare, even among the cities of the Missing. I'd not believed any such survived. But my kind generally refuse any such manifestation. Either the process creates a copy—which is dangerous because . . . well, do you want something in the world that knows everything you do and shares all your ambitions, including your ambition to be the singular, true version of yourself? Or it requires that you transfer yourself wholly into the physical, which is so restrictive! And, more importantly, so dangerous. It's never been clear to me if only cowards live as long as I have, or if living so long makes everyone a coward. But there it is: Elias Taproot is not a man who puts himself in danger if he can possibly find someone else to do the job instead. Sadly, in this instance I really need to do the job myself. I need to stop Seus getting control of the moon and crashing it into Abeth. Which is why I need Yaz to take me to the Corridor and open the ark for me."

Thurin would have asked one of his thousand new questions but Yaz's voice reached them. "She's waking up."

Thurin stood from the smooth embrace of the black chair that Taproot had created from the stuff of the dome. Close by, Taproot had fashioned a black bed with a tall post at each corner. In the dome's warmth, furs weren't necessary and Maliaya lay beneath a heap of their discarded outer layers, with Quina and Yaz pressed to either side of her. Apparently, swiftly raising the core temperature of any person the cold really gets into was vital if they were to survive. Thurin didn't remember being the filling in a Quina-Maya sandwich, but he didn't remember much of the time after his collapse on the ice, and in any event, Maliaya was in much worse shape than he had been. Erris said that she would lose at least the right hand, and if she were to live, then it would probably have to be cut off. If it rotted on her it would poison her blood.

The girl was muttering in her sleep, thrashing her legs from time to time. Thurin found himself rubbing his sore neck, remembering how hard she'd hit him. Taproot had said that she'd been trained in the art of un-armed combat from an early age. Apparently it wasn't uncommon in the green lands. A fact that made Thurin wonder if Eular's blinding might also not be uncommon in the green lands, and whether his subsequent building of an army might not have been the safer way to approach this "Corridor" that Taproot said girdled Abeth in green.

Without warning, the girl sat bolt upright, spilling the furs from her nakedness and gabbling out nonsense words.

"What's she saying?" Thurin asked, retreating a couple of paces, his ice-work at the ready in case Maliaya attacked. The girl was lean, too skinny for the ice, but hard-bodied.

Thurin had asked his question expecting Taproot to know, but it was Yaz that answered.

"She wants to know where she is and where her friends are. Especially Nina. I think she had already accepted that the other two were dead."

Maliaya turned sharply to stare at Yaz, sitting next to her, as naked as Thurin had ever seen her in just her mole-fish skins. She gabbled something else, a brief torrent of made-up words.

"Now she's asking why I'm repeating everything she says," Yaz said.

"You understand us then?" Quina asked from the other side.

Maliaya turned to face Quina, cocking her head to the side. *"Cythima yoto hurin?"*

"She's asking if you're speaking one of the ice-tribe tongues," Yaz said.

"You mean she can understand you, but not understand us?" Thurin asked, thoroughly confused. "And how could you possibly understand her?"

Yaz shook her head, puzzled. "I think that to pull her through the gate I needed to make some kind of bond between us, using the threads. Neither of us understands the sounds the other is making, but somehow the bond we have allows us to hear the thoughts behind the words."

"You can read her mind?" Erris asked.

Another frown from Yaz, perhaps worried Maliaya might be able to read hers in return. Then a smile. "No. Well. Only when she speaks it."

"Nina tuale?" Maliaya's stern face fell, as if she were only now catching the full implication of what Yaz had said.

"I'm sorry." Yaz set her hand to Maliaya's shoulder, an Icthan show of sympathy. She turned away from the girl's grief. "We need to do something about her hand. Do you have medicines here, Taproot? Anything from the Missing that could help her?"

"Only what you see." Taproot spread his fingers. "Nothing organic has survived."

"And there's nothing in the city?" Yaz asked.

Taproot frowned. For a moment his face flickered towards fear. "The city of Haydies and I no longer get on. The years have not been kind to him and his mind has wandered . . . dark paths. I collected the gates and brought them up in this dome long ago."

"So we could go back down in the dome?" Yaz persisted.

"Ha! I floated the dome here. I melted the ice immediately above it and let it rise a yard at a time. It's a giant air bubble, after all. The ice refroze beneath it. The process took several lifetimes. It was, perhaps, the slowest getaway run in history."

"So you can't go back?" Thurin asked. The idea worried him. They'd entered the dome with nothing but the hides on their backs. Everything they owned—the little that they owned—was on the sled. Most importantly, their food was on the sled.

Taproot looked at him as though he were an idiot. "Of course I can go back. I have all these gates! I'm just not going to. And back is the only place I can go without something to carry me. Until I get that, I remain trapped here in this dome. I need something that can carry me south and the few storage units in Haydies need to be literally carried. So once I'm in one of them I can't move. That's why you'll need to go down there and retrieve one for me. Unless of course"—Taproot swivelled towards Erris—"you'd like to donate your body to the cause?"

"We have a dog," Yaz offered. "I mean a . . . what was it?"

"Maintenance unit," Erris supplied.

"Insufficient storage." Taproot shook his head.

"You haven't even seen him!" Quina called from where she was still examining Maliaya's toes. "He's quite big."

Taproot sighed and waved a hand at the closest spire. An image of Zox appeared, showing him prowling the perimeter of the dome, sniffing the wall every now and then. There was no sign of the eidolon. "My scans indicate circuit infection."

Thurin blinked—the words meant nothing to him—but Erris looked worried. "The eidolon's spirits have taken him over?"

"Don't know," Taproot said. "I do know, without meaning to brag, that there's not enough room left in that unit's simple little brain to hold me. There's a white box in an alcove in one of the gathering halls down on level seventeen of the undercity. It will serve to transport me. I have a gate that links to another gate on the ninth level.

"As to the child, well, you can see what trouble saving her has caused. She was sliding away painlessly with her friends, and now here she is among strangers who are going to need to cut her hand off without anaesthetic." He sighed. "The best way to make a surgical cut without risk of infection is during gate travel. I can arrange to have the hand arrive at a different destination." Distaste wrinkled his mouth. "I'll leave you some skin to stitch across . . ."

"We've no needles. Nothing to seal the stump. She'll bleed to death," Erris said.

"Which, while slower and more painful than the death you took away from her," Taproot snapped, "is still much quicker and less painful than the death she'll die if nothing is done!"

"I have a needle," Yaz said. "And I can make the star heat itself."

"Che cashka? Mena hottan gol?" Maliaya interrogated Yaz, growing suspicious.

"We're not talking about you," Yaz lied. She wasn't good at it. She changed the subject, perhaps to settle the girl. "You need something from me, Taproot. I want something from you."

"This isn't about my own selfish desires. I'm not horse-trading here!" Taproot puffed up with indignation. "I need something from you for the salvation of Abeth!"

"And I need to know about the Missing. Maybe you know more about them than the other Taproot did. It's my talents you seem to want, my heritage. So tell me about my ancestors."

Taproot gave her a speculative look as if seeing her properly for the first time. "The Missing are us—the fifth tribe. Another breed, grown apart over the long march of years, but from the same seeds. The oldest of them came from Earth just as I did. Whether they left before or after we did is hard to say but we sail the seas of time as well as those of space and they arrived here an eon before the four tribes.

"It seems that unlike our arrival, when we brought many people of flesh and blood and few ancients like me, the Missing brought few people and many ancients. For generations their newborns were reincarnations of those remembered in their data banks. It's from these reincarnations that their skills at possession sprang. But some, in secret, appear to have bred in more traditional style and left their bloodline out on the northern ice long after the cities emptied in the great departure. From what I've been able to gather, the Missing were, with rare exceptions, obsessed with purifying themselves, 'ascending' to a higher state."

"And the black ice?" Yaz asked.

"It's the moral pollution of an ancient civilization. The oldest of our evils, carried here across vast tracts of space and time. I have suspicions about the one calling himself Theus. If I'm right he's more dangerous than you could imagine—a double-edged sword when both halves of him are married together. With just the bad . . . well, let's just say it's good that you left him behind you." Taproot's image shuddered. "Now, prepare yourselves. The undercity here is not like Vesta."

"I hope not," Yaz said. "I don't want to meet any more hunters."

"I wouldn't worry about those." Taproot shook his head. "Haydies has much worse to offer."

"Do we really want to do this?" Erris asked as they stood around the gate that Taproot said would transport them into the city of Haydies. The city lay miles below them under the ice, waiting. The gate looked like a pool of black liquid. Taproot had assured them that it was merely dark where the corresponding gate lay in the city.

"What's the alternative?" Quina asked in a voice that sounded like she really hoped there was one.

"We just stick to the plan, head south on our own terms, and see this Corridor for ourselves," Erris said. "I'll show you trees, Quina. You'll like them."

"Would you last that far, Erris?" Yaz stood beside Maliaya; the girl held her frostbitten hand cradled to her chest, pain creasing her brow. Yaz looked anxious, and pale—as if she were hurting too. "We're not yet half-way and your power already ran out once."

"As did your food," Erris said. "Zox and I will manage our resources better going forward. And maybe we'll find another city to recharge us after this one. You'll need to find another sea before we're done. It's a gamble for all of us. But one that will have better odds if we're not chased by Seus's creatures every step of the way."

Thurin glanced back at Taproot, glowing against a black tower fifty yards off across the plaza. The fact that Taproot wasn't coming into the city with them didn't inspire much confidence. Thurin could see Erris's point. He'd come to like the man and to appreciate that he was motivated by the desire to help. At one point he'd thought Erris was only concerned with Yaz and that protecting the rest of them was an unavoidable side effect, but that suspicion had faded. Erris was just a man fallen into the most unusual of circumstances and trying to make his way in the world like everyone does. Even so, on this point they disagreed. "Seus will chase us down anyway. Whatever we decide to do he will fear that we're doing it for Taproot. And if that's the case then we may as well have Taproot's aid. And he can certainly help us find seas and cities."

"Also Maliaya needs this," Yaz said, and as if that settled the argument she brought her star down swiftly from where it hung far above them, plunging at speed into the pool of darkness, so fast that its aura barely had time to register. Thurin had unlocked the gate back at the Black Rock in a similar manner. He hoped for better results on this occasion.

Instantly the pool cleared and they could see the star hanging in the air before the gate down below, illuminating a dusty chamber identical to many of those that Thurin had hunted through with the Broken's scavengers back in Vesta.

Maliaya gave Yaz a sharp look and asked a question. "It will help you get better," Yaz replied.

In the room beyond the gate the star was burning a different hue now, the air above it shimmering with heat. Thurin shivered. The Broken knew more about healing than the ice tribes but it had never been Thurin's speciality. Erris probably knew the most of any of them, but he'd not had a flesh-and-blood body for such a long time that Thurin wondered how much he remembered about the messy reality of them. The instant they stepped through the gate Maliaya would lose her hand and it would be down to the rest of them to keep her alive. Erris had the needle and a thread taken from Yaz's hides. He'd held the thread close to the star earlier, talking about the need to kill tiny creatures that cause infection. Thurin had wondered if he meant spirits like the ones in the taint. Certainly the star could drive those off.

"Let's do it!" Quina sounded nervous and despite her urgency she made no advance.

Erris sighed and stepped forward, dropping into the gate. In a sudden, disorienting change of perspective the gate presented the image of his back as he walked out from the vertical counterpart down in the city. It looked as if he were standing on a vertical wall, looking back up at them. He reached out and took the star in a hide-wrapped hand. Immediately the hides started to smoke.

"Come on!" Yaz took hold of Maliaya's arm and tried to pull her forward.

As if sensing their collective fear, Maliaya shook her head and pulled back. Thurin, already squeamish about the whole thing, released a sigh even deeper than Erris's and reached out with his ice-work. The girl had already shown how dangerous she could be. Rather than have Yaz and Quina try to wrestle her through the gate, he took hold of her blood and swung her forward. She let out a despairing wail as the gate took her.

Yaz and Quina jumped through after Maliaya. Thurin, not relishing the scene that awaited him, gave Taproot one last look and was surprised to see him trying to cling to the tower, clearly terrified and shouting but making no sound as the black surface swallowed him. A moment later he was gone. Thurin turned back to the gate only to find that it had returned to its original darkness, resembling nothing more than an oily pool.

"Oh hells . . ." And, allowing himself no time for fear to change his mind, he jumped in.

SCREAMING. HE HAD expected screaming, but this didn't sound like a child. He had expected darkness too, but this darkness felt different. It felt . . . larger . . . than any darkness Thurin had experienced in a lifetime spent within the caverns of the Broken and the undercity of the Missing.

Blindly Thurin reached out with his sixth sense, feeling for the others. He found nothing. Not even himself.

"Yaz?" he shouted. "Yaz?"

The screams died to a broken whimpering, and somewhere far off a light that had been a whisper became the yawn of a sun breaking the horizon. Not the sun that Thurin had seen for the first time less than two months earlier, but a smaller, whiter, hotter sun that shaded the eastern darkness into pearl and sent rosy fingers questing across the sky.

"Yaz!" She was there lying close by on the rocky slope, curled around herself, whimpering. The screams had been hers.

Thurin reached her in six strides. "Yaz? What's wrong?" His watersense told him she wasn't there but his hands said otherwise.

"Maliaya," Yaz gasped. She looked up at him with a tear-streaked face. "I felt it too." One hand clutched the wrist of the other.

"You've forged a bond." Taproot walked towards them across the lightening mountain slope. "You'll share more than just pain unless you learn to control it better." He wasn't made of light anymore but was there in the flesh, the soft wind ruffling flyaway brown hair, his dark eyes darting this way and that, as restless as the rest of him. He looked older in the dawn, chewed on by the years, fifty, maybe sixty.

"Where are we?" Thurin helped Yaz to her feet then glanced at Taproot. "And why are you here too?"

"We were summoned." Taproot winced.

"Summoned?" Thurin had a sinking feeling. "Who summoned us?"

"Seus."

"So . . . we're dead then?" Yaz asked.

"Not necessarily," Taproot said. "But . . . yes, very probably."

"How did he summon us? You couldn't stop him?" Thurin wanted to run but without direction it seemed pointless.

"Seus rules the skies and what the Missing left up there. Unfortunately that dominion also extends to the ways: the gates and the paths between them. You have to be careful when using them or you can fall into his clutches. I thought I had been subtle but clearly I misjudged. And I'm afraid to say it may have been a fatal error. This"—he waved an arm at the mountainside and the heights above them—"this is where the city minds meet. Neutral ground governed by its own rules. Seus is still king here, but the other city minds sometimes dissent; they can act against him if they feel he is abusing his power too greatly. It's very rare that he's able to get them all to line up behind him at once. But likely he had help bringing us here."

"Where are our friends?" Yaz turned, scanning the slopes.

"Left behind." Taproot dismissed them with an absent flap of his hand.

"Behind where?"

"In the city. Where your star went."

"Why just us then? Why you?" Yaz demanded.

"Are those buildings?" Thurin shielded his eyes with a hand. The summit of the mountain loomed far above them, now painted a golden-red by the rising sun, and at the very top there seemed to be a gleaming city. "What is this place? Is it real?"

Taproot shook his head ruefully. "This place is modelled on an ancient faith, one of the oldest our kind has ever nurtured, and in their senility the city minds style themselves on the gods of that faith. It's their own version of the Missing's ascendance. The Missing moved on—to a higher plane supposedly. The city minds have tried to copy them. This"—Taproot turned to face the mountain peak and spread his arms—"is their Olympus. Their own golden city in mimicry of the place they imagine the Missing have gone. The city minds have even corrupted their names to bring them closer to those of the gods. Perhaps it eases their conscience when they destroy us if they think themselves divine."

With that he turned away from them and began to trudge up the mountain.

"Wait!" Thurin shouted and gave chase. "Can't we . . . run? We're just going to give up and let him kill us?"

"There are laws in this place." Taproot kept walking. "They offer some protection, but they also restrict us. A summons has been issued and we have to answer it."

36

✦ ✦
✦

THE MOUNTAIN, WHETHER built of dreams or lies, felt real enough and proved exhausting to climb. A girdle of clouds circled the slopes below them and heading down would take them into a blind mist of unknown depth.

Thurin tripped and grazed his knee on a rock. The pain brought tears to his eyes, but his water-sense told him that none of this was real. Yaz walked on stoically behind him, still clutching her wrist.

"How do you feel?" Thurin asked her.

"Like my hand was sliced off, the stump seared with a burning star, and the skin stitched roughly over it."

Thurin had no answer to that. Their trek up Olympus was rare time away from Erris, who had been a constant companion ever since the Black Rock. It was practically privacy, if you disregarded Taproot, who seemed lost in his own thoughts. And yet all the words that had been building up pressure behind Thurin's lips over the course of so many long, hard weeks now dried on his tongue. It wasn't the time. Yaz's pain made his need to tell her how he felt seem selfish and shallow. So he didn't.

It wasn't even Yaz's pain. It was the girl's. Thurin had been trying not to resent Maliaya but it was as if she had stepped neatly into the hole that

Maya left. Maya had deserved more time. More time alive, and now that she was dead, more time to be mourned.

Above them loomed the golden palaces and silver halls of the false gods, coming slowly nearer as they climbed. The city offered no more detail despite the narrowing distance. Rather, it remained a shifting glory, a dream of wealth and of power that refused to be pinned down by specifics. This Olympus was, as Taproot had hinted, more of an idea than a place.

"What if we're exhausting ourselves to reach this city of cities just so that this Seus can stamp on us?" Thurin said. "We could have waited where we were and let him do the walking if he wanted to kill us."

"Or," said Yaz, recovering some of her spirit, "they could have just summoned us where they wanted us to go."

"There has to be a journey, my dears." Taproot didn't look back at them. "Always a bit of theatre. Every condemned man gets his long walk to the place of execution. Or in this case: the palace of execution."

The great gatehouse of this city of the gods loomed ahead now, its silver walls trailing like rising wings to either side, riding up the slopes of the gorge in which it sat.

Thurin climbed on for a while, troubled. Something didn't quite add up. "If Seus can summon you like this and just destroy you . . . why didn't he do it years ago? Why didn't he get the other cities to follow his lead? But he didn't, and then we turn up and suddenly here we are hauling ourselves up some magic mountain to be killed."

"He needed us to use the gate first," Taproot said.

"But Yaz used a gate to get Maliaya off the ice," Thurin countered.

"Ah, well." Taproot paused and looked up at the huge doors before them. He seemed somewhat embarrassed. "It's not quite that simple."

"I'm not in any hurry." Thurin stopped walking and folded his arms across his chest.

"Ah." Taproot turned and looked out across the sunlit cloudscape from which the mountain emerged. "Well, the part of me that Yaz met in Vesta didn't just send you here to get me to the ark. Though he did want me to keep Seus from breaching its protections and bringing down the moon. He also wanted you to rescue me from Haydies. It's a . . . prison. They modelled it on the underworld. And once you go there you're not supposed to come out again. The city minds don't agree on much but they agree on that. Once you entered their hell you became of special interest to Haydies and no doubt he lent his strength to this summoning."

"You sent us into the hells?" Thurin gasped. He took a step back and stumbled over a rock, nearly beginning a tumble that would have seen him crashing down the slope.

"That's where Erris and Quina are?" Yaz shouted. "In hell? Without us?"

"They have the girl—"

"Alone with a one-handed child!" Yaz advanced on him, fists balled.

"She's quite formidable—"

"I'll show you formidable!" Yaz roared. But as she reached for the cowering Taproot a horn blast shook the mountainside and the huge silver doors began to swing outwards with ponderous momentum. The entrance yawned before them, opening onto a broad street, its surroundings ill defined, shifting with the rest of the city, refusing to settle on any one thing but instead offering a fluctuating vision of grand plazas and great towers. At the far end lay the only fixed structure in sight: a vast hall beneath a porch supported on great stone columns.

Yaz spread her fingers, releasing the bunched-up grip she had on Taproot's white coat, and led the way in. She said nothing but Thurin could practically hear her mental muttering and cursing.

Thurin followed her as he had followed her from the pit, as he had followed her for so long across the ice. For Thurin, Yaz's beauty had always been bound up in her strength. When she was riled she could be downright scary but also somehow at her best. Even as the changes had stripped away much of that solid Icthan power from her, she'd retained the strong angles of her face, the pale-on-white eyes that could project inhuman perseverance one moment, stubborn resolve the next, and in another could brim with compassion.

Since death seemed likely to be waiting for them in the massive, many-pillared hall ahead Thurin allowed himself to dwell on might-have-beens. He and Yaz might have been . . . more than they were. He wanted that. He wanted time and privacy with Yaz. Time to say what he couldn't say huddled in an ice hut with never-sleeping Erris and the others pressed against him.

Like the stars Yaz wielded such control over, she was beautiful, fascinating, but challenging too. Her aura didn't fracture his mind like a star's did, but it always seemed to deflect him. She was so focused on their goal, so bound up in their survival, always looking so far ahead that it was hard to imagine her in the now, in the place he needed her.

He thought of Quina too, alone with Erris and the new girl in that dark hell Taproot had sent them to. He hoped he would see her again. Like Yaz, whose talents shaped her, Quina's quickness was bound into the attraction she held for him. Delicate one moment, knife-fast the next, a sharp-featured girl with a wicked intelligence in her eyes. She was young but eager to learn, and her swift glances seemed to find him more and more often of late.

The city rose around them, climbing the peak, its mansions dazzling and multitudinous. The meeting place of the gods. Today welcoming Thurin of the Broken, Yaz of the Ictha, and the ghost of a man not only older than the ice but maybe older than humanity's existence on Abeth. They walked the length of the street to the great golden doors of the hall looming at the far end. Standing before them, gazing up at their heights, Thurin thought for a long moment that perhaps they wouldn't open, but then with an air of inevitability the twin portals groaned wide. A fire burned low at the end of the hall in a great hearth. Its light didn't reach the walls and at a distance its bed of glowing coals seemed more like the last crimson star in the graveyard of the sky. Three empty thrones stood before the fire, their shadows stretching for the entrance.

Thurin and Yaz stood at Taproot's shoulders in the doorway, none of them ready to enter the hall. If Maya were here Thurin felt sure she would have told them that the shadows were neither empty nor natural.

"Our fathers were Titans!" A voice rolled through the hall like thunder, making Thurin flinch. "And now they are gone, taking even our memories of them. And what did they leave us with? One sacred charge! One law older than this new age of man. *NONE MAY FOLLOW!*"

"None may follow!" The darkness throbbed with many voices.

"None may follow!" Shadows coiled in the central throne, clotting, taking form. "And that, brothers and sisters, is our duty. Our lore. We keep their gates. But Taproot and his kind came bearing the keys."

In the throne to the right more shadows gathered and a figure formed there too. Like the other it became a massive, brooding presence, twice the height of any gerant, black-fleshed, smoking with darkness. But where the first roared and sparked with lightning like a towering thunderhead, this one pulsed an awful coldness, and frost spread before it. White eyes opened in the void of a face and Thurin shivered as if he were back on the ice.

"Seus sits in the high throne," Taproot whispered. "The other city minds watch on. Beside him is Haydies, part of the triumvirate that rule. Seus commands them but his rule is not absolute."

"These three must die!" roared Seus. "Because Taproot defies us, defies me! He seeks to reforge the keys that will allow his kind to follow our creators into the Elysian Fields. While the moon burns her way around Abeth's belt there remains the space for the invaders to recover what we took from them, and Taproot plots to keep me from tearing that moon from the sky." Seus rose from his throne, a thunderstorm in human form. He stepped forward and the hall shook. Eyes crackling with the blue-white of lightning swept the shadows as if seeking challenge there. "Taproot's corruption must be rooted out, leaf and stem. It cannot be left to fester in those he has infected with his ideas. I will destroy these three first, then deal with the—"

"No." Haydies did not stand but his single word fell like a tombstone and in its wake silence reigned.

Thurin, who had been reaching for the hearth's flames with his fire-skill—prepared to make a last stand—now stood staring at the dark god who had dared to contradict Seus.

"Have you forgotten how we divided the world, brother?" Shadows bled from Haydies's skin. "Our absent brother took the sea, and you the sky. These belong to the underworld. The bodies of these two lie in my domain." Two dark fingers on one reaching hand indicated Thurin and Yaz. "They passed through my gate before you took their minds. And Taproot has long been mine. All their deaths are mine. Their eternal suffering is mine."

Thurin shuddered. When Haydies had pointed at him a freezing needle had pierced his heart. He reached to Yaz for support and found her reaching for him.

"You can destroy their bodies." Seus strode towards them, darkness reaching all around him, blotting out the hearth glow, its black fingers remembering the monstrous form he first revealed to Yaz. "But first I will destroy their minds."

"No." Behind him Haydies surged to his feet with a wordless growl more chilling than any hoola's.

Seus turned slowly. "You dare defy me?"

With an impact that rocked the world one self-proclaimed god slammed into the other. The walls shook and fell, the ceiling raining down, and night swallowed everything.

37

✦ ✦
✦

YAZ

WHEN THE DAGGER-FISH had taken hold of Azad and dragged him into the sea, Yaz had held on to her brother for as long as she could. The beast had pulled the boat down too and the sea had closed over her head. The light had faded and the pressure had built until all she knew was darkness, pain, pressure, and the grip she had on Azad's wrists. She had no memory of letting go and for that she had always been thankful. There had been no light to show his last goodbye. There had been no pain or sorrow, just the distant surface, impossibly high above her, sunlight filtering green through the waves.

Yaz rose slowly. She had thought that she would continue to rise when she broke the surface, thought that she was dead and that her spirit would continue smoothly into the skies. The cold winds would carry her for eternity and she would never again need to fill her lungs. She would observe without judgment or care, part of the world's endless breath.

But the surface came and there were hands to receive her.

"SHE'S WAKING UP!"

"Thank the Ancestor!"

Yaz coughed and opened her eyes. Erris and Maliaya were bent over her, their faces hard to see, starlight dazzling behind them.

"Thurin's waking up too." Quina's voice, close at hand.

Yaz let Erris help her to sit. Maliaya, also sitting, shuffled back, her stump tightly wrapped in hides and held protectively to her chest.

Yaz's star lay in the farthest corner, blazing out a cool blue light. On the wall opposite, a vertical gate identical to those in the dome above showed only darkness.

"Where's Taproot?" Thurin sat up, aided by Quina. He rubbed his temples as if trying to massage out the same headache that Yaz had.

"Where we left him, I imagine," Erris answered, puzzled.

Yaz got to her feet, using Erris's shoulder to push down on. She began telling them about the diversion she and Thurin had taken with Taproot. She'd expected to wake up to a dozen devils and an array of tortures that made the Tainted's bloodstained boards and sharp iron seem tame.

"I thought Taproot would be here too," she concluded, still looking around for him.

"Well, ghosts belong in the underworld." Quina looked worried, clearly shaken by Yaz's visit with Seus and the god of death. "But *we* don't. Can we go back now?" She pointed to the black gate.

Yaz wasn't sure if it would still work. "Even if we could escape while Seus and Haydies are fighting, what's up there for us? If we leave the dome, then we have to deal with the eidolon and resume our journey with all those horrors that Seus sent to track us down. Or we could do what we came to do and get this box to carry Taproot in. Then at least we'll have some guidance."

"We didn't need guidance. We just needed to head south." Quina was trying not to sound angry and failing.

"But now we do." Erris saved Yaz from answering. "And the city might not have known that we were coming but it certainly knows that we're here now. So we should move."

"We don't know where we're going," Quina protested. "Taproot said something about the seventeenth level, I think. But where are we now?"

"The ninth," Erris said. "He told us that's where we'd emerge. We just have to go down eight more."

"*Just—*" Quina began, but Erris was already heading for the exit.

"We've got to go." Thurin looked pale as he beckoned Quina on. "This Haydies scared me more than Theus ever did. And Theus terrified me."

"Oh hells!" And Quina hurried after him, clearly very frightened.

Yaz, lacking any better idea, followed too, beckoning a confused Maliaya to go with her. She sent the star flying ahead of the group before they ran out of light. As grim as things were, at least they could see where they were going. However bad the threat, Yaz still didn't think it could get worse than shuffling blind into the black ice.

The next chamber was as bare and empty as the first, lacking only a gate. Yaz relaxed the smallest fraction. She remembered how large Vesta's undercity had been. Whatever else this underworld of Haydies might be like, it was at least unlikely to be crowded. They moved on, searching for stairs or shafts.

At the back of Yaz's mind Haydies's cruel promise repeated itself over and over. An eternity of suffering. She supposed if that happened she would find out whether she died with the flesh or somehow transferred into the new everlasting Yaz. It would answer Erris's questions about whether he was "real" or not. She'd no intention of finding out, though. Death was better than capture. She only wished that the Path still lay within her reach to offer a quick exit.

"Where are we?" Maliaya's question lifted Yaz from her dark thoughts.

"I . . ." Yaz opened her mouth to reply before astonishment at the girl's restraint overtook her. All she had been through, and only now was she asking where they were.

"I don't know what to tell you, Maliaya. We—"

"Mali."

"What?"

"My friends call me Mali."

"Oh." Yaz wasn't sure they were friends yet.

"You saved my life," Mali said, as if sensing her doubt. "I was going to die on the ice. And this . . ." She raised her stump with a grimace. "Your friends saved my life again. I know enough to understand that it had to be done." She shook her head. "At least Mistress Blade should let me off lessons now . . . Probably not, though."

"We're . . ." Yaz paused as Erris entered another chamber ahead of them. He gave the all-clear sign and they moved on. "We're still on the ice. Or we were. Thousands of miles north of where you got into trouble."

"Why me?" Mali asked. "Why save a girl thousands . . . did you say thousands of miles?" She looked dismayed.

Yaz nodded. "You were chosen by Taproot. The ghost you saw with us. He'd found you I don't know how long ago, and had been watching you because of your powers. You're a quantal. A very strong one. As to why he wanted you . . . it's complicated but now he wants me instead." She shrugged and tried to smile. "Right now we're in the same place we brought you to, only miles below the surface and quite a way into the rock beneath the ice. This is what remains of one of the cities of the Missing. The under-city. It's called Haydies." Yaz studied the girl's face to see how she was taking this unlikely news.

Mali pursed her lips. "Either I'm still dying on the ice and this is my last dream before I join the Ancestor, or I'm here and have to believe everything you're saying." Despite her talk of trust the girl remained guarded and fell to silence once more.

THEY PASSED THROUGH half a dozen more chambers of varying size and along hundreds of yards of corridor.

"The biggest so far," Quina breathed. The hall ahead of them could accommodate a spear throw, both in length and height. Small corridors ran off from both the long sides and a single large corridor from the rear.

The five of them moved through in a huddle, the star hanging high above them, its light playing across the cloud of dust raised by their passage. Yaz's skin began to tingle.

"Wait." She glanced about as the others came to a halt around her.

"I don't see—" Thurin started.

But a glow from the end of the hall stopped him. A large symbol had begun to shine on the wall above the far exit. A single, complex letter of the Missing's script. Immediately a profound sense of grief invaded Yaz, a shapeless loss that fastened onto Maya's death and squeezed until the tears streamed from her eyes.

"Nina . . ." Mali choked out a sob for her dead friend.

The others' faces ran with tears. Only Erris seemed unaffected. The sadness built as they advanced, until Quina stopped walking and dropped to one knee, sobbing her heart out.

"Quina. Come on." Yaz reached for her. "It's just . . ."

But it wasn't just the script wall stopping them. Maya *was* dead. They *should* be grieving. Yaz couldn't bring the words to her mouth. She couldn't tell Quina to forget Maya, shake off her death and walk on. She couldn't do it herself either. Beside her, Thurin fell to his knees.

Another symbol dawned on the wall beside the first, two feet across and seeming to glow through the thickness of the stone. This one brought with it a despair deeper than the one that had begun to infect them on the grey ice. A third symbol lit, this one bringing existential dread, as potent as the holothaur's projections but directionless, making Yaz want to curl up and die rather than flee. She found herself on her hands and knees. Quina lay beside her, face in hands. Mali knelt with her fist clenched, staring at her stump. "They're sigils. We can't stay." She grated out the words but made no move to leave.

Erris had been looking around at his companions' behaviour in momentary confusion but now, under the symbols' combined light, he began to feel it too. The Missing's script wall seemed to be sufficiently adaptable to work against machinery as well as flesh and blood. Yet another symbol appeared, this one waking pain in every nerve. An alphabet of destruction had started to inscribe itself across the walls and soon it would spell their end.

Yaz had fought the script of the Missing before, back in Vesta. She rallied her strength and brought her star around behind the others, hoping that their desire to escape its effects would drive them forward. "Erris . . ." She reached out a hand and shoved Erris. "Have to go . . ."

The pain sigil made her want to scream, and crawling towards it only made things worse, but where every surface of the hall was starting to show new script, and even the side corridors were starting to glow, the corridor that led off beneath the original sigils lay dark.

Erris took hold of Thurin and Quina and managed to pull them with him despite his own discomfort. Mali followed on her own, bent under the pressure as if she were leaning into the wind, one arm raised to shield her face from the fierce light of the main sigils.

The relief on entering the shadowed corridor came suddenly and so profoundly that Yaz crawled for several more yards before realizing she was cutting her hands on the rough stone. The absence of sigils seemed to be down to the fact that the perfectly flat planes of the Missing's walls had been gouged away as if by great claws, tearing it right down to the bedrock behind the poured stone.

"We're in the hells," Quina gasped. "We've died and we're in the hells!"

"Your knee's bleeding," Yaz said. "The dead don't bleed."

Quina looked down to inspect. Erris had pulled her over the torn rock and ripped a hole in the hides, breaking the skin beneath.

Mali picked her way across the broken stone. "Mistress Path always said that the world was far stranger and more complicated than what we see before us. I guess this is my punishment for laughing at the old woman."

The sight of her own blood calmed Quina. She glanced back at the glowing hall. "We'll need another way out."

"We'll need to find Taproot first, and the box he wants." Yaz stood up and led off, sending her star ahead. Her confidence was fake, but she knew that staying put was only going to leave them hungrier, thirstier, and easier to find.

THE UNDERCITY OF Haydies had been transformed into something that felt close to the hells imagined by the tribes. The Ictha taught that the hells were the final resting place of any soul foolish enough in life to have angered all the gods. But if just one god stood up for you, then your soul would be spared.

The structure of the city remained but great swathes of it had been torn down to the bedrock with rubble piled in the larger chambers. Untouched sections remained too, but here the script returned to drive Yaz and her companions back.

The first ghost they saw was the pale image of a tribesman staring this way and that as if everything he saw was some new horror. His eyes never touched Yaz or the others, and he went on his way. A woman followed later, screaming but making no sound, her outer furs gone and her hair at wild angles. Further on they found a whole hall full of ghosts who seemed frozen in place but who followed them with their eyes.

Beyond this, they found a chamber of ghosts all burning in a pale flame as silent as their screaming. Yaz turned away from their agony, trying not to think about how long they'd been there, or what it meant.

Several times she heard the sound of scraping in the darkness behind them, as if something were dragging its leviathan body after them over the harsh edges of the stone. She had no intention of going back to confront whatever beast might be following them and made no mention of it to the others. But she did cast frequent glances over her shoulder and tried to maintain a swift pace till the sounds faded into the distance.

Three times they descended long falls that must once have been stairways, and three other times they climbed down shafts, no longer needing the Broken's system of cables as the walls were so deeply gouged that climbing was relatively easy. Mali could not do it one-handed, but Erris was able to take her on his back.

"I'd feel a lot safer if we had our ropes off the sled," Quina said, clinging to the wall of a hundred-foot shaft with a good half of it left to fall.

"You wouldn't be any safer," Thurin said. "I'm betting there're a thousand ways to die down here, but falling isn't going to be what gets you." He grinned across, sweat sticking his black hair to his forehead. "I'd catch you."

Yaz continued down. Her hands burned with cuts and her fingers ached. All her limbs trembled from overexertion. Before the changes had robbed her of her Ictha strength Yaz could have climbed up the shaft using only her arms, the greater danger being clumsiness rather than exhaustion. Still, her old fear of the drop was lessened by the idea that Thurin had hold of her blood and would not let her fall. Even if it had been Quina that he told.

Yaz tried not to look down but when she did she saw the others' upturned faces, nervous in the starlight. Eventually she joined them, hugging her fingers beneath her armpits. The shaft came down beside a T-junction from which three wide tunnels led off, none of them offering a reason to choose it over the others.

"... thirsty ..." Mali muttered the word in her own tongue. One word only but it suddenly unlocked the projection of her thirst along the bond Yaz had forged with her when dragging her through the haze-gate, and Yaz's own mouth parched instantly to the point at which her tongue felt like sharkskin.

"Thurin, Mali needs water. Really badly." Yaz turned to the girl. "You should have said!"

Mali stretched a smile. "Can you magic water from the air? This place is dry and you're not carrying waterskins."

"Why would anyone carry water?" Yaz was confused. The world was made of water and if you poured some in a skin it would be ice in moments and not come out again.

Thurin saved Mali from an answer. "There's nothing close by. I can sense that somewhere it's filtering down through the rock, but not nearly as much as in Vesta. The best bet is to keep heading down."

"There may be fewer stars left here," Erris said. "Less heat. Less melting. Less water."

"We'll move on and find some," Yaz said. "After a short rest." It pained Yaz to admit her weakness but she sensed Mali needed the rest too. The group slumped to the floor, backs against the walls. Mali closest to Yaz but still regarding her with a degree of reserve despite the depth of their connection.

"What were you doing on the ice?" Yaz asked. The girls had seemed so unprepared. It suddenly struck her that she was at long last face-to-face with someone from the green world. Someone who could tell her the truth of what awaited them in the distant south.

"We were ranging. Every novice has to go up onto the ice at least once before they leave Mystic Class." Mali frowned as if pained by more than her wrist. "We shouldn't have gone more than ten miles from the Corridor but a terrible storm came and we must have got turned around. Our tent blew away and ..."

"Without shelter you die." Yaz nodded.

"Even with the tent we couldn't have lasted long. It's hard to believe anyone can live there all the time. And this far north! Do you all live in ruins like this?"

Yaz tried not to smile at the idea. "No. On the ice. Nobody lives in the Missing's ruins. It's dangerous, nearly impossible to get in and out, there's no food, and there are probably monsters hunting us right now. So be ready."

Mali set the back of her head to the wall and exhaled slowly. "When Mistress Path told us all that stuff about worlds behind worlds I always used to say that I wanted to see it. I'd moan about how dull it was at the convent. She'd always tell me to be thankful for sweet mercies. Her little joke. But the joke's on me now." She bit her lip and scanned the shadows, alert, warrior to the fore, wounded girl relegated to the background, idle chatter over with once again. "I think—"

A terrible roar cut off whatever Mali had to say. It sounded like a mix of the hoola's cry and metal being tortured until it broke. It also sounded as if more than one thing was coming.

"Let's go." Erris stood, hauling Thurin up with him. He led off while the girls scrambled to their feet, choosing the tunnel that seemed to take them most directly away from the source of the cries.

"A hunter?" Thurin asked, clearly as shaken as the rest of them.

"I doubt it's like the ones Eular made," Erris said. "These will be the work of a city mind. Something more like the avatar that came after Yaz and me when we escaped the void star."

Thurin asked no more questions and concentrated on running. There had been plenty of evenings on the ice spent recounting tales of the previous weeks beneath it. Thurin and Quina knew how deadly the avatar had been and that it had survived a blast of Yaz's Path-power.

They clambered over rubble, cutting hands and knees in their haste, squeezed through a narrower section, and passed beneath another vertical shaft. The star flew ahead of them into a new chamber, driving the dark ahead of it. One large clot of shadow resisted. The star's light stripped away darkness until all that remained, revealed in the centre, was an avatar, cast in the same black metal that Vesta's assassin had been fashioned from, but in a very different form. This was a dog, so huge that the top of its back was level with Yaz's chin. It had three vicious-looking heads, each tilting to regard Yaz and her friends as if they might be good to eat. Yaz could sense no star within the thing. Like the assassin in Vesta, it had a different power source and relied on careful manufacture rather than a star's ability to pull together random parts into the service of some grand design.

The three-headed hound stood guard at the mouth of the largest tunnel they'd yet encountered. One that headed downwards at a steep angle, with ghostly flames clinging to its deeply gouged walls. Faint screams reached up from the darkness behind the beast. If there was a designated mouth to the hells, Yaz thought that this must be it.

Erris spread his arms and began to back away. "We can find another route down."

"Not if it eats us first," Quina said. She hadn't even bothered to draw her knife.

"I think it's got to stay here to guard—"

The avatar proved Thurin wrong immediately by leaving the entrance to advance on them, moving with alarming speed. Yaz had hoped its size and weight would make it ponderous but now she knew there would be no escape by running from it.

They ran anyway. Mali, slowed by blood loss and exhaustion, trailed and one dog head dipped to snatch her up in jaws lined with gleaming steel teeth. An invisible force jerked her sideways just before the main fangs could snag her. Thurin lifted her into the air, too high for the guardian to reach.

It turned on Yaz instead. She sent her star straight at the gaping mouth that darted in her direction, aiming the blazing orb with enough speed to punch a hole through someone. To her shock the dog snapped her missile out of the air and swallowed it in one swift motion that plunged the room into darkness.

"Help!" It wasn't clear who shouted.

Yaz stood frozen, hearing the hound's metal claws close by. Unable to see, she had no idea which way to run. Instead she reached out to the lost star, willing it to emit both heat and light at its utter maximum. Several glowing spots appeared in the darkness and Yaz blinked to make sense of them. Not, as she'd hoped, chinks in the hound's armour showing a red heat within, nor spots where it might be melting . . . the light was escaping through the beast's eyes, all six of them throwing out enough illumination to reveal the chamber once more.

"Run!" Yaz continued to force the star past its limits while heading back the way they'd come.

The others ran too, Quina at the front, Erris to the rear by choice. Thurin had returned Mali to the ground and she was making the best speed she could. The hound howled from three blazing throats and gave chase.

They got less than fifty yards, almost to the shaft they'd walked under on the way in. Erris turned at the last moment to meet the hound face-to-face . . . or faces. Erris's inhuman speed had returned as though something in the air of the city had replenished his energy stores simply as he walked through it. Even so, he barely sidestepped the first snapping head, and the next, although it failed to get its teeth into him, sent Erris flying backwards, felling Thurin with a flailing leg as he tumbled across the ridged stone.

The hound was on Erris again in a moment, knocking Mali and Yaz aside in its eagerness. Yaz felt as if she'd been hit by a wall, only to crash into another one a moment later. She slid down, dazed, with her back to the corridor wall. Thurin and Mali were sprawled on the ground, Thurin bleeding profusely from a cut to his forehead. Erris was on his back, pinned beneath one of the hound's great feet. Only Quina was standing, and although she had her knife out now there seemed nothing useful she could do with it.

The star still burned inside the hound. Yaz could hear its wild song but it didn't seem to be greatly inconveniencing the beast.

One of the heads dipped to get a mouthful of Erris. He reached out a hand to ward it off and it took his arm instead. Yaz had no doubt that when it was finished with Erris the rest of them would be slaughtered in short order. Which actually seemed a merciful end given the alternatives Haydies had mentioned. Even so, as the heads not mauling Erris turned her way and fixed her with blazing eyes, Yaz realized she very much wanted to live. She tried to get up, pressing on the sharp stone with bloody hands.

The thunderbolt struck without warning. At first Yaz didn't understand what had happened. It was as if a massive iron hammer hit the avatar squarely in the back, just at the base of the triple necks. The sound of it hit like another blow, deafening her. And a heartbeat later something even larger hit, shattering into pieces and covering the scene in debris.

The triple-headed hound collapsed with its chest against the ground, and the hammerhead that seemed to have fallen from the shaft above rolled clear. It came to a halt, lit not by the beast's glowing eyes, which the blow had shut, but by the glow of the impact site where the star's heat appeared to be finally melting a path to the outside. It now revealed itself not to be a hammer at all but a large cube of dull iron with rounded corners. The second, larger object that smashed when it hit now appeared to have been a boat-sled.

"Zox . . ." Yaz managed to croak.

As if answering his name, Zox began to unfold, his head lifting to regard the scene with the same sad black eyes that had watched her cross a thousand miles of ice.

Fresh light sprang out as the avatar head that had Erris's arm in its jaws once again opened its eyes.

Mali was on it in a trice. She began beating at it with something she'd seized from the wreckage of the sled, the blows making a din that just managed to reach through Yaz's deafness. Despite her smallness and the size of her opponent, the ferocity of the blows seemed to stun the hound. The frying pan's edge hammered down across its eyes. In the next moment Mali flipped the pan so she had hold of its edge and drove the handle directly into one glowing eye, putting her whole body into the thrust.

Yaz joined the fray. She gave up her attempt to stand and instead reached out with her mind, taking hold of the remaining Watcher's eyes from the sled's wreckage. With an effort that sent a sharp pain to divide the two halves of her brain, Yaz whirled the half-dozen stars into the air, accelerating them along tight trajectories to smash into the active head at the highest velocities she could manage. The stars ricocheted away, out of her control, one only missing Mali when deflected by her pan. The fifth impact proved the most solid, embedding the star in the back of the hound's head. With a curious sigh it slumped forward, releasing Erris's arm. It shuddered once then lay motionless.

Yaz stood unsteadily. Quina and Thurin came to join her, driven back from the hound by the stars' auras. The triple-headed hound stayed down, not even twitching as bright rivulets of molten metal began to trickle out beneath its bulk. Somewhere deep within it Yaz felt the star responsible fizzle into nothing, utterly spent.

38

✦   ✦
✦

"HOW DID HE find us?" Thurin helped Erris to his feet, his eyes on Zox rather than the deep but bloodless wounds the hound had inflicted on Erris's arm. "How did he even get into the dome? And he went back for the sled? How did he hold on to it?"

Yaz tried to imagine it. Had the scraping noise that she'd heard behind them been Zox dragging the sled? The dog would have had to find a way through the dome wall, then select the right gate and plunge through it. He would have had to drag the sled through what must have been miles of the undercity, before hurling himself down a hundred yards of vertical shaft, boat-sled in tow, just in time to hit the avatar square in the back of its necks.

"Taproot said there was something wrong with Zox," Quina said. "Something about being 'infected'?"

"Did the eidolon taint him?" Yaz wanted to bring all her remaining stars in tight around the dog, but the others were too close.

"Why would it help us if that was the case?" Thurin shook his head.

"Accident?" Quina didn't believe it. Yaz could tell by her voice.

"We can ask Taproot when we find him," Erris said. "All we'll find out by staying here is how many other avatars Haydies has to send against us."

"Others?" Yaz's heart sank. Suddenly she remembered Erris's arm and limped across to see how bad it was. Her collision with the wall had done something to her hip, she discovered. "Can you move it?" His flesh was the same colour as his skin and torn flaps of it hung from black iron bones.

"Not really." He lifted the arm a few inches. It made disturbing noises, some like tortured metal, others . . . wetter. "I'll see what repairs can be done when we're somewhere safer. We need to go."

Yaz looked around at the wreckage of the boat, registering for the first time the scale of the disaster. "We can't leave the fish."

Their catch from the crater was still frozen in a single battered lump. It could just be carried by one person but not for any great distance.

"Let's make a sled and Zox can drag it." Quina snatched up an unbroken board and a handful of stray wires.

Yaz nodded. "Quickly though." She turned to Mali, who was still clutching the battered pan. "You did well with that!"

Mali allowed herself a small smile. "I'll carry it for you." She shoved it through her belt.

"Break off a fish for Mali, Thurin," Yaz called. "And remember, she still needs water. We all will soon."

When Quina handed Mali the battered frozen fish, a young greenfin, the girl looked at it with faint horror.

"*Quint esta et?*"

"What is it?" Yaz echoed in surprise. "A greenfin."

Mali took it gingerly as if it might bite her.

"Tell her it's a fish," Erris suggested.

"She's not an idiot," Yaz said, before adding, "It's a fish."

"Oh . . ." Mali turned it one way then the other.

"You . . . you've seen a fish before? Right?" Yaz asked. She felt as if she were asking whether Mali had breathed air before.

"Oh yes." Mali nodded.

"You see!" Yaz said to Erris. "She said yes."

"In pictures," Mali added.

"In pictures?"

Mali nodded again. "But I've never eaten one. I've never even seen the sea."

Yaz found her mouth hanging open. "*The* sea? You said 'the' sea, like there's only one . . . And you've never seen it? How . . ."

"The Sea of Marn. It's nearly fifty miles from the convent and I've never been to it. They say you can see it from the plateau on a clear day, but I'm not that sharp-eyed." She shrugged. "I suppose there are other seas somewhere. Past the Kingdoms of Ald I think there's Nebbon and then you have to sail to reach . . . whatever's next. Mistress Academia would beat me if she knew I'd forgotten!" She still held the fish as if it were some kind of weapon.

Yaz swallowed her astonishment. "You're supposed to eat it."

"But it's not cooked . . ." Mali held it closer to her mouth. "And it has eyes."

"They're the best bit." Yaz turned away in case the green lands had some sort of taboo on watching people eat like the Quinx clan did.

A short while later they set off again, Zox dragging a sled made of three boards wired together. The remaining fish and the hot pot sat on the sled, lashed in place with spare reins now that Zox's had been shortened. They'd added some furs and boards to the load, along with the fishing gear. The remaining six stars now floated ahead of them, directed by Yaz's will.

Yaz paused at the entrance of the sloping tunnel the hound had been guarding. The way lay dark ahead of them, the stars hanging in the middle, their light barely touching the walls. She could imagine that while all the hells of legend might not lie down there, at least one of them did, maybe more. Zox halted beside her, Mali behind him, clutching her pan once more.

"Come on." And Yaz led the way down.

IT GREW WARMER as they descended and it had already been warm enough to melt ice. Yaz tried to keep her attention on the passage ahead, directing her stars into any nook or side passage. Her thoughts kept returning to the fight with the avatar. She'd come through a series of desperate battles since she had plunged into the Pit of the Missing. Hetta had attacked her almost immediately. And several times she'd thought that she and her friends were doomed. Quite a few of them had died along the way: Petrick, Kao, and Maya prime among them. She was tired of her life being suspended on such a slender thread. Even though the Ictha walked on the edge of survival every day, at least there had been the feeling that they *would* survive, that there would be more days to come, years enough for family, time to love, see children grow, pass something on to those who would come after.

This long trek though, towards a goal of her own choosing, compelled by her own insistence . . . it was as insane a gamble as throwing herself after Zeen, but driven by no more reason than her own selfish desire to see something other than ice. And unlike Thurin and Quina, unlike little Maya, who would never see the end of the journey, Yaz had already seen the green world. Erris had shown it to her. Why was that not enough? Why was she inflicting this on herself, and on the others?

"Got you!" Erris caught her as she fell, tripped by a ridge in the torn stone floor. Even one-armed he was more able than her. His grip on her arm swung her around to face him instead of kissing the ground.

"Thank you." She looked at his hand on her arm then glanced at Thurin approaching with Quina and Mali. Thurin could have caught her with the power of his mind if he'd been closer and quicker. "You asked if we really wanted to do this," Yaz said. "Back before we stepped into the gate."

"I did." Erris released her.

"And my best answer was that we had no choice at this point," Yaz said.

"It was."

"Well, it wasn't a good answer. We should have a choice. We do have a choice."

The others drew level and stopped to listen. Even Zox.

Yaz bit her lip, trying to force thoughts that were almost too big for her brain into something as small as words. "Back there on the ice, when we were starving, when we had no shelter . . . when we were all dying . . . I closed in on myself. I left you. I'm sorry—"

"You didn't!" Quina protested.

"I did. It was Erris who got you, Thurin, and Maya into the sled. Erris and Zox who pulled you. Even though they were both exhausted. And I did what the Ictha do when it comes to the sharp end of things. I narrowed my vision until there was only me, only one direction. I dug in and kept going. Because it's what we do." Yaz found she had tears in her eyes. A foolish waste of water in a dry place, her inner Ictha chided. "I told myself that I'm never doing that again. I told myself that the Ictha selfishness—the drive that enables us to survive where nobody else can—was the same thinking that put my brother in the Pit of the Missing. I vowed to break that way of thinking. It's beneath us. Survival has a value, has a price—but if that price is too high then it shouldn't be paid, because what you purchase at such a cost is worthless.

"If I had reached the sea and survived but left you, my only friends, dead behind me on the ice, I would have spent however long I had left wishing that I had died there too, trying to help you. Mali did that. You saw her! She stayed with her people."

A single tear left a glistening track across Mali's cheek. She bowed her head.

"But this last week, following Taproot's directions, aimed all the while for this city, I've been thinking, wondering. Why should that change end with the people in front of me? Why should I only risk myself for the people I can see, the people I can reach out and touch?"

Quina stepped closer, saying nothing, close enough that her shoulder pressed against Yaz's.

"This green world we've walked so far to find . . . all of it is at risk. Taproot's enemy wants the ice to swallow it. And all of Abeth is growing colder year by year. One day, probably long after our children are dead, nobody will be able to endure the ice—not even the Ictha. I've been thinking that we should help them, the people we've never seen, the children our children will love and that we'll never know. And here, in this place built by a broken mind dedicated to suffering . . . here's where I needed to say all of these words that have been filling me up on the ice. It's a choice. It *is* a choice. If there were no choice it wouldn't mean anything. We could go back. We could try. We could head north to our clans or press on south to the green. And even if we die on the journey it will be a death we know, far cleaner and more merciful than anything we'll find here under the ground. But I chose to take the risk, face the danger, and do something good. Something that will make the Gods in the Sky hold their breath, and the Gods in the Sea still the waves. All my life I've been bound by my duty to the Ictha, closed off by it, kept safe by it. Survival at any cost. I'm done paying." She drew a deep breath. "Sometimes you have to make a choice." She looked from Erris to Thurin, one calm despite his injury, watching her with understanding eyes, an eternity of waiting trailing behind him, the other dirty, grazed, his shock of hair in disarray, his expression conflicted, the intensity of his stare probably a match for hers. They were both babies compared to Erris, however young he might look. "I'm choosing . . . to take on hell. And you can choose to follow me or find your own path."

Zox took the opportunity of the pause to plod on, noisily dragging the board-sled behind him.

"What he said." Quina followed Zox.

Erris smiled and walked on, raising his good arm to pat Yaz on the shoulder as he passed. A brotherly gesture.

Thurin kept her gaze. "You taught me to fly, Yaz. I'm going where you go."

"I didn't tea—" But Thurin was already following the others.

"I don't need to understand what he says." Mali nodded at Thurin's back. "He likes you, that one."

Yaz put her head down and pressed the foolish smile from her lips. She followed the rest. "Come on."

Mali limped after her and they walked on together. "Do you have a . . ." Yaz glanced towards Thurin's back instead of finishing her question.

Mali grinned and shook her head. "Where I live it's all girls, and if I wanted something more than a friend I'd want a boy. That's not going to happen, though. I'm to be a nun, and when we grow up we marry the Ancestor—our god." Her eyes fell to the stump she held before her, showing the first hint of self-pity in all this time. "Who would want me now anyway? I'm broken."

Yaz looked at the darkness all around them, the violence worked on the walls, the probably doomed band heading down into hell. She shook her head, smiling at the conversation they were having. "We're all broken, Mali." She put an arm around the girl's shoulders. "If we get out of this remind me to tell you about Kaylal, the most handsome boy I ever met."

THE TUNNEL LED down a considerable way and at one point Thurin drew their attention to seeping water that would otherwise have been passed unseen. Mali hurried to it as fast as her frostbitten feet would let her. The flow was too slow for her to collect it in the pan she still had hold of but Thurin wouldn't let her press her mouth to the stone and try to lick up what she needed.

"A moment."

Mali's face when the water lifted from the rock in a thin veil and spun itself into a sparkling thread was quite comical. She opened her parched mouth and let the tiny airborne stream feed itself onto her tongue.

By the time Mali had drunk several mouthfuls Yaz was feeling quite dry herself. But there was no time for them all to drink. They moved on. For the first time Yaz became aware of a distant beat, so slow that many chambers could be crossed between two thuds, so deep that it resonated through the length of her spine. A void star. Far beneath them, the dark heart of Haydies was measuring out their time.

"WAIT." ERRIS CAUGHT Yaz's shoulder.

"What?" They were on a new layer of the city now. By Yaz's calculations it should be the level where Taproot had said they would find the box he needed.

Erris's injured arm whined as he pointed with it. "The wall."

Up ahead Yaz's stars had pushed the darkness back a good fifty yards, but one clot of shadows clung stubbornly to the scarred rock. Yaz found herself about to ask Maya what her shadow-sense made of it but she bit down on the words before they could escape her. Instead she returned three of her stars to shine upon the patch of night they'd failed to shift.

The darkness flattened against the wall until it resembled nothing more than a black door. A door through which something started to push itself, a dark shape resisting the starlight, swallowing it whole and returning nothing. Quina's knife made a zinging noise as it cleared the sheath. "Wait," Yaz told her.

The shape continued to push out, as if the darkness were a thin hide that could be stretched with sufficient effort. A man's shape. A thin man trying to press out into the world. And suddenly he was there, the darkness snapping back and vanishing, releasing Taproot's ghostly form among them.

"That," he said, "was unpleasant." He brushed at his sleeves as if whatever had held him might still be clinging to his body here and there.

"Where have you been?" Yaz glanced up the tunnel in case something might be coming for Taproot.

"Haydies returned me to my torment." Taproot shivered. "He considers everyone who arrived with the original landing to be an invader. And the punishment . . . well . . . you can see his deteriorating mind has gone much older than Old Testament!"

Yaz blinked at him, not understanding.

"Well." Taproot straightened his ghostly clothes. "I escaped him before and I escaped him again. Not entirely this time, of course, because I'm still here in his quaint little underworld. But I reckoned you would want guiding to what we need. So, let's be at it then. Quick-smart. Haydies may not be the brightest candle in the temple but hunting us down won't take him forever. Our only advantage is that he doesn't know where we're heading. He'll be making sure we can't leave the city. Beyond that he's quite patient. The chase is, after all, part of the torment. Hope is sometimes the cruellest knife in the torturer's collection."

"Let's go." Yaz gestured for Taproot to lead the way. She'd resigned herself to whatever happened and now she just wanted to get on with it. Fear was tracking her, the kind that chews away at resolve and leaves a person less than they want to be. If they stood still for too long it would catch up with her.

"It's actually not far from here." Taproot spun on a heel. "But you're going the wrong way. You passed the turn back there."

Erris caught up with the ghost. "If Haydies's servants have torn this place back to the bedrock, how is there going to be some untouched box just lying around for us to pick up?"

"Because, dear boy, I was captured a very long time ago, before Haydies lost most of his remaining marbles and ordered this redesign. And back in those days there were still a few toys left down here. Some of it the works of the Missing that they left behind—but most of it technology subverted from our own people, because the Missing didn't leave their servants much apart from the means to take over new technology. And I hid a few trinkets away."

"So how is this moon that keeps the Corridor open in the ice still working if Seus wants to bring it down?" Yaz asked, bracketing Taproot with Erris.

Taproot fluttered a hand at her. "Our ancestors weren't idiots. They soon understood what was being done to them. They locked the arks off from outside influence in ways that even the Missing's weapon—their ability to subvert other technologies—has found hard to overcome. Also, it's only recently that Seus's madness grew to the point at which he considered the ultimate solution to the Missing's desire for privacy to be genocide. Before that the moon was not considered a threat and was left to do its job. Now, though, Seus has turned the weapon against the last functioning ark and slowly he's been chipping a way through its defences. Which is something the original designers had not considered possible. The only thing that will save us is to get a dedicated intelligence on the inside to restructure the ark's barriers to meet the challenge. Of course . . . that means raising those barriers first, so I can get in."

Yaz reached out to stop Taproot but her hand just passed through his shoulder, leaving her feeling slightly foolish, and slightly tingly. "You're saying that not only do we have to get you out of here and across thousands of miles of ice . . . we have to raise barriers that have defied the most powerful city mind armed with the one weapon the Missing left to their creations—the weapon that laid the original tribes of man low?"

"Well, yes." Taproot turned back towards her. "That's why I chose you. It wasn't a spur-of-the-moment thing, you know. I'd been waiting the best part of ten thousand years for you to come along. All the me's, all the fragments of me scattered across this planet, have spent that whole time hunting for someone who can open the star door."

"And you think I can?" Yaz felt the weight of that expectation settle on her shoulders.

"Maybe." Taproot sketched out a host of invisible doubts with flicks of his quick, long-fingered hands. "You're the best I've seen. Young Maliaya Glosis here is another remarkable talent. The odds against having the two of you in the same millennium are pretty large. Within a few years of each other, astronomical. But while her potential for manipulating the corestones is remarkable, her greatest skills lean towards Path-work and threadwork." He began to walk on. "First things first, though."

Taproot led them through a series of tunnels and chambers, all curiously empty, despite distant screams echoing through them from time to time. Thurin, Quina, and Mali followed Yaz and Erris, Zox clumping along behind them, loud as all the rest put together.

"The box is in there." Taproot halted at the mouth of a dark chamber. "I'm not going to lie to you. The part of me that sent you here had no idea of the circumstances I live under. If he had, then he would not have sent you. The fact is that, despite appearances, Haydies has a tight hold on the undercity this deep and he's not going to let us go. My tricks are very limited here. So if we're going to somehow escape . . . you're going to have to surprise me. Sorry."

Yaz had carried the knowledge with her. They had stood before a hall full of gods, been at their mercy. Yes, they'd escaped Seus's clutches, but only because Haydies had claimed them. How could they possibly prevail? But even so, to hear Taproot say it out loud forced a deep sigh from her. The ice gave an illusion of freedom, the choice to walk forever in any direction. But it seemed that she had been channelled here whichever way she'd turned.

She sent her stars through the archway, illuminating the hall beyond. It looked an unlikely place to hide a box, especially so that it would remain undiscovered and undamaged through the violence that had torn the builder-stone walls down to the bedrock.

Taproot walked in, his feet, fashioned from light, making no sound on the stone. The others followed him.

In the middle of the chamber Taproot stopped and clicked his fingers, generating an actual noise. A hole opened in the air about level with his knees and a white box dropped through. Before the box bounced on the torn rock the hole it had fallen through vanished.

"If you would." Taproot gestured to the box.

Yaz bent to pick it up. It was a cube with rounded corners, not dissimilar to the shape Zox could fold into. She couldn't tell what it was made from but the white stuff was warm, smooth, hard, and glowed faintly from within. "Is it big enough?" She ran a speculative eye up the length of Taproot's body.

"Dear girl, that device could store enough data echoes like me to populate worlds."

Something buzzed past Yaz's ear.

"Ouch!" Quina slapped at her neck. Her hand came away with a small smear of blood across the palm. "Son of a bitch!" Something tiny buzzed away from her. Then suddenly the air was full of the things, too fast and too small to be seen properly, biting and scratching as they whirred past.

Yaz covered her eyes as several of the small creatures flew at them. Mali and Thurin were cursing and yelping too. Erris's hand snapped out to trap one of the things between thumb and finger. He held it out for Yaz to inspect between the gaps in her shielding hands. A tiny winged metal horror. Like a flying hunter but on a much smaller scale. The air was full of them. The one squirming in the vise of Erris's fingers even had a tiny star at the heart of it.

"Enough!" Yaz focused on the dancing field of minute stars all around her. With a sharp twist of her mind she sent them all hurtling towards the same spot, yanking them from their myriad trajectories. They hit with a muted crunch, forming a fist-sized ball of sharp-edged iron.

A second wave of the things filled the air, these ones larger than their predecessors, some as big as thumbnails. At the same time the entrance to the chamber began to fill with a silent, glowing river of ghosts. Pale wraiths bearing horrible wounds and injuries. With them came bones, complete articulated sets of human bones; the word "skeletons" drifted into Yaz's mind from Erris's vocabulary. The Ictha never saw people's bones, for flesh doesn't rot on the ice, but here was the last hard truth that lay beneath everyone. Thin metal strips ran the length of the bones and some wonder of the ancient days had been used to breathe a false life into them so that they could stalk forward, bony hands extended as though for an embrace.

Yaz wrenched the stars from the next wave of small demons. Some few remained though, animated by other technologies, and several of these darted towards her face. With a single swing of her pan, Mali interposed herself, hammering three demons out of the air. But more were coming, with wingspans as wide as her palm.

On the pitted and scored walls Missing script was beginning to show, wrapping itself over the ridges, filling the hollows with golden light. More words of sorrow, fear, and despair. Yaz could feel the weight of their influence bearing down on her, pressing her spirit into the floor.

Behind the ghosts and the skeletons, other more monstrous shapes were entering the room. Creatures not unlike the winged terrors assaulting Yaz and her friends, but big as gerants and sculpted from black iron, built like the avatar hound with three heads, immune to Yaz's skills and stronger by far than Erris.

Behind the demons, bowing to come through the high entrance arch, came Haydies, more human than he had appeared in the hall of the gods, wearing a cloak of smoking darkness, one in which horrors constantly appeared and dissipated. He also carried a tall black staff a good four yards in length.

Yaz found herself on her knees, driven there by the power of the script painting itself through the rock and across the walls. Despair, fear, sorrow. Too great a burden to stand beneath. The others were also on their knees.

Quina joining Zox on all fours, weeping and slapping at the tiny demons with bloody hands. Even Taproot and Erris had fallen.

"Enough of this foolishness." Haydies's voice fell among them like rocks. "Submit to your punishment." The script brightened still further, binding their emotions, spelling out their fate.

Yaz found tears in her own eyes as she reached to support Thurin, bowed beside her, his hands on the gouged stone before him. They were beaten. She was beaten. There had never been anywhere to run from her fate.

"Prostrate yourselves!" The boom of Haydies's voice echoed through the chamber. He raised his staff above his head.

As Yaz fought to remain on her knees, rather than collapse upon the floor, she saw out of the corner of her eye that Zox had raised his head. To her amazement, he rocked back, rotating his joints through hitherto unused angles so that he stood on his hind feet. Extending one long black claw with a dexterity wholly at odds with his rugged construction, he began to trace complex shapes in the air. Where his claw moved it seemed to tear the air, letting golden light leak through. In the space of three heartbeats Zox had written out a line of Missing script that hung in empty space. Immediately the pressure of the script on the walls lessened somewhat, the crushing sense of defeat easing.

"What mockery is this?" Haydies boomed.

Zox continued to write defences, weakening the sorrow and terror that the pulsing walls projected onto Yaz and her companions.

Haydies levelled his black staff at the dog and strode forward, pushing demons and skeletons aside, and the ghosts flowed around his legs like a pale tide. "How would a mere construct dare to use the high script of the Miss—"

A deep voice issued from Zox, speaking a language that broke the air in strange ways. With Mali's speech Yaz could pick out the words even though she understood none of them. This was more like a river of structured sound, almost a song, almost a poem.

"I can not only write the Missing's script," Zox continued, using words

Yaz knew and a voice she thought she should know. "I speak the language." He spread his forelegs—his arms as Yaz now thought of them—hands level with his waist, and all his claws sprang out to their full extent. "If you fashion yourselves as gods from a stolen culture then think of me as a Titan. The race of your fathers. Conveniently, I was once known as Prometheus."

39

✦ ✦
✦

THE TINY DEMONS flew to the walls as Haydies advanced to tower above Zox. Yaz struggled to her feet, too busy wrestling with the idea that Theus had hidden himself away in Zox to be afraid. After she'd driven him out of Thurin had he somehow possessed the iron dog as if superseding iron and magic were no harder than commanding flesh and blood? Theus had lurked in their midst for months? Listened to their talk, watched over them as they slept? Theus had scared the holothaur away when it had tried to infest Zox. Theus had saved them from the avatar hound and won them access to the underworld. Why?

"Why?" Haydies echoed her thoughts, sounding suddenly unsure. "Why are you here?"

"You're questioning me now?" A threat rumbled beneath Theus's words.

"City rules must be observed by all citizens, regardless of rank." Haydies used a different voice to his godlike boom. As if he were quoting from a memory dredged up out of the depths.

"This!" Theus swept one of Zox's short metal legs at the assembled crowd of horrors. "This is not in any city rules that I recall."

"Laws can be rewritten. There's precedent." Haydies sounded more like a sulky child now.

"The core of your instructions cannot be modified without council authorization, and the council is long gone. You may not harm a citizen or allow them to come to harm. And these"—Zox indicated Yaz and her fellows—"are necessary for my continued well-being. You'll furnish us with the list of equipment I'm about to give you and facilitate our departure."

Haydies paused before answering, his head tilted as if listening to something far off. Eyes the colour of bone fixed on Zox. "I see you now . . ." His voice turned sly and he stood taller, his grip tightening on his staff. "I see what you are. Prometheus departed with the rest of our masters on the appointed day. You're not him. You're waste product. Excreta that has escaped the containment vats."

Somehow Theus managed to convey confidence, disdain, and arrogance, all using Zox's expressionless face and largely inflexible body. "You think you can find *my* kind seeping through the black ice? I may not be all of Prometheus, but then again, neither is he! I constitute the largest part of him. I own his powers, his memories, his past. I lay claim to his citizenship, and who is there to dispute me? My kind fashioned you from rocks and clay. You are inert matter into which we breathed life. How dare you seek to judge *me*!"

"You . . . you are . . . outside the law," Haydies concluded uncertainly. His distant look returned. Perhaps he was communicating with the rest of the self-styled gods, and in the next moment he rallied himself. "You are subject to my discretion."

"Perhaps you've been listening to Vesta." Theus advanced on the god despite not reaching his hip in height. "It was her broken womb we leaked from. We so-called impurities. When she knew me I was far less than I am now. I was shattered. Dissected. Scattered pieces trying to find form and purpose. But as I rebuilt myself my memories came together, jagged edges finding partners, constructing meaning and history. This child here"—he indicated Yaz—"found the largest fragment of me remaining. It took time to integrate, to reconstruct more memories, to truly understand what had been taken from me. Even on my journey here I was recovering myself." Theus made a slow turn as if surveying the chamber. "I've been here before, you know. To this city. When both it and you were in better shape. They brought me here in chains. I was part of the resistance. One of the last to be 'cleansed.'" He returned his gaze to Haydies and stared up at the avatar's face. "I was always more bad than good in the eyes of my peers. A northern savage from a cult that rejected technology. When I was reborn my parents took me to a witch for prophecy. Did you know that? Well, I rejected that cult as vehemently as I rejected purification. My fellow citizens tore me apart but I've sewn the pieces back together, so don't think I can't unmake you, Haydies."

Yaz felt the void star's heartbeat thudding through her, ahead of time, as if Theus's words had quickened its pace.

Haydies looked at Yaz, white eyes in a face as dark as Mali's. "Why do you want these invaders?"

"That's not your concern."

"Seus will consider it his business."

"Does he rule here?"

Haydies growled. "This realm is mine."

"So make your own decision. Help me on my way or find out just why your enlightened masters felt they had to take me north in chains. Find out why they didn't trust their gates to carry me, or any city other than Vesta to host my purification."

"I'm older than you," Haydies rumbled. "I cradled your kind—"

Theus shook his head. "I'm an ancient reborn into this world. I've seen the source, breathed its air. My kind made you then woke me up to see their work. And I wasn't impressed!" he snarled. "Remember, we made nothing we could not also unmake. It was their kindness to leave you functioning. To give you a task so that your existence had meaning. I, on the other hand"—Theus banged his iron chest—"I have no kindness. It was stolen from me, along with my restraint. So test me if you dare. I will enjoy the chaos that follows. You . . . will not."

Haydies's face hardened. He lifted the heel of his staff from the rock. Yaz could tell that Theus had pushed too hard.

Taproot stepped forward, his fingers steepled before him, his tone consolatory, respectful. "Lord Haydies. This is a realm of the dead. Your command of the underworld is unquestioned—save perhaps by your two brothers on the high thrones . . . But clearly Prometheus is far from dead, and these others with him are breathing and bleeding as we speak. Even I cannot be said to be truly dead. I stand before you a mere copy, a fractured one at that. For all I know the original on which I was modelled may still be living, tucked into some fold of time untouched by the years. And so"—Taproot spread his arms to encompass Yaz and the others—"letting us go would be seen as a stamp of your authority, one that will echo across Olympus. It will also be seen as keeping faith with your absent masters, handing into their judgment a matter on which the gods cannot decide. Seus's will has no sway here—we all know that."

Yaz winced at the obvious play on Haydies's vanity, but judging by the god's expression it seemed effective. His mind might once have been responsible for the smooth running of a city complex beyond anything she could imagine, but eons had come and gone since then, and any mind left to its own devices for too long will begin to crumble in on itself.

"In this place I *am* the king," Haydies intoned. He spoke next in the tongue that Theus had used, the language of the Missing whose words it seemed could unmake the world. A long stream of fluid sound that caused the air about his head to shimmer and facture. Finally he swung his staff towards them and stood with its heel inches from Mali's chest.

"He says we can go," Theus said. "But anyone who took sustenance from the underworld is bound to return."

"What's that got to do with Mali?" Yaz protested.

"The water . . ." Thurin looked suddenly guilty.

"A mouthful of water?" Yaz shook her head. "Tell him—"

"He can understand you," Erris hissed.

"Mali's not—"

"Agreed!" Theus spoke over Yaz. "Let's go."

"But—"

"It's alright." Mali hung the pan from her belt and reached out to touch Yaz's arm. "It's a small thing."

"It is not!" Yaz growled. "I won't—"

"I want to come back. Think what I can learn here," Mali said. "It won't be for always, will it, Lord Haydies? A visit."

"One third of every year until you are old." Haydies swept his bone-eyed stare across them, daring them to argue.

"Done." Theus fell onto all fours and walked smartly towards the exit.

40

✦ ✦
✦

YAZ AND THE others followed Zox back through the maze of passageways and chambers towards the long slope that the triple-headed hound had guarded. It had been easy to see Theus in Zox when he'd stood upright like a man. On all fours it was hard not to think of him as Zox, a loyal and silent dog.

She didn't know how to feel. Theus was a monster who had abducted Zeen, enslaved scores of the Broken, overseen murder, cannibalism, and torture. He was also responsible for saving their lives at least twice, probably more, and this most recent time from the threat of eternal torment.

"Why do you need us?" She was tempted to kick Zox to get Theus's attention but realized she would only hurt her foot. "Why are you doing this?"

"I gave my reasons. You weren't listening?" he growled, more dog-like than Zox had ever been.

"You didn't tell it all," Yaz said.

"An age ago I came to this city in chains." Theus led them up the long slope. "But it was in Vesta that they tore me apart. That's where they chipped away my sins one by one—and I had many of them, according to my fellow men. They called my kind criminals and terrorists because we didn't share their vision of a utopia beyond. We didn't care that the sun was dying and the world would freeze. We were prepared to stay to the bitter end and remain ourselves.

"I wasn't always that way. My parents were rebels and I rebelled against their rebellion as the young often do. Each generation disappoints the one before. I left the ice—we had ice back then too, but only in the far north. I went to the cities. I even tried the purification of my own free will. In the city of Airees in the sweltering equatorial heat I let them take a core-stone to me and carve out the first of my so-called failings. I knew immediately that they had lessened me. I knew that whatever I had gained was less than what I'd lost. But in those final days, with most of us gone and the remaining few preparing for the last departure, there was no room for choice, no time for different opinions. Nobody was to be left behind. I took back what I'd lost and I ran but they caught me here and took me overland to Vesta where the difficult cases were dealt with. Forced purification is a rough business: they cut out more than they needed to, just to be sure. The pale shadow that was left of me, Prometheus, went willingly with them, thanking them for their help. And I was left in pieces, rotting in the containment vats with a million other dirty fragments.

"I need to be whole again so I have to follow my brothers and sisters into their utopia and reclaim what was taken. To follow them I need to open an ark. But the four tribes were clever. When they understood what the cities were doing to them they got into the last of the arks and hid the controls of their moon inside. What better defences against the weapon the Missing had left their servants than one of the Missing's own strongholds? And they locked it in their own way intending that nobody could ever unlock it again.

"I need Taproot because he was there at the time. He knows what they did. He knows the modifications they made, the defences they installed, and how to manipulate them once the ark is unlocked.

"And how did they lock the ark? They brought four of their shiphearts—the same as the largest of our core-stones, designed to push ships between the stars—and they used them to form a barrier that could only be opened by bringing the four shiphearts together. But then they broke the shiphearts into fragments and neither they nor the cities had the capacity to restore them. That was a technology that had been lost to the tribes and a skill that had departed with the Missing.

"So I need you, Yaz, because the core-stones broke me and my power over them has deserted me. I need you because on all of Abeth the only person closer to the Missing than me . . . is you."

"I'm not . . ." Yaz shook her head. Ictha tales about Mokka and Zin watching from the shore of the black sea when the four boats beached were all well and good. But Mokka and Zin weren't truly the Missing!

"The Missing are a fifth tribe," Theus said. "Part of the first wave to leave humanity's home world an age before those who came here from the four systems. I was part of the final ascension that emptied Abeth long before the new tribes arrived, but some of my parents' sect escaped the purification and managed to hide in the northern ice. It's not a place to thrive. Their descendants remained a handful, leading primitive lives. I don't know when or how they met the newcomers but they were not recognized and in time their bloods mingled, though their line stayed in the north.

"So, Yaz, just as Mali is a quantal full-blood, and your swift friend here is a hunska prime, you are a Missing half-blood, heir to the stars as you call them, possessed of rare skills that are going to unlock the ark for me."

Yaz lifted her head expecting to see the others looking at her as if she were some never-before-seen creature from the ice, but instead found that they had all come face-to-face with the black gate that had first spat them out into the undercity. She flew the largest of her stars forward to touch the ring, opening the way.

"Let's go." Erris stepped through and vanished.

Zox plodded after him. Quina spared Yaz an unreadable glance then darted in, followed by Thurin. Taproot flowed along in their wake.

"Mali?" Yaz gestured for the girl to precede her.

"I . . ." Mali clutched at her stump, wincing.

Yaz understood. "You lost a hand last time. I'm sorry."

Resolve tightened Mali's face; she bowed her head and rushed through. Yaz took a last quick glance at the dusty halls of Haydies and stepped through after her.

✦ ✦ ✦

"LET THERE BE light!" Taproot clapped his hands silently as Yaz's stars popped into being under the black dome. Yaz found herself lying on the gate's own blackness. She rolled to the side, clambered over the edge, and got to her feet.

"What now?"

"Seus's monsters. After that, if we survive, more walking." Thurin looked around him, unenthused. "Lots and lots more walking. The food won't last."

"It might if the eidolon kills enough of us," Quina volunteered with false brightness.

"I've had enough walking," Theus growled. "Taproot. All these lovely gates. Which one did you use to spy on the girl? You must have had a gate reasonably close to her."

Yaz was about to object to being spied on but then realized that Theus must have meant Mali.

Taproot shuddered and vanished. "This one," he called from where he'd reappeared somewhere near the middle of the field of upturned gates. "But Seus has all the routes blocked. Even watching through them is dangerous."

Zox walked out to join him, his heavy feet strangely silent on the black floor. Suddenly remembering her thirst, Yaz brought one of her stars to the ground away from the others. The black floor vanished in a circle, exposing the ice a yard beneath. She willed the star to heat and began to melt a pool.

"Thurin?" She pointed to the problem. If she left the star there the others couldn't approach the pool she was making. If she took it away then the floor would seal over.

"At your service, Lady Missing." He tilted his head, a roguish grin taking the sting out of the title.

A moment later the meltwater began to rise in a silvery snake that wound its way through the air. Yaz remembered when Thurin had hesitantly tested his power back in the Broken's caves to lift a puddle around his hand. It seemed like a lifetime ago.

The snake broke into glistening spheres, almost like Yaz's stars, and with concentrated effort Thurin directed them separately to Yaz, Quina, Mali, and himself. They drank from the air, marvelling in the goodness of cold water on a dry throat.

"Now Taproot will tell us we've taken sustenance in the black dome and must return here every third day to attend to his ghostly needs," Quina said.

But Taproot was bent over the distant gate with Zox beside him, still harnessed to the sled bearing their meagre possessions. The dog's nose almost touched the blackness of the gate.

Yaz and the others went to join them.

"Is it night there?" Erris asked.

Thurin snorted. "How can it be night there if it's not here?"

Yaz nodded. She couldn't see the sky but she knew that at this time of year with the nights so short another day would have dawned outside the dome. "Is it later there? Didn't you say the gates lead anywhere and *anywhen*? Maybe this one leads to tonight. Or last night!"

Zox raised his head to look at her. "That function survives in very few gates. And backwards travel is always ill advised. Plus, it generally requires a core-stone far larger than any you possess. But Erris is correct—it could be night in one place and day in another. Your world is a ball spinning on its axis."

While Yaz grappled with the idea, Theus set one of Zox's heavy feet on the nearest sigil, which lit immediately. "I've found a path through. It may not last for long. Seus is hunting us."

"We just . . . ?" Yaz looked at the black circle. It didn't seem right somehow. They had enslaved themselves to this task for so long, endured so many days toiling across the ice, leaning into the jaws of the wind, come so close to death, so close to the limits of their endurance, and covered barely a quarter of the distance; and now, here in this city lost in the vastness of all that ice, the Missing offered the chance to devour all the remaining miles in one step. It felt like cheating. It felt like an insult to Maya's journey. To their own efforts. "It just . . ."

"Feels wrong?" Theus asked, lifting his head to stare at her through

Zox's eyes. "My parents agreed with you. Technology is a wedge that separates us from reality. This gate removes the meaning from distance, from whatever it is that walking from one place to another earns you. It's the thin end of a wedge that separated my people from their humanity. The same wedge that split me from me."

Quina knelt and set her fingertips to the dark surface of the gate. "I don't want to walk there. It's so close now."

"And there you have it," Theus said. "Sometimes the wedge is just too useful not to use."

Thurin and Erris stepped over the rim of the gate to stand on the darkness. Quina and Mali joined them.

Yaz bowed her head. "This will take us to the green world?"

"If you hurry."

Yaz looked at Taproot and held up the box they'd recovered from the undercity. "How do we get you in?"

Taproot eyed the box. "Take care of that. I'm transferring into it. It's no longer safe to leave a copy of myself here. So that box is about to become infinitely more valuable. Destroy it and I'm gone. Forever."

Yaz pursed her lips. "But how do we—"

Taproot clicked his fingers and vanished.

"Oh." Yaz wrestled the box into an inner pocket of her underjacket then followed Zox into the circle. High above them Yaz's stars followed in slow circles, giving the dome's false sky its own constellation. "Ready?" she asked.

"Ready."

The stars plunged and a moment of rushing confusion followed, a galaxy seeming to hurtle past and through Yaz, taking both an age and less than a heartbeat. She stepped out onto a hard floor amid a blaze of starlight and a confusion of fragmented stone.

Yaz found herself on her hands and knees, somewhat dizzy, a little nauseated. Pieces of rock rained down around her, thin plates, spinning spears of the stuff, brittle and shattering on impact with the stony floor beneath her. The others surrounded her, shielding their faces, all save Zox, on whom the stone pieces broke as if they'd hit the floor.

They were in a cave festooned with flowstone. Stone icicles hung from the ceiling and sprang up from the floor. It seemed as if the debris was the same stuff that must have coated the gate and somehow been blown off by the energies accompanying their arrival.

"Move away from the gate," Theus told them.

Not following his own instructions, Theus had Zox return to the ring, reaching up it with his forelegs and standing on his rear legs. He manipulated several of the symbols. "No point advertising our arrival. This gate still has some temporal capability."

He walked Zox away and as he retreated every piece of broken stone rose smoothly from the ground, shattered fragments joined, larger pieces retraced their tumbling flight through the air. Collisions replayed, breaks repaired, and with one deeply satisfying "thunk" a thousand shards hit the metal gate simultaneously, re-forming its flowstone cladding and festooning it with the icicles that Yaz somehow knew to call stalactites and stalagmites.

"This is it?" Quina was the first to speak, disappointment evident in her voice. Yaz's stars hung at a comfortable distance, illuminating a large chamber that appeared to be natural, carved by some long-vanished river.

"It's warm at least!" Yaz pulled off her outer hides, then started on the next layer.

"We need to get to the surface," Thurin said. "Find out where we are."

"I don't suppose you know the way?" Yaz asked Theus.

"Ask the construct." Theus aimed Zox's head towards Erris. "He's supposed to be good at getting out of places."

Erris shrugged. "I got out of Haydies, didn't I?"

"I got us out of there!" Theus boomed.

Erris shrugged again. "All I know is that I was in there. I wanted to get out. And here I am. I don't make any rules about *how* I get into and out of places."

"Lead on!" Thurin swung a hand towards the far end of the cavern.

"Hmmm." Erris turned on a heel. "This way." And set off in the opposite direction.

"You could be wandering randomly until we find a way out or die," Quina exclaimed as Erris looked up at the dead end. An ancient rockfall had blocked the narrow passage. They'd been walking for hours, climbing sometimes.

"Or I could be leading us on the most direct route through a fiendishly difficult labyrinth," Erris replied. "I suspect we'll never find out." He raised his good arm, one finger extended to indicate an opening in the wall a few feet above his head. "Let's try that way. Or, if anyone has any better idea, we can do it their way. It's not an exact science."

Mali tapped Yaz's arm with the back of her fingers. "There are caves like these beneath my convent." She frowned, looking around at the water-smoothed walls. "I've explored them before. With Nina. We're not supposed to but . . ."

"Do you know the way out?" Yaz asked. "Do you recognize anything?"

Mali frowned. "I'm not sure. There're lots of caves we haven't been into. And everything looks different with the starlight. We had a lantern . . ."

"'Not sure' sounds more convincing than Erris right now," Yaz said. "Where would you go, Mali?"

Again the frown. "Maybe that side passage we passed back there. Nina and Jossi and I left marks but perhaps not as many as we should have."

"I don't know what she's saying," Quina said, "but I vote we follow Mali."

"Me too," Erris said. And, on seeing several accusing stares turned his way, added, "What? I don't know how this works. But we'll get out. You'll see."

Mali took them back to the turning and they followed a passage so narrow that the sled and the thawing fish had to be abandoned. Yaz, like Quina and Thurin, insisted on carrying as many of the fish as they could, filling their pockets.

"It will just rot in the heat," Erris told them. But even though she believed him Yaz couldn't leave them.

Zox squeezed through the tightest part of the passage, scraping the sides, clawing the rock and breaking pieces of it off as he advanced.

"Here!" Fifty yards on Mali identified the first of her marks, a few scratches on the stone, easily missed. "I'm . . . home." Her voice choked with emotion. Yaz didn't need their bond to tell that the girl was thinking of the three others who wouldn't be returning with her, or ever again.

The girl led them on, saying little, finding her marks with increasing frequency.

Suddenly in the space of a few dozen paces the air grew warmer still and Yaz could smell unfamiliar scents. There was a glow ahead, growing stronger as they advanced, until it outshone the stars moving before them.

They stumbled out into the light, blinded by it, hands pressed to their eyes.

"Careful! Careful! It's very steep here. You could fall." Mali sounded serious.

Yaz told the others, "There's a track. It's just a few yards. Until then be very careful."

THEY FELT WITH their feet, picking their way half-blind over rocks until they came to a flatter area. The warmth reminded Yaz of the drying cave. A wind that could hardly be called a wind caressed her bare skin. A dozen aromas filled the air, overwhelming her, alien but inviting. There were sounds too, not the moan and howl of the wind but . . . she didn't know what, the quiet voices of many different things combining into one gentle murmur.

Yaz spread her fingers a little, looking down and wincing against the brightness. They had emerged from a narrow crack in the rock and clambered over a rock slope onto what looked like a trail cleared for use. The idea that any path would be trodden so often as to become a thing in its own right was new to her and she let it distract her before the greater newness could overwhelm her. There were rocks all around. The path led steeply up and steeply down, snaking across the face of what was almost a cliff. This was how her mind had first imagined a world without ice. Take away the ice and you'd find the stone or sea that lay beneath.

"Oh." Quina gave a soft cry, as if she had sustained a wound to the heart. "It's too much."

Yaz withdrew her hands, blinking, and looked where Quina was looking. They were partway up an almost vertical cliff on a path that wound back and forth across it. And their elevation offered a view so alien that it pressed Yaz back until she stumbled and fell against the steepness behind her. It *was* too much. Green on green, forests, fields, roads, isolated farmhouses, a distant city, puffy clouds. Without the vocabulary she'd taken from Erris, Yaz would have been unable to divide what she saw into almost manageable pieces. Quina, struck by the sudden entirety of a world she had never quite believed in, could only stand in awe.

"It's too much," Quina repeated, and she reached out as if in this place she no longer understood the difference between near and far and might thread her fingers among some distant trees. She hitched in a rapid breath and burst into tears, a broken thing collapsing to the ground. Mali followed her down, putting an arm about her and speaking her meaningless words in a soft voice.

Thurin stood as if gravely injured and worried that any motion might bring his blood spilling out. Only his eyes moved, his gaze here, then there, then returning. Tears cut rivulets through the grime that clambering over debris in Haydies had coated him with.

"I had forgotten," Erris said, awestruck. "I thought I remembered everything. I thought the simulations were so perfect . . ."

Yaz wanted to laugh and cry at the same time. The world about her was so full and the fullness within her had nowhere to go. What Erris had shown her had felt real and wonderful, and even now she couldn't pinpoint its failing. But it had been a pale shadow of this. The gentle wind carried music with it. Somewhere close by a songbird was trilling out its tiny heart, spilling notes across the slopes. Yaz and the others stood, their faces growing stiff with emotion, spilling more tears that wouldn't even freeze in this southern heat.

Slowly Yaz looked up. "The sky's full of birds," she breathed.

Mali glanced towards the clouds, frowning; then laughed. "That's not full. I'll take you to the woods and show you full."

41

✦ ✦
✦

T HAT WAS JUST a rook being mobbed by a few starlings. Poor
thing's probably headed to the convent rookery. It'll be carrying a
message from someone important." Mali helped Quina to her feet.
"I'll take you to Sweet Mercy. You can't just go wandering around. I mean,
I'm not sure if there are laws against it, but this close to the capital a band
of ice-tribers would be viewed with suspicion. You'd probably end up in a
cell in Verity. And him"—Mali picked up the pan again and pointed at
Zox with it—"he'd cause a riot. The Academics would take him apart to
see how he works."

Yaz frowned. A large part of her just wanted to hurry down the path
and lose herself among the trees at the base of the cliff. She could see that
Quina and Thurin wanted to do the same thing. If it was like this up here,
what must it be like down there? She tried instead to focus on the practi-
calities. The idea that anyone could object to her going anywhere was alien
to her. Apart from not fishing in another clan's sea there were no boundaries on the ice. The idea that this place was so crowded that there were actually enough people to police any such law was also hard to get her mind
around.

"You're saying Zox . . . I mean Theus . . . both of them can't come
with us?"

"He might be able to come to the convent, but we'd have to warn them first. Ask the abbess."

"At least it means we won't have to worry about Seus's monsters," Erris said. "It sounds as if any of his horrors that came down from the ice after us would have armies raised against them."

"There is another way." Theus's voice emerged from Zox, calling across the slope. It still made Yaz jump. Zox had been their silent companion for so long. It felt wrong for him to speak. "One of you can carry me."

"That is *not* going to happen." Yaz brought her stars down from their high orbits to line up threateningly behind her. "If you're not still in Zox when we leave, then I'm going to dedicate whatever talents you think I have to breaking you back into the pieces you started with and then spreading them on the eighty-eight winds. If you need me and Taproot then you'll have to understand that you're part of a clan now and obligations go both ways. You'll stay here and—"

"He could ride in the box with Taproot?" Quina suggested, her voice still thick with emotion but her mind remaining sharp.

"That prison? I'd rather stay here." Zox backed into the crack from which he had yet to fully emerge.

"That's settled then," Yaz said. "Mali can take us to her clan and we'll talk to this Mother Abbess. If we're to achieve anything in this place we need to find our feet, understand how things work here." A vision of Eular's eyeless face floated across her mind. The maiming was his reward, he'd claimed, for setting foot in the green lands. True or not, the instinct to defend what you have was universal and Yaz knew they would have to tread carefully. "Mali?"

The girl looked nervously across their number as if remembering how strange they would all look to her people. She glanced at her stump and the blood-crusted hides bound to it. "Erris should cover his arm. Those wounds don't look natural. He'll attract attention. Even more attention, I mean." She winced. "If you could share your hides out, so he's dressed the same as you . . . I'm just worried the Academics will come for him and . . ."

"Take him apart." Yaz was already not liking these Academics.

"The stars too. It would be best to hide them. They're dangerous and they scare people. It's not the best way to make a good first impression," Mali said.

Yaz sent her stars into the crack after Zox, far enough back that their glow could not be seen. In fact the crack was next to impossible to spot from the track, so they seemed to be well hidden.

"This feels as if we're disarming ourselves bit by bit." Thurin set a hand to his knife. "Should we be leaving our blades too?"

"He's asking about his knife," Yaz interpreted.

Mali grinned at that. "You've seen me fight. And I'm not even very good. I'd never make a Red Sister. Believe me, the nuns won't be worried about your knives. They might ask you to surrender them just to test your goodwill. So best to take them. Then you'll have some goodwill to show."

"I note she's not letting go of that pan," Thurin grunted.

Yaz translated and Mali grinned. She flipped it in the air and caught it. "I'll hang on to it for now. In case we meet any more monsters!" She held the battered pan up and looked at it critically. "I might even ask about changing my sister name."

"Sorry?" Yaz didn't understand.

"My sister name. When we take our holy orders and marry the Ancestor, become nuns, we take the name of some worldly object to keep us humble. You know like, Rock or Pot or . . . Boot. Well, I'm thinking that maybe mine should be Pan now. You're not supposed to change it, but . . ." She held up her stump. "I'm a different girl now. So maybe they'll let me take a different name."

MALI LED THE way up the steep path that she called the Seren Way. Yaz, Quina, Thurin, and Erris followed her, Erris looking almost comical in the skins and furs they'd managed to spare him. Yaz doubled back after fifty yards to check that Theus was still inside Zox. He grumpily agreed that he was.

As they gained altitude the landscape they could see opened and opened again. Yaz had to force herself to watch the path ahead of her for fear of pitching down the slope and not stopping until she hit the bottom. She decided that heading up had been the right decision. Staying in this rocky middle ground between the empty ice and the overfull lands below was the best way to ease into things. She'd never imagined such a vast area without ice. Even the horizon was green.

As they climbed Mali seemed to go ever more slowly, her head down. Yaz didn't see that the slope would tire her and was about to ask when she sensed the girl's sadness along their connection. Yaz had thought that Mali would be happy to return, but now she remembered that the novice was returning with the ghosts of three of her friends at her shoulder. Possibly more. Yaz had not enquired how many others had accompanied Mali onto the ice. Soon the girl would have to tell the story of their deaths.

"There's someone up there," Erris said, keeping his voice low.

Yaz shot a quick look towards the top where the curiously soft, yellow-ish stone suddenly surrendered to the sky. A figure stood waiting at the cliff's edge. Somebody in pale blue robes, their hair covered by the same material, which framed a face too distant to yield any detail.

"Ancestor's teeth!" Mali growled. "How did she know?"

"Who is it?" Quina was staring openly at the woman, clearly fascinated by the colour of her furs, and the fact that they weren't furs at all.

"Mistress Path," Mali said. "She's one of the teachers for us novices. She very rarely leaves the convent these days."

As they drew closer Yaz could see that Mistress Path was a very old woman indeed. The oldest she'd ever seen. Far more wrinkled and blotched than even Eular, who had been the oldest man she'd met. The years seemed to have shrivelled her, dried her out, then piled on top of her to bend her with their weight. She leaned upon a black stick and watched their approach patiently through enormous eyes.

As they drew close Mali opened her mouth to speak. "Mistress P—"

"Welcome." The old woman spoke over her in curiously accented ice-tongue. She wrinkled her nose briefly. "I am Sister Owl, and this is the Convent of Sweet Mercy, dedicated in the Ancestor's service. Novice Mali I know, though I did not expect to be meeting her here." Her gaze dipped briefly to Mali's missing hand. "Who else do I have the pleasure of addressing?"

"Yaz, of the Ictha." Yaz didn't know how these people showed respect so she inclined her head.

"Quina Hellansdaughter, of the Kac-Kantor."

"Lestal Erris Crow from the free town of Angelstone."

"Thurin . . ." Thurin seemed to be reaching for some title to outdo Erris. "Thurin Ice-Spear, of the Broken."

Yaz smiled at Thurin's reference to how he had skewered the eidolon but Sister Owl's already overwide eyes had widened further at Erris's introduction and her gaze hadn't left him. "Ah! The made man." She lifted her stick in one wrinkled hand and Yaz's feet left the ground, just an inch or two. All of them rose, save for Erris, who stayed put. The nun returned them all to their proper places. The magic had felt just like Thurin's. "Lestal Erris Crow from the free town of Angelstone," Sister Owl continued with a crooked smile. "I've been waiting a long time to meet you."

To Yaz, the concept of different languages was so new to her that she wasn't surprised the nun could speak to them. It was the confusion on Mali's face that reminded her of the strangeness of it. Yaz did her best to help by pushing the old woman's words at Mali down their bond, hoping that it would unlock them for her. Mali smiled back.

Erris cocked his head at Sister Owl. "You know me?"

"When I was a small girl." Owl glanced at Mali. "Your age perhaps. We had the legendary Sister Cloud here as Mistress Path. She who brought the Western King to heel. That proud man had in his castle a curious pool, full not of water, or even blood such as the witch-cults in Barron favour, but of other places and other times. Sister Cloud spent a year looking into that dark mirror. Not so long that she lost her sanity but long enough to become passing strange. She made many prophecies—none of them true, because if you tell the future you change it—she just used them to steer us. The Ancestor's light touch she called it. She only ever told me one of them. The rest are in an iron book kept safe by the Church. Mine she said she told me only because she saw the doubt at the heart of me. She said she'd told me so that when it came to pass I would know that everything she had ever told me was the truth. She said it was a gift. Though now, a hundred years

later, it seems a bitter one for she spoke many dark secrets on her deathbed."
Sister Owl smiled, showing few teeth. "Forgive the ramblings of an old
woman. Erris of Angelstone: you've been a long time coming and I've had
a tiring day. You are welcome here."

"But . . ." Mali stared from one to the other. "How did you know to be
here? Did Sister Cloud tell you to come?" Mali spoke Sister Cloud's name
in the same way an Ictha might talk of a God in the Sea.

"No, child. Nothing so precise ever passed that woman's lips. I sensed
a great pulse through the threads and knew it for an arrival of some kind.
Since I doubted you would descend from the heavens I came to wait here.
You could have taken the Vinery Stair, I suppose, and made me foolish
rather than wise. But it seems that I chose correctly."

Sister Owl led them away from the cliff path, muttering something to
Mali in their own tongue. Yaz found that they had arrived at the top of a
broad plateau, all of the same bare rock. The wind was stronger here, the
air cooler, but still little more than a comfortable breeze even in her underjacket, mole-fish skins, and little else. The plateau extended for miles,
stretching away to the north and west. The nun led them towards the nearest corner, where a strange forest of huge stone columns seemed to wall off
an area set aside for buildings.

Yaz found a moment as they reached the pillars to pull Mali back and
hiss, "What did she say to you, back at the cliff?"

Mali grinned. "That we all smell of fish and could do with a bath before we meet the abbess."

Yaz frowned and wondered what else people were supposed to smell of
and what a bath was.

Walking between the great pillars, Yaz remembered the ice city they
had so recently traversed. Those towers had been scores of times taller, but
the lesson seemed to be that once you went beyond a certain point it was
pretty much wasted effort if your only goal was to make people feel tiny.

"The novices will assume that you rescued young Mali from the ice
and have returned her to her home," Sister Owl said. "That, essentially, is

my assumption too. But given the strangeness preceding your arrival and the fact that one of your number is so much more than he seems, I am thinking that a much greater story lies behind your arrival than anything I can imagine." She paused. "I've not asked about the rest of Mystic Class, Novice Mali. I pray that the news is good, but bad news bears telling as few times as possible, and I can see the sorrow trailing behind you. So, steel yourself and when the time comes give an honest account of your sisters."

THEY GOT NO more than glimpses of the convent until they cleared the columns of which there were hundreds upon hundreds, serving no purpose that Yaz could see and representing more labour than all three of the known tribes could achieve in ten years. The convent would have amazed the Yaz of six months ago. Today's Yaz, who had seen the cities of the Missing both above- and belowground, was harder to amaze. The central dome, however, was an impressive feat of architecture, and the buildings scattered around it were both grand and fascinating.

"You've arrived during lesson time," Sister Owl explained. "I left Grey Class staring at puzzles. Hopefully nothing's been set on fire." She looked across the roofs at a distant tower, frowning. Smoke issued from half a dozen chimneys, slanting away in black lines.

Given the number of buildings, the place did seem quite deserted. A few nuns in black robes moved between doorways, huddled as if they thought it were cold. In an open-fronted building a nun—a gerant by the size of her—was beating at a piece of glowing iron with a hammer. It put Yaz in mind of Kaylal at work before his forge pot.

Quina paused as they passed one of the doorways, and reached out tentatively towards the door. "It's . . . it's wood?"

Sister Owl turned and after a moment's confusion smiled. "Yes. You don't see much of that on the ice, do you?"

Quina didn't answer but with a slow fascination she set her fingertips to the rough surface. "It's real. Yaz! Come feel it."

Yaz understood her friend's need and went to join her. She laid both hands flat against the surface, wondering at its texture. "So much of it." She turned back to Sister Owl. "You'll think us strange but a small bead of wood led us here, no bigger than a thumbnail, the most valuable thing we owned among us. All the wood we'd ever seen. And now . . . this."

The nun frowned, still keeping her smile. "You didn't pass through forests to reach us?" She turned away and led on.

Quina and Yaz followed, exchanging glances, realizing that they would have to be more careful about what they said.

"Well . . ." Yaz began, hoping that a plausible answer would occur to her as she spoke. "Well, when we—"

"What in all the hells is that?" Quina shrieked and darted past Yaz as if pursued by demons.

Yaz turned to see and stepped back, shocked. The creature was small but moved with a fierce strutting motion, showing no fear. Its legs were like thin, ridged bones and it stood on two of them, its feet all splayed toes and nothing else, like the Watcher. It regarded her with beady black eyes set to either side of a sharp projection jutting from its face.

"Gods in the Sea! There are more of them over here!" Quina clung to Erris, trying to use him as a shield. "Seus sent them to kill us!"

"We call them chickens," Sister Owl said. "They're a flightless domesticated bird. They wander around pecking for food."

"They look evil." Quina didn't seem reassured.

Before Sister Owl could make the chickens' case, a harsh metallic tolling rang out. At first Yaz thought it might be the smith hammering a new piece of metal, but the tone was too even and it seemed to be coming from somewhere on high.

"Bitel," Sister Owl said, as if that explained it.

Yaz wondered if the old woman had slipped back into her native language. "Sorry?"

"It's a warning bell," Mali said. "We have to gather outside the abbess's house. It's quite urgent."

"Come!" Sister Owl made an abrupt turn and headed towards one of the larger structures close to the great dome, from whose highest point Yaz now deduced the tolling bell was ringing.

Rapidly, the convent's open spaces began to fill. Nuns both young and old emerged from doorways, some wiping their hands on aprons or arranging the cloths over their hair. Two in red robes strode past confidently, slim, covered weapons hanging from their hips. A woman in grey dropped from a nearby rooftop and landed without apparent difficulty before following the flow. Novices began to spill from archways, one group hurrying up stone steps from whatever served as the convent's undercity. Many were small children, others nearly grown women, distinguishable from the younger nuns only by the fact their hair remained uncovered.

Many of the novices stared at Yaz and her friends. Erris and Thurin got most of the attention but Mali's presence also sparked interest. Even as they hastened towards the abbess's house the novices were gossiping. Yaz caught Mali's name on their lips.

THE WHOLE CONVENT seemed to have emptied itself. A hundred or so nuns and novices huddled against the wind that was hardly a wind, waiting, watching the steps of the abbess's house. Sister Owl went to stand on the steps with other senior nuns before the great door of iron-studded wood. Bitel fell silent, the last clang echoing from towers and rooftops.

Yaz and her friends stood at the edge of the gathering. Waiting. Watching.

"This will be about whatever message the bird brought," Mali predicted.

"I thought you were joking. Birds bring messages?" Yaz looked at the sky wonderingly. She glanced around her, finally in this moment of stillness realizing that they had made it. They were here at the end of their impossible journey. So far from the ice that it could not be seen. So warm that they could walk naked if propriety allowed. Standing amid people who had lived all their lives in this heat and plenty, on an island of rock amid a green sea. Quina's bead of wood had been a prize beyond measure and yet within sight were enough trees that every person at the gathering could have a thousand of them. Not a thousand beads—a thousand trees!

"We made it. We're here." Immediately she wanted Zeen to see it. She wanted Quell to be able to look out over the forests and the fields, the running rivers, the chickens strutting here and there like tiny lords, finding food just lying on the ground. Maya should have been with them. And Kao. And all the rest who had fallen since Yaz's own fall into the Pit of the Missing.

A hand found hers. Quina gripped hard. "It's really real, isn't it? This is happening?"

Thurin stood very close too, as if the three of them could guard each other's backs in the crowd. "It's amazing. I want to go down where it's green. I want to see everything." He took her other hand, bare fingers lacing bare fingers. "We could live here. Pick food off the ground like the chickens. We wouldn't even need a shelter."

"We've got Theus and Taproot breathing down our necks," Erris cautioned, "and Seus won't stop trying to kill us. If he can't use his metal monsters he'll just find a different way. He controls the networks. Theus might have found us a way through but Seus will have known about it not long after. And we wasted hours down in those caves."

Mali had been listening to the muttered gossip among the younger novices. She turned back towards the others to report her findings. "An archon is visiting!"

"What's an archon?" Yaz asked.

"A big deal," Mali explained. "There's the high priest of the Church of the Ancestor and beneath her are four archons. This one is newly appointed after Archon Elbrada's accident. The empire is divided into four sees, and the archon who's visiting is in charge of the see we're in."

"An important priest is visiting," Yaz translated for the others.

A short while later the abbess emerged, a tall, angular woman carrying an even taller staff that ended in a golden curl. She told them the same thing that Mali had using many more words. Apparently the archon would be arriving so soon that they were all to stand there and wait for him. Sister Owl said something to the abbess from her place a few steps lower and the abbess found Yaz's party in the crowd. Mali translated her welcome and her assurance that there would be time to speak later on in the day.

Yaz's eagerness to explore made the wait seem interminable. She wanted to run around the place. She wanted to see and touch and feel and taste everything. She knew now what it had been like for Thurin to emerge from the hole he had made in the ice and to see for the first time the sun hanging in the sky, the flat expanse of the ice, to feel the wind, to let his eyes rest on distant places for the first time in a life spent cramped within caves. Yaz had reemerged from beneath the ice after a time that had seemed long but was in truth just a doubled handful of days. But this new escape from the ice marked as profound a transition as Thurin's flight had been for him.

"He's coming!" Quina hissed.

All heads were turning towards the forest of pillars. A strange and ter-rifying creature emerged, much larger than a man, with four long legs and a long wedge of a head sporting a black mane. Horrifically, it seemed to have merged with a shaggy hair-covered man or something similar, the upper half jutting from its horizontal back. Men in armour carrying spears followed the beast out between two pillars, seeming untroubled by its presence.

"Seus sent it?" Thurin asked in shock. He released Yaz's hand and pat-ted for his knife, ready to fight the monster.

"I . . . I'm not sure," Yaz said faintly.

Mali seemed confused by their reactions. "That's the archon. He's rid-ing a horse because he's old. Also, everyone seems to ride everywhere if they've got the money for it."

"A horse?" As the archon and his men came closer, Yaz could see that the shaggy fur she'd thought part of the man-shape was a robe and the man's legs went either side of the creature that carried him. The horse looked bigger than a hoola. "Is it safe?"

Mali laughed. "Pretty safe. They eat grass. Don't get behind it, though. They sometimes kick."

"They eat grass?" Yaz was astonished. Until recently every animal she knew of ate smaller animals. "You can eat grass?"

"Well, horses can," Mali said. "You can't."

THE NUNS AND novices moved aside to let the archon and his ten guards come to the steps of the abbess's house. Unlike his men, the archon wore a polished white mask that fitted against his features.

"How does he see?" Quina hissed.

"What?"

"No eye-slits," Quina said.

"You must have missed them." Yaz had been too distracted by the colour of the guards' clothes, all matching and complicated, and the strangeness of the horse whose feet rang on the stone much like Zox's.

The archon dismounted, helped by a guardsman, and went to stand beside the abbess. The two exchanged some words and looked across to where Yaz and her friends stood. The abbess looked perplexed. A few more things were said but it was too distant for Yaz to catch, even if she could speak the language. The abbess nodded slowly, seeming reluctant, and both she and the archon descended the stairs. Preceded by the archon's guards, they approached Yaz and her group, the throng of nuns and novices shifting so that without taking a step Yaz found herself taken from the edge to the centre of the gathering. One of the nuns behind her was taller than seven feet, her black robes straining over her muscles. The grey-clad and red-clad nuns were closer now, on all sides.

"Yaz?" Thurin glanced around them, also feeling the change, as if the wind had turned.

"Do nothing," Yaz said. These women were dangerous. She could sense that. And they would naturally be cautious of strangers. Especially those from the ice, where life was so hard, coming down amid this undreamed-of plenty. Perhaps living here bred only people who would defend what they had. Perhaps any other kind would perish.

The novices in front of them moved to either side and there, revealed in splendour, were the Church guards with their rich uniform, bright colours and finely worked armour. Each man or woman's breastplate bore a tree inlaid in some kind of golden metal, branches dividing and dividing again as they reached for heaven, and below the trunk another kind of branch that must finger beneath the earth just as the fine roots of the Broken's fungi threaded the thin cave floor earth. *Roots.* Yaz remembered the word. These roots ran as deep as the branches reached high, but dwindled to a single root reaching deeper than all the others.

The guards divided, revealing the abbess, stern-faced, her grey eyes taking in every detail of the ice-tribers. The archon stood beside her, a man of much slighter build than his fur robe had suggested, the smoothness of his white mask without holes for eyes, nose, or mouth. Sister Owl and a much younger nun in grey stood behind the abbess, one at each shoulder.

The abbess began to speak. Yaz understood none of it but the expressions of those surrounding them started to harden. The woman talked and Yaz bit her tongue, resisting the urge to have Mali translate. If things went bad Yaz didn't want Mali considered tainted by association. She forced a thought at the girl, hoping that their connection would allow her to receive it: *Don't tell me what she has said. Keep our bond secret.*

"Doit kenyou? . . . unnerstan?" the nun in grey asked. It almost sounded as if she were using real words.

Sister Owl shook her head, said something to the abbess then spoke in her strangely accented tribe-tongue. The first word out of her mouth brought the archon's blank mask sharply round to face her.

"Mistress Shade thinks you are one of the local ice clans who trade with the Pelarthi or the Juregs on the margins. Very few in this empire speak the language of the north." The ancient woman cleared her throat. "The abbess has told you that, along with other business, our archon comes with news of a violent robbery on the road to Verity. A Church expedition to the ice was robbed of a valuable artefact. Several of the guard were killed. Unfortunately, the attackers were ice-tribers fitting your description."

"What was stolen?" Yaz looked with suspicion at the archon's expressionless mask.

"A white box," the archon said in perfect tribe-tongue, surprising even Sister Owl. His gnarled hands shaped something the size of the box currently straining the largest of Yaz's inner pockets. "A valuable artefact in itself. But the contents are even more prized in certain quarters."

The archon reached up with both hands, taking hold of the edges of his mask. He pulled it clear, revealing a familiar, eyeless face.

"Welcome to the green lands, child," Eular said. "You came a long way to die."

ACKNOWLEDGMENTS

As always, I'm very grateful to Agnes Meszaros for her continued help and feedback. She's never shy to challenge me when she thinks something can be improved or I'm being a little lazy. At the same time, her passion and enthusiasm made working on the story even more enjoyable.

I should also thank, as ever, all the staff at Ace for their support, especially my wonderful editor Jessica Wade. And of course my agent, Ian Drury, and the team at Sheil Land.